VENGEANCE

VENGEANCE

A REECE CULVER NOVEL

BRYAN KOEPKE

The author is available for select readings and lectures. To inquire about a possible appearance, please contact Writers Cabin Press, Ltd. http://writerscabinpress.com

This book is a work of fiction. Names, characters, places, and events herein are either the product of the author's imagination or are used fictitiously. Any resemblance to actual persons, living or dead, is entirely coincidental.

VENGEANCE

A Reece Culver Novel

Published in the United States by Writers Cabin Press, Denver, CO.

www.writerscabinpress.com

ISBN: 978-0-9915824-1-9

ACKNOWLEDGMENTS

I'd like to thank my wife Ildy for her love and friendship.

My thanks go out to my beta readers – Jean Scriven, Cyndie Burgess, and Patrisa McHone for spending the time to read an early draft of this work, and for giving me their honest feedback.

Thanks to Suz Simone for that great author's photo.

I'd like to thank John Paine for his advice and council.

I'd like to thank my mom and dad for teaching me about life, and instilling the love of learning and an appetite for adventure from a young age.

PROLOGUE

July 9, 2009

AL CULVER WELCOMED the cool touch of the building's stone exterior. An arid summer wind howled, whipping up loose bits of dirt and gravel in a driveway that seemed neglected. Hugging the wall, Al stayed in the shadows as he edged forward. Halfway down the structure he came to a small rectangular window chest high, perfect for snooping. He could hear what sounded like a boisterous party inside as he peered in from the bottom corner, doing his best to avoid detection. Inside, the walls were covered in lavish wallpaper, and a woman in a designer purple outfit sang to a piano on her left. Circular tables inhabited by men in tuxedos and women in the latest fashions stretched toward gambling tables near the center of the cavernous room. Along one wall a long dark antique bar held a line two and three deep of thirsty patrons. Fuel up before you lose everything you came with, he thought with a retired cop's irritation.

Al ducked as a man stood up from one of the tables and stared toward the window. He wanted to take a look to check, but he knew better. Keeping low, he instead passed beneath the window frame, thinking how clever it was to hide a casino in the carcass of a stone farm building this far out in the country.

Yet it was still an easy drive west from St. Louis. Sidestepping toward the back of the building, he reflected back to his days as a detective. He would never have done a reconnaissance like this back then, with no backup or without a single soul knowing his whereabouts. But that was before he spent four hard years relying on a cane. All that time he had been searching for the men that beat him so badly. Al counted himself lucky for spotting them when he had. He owed it to himself to at least confirm that all the rats were in the same cage. Then he'd pull back to a pay phone and call in the others.

At the far corner he peered around to view the back of the large property. No more than thirty yards distant he could see the glow of cherry-tipped cigarettes in the night as two men laughed.

Suddenly, Al heard a noise, much too close, and whipped around.

Cold steel pressed against his right temple, indenting the flesh. He slid his hand down toward the Smith & Wesson on his belt, only to be met by the firm grip of another man. Al thought about spinning to break loose and run, but that wasn't happening. He tried to see their faces, yet as he stepped back, he felt the unmistakable snout of a gun barrel pressing into his back.

A hand patted the left breast pocket of his sports coat, reached inside, and ripped out his wallet, nearly taking his nipple. The powerful white beam of a flashlight illuminated and he blinked at the flash of purple dots. Someone walked to his left, crunching gravel, and he wondered how many he was facing. He still had a snub-nose .38 clamped to his bum left ankle, so he knew he still had a chance.

"Well, well, what do we have here? Al Culver, Private Investigator," a man said in a thick southern drawl. He recognized the voice and felt a shiver part the tiny hairs of his spine.

"Go on, start walking," the voice commanded.

He knew what happened last time he obeyed an order like that. He wanted to run, but knew his damaged legs wouldn't permit more than a hobbling stumble. Fear seeped through him like a cancer. He thought about the voice, and the months he'd spent in the hospital after last hearing it. He cursed himself for going in alone knowing he should have waited.

"Come on already, just shoot the stupid bastard," said a second voice.

"All right, I think I will."

Al squinted into the darkness and realized the large-caliber weapon this familiar person was holding had a suppressor screwed onto its barrel. He cringed, feeling trapped and vulnerable. Death was near.

His thoughts sped up with a sudden burst of adrenaline, and he felt the urge to run. The man in front raised the gun, the muzzle flashed with flame, and Al Culver's chest erupted in pain. His legs went weak and he fell backward into the cold, wet rock. As his vision narrowed he reached sideways, trying to somehow brace himself, but instead he sank to his knees, and felt the moist earth soak through his pants. He coughed and struggled for breath as the kind face of his wife came to him in a parting good-bye.

CHAPTER ONE

January 2011

REECE STARED OUT the large second-story window onto the prominent artery of East Colfax that divided Denver's good neighborhoods from the bad. Two drunks, standing in a couple inches of snow, were pushing and shouting on the other side of the four-lane boulevard. Reece caught a streak out of the corner of his eye and wondered who'd be parallel-parking a red Mercedes convertible in this part of town.

He sat down at his desk and tabbed through a bunch of e-mails he'd received the previous week on his laptop computer. Reece was concentrating on a message from his father's old partner, Haisley Averton, when he heard a distant noise. Someone was walking across the worn linoleum floor that led from the stairwell out back to his office door. A tall figure appeared outside the etched glass that boasted the backward letters that spelled out his business name.

A soft knock penetrated the quiet. Reece saw the silhouette of a female face. He came forward to turn the dead bolt lock and pulled the door open. In the door frame was a tall woman whose face was flushed in the January cold. Her long red hair framed large almond-shaped green eyes. She was a beautiful woman, the kind that would drive a red Mercedes. Reece pulled the door inward and motioned for her to enter.

"Mr. Culver, I'm so glad I caught you," she said, leaving a trail of perfume as she walked past. The tall woman quickly dropped into one of the armchairs before his desk. She wore a baby blue fleece, designer jeans, and a pair of knee-high leather boots flared like the three musketeers'.

"What's on your mind?" he asked, taking a seat at the desk. Reece noticed her watch and wondered if it was a real Rolex.

"I need your help, Mr. Culver. It's my mother," the woman said. He was drawn to the soft skin of her cheeks, the comforting lilt of her voice. She noticed him staring and smiled.

"What about your mother? Is she in some sort of trouble, miss?"

"Oh, how rude of me. I didn't introduce myself," she said, extending a pale hand. "I'm Crystal Thomas, it's a pleasure to make your acquaintance."

He took her hand, gave it a gentle shake, but didn't let go. She had long, slender fingers like a piano player. The citrus scent of her perfume filled his nostrils. He could definitely like having her as a client.

"I was told you specialize in missing-person's cases," Crystal said, leaning forward a little, holding his attention.

"Well, that depends on who's missing."

"There are just some unresolved questions that I'd like to get answered."

He had handled all sorts of combinations, but not any cases of a daughter looking for her mother. "What sort of questions?"

"It's about my mother, Tracey. I want to locate her. I think she might have been kidnapped, or worse, " she said, sounding somber.

Why would she come to see a private investigator about that? "Have you contacted the police?"

She gave an exaggerated look of unease. "No, it was a long time ago. I was young when it happened."

"How young?" he asked, noticing a small scar on the right side of her neck.

"It was 1989. I guess I would have been eight," she said, leaning back languorously. He wasn't about to tell her that he'd bought the armchair at a garage sale.

"When I was on a flight recently, I found an old newspaper in the seat back pocket. In it I read an article about a woman who went missing thirty years ago in Ohio. The case was reopened by the partner of a retired detective, and the woman, who'd run away from her abusive husband, was found alive and well in Texas. The newspaper article sparked off a desire in me, and I've been having dreams about my mother ever since. I know it probably sounds crazy to you, but I think she's trying to reach me, and tell me something."

Reece had investigated some cold cases, but this was bordering on deep freeze. "I've got to tell you, Ms. Thomas, these kinds of cases can be quite intensive. Twenty-two years is a long time, and it could take months, if not years, to find your mother. There's a good chance we won't be able to solve this."

"Mr. Culver, I don't care how expensive it is. I have the money and I want to find my mother if she's alive, and if not, I want closure. I've lived too long with this hole in my heart not to take action."

She was singing the right tune for perennially cash-strapped Reece. "Well, I usually charge $700 a day, which includes all of my expenses, except airfare. I'd need $2,800 to start, and a full week's retainer if it looks like it'll take longer than a couple of days."

"That's fine. This is very important to me," she said, digging into the creamy blond leather of her Coach bag. She pulled out a red leather checkbook and a thick silver pen, and began writing. She recited his name out loud as she wrote it across the check. It sounded good rolling off her lips. It looked even better on paper.

"Where was your mother living when she went missing?"

"We were in Tulsa by then."

That was a start. "Tell me about it. Also, what's your mother's full name and how old would she be?" he said, glancing down, confirming that the amount $7,000 was written on her check. Nice, he thought. Very nice.

Crystal's voice took on a distance as she recalled her past. "I grew up in St. Louis near a highway and a park where we used to play. I remember the arch," she said wistfully. "My mother's name is Tracey Ann Roberts. The last time I saw her, she would have been twenty-seven. I remember from the candles on her birthday cake the month before I lost her."

"You said earlier you were in Tulsa when your mother went missing. Were you on a trip with your parents? Why were you in Tulsa?"

"That was where our mom took us after she left our dad, Owen Roberts," Crystal said, seeming uncomfortable as she mentioned his name.

So, Owen had a motive for making his wife disappear. "I know you were young then, but do you remember why your mother took you away?"

"They were having problems, and Daddy took it out on us kids. I remember my brothers teased me, calling me ratchet mouth. My dad was always telling me to be quiet. He said my voice hurt his ears," Crystal recalled sadly.

Reece decided to get right to the point. "Was your father abusive?"

"Not to me, I guess, but he did manhandle my brothers. The abuse was more emotional for me. One weekend, when my mother was studying for her college exams, he had us kids help him build a room under the staircase in the basement. It was a fun project until he told me to go in, and he locked the door." The corners of her eyes began to well with tears.

"That must have been pretty scary for a little girl your age," he said, wanting to console her, but not really knowing what to say.

"That incident was what led to my mother taking us away. That afternoon my mother came home early from work. I remember hearing her yell out my name, looking all over the house for me. She came down into the basement and heard me crying through the locked door. My mom went berserk and got my older brothers, Julian and Wayne. They pried the lock off the door and got me out," Crystal said in a small childlike voice.

He handed her a Kleenex and wondered if her father had caught up with the mother in Tulsa and done something. Crystal dabbed her eyes, and Reece realized he couldn't press her, not when she was so vulnerable.

"I'd like to set up a time with you to get further background," Reece said, tucking the check into his shirt pocket.

"I have a work trip tomorrow," she said with her lips pursed like she wanted to meet, but couldn't get out of the trip.

"I can get started on things," he offered, "and we can meet when it works for your schedule."

"I could do something later tonight if that works," Crystal said coyly.

"That could work."

"How about I drop by around six? We can take my car, dinner's my treat, and you can get all the background you want."

He wasn't sure of his new client's intent, but he did know that $7,000 was a good reason to be agreeable. "Then that's what we should do."

CHAPTER TWO

REECE GOT UP from the desk and walked over to the tall corner window to watch his new client walk away. The sun was peeking from the clouds, warming the glass. Crystal jumped into her hot red car and roared off. Down the street a jet black Range Rover parked on the opposite side caught his attention. He figured it must be one of the local drug dealers collecting the proceeds from their weekend deals.

Reece returned to his desk, thinking about Crystal. He logged on to the laptop, wondering where she lived. A few minutes of searching the Denver county property records turned up the page for Crystal Thomas. She lived in a downtown Denver loft, which she'd purchased four years earlier for $550,000. Impressed, Reece continued his search and found a newspaper article announcing the death of her husband Nathan in a skiing accident at Vail the previous winter.

He read the article, wondering what other secrets Crystal Thomas had to hide. *Why had she really come to visit? Could she really want to find her mother after all these years?*

Reece caught himself staring at the wall and came back to reality. His checkbook and a pen sat to the right of his laptop computer. He pulled a big pile of bills out of the desk drawer. The balance column on the ledger page read $127.63. He wrote $7,000.00 in the deposit column with a nice big flourish.

He pulled the first envelope off the stack of bills, peeling it open. It was a stern note from the credit card company threatening to turn the bill over to a collection agency. Reece worked his way through the stack, and by the time he got to the bottom he knew he needed to devote all of his time to Crystal's case.

Reece had a few more things to do before his big date, including the duty of walking his dog. After locking up his office, he climbed the circular staircase up to his third-floor apartment. When he popped his head through the floor he found Manchego sprawled out on the couch watching TV. Reece grabbed his brown leather bomber jacket from the hook on the door and pulled out the leash. Taking his cue, the blond Labrador retriever leaped off the couch, pushing it back against the window, and trotted toward him. He raised his finger as if pointing to the ceiling, and Manchego dropped into a sit. The dog's head was warm under Reece's hand. As soon as he'd clipped the leash onto his collar, Manchego was up, tail wagging like a fierce metronome against Reece's leg, eager to get out of the apartment.

Reece snatched his gray cowboy hat from its resting place inside the original bottom half of the box it came in from the mall. He'd figured the top of the refrigerator was as good a place as any to store it. A few years back he'd splurged and paid close to $600 for the Stetson SILVERBELLY 30X Fur Felt hat with a four-inch brim. From that day on it had found a permanent place in his wardrobe.

As he and his dog stepped out onto the cleated steel stairway, Reece guessed the temperature to be in the low twenties. The sky was a bright Colorado blue, and on the way down the steps, distracted by the sky's brilliance, he slipped on a patch of snow-covered ice and almost fell. Manchego stopped, and Reece smiled at him, thankful he hadn't been pulled further off balance. His dog sniffed the air with his blond snout, holding his head up. Reece followed suit and detected the faint odor of burning pine from some distant fireplace. The smell warmed his heart before he located the reason: it reminded him of a camping trip he'd gone on with his father.

He reminisced about those few days while he weaved his way through the streets of the city. By the time he was winding up the dog's outing, the brief glow from his time together with his father had hardened into a frown. Reece was one of those younger brothers waiting hopefully in the shadow cast by the superstar son, Raymond. His brother had settled in the small town of Parker, south of Denver, and the walls of his den were lined with an assortment of sports trophies. His brother had been the captain of both the baseball and football teams at their Saint Louis high school and after being scouted had played football for the University of Kansas until impregnating his girlfriend Gwen and blowing out his right knee in his sophomore year of college.

Unlike most families, it had not been his father that was so enamored of his talented son. His mother was the one that went to all of Raymond's games, and she continued to dote on him even now. Reece had long ago tired of being left out of the special loop between his mother and his older brother. Raymond had taken his father's place after the murder, and these days Reece was always the last to hear about anything. That was just fine with him. He was busy living his own life. Yet on some level he wanted to be there for his mother, Helen. He knew it was hard for her being a widow.

She never turned to him for help, though, and hadn't since that awful day shortly after his father had been killed. Reece had been visiting Raymond when his older brother angrily took him aside.

"Mom got a visit from that FBI agent who was working Dad's case. He's got her all worked up. They have a theory as to why Dad went all alone to that farm on the outskirts of St. Louis."

"What kind of theory?" Reece said.

"When they found his body, they recovered a Nikon camera with shots from in front of a house back in the suburbs."

"Yeah, I know all about those pictures. Haisley got me copies," Reece said.

"Yeah, well, did you know about the broken camera?" Raymond said, clenching his hand into a fist.

"What are you talking about?" Reece said.

"They found a second camera, a Canon digital. It was in Dad's home office in St. Louis. It had your prints on it."

Reece thought back to his father's office and the last time he'd been there.

"Are you with me little brother," Raymond shouted, stepping closer.

"What are you trying to say?"

"The FBI think you went with Dad to take pictures with the Canon camera and somehow, under your watch, it got busted."

Both Raymond and his mother had held Reece responsible ever since for the murder. Reece knew that wasn't right, but the only way he'd ever redeem himself is if he found his father's killer himself. Reece had decided to put the training he'd received in the Air Force during his four years in the security police to use by doing his own investigation. He took a six-week leave of absence from his engineering job at Caulder Space Systems and never returned. A year later, he was still looking.

Irritated by his failure, he decided to get busy. With the cordless mouse in hand he scrolled through half a page of junk before coming to one from his dad's old police detective partner, Haisley Averton. He'd been a good friend of the family for as long as Reece could remember and had stayed close after his partner Al's death.

Haisley answered after two rings. "Hey, buddy, what's going on?"

"Hey, I've got a favor to ask," Reece said.

"What's going on?" Haisley said, sounding curious.

"I've got a missing person's gig. Is there any chance you could get back into that old precinct of yours, and get me a copy of a case file?"

"I could try, but the new chief of detectives runs a tight ship. I'll call someone and see if they'll let me in the back door."

"I'd really appreciate it. The name is Tracey Roberts. DOB is 1962, and I'm guessing place of birth to be St. Louis."

"St. Louis, your old stomping ground."

"That doesn't matter anymore," Reece said, more sharply than he intended. "It's just the source of my next pay check now."

CHAPTER THREE

A WHITE FORD ECONOVAN drove through a large beige-sided apartment complex on the outskirts of Jenks, Oklahoma, just south of Tulsa. The driver eased over a section of speed bumps before parking with the grill of the vehicle facing a grove of cottonwoods. A muscular man dressed in dark blue jeans and work boots got out and gazed at the three-story complex. He pulled the hood of his sweatshirt up over his thick white hair, opened a lighter under the tip of an unfiltered cigarette, took a long draw, and welcomed the taste. He set out past the trees on his way into the adjacent park and spotted a lone figure dressed in black sitting on one of the wooden picnic tables fifty yards distant. The once green grass had long ago turned brown and matted from a lack of moisture and an abundance of children. He took several quick steps toward the tables, puffing on the cigarette before dropping it to the ground. As he closed the gap he noticed the gold weaved trim on the rear of the distant man's vest.

The scent of a cherry-flavored cigar came to him as he approached and confirmed it was Rocco, the blackjack dealer. The driver reached around his back and pulled a large black .45-caliber handgun from the waistband of his jeans. He crept forward happy he and the dealer were destined to meet one last time. The blackjack dealer sat on the top of the picnic table, oblivious to the approaching figure who's gun was held outward at arm's length, aiming at the back of the man's head. The driver advanced until the stout barrel of the gun collided with the rear of the dealer's skull.

Rocco leapt off the table and onto his feet, stumbled, and then turned toward the man with the gun. "What are you trying to do? Scare me to death?"

The driver smiled as he skirted the table and shoved the gun into Rocco's spine.

"Start walking," he said, placing his left hand on the blackjack dealer's belt.

After reaching the parked van, the driver slid open the side door and ordered the dealer inside, encouraging him with the blunt nose of his gun. He followed after and slid the door closed.

Rocco turned toward him, pleading, "I don't know what you think is going on, but you got the wrong guy. I'm on your side. Let's talk about this."

The driver held the gun against the kneeling man's head and pulled a pair of stainless steel handcuffs from a rear pocket of his jeans. He fastened one side onto the right wrist of the dealer and cuffed him to a steel eyebolt on the floor of the van. The dealer protested with a flurry of cusswords. The driver pulled a roll of silver duct tape out of a steel bin on the side wall of the van, tore a length from the roll, and ran it over the man's mouth. The dealer's eyes went wide with fear as the driver held his gun up and then came down hard across the man's cerebellum. Rocco dropped face first into the floor with a thud.

The driver made three revolutions with the duct tape around the unconscious man's calves and crawled toward the front seat. He reached into the console between the front seats and pulled out a large plastic syringe. The driver rolled the dealer over and undid the buttons on the front of his white dress shirt, peeling it down to expose the pale white flesh of the man's shoulder. With the syringe in his hand he inserted the needle into Rocco's shoulder and pushed on the plunger with his thumb, emptying the contents of the hypodermic.

He didn't wait for the drug to take full effect. He started up the van and roared off down the two-lane blacktop road. Soon the white Ford van turned off and barreled, shaking constantly with the ruts, down a narrow dirt road for a couple of miles. The van slowed as it reached a heavily treed area alongside the Arkansas River. The engine ceased and the driver's side door opened, freeing a cloud of cigarette smoke. The white haired driver hopped out and listened until he was convinced he was alone. He went around to the back of the van and opened the twin doors. Inside, the blackjack dealer lay quiet, eyes open, staring up at the interior roof. The drug was doing its job.

The driver slid his hands into a pair of latex gloves, pulled a plastic apron from a white shopping bag, and put it on. He went to the passenger's side door, pulled out a red gas can and a blue and orange cardboard box containing his brand-new Husqvarna chainsaw. He pulled the tab out of the side of the box, thinking he'd keep it to store his new toy when he was done. Looking back at the blackjack dealer, the driver felt a bolt of excitement and tore open the cardboard box freeing the chainsaw. It felt good in his hands. He was powerful. He stabbed it toward the ankle of the still man, scraping his skin. The dealer gave out a muffled moan.

"Next time you'll think twice about opening your mouth. Hell, you had it made working for us and you had to mess that up too," the driver said, puffing on another of his cigarettes. He climbed into the back of the panel van, undid the handcuff from the eyebolt, and fastened it onto a twenty-foot length of bright steel chain he'd bought earlier.

With the chainsaw fueled and resting on the top of a short stump, he stuck the toe of his work boot through the orange plastic handle and pulled the black cord six times. Next, the driver moved the red plastic lever from choke to half. Glancing over at the dealer with a broad smile, he pulled the starting cord a seventh time bringing the chainsaw to life with a roar. He squeezed the trigger and felt the torque of the saw in his arm.

"It's time to do a little trimming."

*

The driver set the shovel down so it was leaning against the rear bumper of the van. The sand he'd shoveled into the top of the blue plastic container would do its job weighting it down once it found its home in the river. He leaned against one of the rear doors, savoring the taste of his unfiltered cigarette and admiring his handiwork. The hard part was over. He grabbed the white steel lid and its clamping mechanism from the rear of the van and walked over to the blue barrel.

With the cigarette hanging from his mouth, he pursed his lips and took one last puff before letting it drop to the ground. The view into the fifty-five-gallon barrel was less than pleasing but held the remains of an honest day's work. The driver pushed the white metal top down onto the plastic drum in an effort to seal it. The fit was tight and he held it down with his hand while fitting the clamp onto the seam between the lid and the top metal flange. It wouldn't close all the way. Something was keeping the lid from sealing.

He pulled the clamp lid off and noticed that one of Rocco's shoes, still fitted onto his big bubous foot, was sticking up out of the barrel just far enough to keep it from closing. The driver grasped the ankle of Rocco's leg and pulled up. He twisted the black dress shoe from the dead man's foot and shoved it back into a void in the top of the drum between an elbow and a hand. It was messy work, but he needed to get it right.

*

Who knows who might come out here on any given day? He remembered back to the days of his youth when he and his friends had ridden dirt bikes along the banks of Lake Michigan. They'd had fun in those days stealing beer and cigarettes from the dime store and then racing off to the next town along the expansive lake to see what new trouble they might find.

He smiled thinking back to all the trouble he'd gotten into and was proud that he'd never seen the inside of a prison cell. He was good at his job. The best there was in his line of business and he was proud of that fact.

With the top of the barrel firmly in place, the driver bent over it and reefed on the steep clamp, closing it and fastening the lid securely in place. He fished the spool of bailing wire he'd brought along out of his back pocket and began twisting the black strand around the steel clamp. He wished he'd brought along a pair of pliers, but his hands were all that he had.

The driver stood admiring the sealed drum and pulled another cigarette out of the wooden container in the rear of the van where he kept his smokes. He lit the end with a blue Bic lighter. The first puff was always the most satisfying, and he welcomed the smell of the burning paper and tobacco. Well worth the hacking cough he woke up to every morning.

With the shovel in his hand he walked past the van toward the hill overlooking the Arkansas River. He'd come a few days before, scouting out a place to dispose of the blackjack dealer.

He was glad he'd caught Rocco in the act and taken care of it before any trouble came to his boss.

The view out over the river was favorable, but he wondered how deep the water was close to shore. He ventured down the river's edge a few hundred feet until he came to a gentle slope. This would be a problem. There was a five-foot wide section of shallow water and then the sandy bottom disappeared into brown murky water.

He picked up a rock and threw it out past the shallows. The splash was high, indicating the water was deep. That was where he needed to roll the barrel. It needed to sink deep enough so that its bright blue exterior couldn't be spotted from on top of the hill. The world was filled with treasure hunters, and he didn't want anyone discovering what he'd buried within the blue drum.

The driver climbed back up the steep slope a ways until he came to a wide shelf of dirt. It was near the bottom of a steep slope. Once the barrel was rolling it would be moving very fast by the time it got this far down the hill. He went to work building a berm. He figured once he got the barrel rolling down the hill, it would hit the ramp and launch off the ground and in doing so clear the shallows on the verge of the river. This job was turning into something way more time-consuming than he'd imagined, but he couldn't stop this far into it.

With a new cigarette smoldering from his mouth he pitched dirt back toward what was quickly becoming a three-foot-wide jump that ran the width of two barrel lengths sideways along the hill. It was a good two feet tall at the high end and spread back toward the slope of the hill, looking like a jump he'd navigate with a dirt bike. He'd had plenty of experience building jumps when he was younger and loved the feeling of going flat out off them. He'd fly through the air aiming for the other side and feel strong doing it.

After climbing back up the hill, he returned to the van. He looked around listening for any signs of company. The job had taken far too long, and that was when you'd end up getting caught in the act by some passerby. He glanced into the van and spotted his big black semi-automatic handgun on the passenger's seat.

The driver tipped the barrel over and smiled at the sloshing noise it made as he pushed it through the leaf-covered grassland toward the edge of the hill. It was heavy and hard work rolling what was now close to three hundred pounds of dead weight. With his left hand on the top and the other on the bottom rim, he pushed out away from his chest, rolling the drum two to three feet with each gesture. His lips were dry, he discovered. He'd need water when he was done disposing of the barrel in the depths of the river.

Finally, he got to the top of the hill and let the weight of the barrel roll back so it was resting against his shin. He stood catching his breath and staring out across the half-mile wide section of river. A breeze ran through the trees behind him and he twitched as it flooded his sweat-soaked shirt and chilled him. He bent over, grasping the barrel, and lined it up, aiming at the jump he'd constructed near the bottom. He rolled it a half revolution forward till it was right on the edge of the dropoff and gave it his best shove. It rolled slowly at first and then picked up speed a third of the way down the steep hill.

He waved the flame of his lighter under a cigarette as he watched the blue container barreling down the slope. It hit the dirt jump, went airborne, and flew a good twenty feet out into the brown murky waters of the Arkansas River before disappearing beneath the water's surface.

He smiled in satisfaction at the gigantic splash it made. That made all of his hard work worthwhile.

CHAPTER FOUR

REECE WAS STRAIGHTENING the books in one of the twin walnut bookshelves when he heard the exterior door slam. The clicking of her fancy high heels on the linoleum confirmed his suspicion of who it was.

"You look nice," he heard her say. Reece turned and liked what he saw as well. She was wearing black tights that left nothing to the imagination and a navy blue silk shirt. Her red hair looked like she'd just come from the salon, and her cheeks were reddened with makeup that matched her lips.

"Could I get you something to drink?" he asked, hoping she liked diet coke or water. He slid open the door of the wooden credenza he'd picked up a few weeks back, and pulled open the mini fridge.

"If you have ice water, I'd take a glass of that," Crystal said in a seductive voice. He filled a glass with ice cubes, pulled a bottle of water from the fridge, and turned back toward her. She had her elbows planted on the desk with her chin in her palms. Reece caught himself staring and quickly poured the water into the glass.

He took a seat behind his desk and handed her the glass. She leaned back and took a long sip.

"So how long have you lived in Denver?" he asked studying her face.

"I've been here since 2004. I followed my husband Nathan here."

"Nathan doesn't mind you spending your Sunday evenings with strange men?" he asked, knowing that where Nathan was, he wouldn't be caring.

"No, I'm widowed," she said with a hint of sadness.

"Oh, I'm sorry to hear that."

"It's okay. I guess I'm to the point where I should be over it. It was an accident. We were skiing in Vail. Nathan was a very good skier, and was always pushing himself to test out harder terrain."

"What happened?"

"We were chute skiing and he made a wrong turn. The winds were up, and it was near whiteout conditions. I was following him, but I couldn't see, so I stopped. I heard his scream. It was horrible. He went off the edge," she said, looking like she was on the verge of tears. Reece pushed the square Kleenex box across the desk, but she regained her composure.

"The sight of him lying there in the boulder field is something I'll never be able to forget," Crystal said.

"I'm sorry about your loss," he responded, though he wondered how she could have seen her husband in a whiteout.

"Was Nathan your first husband?" he asked.

"No, I was married before to Paul."

"Did that end in divorce?" he asked, watching her wad up the used Kleenex and stuff it under the sleeve of her blouse.

"No. I don't really want to talk about that. What do you need to know to find my mother?" Crystal asked.

Reece knew he'd hit a nerve asking about her marriages, and he made a mental note to pry into her past.

"Sorry about that. I guess it's just part of my job. I like to ask questions," he said. "Are you hungry?"

"Yes, shall we go?" she asked.

"Yes, unless you'd like to eat in. Do you like Chinese?"

"Chinese would be good."

He pulled a well-worn menu for Chui's Chinese out of his desk. He knew the menu by heart, having ordered from the restaurant one floor below more times than he could remember.

She took the menu from his hand and studied it, then looked up smiling at him.

"Why don't you surprise me, Reece? I like most everything."

That made his life easy. Picking up the phone, he dialed and ordered up dinner.

"So how about work? What do you do, Crystal?"

"I work for the United States Attorney's Office for the District of Colorado."

"Wow, that sounds pretty important. Can you discuss your work?" he asked, wondering if she trusted him.

"Right now we're working with a multi-state task force. It's a big case, that's about all I can say."

"It sounds very interesting," he said, noticing that she knew how to clam up when needed. He stood up and added, "Would you like to come up to my apartment? I have a full kitchen, and it's probably more comfortable than eating on a desk."

"Lead the way."

He led her through the door to the staircase. On the way up the spiral stairs he remembered Manchego, and hoped his dog hadn't left any surprises. Reece stepped off the top stair with Crystal a few steps behind.

"Manchego," he said, alerting the dog.

"Whose Manchego?" Crystal asked. Reece heard a louder than normal growl coming from the couch.

"He's my watchdog," he said, not sure what was up with

Manchego. It wasn't like his dog to growl unless he sensed danger nearby.

"Oh, I love dogs. What kind is he?" Crystal asked, stepping up into the apartment.

"A blond lab," Reece said, watching Manchego hop off the couch and come toward them. Crystal bent down to greet the dog. He sniffed her hand, gave her a lick, and then one ear went back, and one went forward. The dog hesitated and then withdrew toward the master bedroom. Reece wondered what was going through his dog brain.

He heard a faint knock on the back door and went over to answer.

"I like your place Reece. It's very quaint," Crystal said.

He opened the door and found the young red-cheeked face of Larry Chui's daughter Noi, holding a large cardboard box.

"You want, put it on your tab, Mr. Reece?"

He took the box and handed over the last $65.00 in cash he had.

"Tell your father to close my tab. Thanks for bringing this up, Noi. This is for you," he said, peeling the top five-dollar bill off the stack.

Noi's face blossomed into a huge smile.

"She's cute," Crystal said.

"Yeah, she is," he said, shutting the door and taking the box to the kitchen counter.

She was staring at a row of photographs from his childhood next to the television. He guessed that she might be jealous, since her own childhood had been cut short with the loss of her mother at the age of seven. What kind of mother would abandon her children at such a young age? There had to be more to the story he didn't yet know.

"Noi takes care of Manchego when I travel, and her father

is the best landlord I've ever had," Reece said, breaking the silence.

"It smells like he's a good cook too." Crystal said rising from the couch and approaching him. He noticed her coming toward him and turned away pulling plates and silverware from the cabinets. The small kitchen was in a lot better shape now than earlier in the day when he'd decided to clean the large pile of dishes that had taken up permanent residence in the sink. A mixture of Chinese food smells colored the apartment, but he could still discern the fragrance of her citrus perfume drifting toward him.

As they ate, he learned that she and her boss were catching a flight to St. Louis the next day for a meeting with the FBI. Reece was curious about the coincidence of the same city once again, but for now she was keeping her secrets to herself.

After dinner, they sat on opposite ends of the couch in an awkward silence. Reece noticed her staring at him with an intent gaze.

"I've got a question for you," she said.

"Shoot."

"I read a publicity piece about you and your new office in the *Denver Post* a few months back. I guess that's what brought me here today. Anyway, I was wondering what would make a successful aerospace engineer quit his job and become a private investigator."

"I've often wondered the same thing myself," Reece said, smiling at her. "I guess I needed answers to a couple of questions, and the only way to get them was to go all in."

"I like a man who goes all in."

Reece didn't know how to respond to that. What did his new client want from him, anyway? Did she want him to find her mother, or did she like to tease private investigators?

Maybe that was the way she was with all men. He took a forkful of the chicken kung po and shook his head. He didn't really care—as long as she wasn't trying to lead him into some scheme to break the law. Yes, he decided, he had to make sure he kept his distance with this one.

CHAPTER FIVE

CRYSTAL FINISHED HER bagel, returned her empty coffee mug to the sink, and made one last trip to the bathroom mirror. She guided the gold handled brush her mother had given her as a child through her newly dyed hair, admiring the way she looked as a green-eyed blonde. Reaching across the counter, she retrieved a contact lens case, and tilting her head back, she poured drops of saline solution into each eye. With one of the blue lenses on her index finger she pressed it against her left eye and blinked until it became centered. She took one last glance into the mirror, admiring her new disguise.

She drove the Mercedes from the basement garage of her downtown Denver loft and headed south on I-25 toward Arapahoe Road, glancing down at the letter in the taupe envelope she'd opened earlier. Crystal stopped at the traffic light after taking the exit ramp off the highway, and while waiting for it to turn green she took the letter and stuffed it into the side compartment of her purse. She wondered, *Why now after all of these years?*

The light changed, and she tore off down the three-lane boulevard thinking about the call the day before from the man she called Papa. He was the only man she'd ever felt truly loved her, and she didn't want to do anything to mess that up.

Yet when she had told him she'd hired an investigator to find her mother, he'd gotten angry. She wondered if he knew something about Tracey Roberts he hadn't told her.

She had made the phone call in the first place because she'd come home to find a small box in the mail. Inside was a handwritten note from someone who'd signed it as Papa. Crystal smiled and pulled sheets of tissue off a slender black smartphone near the bottom. *Every time I get mad at him, he does something like this.*

The shrill ring of the desk phone had broken the silence of the room, startling her. She reached out and answered.

"How's my baby girl?" a man asked in a raspy voice.

"I'm good. How about you?"

"Good as well. What are you up to today?" he asked.

"I'm getting packed for a work trip to St. Louis tomorrow," she'd said. "Oh, and thank you for the new phone. I just opened the box. You really shouldn't have."

"You're welcome, dear. A girl can't be without a phone."

"Thank you, Papa."

"So who all is going on your trip?" He said. Crystal listened to him take a drink of something.

"Just me and my boss George," she said, then compared the gold contacts of the cell phone battery to the opening and pressed it in place. "So enough about me, what about you Papa, what's new with you?"

"It's been pretty slow here today, just getting ready for tonight's tournament," he said. She listened to him chewing on something and it irritated her. He always had to eat and drink when he was in the middle of a conversation with her.

"Hey, Papa, there's something I need to tell you," Crystal said.

"What's that?"

"Do you remember when I told you about the investigator here in Denver?"

"Yeah, what about him?"

"I hired Reece Culver to find my mom," she said sounding proud.

"Crystal! What did you go and do that for? That's a waste of time and money. I told you what happened to your mom."

"That's not true. You told me that she ran away. I took you at your word because I was young," Crystal shouted. "You and Diane just took over my life, and every time I asked about my mom you dismissed it. Don't you think I have a right to know what happened to her?"

"Calm down, Crystal. That was a long time ago. Nothing positive is going to come from digging up the past."

She sobbed, and wiped her nose with the sleeve of her shirt, feeling angry and sad all at once, tired of his manipulation.

"Why can't you just let things be?" he demanded. "Why do you always have to dig up the past?"

"I know what you told me, but I want to find out for myself. I need the truth."

The memory faded as she reached the entrance of Centennial Airport. She followed the road south and watched the big American flag in front of her destination stretch toward the east in a strong gale. Crystal leaned into her turn at the Y in the road and drove toward the control tower.

She parked in the first row of cars at hangar seven. After using her badge to get into the side door, she saw the familiar face of her boss, George Kendall, the U.S. attorney for the District of Colorado. The square-faced man had a refined nose and a full head of gray hair. He looked important propped against the wing of their government-operated Hawker 4000 jet. He noticed her arrival and she glided across the polished white hangar floor, knowing she had his full attention. Crystal wondered if the navy blue business suit she'd decided to wear was conservative enough for their meeting. Her skirt had a mid-knee slit and he seemed to find her outfit intriguing.

"Crystal," George blurted out. His voice echoed off the walls of the enclosed hangar. "Shall we take a walk while they get our ride prepared?"

She smiled at him and walked past, dragging a small-wheeled red suitcase. After stopping to leave her luggage next to the jet, she turned back toward him.

They fell into a cadence as they walked toward the space between the two tall hanger doors. To the west a thick veil of sculpted white clouds covered the foothills that had been bathed in sunshine when she left her loft. The winds were up and she worried that the trip might be delayed.

"George can we fly in this?" she asked in a submissive voice as they walked out onto the asphalt ramp in the strong wind.

"Oh yeah, we've got a jet. We'll be up and out of this in no time," George answered reassuringly. He had only a limited amount of small talk in him, though, and he quickly turned to their business at hand. "I wanted to make sure we're both on the same page, Crystal. I've been following Sam Shanks for over a decade, and I don't want St. Louis trying to take our case." They rounded the south side of the hangar, taking shelter from the gravel being stripped from the pavement and flung toward them in the wind.

"I'll follow your lead, George. I was under the impression, from your phone call with Stephen Cox, that this trip was just to confirm our information."

He leaned forward, pressing his hand on the side of the hangar as he turned toward her. He was close enough that Crystal felt uncomfortable and thought about moving away.

"Good, we definitely don't want to fill in any blanks for these guys. I don't trust any of them."

What you don't know, George, she wanted to say, is that the person you shouldn't trust is me. I have a keen interest in Sam Shanks myself—a keen interest in making sure the investigation of him goes nowhere.

CHAPTER SIX

THE NEXT MORNING Reece rolled onto his right side and grabbed the edge of the mattress, trying to avoid hitting the floor. Manchego had taken up most of the bed, leaving his master to the two-foot-wide section he'd decided belonged to the guy that fed him. Reece made his way to the living room, where he slid into last night's clothes and pulled on his favorite cowboy boots. The leather felt cold on his calves. He sniffed the air and caught the strong scent of Crystal's citrus perfume that had infused the surroundings. He dug through the wicker basket and found Manchego's leash.

As Reece walked his dog down the stairs, he heard a fire truck going down 17th Avenue in an awful hurry. He wondered what was burning at six in the morning, and then remembered where he was. Manchego stretched the leash to its full length and squatted on the first piece of grass he could find. Reece waited, sniffing the cold morning air and welcoming the mind-clearing chill. They headed back toward the apartment, and when he got to the stairs out behind Chui's Chinese he saw Larry Chang, the day cook and owner.

"Hi, Reece," Larry said reaching down to give Manchego a few pets. "Thanks for paying off your food tab last night. Noi is still talking about the $5.00 you gave her."

"Do you think Noi would like to watch Manchego for a few days? I've got a work trip," Reece said.

"When are you leaving?" Larry asked.

"Probably later today."

"Reece, there's one more thing," he said. "Rent's due a week from tomorrow. I need you to pay last month's rent too."

Reece smiled at him and nodded. "I've got you covered."

After returning to the apartment he spent the next few hours packing and getting Manchego's food and gear situated so that Noi could take over her duties easily. He walked down the street to the bank, and as he entered, he caught the security guard's disapproving look as he pulled his carry-on suitcase with a camouflaged backpack slung over his left shoulder. He had to get a wad of cash because when he'd tried to buy an airline ticket on the Internet, his credit card had been declined. With his business at the bank completed, he went out onto Colfax to hail a cab.

On the cab ride to Denver's International Airport, he perused the notes he'd started on Crystal's missing mother Tracey, but soon his mind drifted. The sights reminded him of the day his father had picked him up from the airport back in July of 2009. That in turn took him back to that day his father and he had followed Anthony Zimeratti's blue Corvette through the streets of downtown St. Louis. His dad had handed him a Canon digital camera, telling him to snap pictures of Zimeratti with his mistress. It was the last piece of evidence Reece's father needed for his PI divorce case.

He'd set the camera down on the seat as they sped up to catch Zimeratti. The blue Corvette was faster than his dad's GTO, and Reece remembered his dad punching it and doing a power slide around a corner. The camera slid off the seat into the floor well, and Reece wasn't fast enough to grab it. When he did pick it up, he looked through the viewfinder and everything looked fine. He ran his hands over the plastic camera body, thankful it was still working. But now he knew it had in fact broken.

They caught up with the Corvette. It roared along in the left lane and they were two lanes over to the right. Reece took four or five good shots of a hot blonde in the passenger's seat kissing Zimeratti all over as he sped down Broadway. Reece remembered zooming in on the woman and realizing her shirt was unbuttoned down to her waist, exposing her breasts. Reece and his dad started laughing, having a good time. They eased back satisfied they'd captured the evidence Al Culver needed.

Reece felt the jerk of the cab's brakes and looked up, letting go of his daydream. The taxi had pulled up to the curb at DIA, and he got the feeling someone was watching him. Someone was. He saw the driver's grizzled face in the rearview mirror "You owe fifty-four. I take cash or credit card."

"Yeah, I got it. It's not like I can't see those big red numbers on your toll taker," Reece said, leaning back to grab the wallet from his back pocket. He handed the guy sixty bucks. The cabbie took his time counting out the six dollars in change, and his attitude took away any chance of a tip.

Reece paid cash for his airline ticket at the counter and checked his carry-on with the locked gun case for his Smith & Wesson .357 Magnum inside. He liked his Model 686 Plus and the idea of having seven bullets instead of the usual six. He wasn't the best shot with a handgun, but if need be, it could be gripped by the barrel and used as a club.

"That's all you're checking in?" the ticket officer asked.

"Yeah, that's it."

*

Once he landed in Tulsa, he ended up renting a blue Mazda 6.

The car's acceleration was responsive as he pulled out of the airport and merged into the northbound lane of the highway. Reece dialed Haisley to see if he'd turned anything up on his missing person, Tracey Roberts.

"Haisley, what's going on?" Reece asked.

"Culver, where are you?"

"Just flew in to Tulsa. Did you get the file?"

"I did, but it's a dead end."

"Dead end, what do you mean?" Reece asked, annoyed.

"There is no file. All I got is the folder jacket. I convinced Darla over at Riverside to let me look myself, but that's all I came up with."

A file missing from the archives? "Is there anything written on the jacket?" Reece asked, knowing that sometimes detectives would write investigative notes inside the cover.

"All I got is a photograph of a green and white house, plus the name Ann Fletcher. I wish I had more for you, Reece."

"Spell the name for me," he said, pulling his notebook out of his bomber jacket.

"It's spelled just like it sounds," Haisley said.

"How about the picture of the house? Can you tell where it's located?" Reece asked, hoping for something.

"It could be anywhere. There's a green lawn, and the house is a ranch style with white wood siding and green trim. The neighborhood has lots of trees. There's really nothing else to add."

"Well, I guess having a name is better than nothing," Reece said.

As he continued onward, he kept considering why the file of a long-cold missing-persons case would be missing. It could have been misplaced. That sort of stuff happened. But it stuck in his craw, all the same. This attractive woman decides after all these years to look up her mother, and that happens to be a file that is missing from the police records.

Well, he thought, sighing, he knew the woman worked in health care. He'd just head over to the hospital. They'd have records on Tracey Roberts—or at least he hoped so.

CHAPTER SEVEN

A NEW WHITE FORD van took the Garnet Road exit, southwest of Tulsa. The driver eyed himself in the rearview mirror and smoothed his shaggy windblown hair with the palm of his hand. He turned into the Motel 6 he'd spotted and parked near the entrance. The driver pulled a large black handgun from the center console and shoved it into a black leather satchel on the passenger's seat.

He pulled the hood of his dark gray sweatshirt, a twin to the one he'd bought for Owen Roberts, over his hair and got out. He walked with an air of purpose into the motel office. He frowned when the young acne-faced clerk asked for his driver's license and credit card, and instead slid a crisp hundred-dollar bill across the counter.

"This should take care of one night, and the rest is yours," the man said, staring at the young clerk coldly. He instantly jotted down the name John Doe in his motel log next to room number fifty-six, and slid a green fobbed room key across the counter.

The driver made his way to the bright orange steel door of the motel room and, once inside, went immediately to the window to close the curtains. He turned on the light and retrieved a towel from the small motel bathroom. After placing the towel lengthwise on the bed, the driver took his clothes off and folded each article into a neat pile on the towel as he undressed.

The hot water of the shower felt good on his muscled frame, but the cheap motel soap was hard to work into a lather despite the massaging of his strong hands. He rubbed the bar firmly upon the thick white hair of his scalp, trying to loosen any remnant of blood spatter that remained after dismembering the body. He'd caught the blackjack dealer writing e-mail to the Federal Bureau of Investigation. What kind of crap was that? he thought as he continued washing. A grim smile lit his face as he pictured the chainsaw he'd purchased at the hardware store. That made the task of inserting the dealer's six-foot frame into a blue plastic fifty-five gallon drum manageable. Now he was sucking up fish food in the Arkansas river.

The driver emerged from the steam-filled bathroom energized and pulled on a fresh pair of underwear and a white button-down shirt he'd picked up. The garment bag he'd brought with him in the van had a lone drip of dried blood, but the navy blue suit coat and matching dress pants inside the bag had remained pristine. He wrapped the towel on the bed over the his old clothes and placed them into the clear plastic garbage liner from the cheap brown wastebasket next to the TV stand.

He doubted anyone did any diving into this motel's Dumpster.

CHAPTER EIGHT

THE LARGE HOSPITAL where Tracey Roberts had once worked in the ICU took up half a block or more on the east side of 61st Avenue. Reece found a spot in visitor parking, and made his way into what looked like the administrative section of the mammoth red brick building.

He found a receptionist's window with the title "Medical Records" and approached.

"Excuse me, I'm looking for some employment records," Reece said. "Would you be able to help?"

"It depends whose records, and how old they are," the woman snarled, pushing up her bifocals.

"The records are for a client of mine who worked here. A nurse in the ICU," he said, holding up his identification.

"What were the dates of employment?"

"She worked here during 1989," he answered. He had barely finished when he was greeted with a cackling laugh. The woman turned her back and wandered off down a long aisle.

Reece stood at the window, not sure if she'd return. He had a mind to walk though the door labeled "Records" to his right. He heard what sounded like the same woman talking in the distance behind several large shelves. He heard her say "1989" and break into laughter.

Reece clenched his fist. She was patronizing him. He hated that and considered hopping over to the other side of the counter to shake some sense into this rude person. *Why walk away and blow me off?*

Instead, he left the counter and continued down the hallway looking for help. An older woman was coming toward him with a stack of medical records under one arm. She was short but sturdy with gray hair and thick glasses hanging from a chain around her neck.

"Excuse me," he said, reading the name Joan off of her badge.

"Yes."

"I'm looking for a historical employment record. Would you be the right person for that sort of thing?"

Joan walked off without saying a word, and Reece wondered if the hospital was going to be a dead end. He watched her open a door on her right and turn back.

"Come this way," she said. They walked by several rows of records neatly stacked in large yellow racks.

"What year is your historical record?" Joan asked.

"It's 1989," Reece answered, smiling at her.

"I was here then. What was the employee's name? I might have known him."

"Tracey Roberts. She was a nurse here for a short time."

"Doesn't sound familiar," Joan said. "That's a long time ago, however. If we still had those records they'd be downstairs. I was going to take lunch now, but if you have a few minutes we could go take a look."

"Sure," he said. They went to a reception desk, where he signed in and was given a visitor's badge. They walked down long hallways filled with sick people lying on gurneys, and Reece remembered why he disliked hospitals so much. Almost all of his previous visits were associated with pain, with damage to some part of his body, and the only thing that stayed the same regardless of which hospital he'd visited was the smell.

They took an elevator down for what seemed like twenty minutes, and on the way Reece learned that Joan had worked for the hospital for thirty-seven years, and was going to retire soon up on Lake Ten Killer. It made him think of his mother, who had recently bought a home on Keystone Lake west of Tulsa. He made a note to visit her while he was in town.

The elevator doors opened and they walked down a dark damp hallway toward a distant room she said was where they archived the records.

"The morgue is over there to the left down that hallway. I hate coming down here alone. You'd think I'd get used to it, but even after all of these years this place still gives me the creeps."

They passed a narrow passage leading to the morgue. A shrill wine came at them from nowhere. They stopped, and he tried to place the sound. Joan looked over at him with wide eyes.

"Sorry," she said, and then turned and hustled back to the elevator. The noise was continuous, as when construction workers rip sheets of plywood. Reece watched Joan disappear into the elevator. He guessed it was the kind of saw they used to cut open bodies during an autopsy. He continued down the hallway until he came to a single steel door with the words "Records Archive."

Reece tried the handle but it was locked. He walked to his right, down another hallway that seemed to lead to some unfinished part of the hospital. There were no doors, so he turned around. He searched the basement for a quite a while, and was about ready to call it quits when he found a door that exited into the back alley behind the building.

He stepped out welcoming the bright afternoon sunshine, and followed the red brick exterior toward the area where he thought the medical records might be. Reece came to a loading ramp with a door beside that read "Medical Records Archive". He rang the bell and waited until the door cracked open and a face appeared. "You got to go around to the front, mister," a short, pudgy man with wisps of blond hair on the sides of an otherwise bald head said.

Reece put his hand against the door to avoid having it slammed in his face. He knew enough now to fabricate a plausible fiction.

"I've been up front. I checked in with Joan in Medical Records. I'm here to continue my search."

"What did you say your name was?" the man asked, pulling the door open a little farther.

"Reece Culver."

"Are you with the hospital?"

"No, I'm an investigator," Reece said, holding up his ID.

"You working some big murder investigation or something?"

Reece kept quiet and followed him through a second door into a football field–sized room with high ceilings and tall steel shelving units that reminded him of the aisles at a warehouse store. He stopped and turned back toward the janitor.

"There haven't been any murders in the case that I know of."

"Okay, mister, I got work to do. Don't take anything, but if you need to make copies, you can use the copy machine over there," he said, pointing at an office area on the far side of the room. "You can let yourself out the same way we came in."

CHAPTER NINE

A BRIGHT YELLOW CAB pulled to the curb. George Kendall and Crystal stepped out from under the covered atrium outside the Omni Majestic Hotel in Saint Louis. Large drops of rain pelted George's gray raincoat. He grabbed the door and waited for Crystal to go in. He followed her into the cab, and after slamming the door said:

"Take us to 2222 Market Street, please."

The driver headed away from the curb with his windshield wipers working wildly to clear the rain.

"You two don't look like G-men to me," the driver, said looking at them in the rearview mirror.

"We're worse than G-men. Now mind your damn business, and take us were we want to go," Crystal said, smiling at George. The cab pulled up to the curb in front of the FBI building, and Crystal stepped out. George reached over the seat to pay and joined her on the curb.

"Are you having a bad day or something?" he asked, following Crystal into the lobby. She stopped, looking at the interior of the building. George caught up with her.

"I'm fine, I just hate this town. It's either six hundred degrees outside or raining cats and dogs."

"St. Louis is a fine town. Besides, a few days here will help you appreciate what we have back in Denver."

They went to the counter and signed in. The clerk asked to see two forms of official identification. Crystal looked at the man and he pointed to a posting of acceptable credentials. She read the list - "US Passport, Birth Certificate, Voters Registration Card, US Government ID badge, Social Security Card".

"Here use this," George said sliding his Denver federal center Id badge and Social Security card toward the clerk. Crystal reached into her coat and found her badge and after a quick search located a Voters Registration card in her purse. The clerk signed them in and told them that Special agent Stephen Cox was waiting for them in the Dovetail conference room on the forth floor.

Crystal and George stepped off the elevator each wearing blue and white visitors badges. George recognized Cox's secretary Rhonda, and they followed her into a large room with a conference table, and fourteen blue chairs. At one end there was a computer desk beside a gray steel file cabinet with a red and white magnet in the center of the top drawer that read, "Classified." Crystal took a seat next to George, who sat across from a stocky man with bushy gray hair and thick glasses, reminding her of Theodore Roosevelt. At the head of the table sat Special Agent Cox, the District Commander of the St. Louis FBI Organized Crime Task Force. He had a blond buzz cut and a gaunt face that she knew was a artifact left over from his days as a long distance runner. On the opposite side of the table sat three other men.

"I'd like to thank everyone for coming to this meeting. I wanted to get all of you together so we all have the latest information. I'd like to go around the room and introduce everyone. On my right is St. Louis Chief Detective Mike Mobley," Cox said referring to the man who resembled Teddy Roosevelt.

"Across from him is George Kendall which all of you are acquainted with, and his assistant Crystal Thomas. Across from Crystal is Jim Messerman from the Tulsa branch of the FBI. Agent Messerman is an expert in illegal gambling operations, to his left we have Detective Ed Stevens from the Tulsa Police Department, and finally Nathan Hawk, our St. Louis–based federal prosecutor," Agent Cox said.

Hawk and Stevens looked like garden variety businessmen dressed in inexpensive blue suits that might have come from Sears or Pennys. Agent Messerman had deep set black eyes, high cheek bones, and jet black hair that he wore parted to one side. His business suit had a sheen to it making it looker more expensive than the others.

"I brought you all here today to bring you up to speed on some new information we've obtained. During the past year Agent Messerman has infiltrated the operations of Sam Shanks, and we now have a dependable informant."

His secretary Rhonda dimmed the lights, and the projector screen at one end of the room lit up with a photograph of an elderly man. Crystal looked over, and saw her boss sneering at agent Cox in the dark.

"Ladies and gentlemen, this is a picture of our latest asset, Owen Roberts," Agent Cox said, motioning to Rhonda. The secretary carried in a large blue plastic tray covered in muffins, donuts, and tall cups of Starbucks coffee. Crystal smiled at Mike Mobley as his eyes followed the tray of food. Mobley seemed to notice the smile and gave a grin through his bushy mustache. With his lamb chop sideburns and bright red cheeks, he resembled a department store Santa Claus.

"Everyone, help yourself," Cox said, grabbing the largest of two apple fritters. He bit into the concoction of apple, sugar, and dough, and seemed surprised when it broke in half, with one piece nearly missing his coffee cup. Agent Cox set the donut down, still chewing, and licked his fingers, then began talking with his mouth full.

"This photo of our confidential informant was taken in 2005, when he was brought in for questioning by the Tulsa PD." Crystal studied the picture, and thought grudgingly that Owen looked good for his age. She pressed a fingernail under the bed of the adjacent finger and concentrated on the pain, feeling like she could break into a cold sweat at any moment. Having Owen Roberts' picture on the screen at the front of the room was a little too close for comfort.

"Owen L. Roberts grew up in St. Louis, Missouri, and we speculate he first met Sam Shanks in the late 1970s after becoming a regular customer at one of Shanks's gambling establishments," Cox said, motioning for Rhonda to go to the next slide.

"Here's a photo of Roberts playing poker with some as of yet unnamed companions."

As Crystal studied the photo of her father, she fought to control the rumble in her stomach. *What if they found out?* She clenched her sphincter and prayed. *If I run for the bathroom they'll know something.* She nibbled at the dry skin on the top of her bottom lip. Mike Mobley stared at her from across the table. She looked past him, trying not to make eye contact.

Agent Cox nodded his head, and Rhonda brought up the next slide. It was a family portrait in the front yard of a white house with green trim. The house Crystal grew up in with her parents Owen and Tracey Roberts. She stared at the picture wondering where her brothers Waylon and Julian were. It had been so long since she'd seen them. She felt like crying, but instead drifted into a daydream about the day they drug her away from her brothers. She'd later been told they went to a separate orphanage in the country south of Tulsa.

"This photo, taken in 1987, shows Owen Roberts, his wife Tracey, and their three children during happier times. His wife, Tracey took the kids and left in 1989,"

"Where was this taken?" George Kendall asked studying the photo. Crystal looked at her childlike visage in the picture and resisted the urge to bolt from the room. Her hair was dark red like her mother Tracey's, but with her dyed blond locks and the pale blue contact lenses she regularly wore to the office, she hoped no one would make the connection.

"That was in St. Louis," Cox said, gnawing on his second pastry, this one a Danish. He followed with a long sip of coffee, set down his coffee mug, and still swallowing started to speak. Crystal stared at Cox, wondering why he was in such a hurry to speak that he never finished chewing. That was what drove her so crazy when she was talking with the man she called Papa.

"Tracey Owens took her kids to the bus station on August 9, 1989. She left them by themselves supposedly to run an errand, and was never heard from again."

"How do you know where she left?" Nathan Hawk asked.

"The oldest sibling, Waylon, told us what she said before leaving. Owen Roberts is still the prime suspect in her disappearance, but the crime was never solved," Cox said wolfing down the last of his Danish in the dim light.

Crystal rocked forward in her seat. "Was she ever located?"

"No, Ms. Thomas. We didn't receive notification until a few weeks after her disappearance, and by then the trail had gone cold. Are there any other questions?" Agent Cox asked.

Crystal sat back, fidgeting with her hands under the table. She pushed hard and felt the tip of her thumbnail lift. The pain was strong. If she continued, it would bleed. Yet the pain took her away from the fear. She remembered learning the habit in the orphanage.

"Over the past year we pieced together Owen's story. He's a compulsive gambler, and we think he became indebted to Shanks between the years 1980 to 1989. Shanks put together some kind of deal with Owen. There was one theory that his wife's disappearance was the result of the deal. We're still speculating on what happened to her, but sometime between 1980 and the present Owen went to work for Shanks," Cox said, picking up his coffee mug.

"Next slide, please. Okay, here's a series of aerial photographs showing the property that Shanks and his crew call home these days. We've got a man working for us down in Tulsa who's observed the operation at night. Our Tulsa man is a regular at a Thursday night poker game."

With the new subject Crystal felt relieved, but she still worried that her boss George Kendall would make the connection between her and Owen. She panned the faces of the men across the table and all eyes were on the detailed map of Shanks' Tulsa casino. From the air it looked like a series of farm buildings about a half-mile in from a small two-lane road to the north. A small creek paralleled the property on the west and that area appeared heavily wooded. A neighborhood of houses abutted the plot on the east, about a mile or so from the main casino building. From what she could see in the pictures the large expanse of land seemed like the perfect place to hide a casino.

"Have you confirmed that this is indeed an illegal gambling establishment?" George Kendall asked.

"Yes, like I said earlier, Agent Messerman has a man that's been a regular at the property for the past three months. Agent Messerman, would you like to add to that?" Cox said as he slid the laser pointer across the table.

"Here's a map we've made of the property. This brick building here is the main casino, and the other buildings service a working farm on the property," Messerman said, aiming the red laser pointer at the screen.

"The last time we met with the CI, Owen Roberts, he told us Shanks is pulling the plug on the place. He's got a big party planned for Saturday night, February 5. We're going in two days before this coming Thursday night. It's the night of their weekly poker tournament, and the place will be a zoo. It's the perfect time to blend in and pull this off," Cox said running a hand through his short buzz cut. "Okay, the raid will go like this."

CHAPTER TEN

ONCE INSIDE THE archives, Reece walked down the first aisle. The shelves were filled with stacked cardboard records boxes with large labels listing a range of names housed inside. He could see that most of the boxes were arranged alphabetically, so when he got to the end he made his way toward the "R's". The section that was labeled with a large green "Q" was narrower than the one before it, which seemed logical.

Reece walked down the next row looking for a name that started with "Roberts", but by the time he'd gotten to the end he'd only found "Reynolds". He turned the corner and was in the "S's". Turning back he looked up toward the top of the shelving where he could just make out a box with the name "Roans" midway down from the very top shelf. It was a long way up and he wondered if he could climb the tall metal shelving to reach the top shelf. Reece took hold of a steel beam that supported the next row of shelves just above his head, and began to pull him self up. Just then a door slammed on the other side of the cavernous warehouse, and he thought better of the idea. He didn't want anyone looking at him like a cat burglar.

He stepped down, walked out into the aisle, and searched for a way to reach the top. Down toward the end he saw a tall steel staircase ladder with two wheels on the backside, and rubber feet on the front. He sprinted to the ladder, tipped it back onto the wheels, and rolled it back into the aisle. He looked up at the area of the top shelf guessing it contained Tracey Robert's employment file, and positioned the ladder. Stepping down on a bar that ran parallel to the wheels, he locked the brake and started upward.

The ladder held his 195-pound frame with ease. He searched for the box he'd seen earlier labeled "Roans." He found it straight above and started to climb toward it. On the way up he got a sense of just how high he was. He'd never liked heights, at least not since falling out of the top of a tree in the backyard of his St. Louis home at the age of nine. That stunt had cost him his run for the spelling bee championship and resulted in a blue cast that at least won him lots of sympathy and signatures from his classmates.

Reece rolled until he saw a box labeled "Roberts – Rogolan." He stood on the top step of the ladder and reached out toward the box, but was a couple of feet shy. A door slammed in the distance, and he wondered if the janitor had left for lunch. Reece looked back over his shoulder and could see all the way to the other side of the room. He was alone.

The shelving lacked much to hold onto. He stuck his right foot into the angle brace, hoisted himself up off of the ladder, and onto the top shelf. The structure wiggled in a wide, unnerving manner. He knelt down on top of a box, crunching his knee through its cardboard lid, and waited for the shelving unit to settle.

In the distance a loud voice broke the silence. Reece froze, ducking down until almost lying flat on the tops of the boxes. He thought he heard the familiar voice of the janitor. It sounded like he was arguing with someone. The second voice sounded deeper with a thick southern drawl. Reece lay there trying to discern what the two men were yelling about.

"You don't belong here," he heard the janitor yell. Reece had no idea who he was yelling at, but he didn't want to linger and let the intruder discover him. Reaching into the records box he'd seen earlier, he sorted through the names, but kept low to avoid detection. He found a manila envelope with a green tab labeled "Roberts." Reece pulled it out and flipped the thick file open. He saw the name "Nester Roberts" and dropped it to his side. The next file folder had a similar green tab with the same name.

Reece heard the voices coming closer and froze, hoping they wouldn't see the ladder. The janitor let out a loud scream—"No, don't you—" that echoed off the ceiling above.

A long bout of silence followed. Reece didn't like the sound of that. He listened intently, wondering what was going on below. He couldn't see much from his vantage point, so he knelt up and looked over the top of the boxes to his right. The janitor was lying haphazardly on the cement floor a couple of rows over. A small puddle of blood was forming near his face. *What the hell is going on?*

A mechanical noise erupted down on the floor behind him. He heard a "clang" and recognized the noise from when he'd stepped down on the brake of the ladder he'd used to climb the shelving unit. Reece heard the squeal of a wheel bearing. He crawled closer to the edge and looked down. Someone was dragging the ladder around the corner at the end of the aisle. He was trapped.

Reece warily climbed back toward the other side. As he spotted the janitor lying on the floor, he saw someone jogging in his peripheral vision. A figure in a dark gray hoodie passed the next shelving unit before running out of sight. It looked like a man, but he couldn't be sure. He had no time to waste. He had to finish up and get out of there before the guy that stole the ladder found him.

Reece tore into the box flipping through records. At last he spied the name "Tracey Roberts" on an orange tab and pulled it out. He opened the folder and saw the date August 19, 1989. It had to be the right one. Reece folded it in half and shoved it into his pocket. He heard a low, growling electro-mechanical sound, like a piece of industrial equipment. Standing slowly, he braced himself on the top of the shelving unit. He stepped forward a little too aggressively and felt the shelves buckle.

The mechanical noise was drawing closer, changing tone in a Doppler effect. It was moving along the ceiling with the low musical grind of a large electric motor. *What the hell is that?* He took a couple of steps forward, trying to see past a pile of boxes that were taller than the rest on the adjacent shelf. He felt the swaying movement beneath his feet and knew he had to take slow steps or risk toppling the shelving unit. Finally, he saw the source of the mechanical noise. It was a large yellow bridge crane spanning across the ceiling. The center had red numbers painted on it that said "50 Ton." He looked down toward the door through which he'd entered and saw the guy in the hoodie. He was holding a yellow box at the end of a pendant that ran up to the crane. It was the control box.

The crane was gaining speed, getting closer by the second. The carriage for the crane was moving sideways. It looked to be a mere forty feet away. He saw a big gray steel hook hanging down. Reece took hold of the shelf, grabbing the steel braces with his hands in an attempt to climb down. His weight made the unit wobble. He swung down to the next row of shelves, and lost his grip, slamming down sideways into a pile of cardboard boxes.

The crane was getting close and sounded like it was traveling at full speed. He wondered who the man in the hoodie was. *Did he kill the janitor and why? What did he want?* Reece reached to his waist for his gun and realized he'd left it in the car. He slid his foot into the brace under the shelf and looked down at the concrete floor forty feet below. He was high enough that if he lost his footing and fell, he'd be severely injured if not killed. The crane was getting closer. He had to hurry if he was going to get down.

Reece climbed down the green steel shelving. He grabbed the edge and felt for a cross brace underneath, but there wasn't one. He leaned over the side of the shelf, looking down. The space between the shelves was a good ten feet. He grabbed the shelf with both hands and lowered himself.

With a forceful whack the crane collided with the top of the shelving unit. His feet swung out away from the next shelf at a forty-five-degree angle. Squeezing his hands, he tightened his grip. He looked up at the ceiling and could see the entire shelving unit tipping over toward him. *I'll be smashed.*

Reece let go. Time slowed as he fell. He hit something hard and felt an explosion of pain in his side. The blow knocked the wind out of him and he fought to breathe. A mountain of boxes crashed down. He heard the steel shelving unit crash to the concrete floor and cringed, hoping it wouldn't hit him. He lay still, listening to the sound of boxes smashing dully to the floor all around him.

When the bombardment was over, Reece opened his eyes and found himself blinking at darkness. He was lying underneath the mountain of boxes he'd been climbing among earlier. He lay silent, thinking about the crane. He took deep breaths, forcing away the pain he felt in his side. He thought about the man with the control box. He had to climb out of this mess and get out of here before the guy came after him. He heard a box sliding to the floor a few feet away. Someone was walking toward him.

The only thing he could do was ready himself to launch a surprise attack if the wrong boxes were flung aside.

CHAPTER ELEVEN

A BLACK STRETCH LIMOUSINE glided up in front of the Philbrook Museum of Art under a cloudless sky in Tulsa. The rear door of the car swung open, encouraged by a pomegranate colored Berluti loafer. The shoe retracted from the leather interior armrest followed by a man whose stature was less than average. He wore a long black wool overcoat topped with a scarf that matched his shoes, and provided warmth to the sides of his prominent hairless head. The limo driver stepped out to get the door, but the man waved him off as he reached for the pale outstretched hand of a young woman.

The man pulled out a tall brunette with quaffed hair, bright blue eyes, and well-toned legs. She wore a crushed black taffeta dress with short black sleeves. The man in the overcoat turned toward the limo driver.

"I'll call you when the party's over," he said in a Chicago accent.

"Very good, sir. If anything changes, just use this number," the driver said, handing him a business card. The passenger shoved the card into the breast pocket of his William Fioravanti suit and slid a hand under the woman's right arm. They walked toward the entrance of the museum, where two doormen dressed in matching black and gold suits were positioned on either side of large double doors. Sam Shanks grabbed the ornate black steel of the stair railing with one hand and undid the buttons of his overcoat with the other as he and his date ascended the steps.

Shanks had always admired the look of Villa Philbrook, a structure originally constructed in 1927 as the home of oilman Waite Phillips. Shanks knew the story well. Phillips had hired Edward Buehler Delk, a Kansas City architect to design an Italian Renaissance villa on the twenty-three-acre plot as a place for their two children to entertain friends. In 1938, Phillips announced that he was giving the seventy-two-room mansion and surrounding grounds to the city of Tulsa as an art center.

Shanks had a dream of doing something similar someday at a place far from here. He led his twenty-something date through the museum lobby toward a group of patrons dressed in similar fashion. A gray-haired man dressed in a tuxedo took a close look at them and said.

"Mr. Shanks. Welcome, it's good to see you. I trust you had a good flight."

"Very good," Shanks said, knowing he'd not been on an airplane in months.

"May I take your coats?" the man asked. Shanks slipped out of his overcoat, handing it to the man, and led his date across the yellow marble tiled foyer toward a room where the group had arranged to meet.

"Sam, I'm so glad you could make it," a tall woman said, approaching the couple. She wore a dress of white silk with a bright yellow scarf draped over her right shoulder. "We've got a great group. Would you like a glass of champagne?" she said, snapping her right finger skyward.

"Do you know any of these people?" Shanks' date said, biting her lip.

"I know everyone that's anybody in the art world, my dear. It's what I do," Shanks said. A tuxedo-clad waiter appeared with a tray covered in glasses of sparkling wine. He helped himself to a glass and handed a second flute to his date before joining a large group of people who were milling around in the main area of the museum. The walls were lined with a collection of mid seventeenth-century Italian artwork.

Shanks spotted Dominic Vance and nudged the arm of his date. She turned toward the approaching man like a fine diamond being shown off by its proud owner. Shanks watched the man's eyes take in the lovely piece of arm candy he'd brought, and for a moment it helped Sam feel superior to all of the other well-heeled gentlemen in the museum.

"Who do we have here?" Vance said, extending his hand.

"Dominic, I didn't see you. You look well. Let me introduce you. This is Candice," Shanks said, pushing the woman toward the Manhattan gallery owner. He took her right hand, kneading it like a piece of molding clay.

"It's so nice to meet you, Candice. Do you have a last name?" Dominic said as the woman pulled her hand as if from a snake.

"Just Candice."

"Very well, then. Sam, there are some collectors here I'd like to introduce you to. Come this way."

Vance passed in front of the couple and led them toward a corner where a small group including the woman with the yellow scarf and two other couples dressed in drab business attire were admiring a large fresco.

"Excuse me, this is the man I was telling you about earlier," Vance said as they approached the group. "Mr. and

Mrs. Phillips, this is Mr. Shanks and his date, Candice." They exchanged greetings and Vance introduced the second couple as Mr. and Mrs. Shimmer.

They headed as a group through the marble-floored rooms of the museum looking at fine art. Sam Shanks was looking over Mrs. Phillips—an obvious trophy—when he caught Melvin Phillips staring at him. The man's wife was in her early forties with long blond hair, high cheekbones, and piercing blue eyes. Her husband was closer to sixty and walked with a noticeable limp. Phillips pulled two cigars from his inside breast pocket and nodded toward Shanks as if to say, do you want to join me? The two men left the group and walked out the side door toward the extensive gardens.

"It's a great day to be outdoors," Phillips said, handing one of the Arturo Feunte cigars to Shanks and then holding up a torch-like stainless steel lighter.

"It is, Mr. Phillips. Thanks for the smoke," Sam said, lighting his cigar and taking several puffs as the end started to glow. Sam held in one of the puffs, enjoying the flavor, as Mr. Phillips lit his own cigar.

"I've got to ask you, Phillips. Are you any relation to Waite Phillips?"

"No, I'm afraid not. All we share is the same last name and a fondness for beautiful things."

"I've got to bring a camera next time I come here. I'm building a new home down south, and I could definitely take some cues from this place." Shanks said.

"Down south. In Texas?" Melvin asked.

"No. The land I own is on a whole different continent," Shanks said.

"Yes it's always good to have multiple homes. We've got a few spread out across the country, and then there's our villa in

Tuscany," Melvin said, sounding competitive. "So Mr. Shanks, are you a collector?"

"Very much so. How about you, Mr. Phillips?"

"Call me Melvin, and yes, my wife and I are very active."

"Do you have a favorite artist?"

"It varies, but these days I'm looking for a Van Gogh."

"Anything in particular?" Shanks said.

"Something small and priceless."

CHAPTER TWELVE

REECE TRIED TO hold his breath, but his side hurt. The footsteps on the concrete went around him. He heard the sound of boxes being thrown and crashing down in the distance. The killer would soon be digging him out. His heart pounded in his chest, feeling helpless as he hid under the boxes pushing down on him. Yet whoever was stalking him apparently came to the conclusion that he must have already left before the shelf units came crashing down. Because he heard more steps. The person was walking away.

Reece didn't budge. He felt the adrenaline pumping through his body and took slow calculated breaths, calming himself.

A heavy door slammed in the distance. He was reminded of the janitor and quickly came to the conclusion that he might still be alive. Using his shoulder to nudge the boxes aside, he soon was able to stand up among the wreckage of cardboard. He hugged the wall and came to the spot two aisles over where he'd seen the janitor. He was gone. There were drag marks where the Frisbee-sized puddle of blood had been smeared toward the center aisle. It was obvious that the killer had dragged the body away to hide his handiwork.

Reece took his time walking toward the back door. Seeing a green desk phone on the janitor's desk, he lifted the receiver and dialed 911. He set it down just as the operator answered, knowing that the number alone would alert them to dispatch someone. With extreme caution he stepped out of the second door, looking both ways. The alley was empty.

His legs hurt like someone had hit it with a baseball bat. He felt a nagging pain in his right side that he worried might be more serious. Reece walked up the steps to the rental car, climbed in, and drove out of the parking lot, blending into traffic on Memorial Boulevard. He wanted nothing more than to put a few miles between himself and the crime scene he'd just departed.

Yet he'd accomplished what he'd come for. The folder he'd dug out of the records box was lying on the passenger's seat beside him. As he stopped at a traffic light he glanced down and saw that Tracey Roberts had used her aunt, Mary Ann Fletcher, for her emergency contact. After pulling his cellphone out, Reece flipped it open and dialed the number Crystal had given him when they'd parted ways.

"Hello," Crystal answered, sounding stressed.

"Crystal, it's Reece Culver."

"Oh, hi Reece, where are you?"

"I'm in Tulsa. How's your business trip going?"

"Oh, it's just the usual boring stuff," she said. "How's the investigation going, Reece? Have you found anything yet?" He thought about what had just happened, but thought better of telling her.

"Crystal, do you remember the street you lived on back in St. Louis, before Tracey took you and your brother's to Tulsa?"

"Let me think. Calvert maybe?" Crystal said. "Yeah, that's it. No, no, it's Calvin Ave. Our house was on the left side of the street three houses down from the park with the big tree," Crystal said. "I miss that place."

"Okay, Calvin Avenue. Do you remember anything else about it?"

"No, not too much. It was a long time ago. Are you going there?"

"Yeah, I've got an errand to run first, but I'll probably head there tonight. When are you planning to be back in Denver?"

"It depends how the meetings go, but I think I'll probably be home Wednesday. I'd really like to see you, Reece," she said. "That night in your apartment. The second time we met."

"Yeah," he said, not sure where she was leading, but wanting to find out.

"For a while there it seemed like something was happening," she said.

"Yeah?" Reece said, letting her talk.

"Reece, I know you felt it too. Something was happening between us."

"Like some kind of connection?" Reece said.

"More than that."

That purr she got in her voice was back again, and Reece couldn't help feel stimulated, even though the phone. The entire mess he'd just been through slipped from his mind as he waited to hear more of that purr. But it didn't take him long to realize she'd already hung up.

CHAPTER THIRTEEN

CRYSTAL THOMAS STEPPED from the curb into the cab, thankful the rain had stopped. George Kendall had let her skip their afternoon meetings with the Missouri federal attorney. He'd told her he would call when he returned to the hotel, so they could have dinner together.

The inside of the taxi had the faint smell of cherry pipe tobacco. Crystal ran her hand over the smooth black vinyl back seat. She noticed the driver's hair was gray on the sides and thinning with wisps of white on top. She wondered if her father Owen's hair might look the same. He would be sixty or so about now, so he would have lost the thick brown hair she had patted with her small hand as a child. After the meeting today she felt conflicted, having hated him all these years for what she'd imagined he'd done to her mother.

His compulsive gambling most likely ruined the marriage. The family as well. She thought of her brothers Julian and Wayne, and wondered where they were. Soon enough, though, her mind turned to more immediate circumstances. She had to watch out that someone in the investigation might connect her to her father, and suspect she was trying to sabotage the investigation.

She felt the cab slow and come to a stop. They had arrived in front of her hotel. She smiled at the driver, handed him a fifty and said, "Keep the change." The driver got out and opened her door.

"If you need any more rides during your stay, here's my card. You can reach me on my cell twenty-four hours a day." Crystal took the card, looked at the name, and said. "Thanks, Charlie. You never know what I'll need."

"Give me twenty minutes, and I'll be here. I can take you anywhere you need to go," the cab driver yelled as she walked toward the front entrance.

The lobby was paneled in fine wood and a large clock on the wall near the entrance to a bar told her how much time she had to prepare for the sting she was planning. She took the elevator up to the third floor, and once she was inside her room she tossed off her long gray raincoat, and plopped down on the bed. She ran the back of her hand across the cold cotton pillow. The cool cloth felt good and reminded her of her mother's soft skin. She remembered her mother holding her against her shoulder when she used to iron Owen's dress shirts. Her mother was so kind and loving. Crystal had kept the letters she'd been receiving the past couple of weeks in her purse.

The first taupe envelope she'd received looked like a wedding invitation. None of the letters had a return address and the postmark was always from a different city. Tears welled up in her eyes as she grabbed her purse and pulled the latest letter she'd received from the person she assumed was her mother. She wanted to be reunited with her more than anything. They had so much to catch up on.

Crystal got up off the bed and went to the closet, wondering what to wear for dinner. She paged through the hangers, stopping to examine each piece of clothing. She passed by a green wool sweater, a pair of khaki slacks, a dark gray hooded sweatshirt, a beige collared satin top, and a short blue skirt.

The satin top was a definite possibility. *Was it conservative enough?*

Crystal reached into her suitcase and dug out her new Samsung smart phone. She scrolled through the numbers, found the one she was looking for, and pressed send. The phone rang twice and went to voicemail.

"I'm sorry to bother you, Papa, but I need to talk," Crystal said in a soft voice. She ended the call and, holding the phone, she remembered the starring role it was going to play tonight. She pressed the blue applications icon on the display. Scrolling through four pages of icons, she came to the one for the camera. With her index finger she tapped the tiny camera button and the viewfinder opened up, displaying the hotel room's brown shag carpeting. Crystal held the phone sideways, aiming at the dresser mirror across from the bed. The image was clear and, with a little light, would be perfect. She pressed the gray camera symbol on the top right, and the mode changed to video.

That's what she wanted: a recording of her married boss engaged in sex with another woman.

Crystal set the camera on the dresser across from the bed. To stabilize it, she propped it up with the Bible behind, and a *Cosmopolitan* magazine in front. She clicked the red button, and the phone chimed. The counter on the top right of the screen counted the seconds of video. Using her finger, she stopped the recording and played it back. Crystal tapped one of the four buttons on the bottom, put the phone into silent mode, and left it sitting sideways on the dresser. It was all ready for the fireworks display.

CHAPTER FOURTEEN

REECE DROVE EAST toward Broken Arrow, Oklahoma, eyeing the moisture-laden clouds that hung from the sky, in places hugging the ground. He had a vivid flash of the janitor splayed out on the cement floor and hoped he hadn't died. He wondered who was trying to kill him.

He'd caught a lucky break with the employment records from the hospital, and was hoping he'd be able to learn something from Tracey's emergency contact, Mary Ann Fletcher. Reece held up the scrap of paper from the hospital and read off her address. He drove past an assortment of small well-kept yards. Spotting her address, he drove into the driveway in front of a beige house with red trim that was in need of a paint job. The small porch was covered with more than a week's worth of yellowing newspapers and an assortment of white plastic trash bags. He didn't care to guess what the trash bags contained, but figured it was dog poop.

He pressed the doorbell, and heard its echo through the small single-story home. Reece took a deep breath, preparing himself, and the faint smell of mold came to him. He was pressing the bell a second time when he heard someone fumbling with the knob. It seemed like whoever was inside the home wasn't exactly sure how to open the front door. An elderly woman with a nasal cannula shoved into her nostrils and threads of stiff white hair sticking out at odd angles from beneath a yellow scarf popped out. She stood staring at him with deep-set gray eyes as if he'd been the first to ring her bell in years.

She began to look ill, and then a slow billow of smoke rose from the corners of her mouth. In the fingers of her vein-covered purple paw she held a long cigarette with two inches of ash about to drop at any moment.

She brought the cigarette to her lips and sucked until the hollow parts of her cheeks drew in toward her mouth. The sight caused Reece's throat to constrict, and made him feel like coughing.

"What do you want?" the woman hollered in a voice louder than warranted.

"Mrs. Fletcher, my name's Reece Culver," he said, holding out his private investigator's license.

"You're from Colorado. What do you want with me?" she said, more observant than her physical demeanor indicated.

"I'm investigating the disappearance of Tracey Roberts. She listed you as her emergency contact at the hospital in Tulsa," Reece explained, hoping she'd invite him in. The woman stood looking at him, like she was trying to decide what to do next. She took another drag on the cigarette, and he watched the ash break off and drop onto the toe of his shoe. Finally, she retreated backwards into her home, waving him in.

Most of the furniture was covered by dull yellow sheets with a thick covering of dust. The walls were decorated with brown striped wallpaper, and the air smelled like a mixture of cat urine, cigarettes, and something sweet that he couldn't identify. The woman parked a green oxygen tank by a gold recliner covered in cat hair. As she slowly sat down, she displaced a small cloud of dander.

"Take a seat, Culver," she said, pointing to a matching recliner. Reece sat down amid a huge cloud of rising dust as he sank into the worn chair. He fought off a sneeze and realized the noise he'd heard when he'd first arrived was coming from a television set on its loudest volume. Noticing it at the same time, the woman dug the remote control out from under a stack of used cigarette packages and lowered the sound.

"What was it you were looking for, Culver?" she asked in a sarcastic tone.

"I'm working on a missing person's case," he answered. "I'm looking for Tracey Roberts."

"After all these years, why bother? If she'd wanted to be found, she would have called," the woman said in an annoyed tone, blowing smoke from both nostrils. "Who's turning that stone back over? Let me guess: it's got to be Crystal."

"You know Crystal Thomas?" Reece asked.

"Is that what she calls herself these days?" the woman asked. "That damn child never could let anything alone."

She took another deep drag of smoke. "That Crystal has had more men than I have cats. What's that silly child looking for now?"

"Did you spend much time with Crystal when she lived in Oklahoma?" he asked, getting the feeling that if he didn't change the subject he was going to waste half a day listening to what she thought of Crystal.

"No, not until she got into boys. She used to come for the weekend and stay with me. I liked her company at first," the old woman said.

"Did something happen to change your mind?"

"She met a boy from another school. He was two years

older than her, and I wondered what a sixteen-year-old boy would want with a fourteen-year-old. Of course, it didn't take much imagination to figure that out. Crystal was one of those girls that developed early, like her mother. At least she didn't get herself pregnant like Tracey did," she said, adjusting the oxygen cannula in her nostrils and inhaling more smoke at the same time.

Reece could feel his eyes starting to water and wasn't sure if it was from cat hair, dust, or smoke.

"Oprah's on. You ever watch her? She's great," the old woman said. She picked up the remote and began increasing the television volume.

"Can I see the room Crystal stayed in when she came to visit?" he asked.

"Yeah, it's that one down the hallway. Help yourself. It's time for the show."

He walked down the hallway, passing an assortment of black and white photos, and idly wondered where the cats were hiding. He came to a door and reached for the handle.

"Not that one. At the end of the hall," the old lady shouted.

Reece followed her directions and turned the brass knob of a light wood door. He walked in and looked around. The walls were pink, and a window at the top of a queen-sized bed was covered with yellow drapes. The walls were covered with an assortment of movie tickets, ribbons, and school photos. Reece studied them, and noticed how different the clothing back then looked. By the closet he saw a corkboard covered with pictures.

Reece came upon an eight-by-ten photo of a woman with long red hair and bright blue eyes —was that Tracey Roberts? She held a small girl in her arms, and two older boys stood to one side. A man on the left had left a noticeable gap between himself and the others. He had a slight build with curly brown hair and a muted smile. The kids looked sad, but for some reason the mother looked proud. He was guessing the look was put on for whoever was taking the photo, and had nothing to do with how she felt.

The picture was taken in front of a single-story house with green window trim and white siding. He guessed from the ages of the children that it had been taken in the mid eighties. The corkboard was filled with other photos of Crystal and her friends. In one photo she stood with a boy in an Edison High School football uniform. Reece guessed that was the boyfriend Mrs. Fletcher had mentioned earlier. Crystal was holding a football, and the boy had his arms around her and was kissing her on the cheek.

He was looking at a bunch of old movie tickets stuffed into the edge of the frame when he spotted what looked like a Rolling Stones concert ticket. It looked older than the rest, and he doubted Crystal had gone to Rolling Stones concerts as a child. He plucked the ticket from the wood border, and read the date. It was from the November 1981 concert in St. Louis. He did some quick math, and confirmed this must have been a keepsake from one of her parents. Crystal wasn't born until August of 1982.

He stuffed the ticket into his pants pocket, and as he turned to go, he found Ann Fletcher standing a few steps behind him. *How long had she been there?*

"I hope you aren't taking things," she said.

"Mrs. Fletcher," he said, trying to deflect her attention by pointing to a large group photo he'd seen earlier, "who are these people?"

"That's the family," she said, walking up, bringing a trail of stale smoke-filled air with her. "That's me and my husband Fred. That man there is Owen Roberts, Tracey's husband."

"Do you remember what year the picture was taken?" Reece asked.

"I'd guess 1985," she said. "If I were you and I really wanted to find Tracey, I'd concentrate my energy on locating Owen. He's the only person I can think of that would have something to gain."

CHAPTER FIFTEEN

GEORGE KENDALL WALKED into his hotel room, bothered by the name Owen Roberts. He'd been considering that last name since leaving the earlier meeting. Kendall sat on the bed and saw a row of pigeons on an adjacent roofline. Things hadn't gone well for him in the afternoon meetings at the federal building in downtown St. Louis. Special Agent Stephen Cox had appointed himself lead and Kendall was pissed. It had been the Missouri federal attorney's idea to include the FBI in their investigation, and now they were taking over the case. He was no longer sure he'd be the chief prosecutor.

Kendall opened his laptop, and while waiting for it to boot up, he went to the bathroom for a glass of water. When the cold water washed over the new crown in the back of his mouth, he made a funny face. He set the glass down a little too hard, enough to crack it.

Returning to his laptop, he scrolled down a list of websites until he came to the Colorado Bureau of Investigation. He went through a series of login screens until he found the directories he was looking for. It had been standard protocol for the CBI to run an extended background check on all of the personnel working in his office. He scanned the entries until he found the original folder for Crystal, dated September 23, 2007. He opened the folder and clicked on her file, looking for the list of relatives she'd provided.

He found the heading Birth Parents and read the names Tracey and Owen Roberts. He stared at the names, thinking back to the meeting he'd just come from with the FBI. How many men named Owen Roberts lived in St. Louis?

*

Crystal splashed water on her face and glanced down at the skimpy black thong she'd picked for dinner, knowing the task ahead would be easy. The collar of her blouse was slightly crooked, so she adjusted it, lining up the red silk edge just above the black lace of her bra. With both hands cupping the undersides of her breasts, she pushed up. She stuck her plump lips outward, puckering at the mirror, and applied one last coat of restless red. Staring at the full-length mirror on the back of the door, she looked down at her bare feet and then upward to her forehead, then squeezed her buttocks tight, pulling in her stomach. The skirt she'd laid out earlier was sitting on the bed.

The phone rang, startling her.

"Hello."

"Crystal, it's George. I'm down in the Clock bar. Will you come join me for a drink?"

"Oh, okay, I was reading a magazine, but I guess so, George," Crystal said with simulated hesitation. "I'll be down in a few minutes."

Bingo. She hung up the phone, pulled the skirt off the bed, and stepped into it, looking sideways at the mirror. After taking a seat on the edge of the bed she slid her feet into a pair of three-inch black high heels. Crystal plugged the charger into the phone, clicked on the lamp next to the bed, and left for the big date that would compromise her boss for good.

CHAPTER SIXTEEN

REECE WAS TIRED of chasing pavement and yearned to stretch his legs. He took the exit off the Mark Twain Turnpike and entered a neighborhood where the vast majority of the homes had plywood nailed over their windows. He soon spied Calvin Avenue, where Owen and Tracey Roberts chose to live on while raising their three children. He followed the directions he'd copied onto the lower half of his grease-stained McDonalds bag, past 1960s-era houses that looked like abandoned remnants after some toxic chemical spill.

He parked in front of the house listed as 4867 Calvin Avenue. When he killed the car's ignition, he was met by the howl of semis coming from the highway he'd just exited. It seemed like a horrible place to raise a family, but maybe the highway hadn't been around then.

Reece switched off the headlights and sat in the car with the doors locked. The street was pitch black, and he had a funny feeling about approaching the house. His cellphone buzzed on vibrate mode in the front pocket of his jeans. He pulled it out and answered.

"Reece Culver Investigations."

"Reece, it's your mother. Where are you?"

"I'm parked on a residential street on the north side of St. Louis. Why?"

"What are you doing there?"

"I'm trying to locate a missing person," Reece said. "I'm working a case."

"Oh, is Haisley with you?"

"No, why would Haisley be with me?" Reece said.

"I don't know. I guess I just thought he might be."

Reece was irritated by his mother's remark, and he stared toward the lone illuminated house at the end of the street.

"You're not still trying to solve your father's murder, are you?"

"No ... well, yes, I am still trying to solve that," Reece said. "But no, that's not what I'm doing right now."

"I've told you time and time again to leave that to the authorities," she said. "I mean it, Reece. The men who killed your father—"

Reece had heard this lecture so many times, and after his long drive he was not in the mood for it. "Look, Mom, I said I'm on another case. This has nothing to do with Dad. This is an investigation, for which I'm being paid good money, I might add."

"Well, all right, then," she said, and from her tone of voice he could tell she didn't think that added up to much. Not like his wonderful older brother. "I thought you were coming to visit me when you were in Tulsa," she went on.

"I can still do that," he said, wanting to get her off the phone. "I still have unfinished business down there, and I'll give you a call when I'm in town."

"You make sure you do. It's hard enough being all alone after the death of your father, but when your children never come to visit—"

"I said I'll call," he said, trying to stop a new torrent of complaints. She'd never paid him a lick of attention when he was growing up, but now that she was lonely, he all of a sudden was to blame for not visiting her. "Do you have any plans tomorrow night?"

"No, I guess not," she said slowly.

"How does six work? I'll drop by and we'll go to Jamils Steakhouse. My treat."

"Okay, Reece. That sounds good." For the first time she sounded happy. She'd gotten her son to do what she wanted.

"I gotta go," Reece, said. "See you tomorrow."

He sighed as he clicked off. He shouldn't be so hard on her. He should try to act more like a comforting son. That's what he told himself, anyway. It wasn't his fault she could so conveniently forget the past.

Opening the glove compartment, he pulled out his holster and the .357 Magnum he always carried, figuring it might come in handy from the looks of the area. He kicked the door open a little too hard and wished he hadn't when the large green door springs popped it back toward him. He pulled his foot back into the floor well just before the door slammed shut with a loud "clank." Why did his mother have to call? he thought as he got out of the car.

He walked onto the unkempt lawn, adjusting his eyes to the dark. He studied the lit-up house across the street, wondering if they might have known Owen or his missing wife Tracey, but decided he'd hold off on knocking on any doors. As his attention turned to the front of the Roberts home, he saw that the slender windows on each side of the front door had been covered in plywood from the inside.

With the trunk of the car open, he pulled out his nine-inch LED Maglite and lit the street behind the car with its strong white beam. Satisfied that the light would guide him through the darkness he extinguished it and pushed the trunk closed.

Reece walked toward the front door, feeling the weeds scrape his pants with their rough edges, and noticed two ancient oil stains where a car had once parked. He walked up on the porch, and listened, half wondering if Owen might still inhabit the place. Reece thought he heard a noise coming from inside, but wasn't sure. He tried the doorknob and found it was locked. Leaning back, he slammed his left shoulder against the front door, but it didn't budge. Maybe he'd have better luck trying the back.

Making his way across the front yard, he saw a faint glow coming from the front room of a house down the block on the opposite side of the street. Maybe those neighbors had known the Roberts family back then. He'd come back the next day to canvas the neighborhood.

Reece walked around the house until he came to the man door on the side of the garage. Inside he saw the remains of a motorbike. Pressing down on the Maglite, he shined it inside. The motorcycle was an old Honda seventy with flat, rotted tires and a rusty seat stained from the springs below. The engine was badly coroded and he wondered if Crystal or her two brothers had once ridden last. He painted the side of the garage with light, and saw bare weathered wood with peeled paint stretching outward.

Reece switched off the Maglite and made his way into the back yard, adjusting once again to the darkness. The stars were peeking out from the clouds, and he could just make out the back porch, a triple-stepped concrete slab. He tried the doorknob, but it wouldn't budge. He stepped back and gave it a savage kick, knocking it open just enough to enter. Something was blocking it from the inside. Reece squeezed past the door, and immediately the stench of rotting garbage filled his nose.

He turned his head and retched, almost losing his dinner. At least he knew the garbage was recent.

With the flashlight on he saw a sea of broken bottles littering the floor. Long strips of wallpaper curled down the walls. Reece slid his feet as he advanced, pushing aside glass shards and who knows what with every step. The room was pitch black and the small beam of light lit a patch just a few feet wide.

The first room he came to was the kitchen, off a short hallway from the back door. A table with long aluminum legs and a yellow vinyl top sat in the center, covered with an assortment of beer cans and bread wrappers. He lit up the cupboards, noticing the absence of doors.

Reece heard something from the next room. That was definitely someone. He started forward, dropping his hand to the grip of his revolver. The floor in the next room was covered with trash, and in the center of the room sat a red flyer wagon piled high with the burnt remains of the doors from the kitchen cabinets. He swept the room with light, looking for clues. He heard a creak in the distance and he knew he had company. Reece pulled out his gun and held it down to his side. A few more steps and he came to a doorway that led into another large room. He doused the walls with the flashlight's beam, looking for the source of the noise, and sensed movement to his left.

He turned in that direction, leading with the light. Someone grabbed his right wrist, and he swung the revolver up, making contact. He heard a grimace of pain as he brought the flashlight around and saw he'd knocked a vagrant to his knees. The homeless guy looked up at Reece, clenching his chin. A thin bead of blood oozed between the fingers of the man's right hand.

"Why you do that? I just tryin' to hep you," the man mumbled from his crouch. Reece brought the gun up, drawing a bead on the guy's forehead and said, "Stay put unless you want something a whole lot worse."

He continued toward the next room with his gun pointed out. Painting the walls of a smaller room with light, he spotted a lone dresser in the corner. The floor was covered in old aluminum beer cans and yellowed newspaper pages. Reece walked to the dresser. He opened the top of four drawers and shined the narrow beam inside, seeing nothing but the wood bottom of a well made tongue and groove drawer. He worked his way down the chest.

The bottom drawer was heavy to pull out and contained an assortment of junk he guessed might have been left over from the house's last occupants. There were batteries, rubber bands, Band-Aids, playing cards, and stacks of poker chips. Reece brought one of the chips up to his face, shining the light on it and read "Malum Farms Casino."

He felt a chill run down his back. That was the name of the place where they'd found his father's dead body. He pocketed the chip and continued rummaging through the drawer.

At the bottom he spotted a legal-sized manila envelope. He pulled it out from under the three inches of junk that lay on top. One of the corners had been burned and the black ash remains crumbed off as he bent back the copper clasp that held the top flap closed. Reece pulled out a thick stack of documents and laid them down on the top of the dresser. He paged the first document off the stack and set it down beside the others. His flashlight illuminated what looked like a checklist written across a single sheet of paper. It looked like a man's cursive handwriting.

Duct Tape
Rope
Box Cutter
Tarpaulin
Map
Gas Cans
Tie Wraps
Canteens

The last words ran into the burned area and looked like the description of something. Reece stared at the words and wondered if Owen had written the list the day his wife went missing. He took the next piece of paper off the stack of documents and saw a hand-drawn picture of the southern U.S. He set it aside and spotted an old travel magazine folded open to an article about a Mexican fishing village named Cabo San Lucas. Reece scanned the article, familiar with the location, and figured back then the town had little more than its marina and fleet of fisherman. He pulled several more sheets of meaningless paper off the stack, shining the light at each and came to a map. He opened it and panned the light down at what looked like magic marker running down the highways from St. Louis, Missouri, to Tulsa, Oklahoma, over to Oklahoma City, and then south through Texas to Brownsville.

Reece shoved the documents back into the envelope and stashed it back into the drawer, thinking he'd come back and get it on his way out. He was just about to shove the drawer closed when he spotted a small black book. The first couple of pages were empty and then he spotted what looked like a ledger of gambling losses. Each entry read like (lost $450 – Owe S.S. 9/23/82). Reece thumbed his way through the book, and after a few pages of similar entries showing wins and losses, he came to more blank pages. Shining the flashlight into the drawer, he found what looked like a legal document under a stack of yellow cocktail napkins. He pulled it out and read over the paperwork for a second mortgage on the house he was standing in. The date on the top was written in cursive and looked like July 20, 1989. Near the bottom of the last page Reece saw the loan amount $45,000.00 and the signature Owen L. Roberts.

After putting everything back as he'd found it, he pushed closed the dresser drawer and left the room. Reece came around a corner and walked through a doorway into what looked like the den. He shined the light along the walls, not wanting a repeat of what he'd experienced earlier with the vagrant. On the far side of the room he spotted something. It was a person standing behind what remained of a burned-out sofa.

The figure was tall with a long gray trench coat, black gloves, and dark combat boots. Reece studied the stranger, shining the light upward toward his face, and saw only a narrow chin, which made him wonder whether it was a man or woman. The cheeks were reddish, and the wide-brimmed black hat covered the eyes.

"What are you doing?" Reece asked, lowering the light so he could still see the figure but not blind him. He heard a scratch on the floor from behind and half turned, still keeping his eyes on the stranger by the couch.

Reece felt sudden harsh pressure on his left wrist and the flashlight was stripped from his hand, falling to the floor with a loud clatter. He gripped the gun, pulled back the hammer, and held it outward, ready to fire. He heard footsteps rushing toward him from behind. He held his gun up and fired into the ceiling.

Reece heard the back door slam open with a chorus of

footsteps, running toward the kitchen. In the errant beam of his flashlight, he noticed that the person in the trench coat he'd seen earlier was gone. Reece had six more rounds in his Smith & Wesson 686P, but for the first time he felt vulnerable. For all he knew the house was still full of vagrants. He needed that light.

Reece wanted to bend down and grab the light off the floor, but he also wanted to ensure he was alone. The room was quiet. He bent down on one knee, hoping some addict's dirty syringe wouldn't stick him. He reached out for the Maglite, feeling the cold hard surface of the floor penetrate his thin pants. The flashlight was just beyond reach. He stretched out farther to snatch it. He heard a faint skid a few inches behind.

Searing pain ripped through his skull, and Reece bit the tip of his tongue, tasting blood. He tried to brace himself but collapsed to the floor, pinning his hand under his shoulder. *My gun,* he thought, struggling to push back up, but the room was spinning crazily and his strength was gone. Reece looked along the beam of the Maglite just beyond his outstretched left hand. He sniffed the wood floor fighting to remain conscious and the smell of urine filled his nostrils. He felt something wet running down the left side of his face, turned his head in that direction, and saw combat boots striding toward him.

CHAPTER SEVENTEEN

OWEN ROBERTS DROVE his boss's prized black Range Rover south out of Tulsa in the black night on his way to a place he'd called home for the past several years. He'd once entertained the thought of driving south and stopping for nothing until reaching Mexico, but that thought had failed to return since the day his boss caught up with him two hours east of Amarillo, Texas. Two chops of a meat cleaver cost Owen both of his pinky fingers, persuading him to never attempt such pursuits again.

He pulled off the two-lane blacktop onto the single-track road that looked like an entrance to a farm. Tall plants grew on both sides of the trail, and it seemed like forever until he saw the lights and parked cars of the casino rising out of the overgrowth in the distance. Owen drove the Range Rover behind the single-story red brick building that looked nothing like a gambling establishment.

A chill ran down Owen's spine when he pulled in to park next to the bright white Ford van he'd earlier noticed was missing from its parking place. Owen had heard a rumor from the one of the female bartenders that Rocco, the blackjack dealer, had insulted their boss one too many times.

Owen Roberts went inside, dressed in pressed black dress pants, a white dress shirt, and a black vest with gaudy gold trim. Greeting several of the regulars, he took up his post behind a green oval Texas Hold'em table. Four men sat in front of him watching as he slapped the shuffling boot and started play.

A few minutes later, Sam Shanks, dressed in a black pinstripe suit, walked past the long bar, nodding at the female bartender. His alligator loafers glided through the thick shag carpeting.

"What's Owen doing working the table tonight? I thought we had agreed Rocco was a better choice," Shanks said.

"Ah, Mr. Shanks I didn't know you were here," Michael Zimeratti said, turning around on a stool to face his boss and sliding a hand over his thick black hair. "Rocco seems to have disappeared, so I made a last-minute personnel change, thinking Owen was better suited for the Texas Hold'em table than the other dealers."

"So who are our guests at the table tonight?" Shanks asked.

"That's Dr. Hank Johnson, the dentist there on the far right. Tavo Sheave, the city councilman, is next to him, Dan Kochi's there, and the new guy, Melvin Phillips, is on the far left."

"Oh yes, good to see Mr. Phillips made it. I met him at the museum. We'll have to keep an eye on him," Shanks said.

"How about the fancy dresser, what was his name? Angelo, was it? Have you seen him around?" Shanks asked, turning back toward the bartender and raising his hand with a wave.

"You mean Angelo Messerman. No, I haven't seen him around lately. Maybe he ran out of money," Zimeratti said with a laugh.

"Good evening, sir, will you be having your usual?" the bartender asked. Both men smiled and nodded, sending her back toward the bar.

"What do you know about this guy named Phillips? He looks well dressed, what's he do for a living?" Zimeratti asked.

"Oil, goes back a couple of generations on his wife's side of the family. They're big art collectors. I get the impression he comes from family money too, but I don't know much more about him. I had him tailed when they left the museum. They have a very big place in Southern Hills, and he mentioned having other homes across the country."

"Sounds like the kind of people we're trying to attract."

Shanks let out a snort. "Sounds like the kind of mark who would like to donate his art collection to us."

CHAPTER EIGHTEEN

THE STRANGER IN the combat boots and trench coat walked toward Reece Culver's unconscious form, shining a large flashlight beam downward. He squashed what remained of a shattered Miller Lite bottle. The room was silent except for the distant moaning of the vagrant he'd paid in methamphetamine.

The old man was still bleeding from the contact he'd made earlier with the steel cylinder of Reece's gun. He slouched on the half burned couch and sucked at his glass pipe. The stranger in the trench coat saw the orange glow cast light on the vagrant's lips.

He stood over Reece and shined the light down. The top of his scalp was painted red with blood from the blow he'd sustained. The stranger smiled, then pulled one of his boots back, avoiding the puddle that was forming from the blood dripping down Reece's face. The stranger bent down and pulled Reece's gun from his side holster. He squatted just to the left of Reece's outstretched body, and laid the flashlight onto the floor with the beam shining toward the vagrant's chest. The room smelled of burning meth, and was filling with a white cloud of smoke.

The stranger grinned at the old man, watching him get high. The addict stared into the light like a deer staring into headlights. The stranger grabbed Reece's outstretched right hand, peeled back his fingers and wrapped them into the .357 Magnum with his index finger on the trigger. The stranger stuck his gloved right finger into the trigger guard and aimed the gun at the old man's chest. The stranger pulled back on Reece's finger and fired twice.

With a comical groan the bum dropped the pipe, and the smile faded off his face.

CHAPTER NINETEEN

INSIDE THE HOTEL bar Crystal spotted George Kendall sitting in the last booth. She walked toward him, checking her navy blue skirt and red silk blouse in the mirrored wall. *I still got it,* she thought to herself.

"I'm glad you decided to join me. Did the headache go away?" he asked, sounding genuinely concerned.

Crystal sat down across from him. "The aspirin did the trick. I feel much better now. Would you like a martini?"

"Yeah, that sounds great. Are you going to join me?" George asked.

"Only if they have Grey Goose, It's the only vodka I drink," Crystal answered. A blond woman wearing a pressed white cotton shirt came to their table with two dinner menus and a wine list.

"What can I get for you?"

"Two Grey Goose dirty martini's," George said.

"Make mine with blue cheese olives," Crystal added.

The waitress nodded, and turned back toward the bar.

"So what did you think of the briefing today?" George asked.

"Agent Cox sounds pretty confident that the raid will be successful, and he'll take Shanks into custody. That wasn't your plan, was it?" Crystal said, hoping he wouldn't mention Owen Roberts.

"No, it wasn't my plan, but this is not over yet," George said, biting his lower lip.

"Good, I'm glad you're not going to let them steal your case."

"I have to say, I got a little uneasy when they brought up the slide of Owen Roberts. I sat through that entire meeting trying to remember where I'd seen his name," George said, staring at Crystal.

She tensed, pressing the nail of her pinky finger under the tip of her thumb, mixing pain with the anxiety she felt coming back.

"When I got back to my room, I went into the employment files, and I figured it out."

"You figured what out?"

"Owen and Tracey Roberts are your parents. It's a conflict of interest," George said flatly. "You're related to a member of Sam Shanks' gang by blood." He leaned forward, sliding his clenched fist along the tabletop.

Crystal threw her napkin toward him and stood up in the booth. "Is that why you invited me down here?"

"Hold it. What are you doing?" George demanded. He reached out and grabbed her right wrist.

"Let me go," Crystal cried.

"Calm down. Let's talk about this," George shouted.

"No!"

"Leaving the table is not a good idea, Crystal."

She lifted her arm, breaking his grasp, and slid back into the booth. She forced some tears to her eyes, making herself look vulnerable.

"It's okay, Crystal. It'll be our secret. The others don't have a need to know," George said. She knew he was lying, but that was okay. She wasn't going to take him at his word, anyway.

"I know your story, Crystal. I know your mother went missing and you were put into an orphanage. I know it's been tough on you, and this job is your whole life," George said in a low voice.

Crystal offered a reason that she knew would make sense to him.

"I'm not a violent person, but if I can track down that son of a bitch, Owen Roberts, I'd…"

She let the words trail off. After a significant pause, she added, "That's why."

*

Later that evening, George and Crystal took the elevator to the third floor. On the ride up George apologized for his earlier comments in slurred speech. Crystal smiled to herself, knowing that the multiple rounds of martinis she'd ordered were to blame. The elevator lurched as it came to a stop, and he lost his balance, grabbing for the side rail. He had no idea that Crystal could drink any man under the table.

She stepped off the elevator and walked ahead swinging her arms with George close behind. She was buzzed, but not to the extent that he was. With the key card pushed into the slot, she grabbed the door handle but it wouldn't open. She pulled the card out, turned it over, and heard the click of the lock open. She turned back toward George.

He had a lustful smile on his face but said, "I'm sorry, Crystal."

"Come on, you're coming with me." She pushed open the door, grabbed him by his necktie, and pulled him into her room, kicking the door shut.

"Why don't you show me how sorry you are, Mr. Kendall?"

she said, wrapping her arms around him, putting her mouth on his, and French kissing him.

"Whoa," George said, pulling away and then moving toward her to kiss her back. They both dropped down onto the edge of the bed. She looked down at the gold wedding band on his left ring finger. That was her ticket out of the mess she'd made.

She squeezed the flab-covered muscles of his upper back, disgusted. How long had it been since he'd set foot in a health club? Crystal slid her tongue back into his mouth and let him have it. She felt his hands slide down, cupping her ass. She tipped back, pulling him on top. She moaned for effect as they made out, and George, who had been way over served, forgot all about his wife and kids.

"Why don't you lose some of those clothes? I'll be right back," Crystal said, sliding out from under him. She walked to the mirror on the other side of the room and activated the video camera feature on her smart phone. She turned back and looked at her pathetic, flabby boss. He was bent over at the waist, struggling to untie his shoes. She walked into the bathroom, hiked up her skirt, and pulled her thong down to the floor before stepping out of it.

Crystal took a seat on the toilet and began to choreograph what she wanted to capture on the video. She returned to the bed wearing only her open red silk blouse and black stiletto heels. She turned on the lamp for good lighting. George stared at her with a devious smile, wadded up his dress shirt, and tossed it across the room laughing.

Crystal stopped a few feet away, reached into her blouse, and began to massage herself. George watched, then began fumbling madly with his belt.

She put a hand on his shoulder and pushed him backward.

He smiled up at her. She smiled at him, running her tongue over her lips. She knelt down between his legs, unzipped his fly, and grabbed the waistband of his trousers above both hips. Then she pulled off what remained of his clothing.

*

Crystal woke the next morning and climbed out from under her boss's sweat-dried body. George grunted, blowing air from his nostrils like a whale breaching, and rolled back over with a hint of a smile on his face. Crystal heard a rattle from the dresser on the far side of the room, and realized it was the vibrating ring of her phone in silent mode. She saw that she'd missed the call.

Crystal gathered up George's clothes and set them in a wrinkled pile on top of his shoes. She went to the closet and wrapped herself in a hotel robe. She looked down at George's half covered body and listened to him snore. She thought how stupid a man could be when offered the naked flesh of a beautiful woman. She smiled, feeling in control again.

She grabbed his shoulder and nudged him. He mumbled something and rolled over, still asleep. Crystal sat on the side of the bed and bent down toward his ear.

"George, it's time to get up," she said, poking him in the stomach with the tip of her index finger.

George blinked and opened his bloodshot eyes. He stared up at her with a sheepish grin, and both of his hands went down to his genitals, trying to cover himself up in a sudden moment of modesty.

"Your clothes are on the chair. I'm going to take a shower. You better go before the maid comes," Crystal said, getting up off the bed and disappearing into the bathroom. She turned on both handles of the shower and took a seat. George was grunting on the other side of the bathroom door, hurrying to get dressed. She heard the door close and was glad he'd gone.

Crystal emerged from the bathroom, opened the door to her hotel room, and put the do not disturb sign on the door handle. She picked up her cell phone and dialed the number for the man she called Papa.

"Crystal, how are things in St. Louis?"

"Better now, but there's something I need to tell you."

"Yeah, Diane and I were just talking about you. We were wondering if you'd like to come down and spend the weekend with us?"

"Oh, Papa, that sounds like fun. Let me see if I can catch a flight out tomorrow morning."

"Crystal, there's one more thing. Would you mind coming to a dinner party with me Friday night? It's black tie."

"That sounds great. What's the occasion?"

He ignored that question, instead posing one of his own. "So, what was it you wanted to tell me?"

"I was in a meeting for work yesterday, and they told us that Owen Roberts is an informant for the FBI. Papa, they're planning a raid on the casino."

*

The flight back to Denver on the government jet was nothing if not awkward. Crystal wore a dull green pantsuit with a choker collar. George sat catty corner from her with his nose firmly buried in the screen of his laptop computer. She congratulated herself on how clever she'd been. George wouldn't be doing any talking now.

The flight touched down on a snow-covered runway at Centennial Airport, and after Crystal emerged from the plane, she took her bag from the co-pilot and started rolling it toward her car.

"Crystal, wait one minute," George yelled. She was standing at the back of her car with the trunk open. Crystal saw George's panic stricken face as he hurried toward her.

"What's the matter, George?"

"About last night. You can't tell anyone. I have a family, and—" George stopped talking. The co-pilot approached carrying the bag he'd left behind in his haste to catch her.

"Here's your bag sir," the co-pilot said, setting it next to Crystal's car.

"Thank you," George said.

Crystal watched the co-pilot walk back into the hangar.

"George, it sounds to me like we both have secrets to keep."

CHAPTER TWENTY

IN A SMALL room near the rear of his casino Sam Shanks was counting twenty-dollar bills. The table was covered on one end with paper sacks of money and on the other with neat stacks of bills. Owen Roberts sat across from Shanks, wrapping a stack of five-dollar bills in a rubber band. Michael Zimeratti was at a desk in the corner of the room in a cream-colored suit, working numbers in an Excel spreadsheet, and with his dark complexion he looked the part of a mob money manager. He had the kind of complex facial structure that was handsome from one angle and devious from another.

"You got any idea what Blackwell did with Rocco?" Shanks asked.

"Whatever he did I can assure you it wasn't good. I seen him stuffing something that could have been a body into the back of the van the other morning," Owen said, looking up from his stack of money.

"That fucking psychopath better get a handle on himself or he'll screw things up here just like he did back in St. Louis," Shanks said, slamming his fist against the tabletop. "Michael, you got any idea what that cock sucker did with our dealer?"

"I saw him hosing out the back of the van last night, so I'd guess your dealer made a mess."

*

Vinton Blackwell drove into the casino property, still thinking about his call from Crystal earlier in the day. He'd always suspected Owen Roberts of being a problem, and he wondered why Shanks had gone to such trouble to keep him around. Blackwell pulled up behind the casino and spotted the cars of Shanks and Zimeratti parked alongside the white Ford van. He walked in the back door and down the hallway toward the big room where the bar was located. Vinton heard voices coming from the money counting room and stopped short. He patted the inside right pocket of his suit coat, confirming he'd brought along his favorite firearm. He could hear Shanks, Roberts, and Zimeratti on the other side of the door talking loudly. As the door opened, he jumped back against the wall and froze.

Michael Zimeratti walked out of the counting room, still looking back toward the occupants inside, and never noticed the large man standing in the dim light a few feet behind him. Zimeratti pulled the door closed and walked down the hall.

Vinton Blackwell watched Zimeratti walk away and waited, still listening to the voices emanating from behind the closed door. He could hear Owen Roberts talking trash about him to their boss, Sam Shanks. Blackwell felt rage bubbling up beneath his skin. He had an impulse to pull his gun and barge into the room. Owen was telling Shanks about what a great guy the dealer Rocco was. "The problems aren't with the people we have working the tables. The problems are with Vinton Blackwell. He's a goddamned psychopath."

That was enough. Blackwell squeezed the doorknob in his hand and swung the door open, almost tearing it loose of its hinges. Sam Shanks, who was seated on the opposite side of the table, looked stunned. Blackwell began shouting. "So, here you are taking shit about me with this scum-sucking bastard. That's just great, Shanks. I guess you might like to know Roberts here has been talking to the FBI. In fact, he's been working for them all along as their informant."

*

Owen looked at Shanks, who was snarling at him like a jackal. Owen pulled an eight-inch filet knife from his waist and lunged at Blackwell, catching him off guard. Shoving inside the killer's large black handgun, he brought the filet knife to Blackwell's neck.

Shanks yelled, "Stop!" but neither man did. Owen had his right hand on Blackwell's gun, trying to keep it out of his face. He pressed into Blackwell's throat and yelled, "Drop the gun or I'll slit you like a fucking cantaloupe."

Blackwell abruptly stopped resisting and tossed his gun onto the money-covered table in front of them. A small trickle of blood seeped from the half-inch slit in the middle of Blackwell's throat.

"You've been trying to ruin me your whole life, Blackwell," Owen yelled. "It was you that talked me into borrowing money from Sam up in St. Louis. It was you that got me in debt so bad that I couldn't afford to gamble anymore." Owen pulled Blackwell's hand down toward his side while still holding the knife to his neck. He twisted the man's wrist, ensuring he had control. Blood from the slit in Vinton Blackwell's neck stained the collar of his white dress shirt.

"You ruined my life, kidnapped my wife Tracey, and caused my children to be put into orphanages," Owen said, shaking his right hand like he might slit Blackwell's throat ear to ear at any minute.

"Get a hold of yourself, Owen. It's not going to do you any good to murder Vinton. If you are a snitch for the FBI, you won't last long," Shanks said.

*

Michael Zimeratti had heard Owen shouting from the counting room. He went behind the long wooden bar and pulled the sawed-off twelve gauge shotgun from the bungee cords that held it in position next to the cash register. Zimeratti pumped the stock, racking a slug into the chamber of the Remington 870, and walked down the hallway toward the commotion. He saw Owen's back facing the open doorway and figured it was a knife he was holding to Vinton's neck.

"You've gone too far, Blackwell. Now it's my turn. I can't wait to feel your blood on my hands," Owen yelled.

Zimeratti leveled the gun at Owen's spine and took a step forward, stabbing him with the snout of the shotgun's barrel.

"Drop the knife, Owen. This little episode is over," Zimeratti said calmly. Owen's mouth opened with a gasp, and the bloodlust fled from his face. Zimeratti looked down at Sam Shanks and gave him a wink. Shanks stood from the table and produced a small silver-single shot pistol from his vest.

"Do what Michael says, Owen. Drop the knife."

CHAPTER TWENTY-ONE

REECE CULVER SAT at a cold stainless steel table staring into a two-way mirror. He'd been in an interview room before, but he didn't know where he was on this particular day. His head was throbbing, and when he looked down at the date window of his watch he wondered how he'd gotten from sniffing a urine soaked floor on Wednesday to sitting in somebody's interrogation room on Friday. It didn't make sense. *What the hell is going on?*

The door sprang open and two men dressed in dark blue suits with police shields clipped to their lapels stepped in.

"Culver, you're awake. You feel like filling us in on what you've been up to?" One of the men asked in a deep raspy voice. He was short with deep-set black eyes, and a square chin. Reece, eyeing his grey buzz cut, wondered if they'd loosened the height requirements the day this guy had signed up to be a cop. Isley, he read on the badge.

Reece kept silent. He wasn't going to say a word until they told him where he was and why his right hand was cuffed to the stainless steel chair his butt occupied. The tall cop, equally ugly, had a dent in the left side of his head that made his thick brown hair set funny on his noggin. He took a seat in front of Reece. This one was Leftwich.

"Culver, I brought you some coffee. You do like coffee, don't you?"

This must be the guy who was to play the good cop.

"Let's see, Reece Culver, age thirty-two, out of Denver, Colorado. You're a licensed private investigator in three states, this being one of them."

Reece stared straight ahead. His head felt funny and specks of memory were returning. He remembered the smell of someone leaning over him. He remembered her perfume. *Had he been in a hospital*? He tried to think back, then thought of his client Crystal and wondered if she had been at the abandoned house. He tried to remember the scent of the perfume. Was it the same citrus smell he'd enjoyed the night she'd visited his apartment? He wasn't sure. Reece thought about the stranger he'd seen and remembered wondering if it was a man or woman.

"You got a problem with the homeless or something?" the short cop yelled, pulling him back to reality.

Reece glanced down at his watch and wondered why it was strapped onto his left wrist upside down. In the glass bezel he saw a reflection of his image. *Is that a bandage?*

"Did one of you do this to me?" he blurted out, pointing toward the bloodstained bandage.

With a long bang Leftwich hit the table closed-fisted in front of Reece.

"Are you some kind of funny guy? You know goddamned well what went down in that house, Culver. I got a dead guy in my morgue with two slugs in his chest from that fancy gun of yours. You got fresh residue all over, and you're asking stupid questions?"

"Why don't you start by telling us why you went to the house in the first place?" Isley asked.

Reece looked toward the door. Maybe it might be a good time to lawyer up.

"You got some kind of drug habit or something we need to know about? That dump we found you in is good for only one thing," Leftwich said, sounding aggravated. Isley advanced toward him and said, "You want to tell us what happened, or should we just charge you with murder and wait until the DA has time to sort this out?"

"Murder? What are you talking about? I want a lawyer and my phone call," Reece said in a low voice.

The two cops exchanged a look. Leftwich got up from his seat, went over to the door, and pounded. A uniformed St. Louis police officer appeared. Reece looked up at the man. He was older with a full head of white hair and a kind face. His nametag read "Felps."

"Let's lock this one back up. Let him sleep off whatever he's on. We'll start this again in the morning."

Reece stared at the two cops who'd been interrogating him. They were hard over sticking him with the murder, but he had no idea who had been killed.

"I'd like my phone call and a lawyer," he repeated.

"We'll get you a call, and we'll get the public defender for you, but I doubt he'll show up until tomorrow morning."

Officer Felps un-cuffed Reece from the table and led him down a hall lined with brown industrial tile. Up ahead he saw a single black phone that looked like it had been put in service fifty years before. As Reece stopped before it, he tried to remember Haisley's phone number. His head started to throb again, and his mind was blank except for the name "Felps." *Why does that name stick out?*

Reece's index finger turned the rotary dial of the phone, dialing area code 918 for Tulsa. Then the rest came to him, and he dialed Haisley's home phone number. Reece listened to the phone ring four times and go to voicemail.

"Haisley, it's Reece Culver. I'm locked up in some St. Louis precinct. I was at the old Roberts house looking for clues. Someone hit me in the head. While I was unconscious, I'm guessing someone used my gun to commit a murder. I need your help," Reece said, hoping Haisley would call back before he spent much more time in jail.

He'd just hung up the phone when he saw a young man dressed in a brown sports coat, dress pants, and reddish brown penny loafers. This guy walked like he was going somewhere.

Reece felt a hand on his shoulder and looked over to see Officer Felps.

"I need you to come in here and take a seat, Mr. Culver," he said, encouraging him into a small room with a single wooden table and four chairs. The link came to him. This guy Felps had worked with his dad back in the early nineties. That would explain his white hair.

"Hey, Felps, do you remember my dad, Al Culver?" he asked hoping he'd say yes. Felps remained silent as he clasped the handcuffs to the leg of the wood table.

"Every one of you guys got a story," he said, then turned and left the room. Reece wanted to go after him, but he would need to take the table with him.

He sat staring at the same tiled walls that he'd seen earlier in the interrogation room. He reached up toward the knot on the side of his head with his left hand and felt a solid bump. He pushed on it and pain shot through his temple. Reece searched his memory, wondering where he'd been the day before. He was almost sure that he'd spent the night in a hospital bed. He remembered a cute, nice-smelling nurse but little else. It was weird. He'd had dreams and fantasies about woman, but this was too real for that, yet he had no other solid memories other than lying on the floor in the Roberts house.

Reece rubbed his wrists and noticed the red grooves the steel had made upon his reddened skin. The door swung open, and someone began talking in a fast high-pitched voice.

"Mr. Culver, I'm your state-appointed attorney, Jed Harris."

Reece sized up his young face, wondering how many weeks it had been since he'd gotten his law degree. The attorney took a seat, setting down a brand-new leather briefcase that matched his loafers.

"Tell me about the events leading up to the homicide, Mr. Culver. What took you to the house on Calvin Avenue the evening of Wednesday, January 26?"

Reece stared at the kid with his brown crew cut, and red cheeks wondering if he was old enough to vote.

"Listen, kid. What's your name? Jed? Is that short for something?" he asked sarcastically. His head hurt. He was sleep deprived, and he was tired of playing games. Reece had a feeling his rights had been violated and he was due to be released.

"Cut the crap and tell me your story, Culver. That is, if you want my help. They got you up on murder charges."

Reece leaned forward, staring through the kid. "What they got me up on is a bunch of lies."

"Not according to them. They got a dead man in the morgue with two bullets in him from your gun. That's enough to put you away for a long time, Mr. Culver."

"The only problem with that story is this head wound here, and the fact I have no memory after I was hit with something last Wednesday night. The other problem is, I'm a licensed private investigator in this state and I have certain rights..." he said, then lost his train of thought. Reece sat silent and then the rest came back to him. "And as far as I can tell, my rights have been violated."

"What do you mean, violated?"

"I haven't been mirandized," Reece said.

"You don't remember meeting with me in the hospital on Thursday morning?" the attorney asked, looking puzzled.

"The only thing I remember is being hassled by those two pricks a few minutes ago."

CHAPTER TWENTY-TWO

CRYSTAL WATCHED THE red Jaguar a few car lengths ahead roll to a stop near the front entryway of the Phillips' mansion. A woman dressed in a stunning black Carolina Herrera stepped out onto the curb, her husband joined her, and one of the valets drove the car away. Crystal's gaze strayed to the Band-Aid in the center of Vinton's throat. She couldn't imagine how he had managed an invitation to an event of this caliber, but wasn't going to risk upsetting him by asking.

One of the valets opened her door, took her hand, and assisted her out of the truck. She joined Blackwell at the curb. "This feels like we're arriving at the Oscars or something, Papa. All that's missing is the red carpet."

"Just look like you own the joint." He took her hand, and they followed the line of guests entering the stone mansion of Melvin and Melanie Phillips.

"Welcome, Mr. Blackwell," a tall man in a black tuxedo with thick gray hair greeted them.

"It's nice to be here, Mr. Phillips. Let me introduce you to my stepdaughter, Crystal Thomas."

Melvin Phillips reached out and took her hand in his. Crystal smiled, despite her irritation that he was staring at her like a piece of candy. She wanted to pull her hand away, but Phillips continued to squeeze it.

"My wife Melanie is somewhere around here," Phillips said. His plump hold finally let go of Crystal's hand, and he passed onto the next guests.

Crystal took a glass of champagne from a waiter's tray and watched in amusement as her stepfather studied a large framed piece of modern art.

"Papa, how do you know Mr. Phillips?"

"I met him at Sam's. The man certainly knows his way around a poker table," he said, moving to the next painting. Crystal watched Mr. Phillips take the arm of a stunning tall blond-haired woman dressed in an emerald gown, and she followed her stepfather toward them.

"Melanie, I'd like to introduce you to Vinton Blackwell and his charming stepdaughter Crystal."

"It's nice to make your acquaintance," the woman said, offering her hand to Vinton, then smiling at Crystal. Crystal noticed Mrs. Phillips' reaction to her stepfather. She'd seen it before. He had the physicality of a much younger man, and that coupled with his chiseled Nordic features made women melt.

"You have an amazing art collection, Mrs. Phillips. It's very impressive."

"Thank you," Melanie said, taking a step closer to him. "It's been a hobby of mine for quite some time."

Melvin motioned for Crystal to join him. She disliked the thought of spending time with the old lech, but walked with him anyway. On her way she spotted one of the waiters with a full tray of champagne and paused to scoop up another glass.

"Tell me about your hobbies, dear," Melvin said, taking a

glass for himself. He brought the glass to his lips and drained it. The waiter stood near them.

"Well, I'm not into art," she admitted.

He gave a short laugh. "I find that refreshing. What is it you're into?"

"Skiing," Crystal said.

"Downhill, cross country, or water?"

"Downhill. I don't have the patience for cross-country, and there aren't any lakes in Colorado big enough for waterskiing," Crystal said.

"Oh, do you live in Colorado?" Melvin asked, eyeing the party. Crystal waited for his attention to return.

"Yes, I live in Denver, and my stepfather and I share a little villa up near Vail."

"That means we're practically neighbors," Melvin said with sudden enthusiasm. She cringed as his hand ran down her back and lingered just above her hips. "I have a house up on the golf course."

Crystal wanted to pull away from his touch, but she knew she'd been brought along to occupy Melvin. She just wasn't sure why.

"Crystal, come this way. There's someone I'd like to introduce you to." Crystal let herself be guided toward a woman dressed in a bright red gown with her back to them.

"Kathryn, I'm so glad you could come tonight," Melvin said. The woman turned to face them. "Crystal, I'd like to introduce you to Dr. Kathryn Anders. Kathryn, this is Crystal Thomas." Crystal smiled at the woman, vaguely thinking they'd met before. "Kathryn has been busy appraising all the pieces we will be auctioning off next month."

"That sounds like an interesting job," Crystal said.

Two young waiters opened a pair of double doors up

ahead. Someone tapped a spoon on a glass, and she saw her stepfather and Melanie Phillips standing on the left side of a large crowd. The room fell silent as Melanie began to speak.

"Melvin and I would like to thank everyone for coming this evening. If you'll come this way, cocktails and dinner will be served in the grand hall, and afterward we have a special announcement to make." Crystal watched the guests flow past Melvin on their way to dinner. She held back, hoping to lose him.

"Would you be my escort, dear?"

CHAPTER TWENTY-THREE

AS REECE BECAME awake, he found himself staring at an unfamiliar ceiling. It wasn't the house he'd entered searching for Owen Roberts. He blinked his eyes and tried to find an escape from the dull, throbbing pain. Reaching out, he gripped the side of the bed and felt cold steel. His eyes slowly adjusted to the dim light, and he realized he was in the same jail cell he'd been led to the previous day. *Fuck, why am I still here?*

He realized he'd missed picking up his mother for their dinner at Jamils Steakhouse in Tulsa Thursday evening. *I hope she's not worried.* Of course she didn't trust him anyway. She never had. That's why she constantly patronized him. *I'll show her. I just need to get out of this damned place. Get back to solving this missing person's case, so I can devote all of my time to finding out who murdered Dad.*

He gripped both sides of his forehead, thinking about what he'd done. *What if Dad went back to get pictures of Zimeratti and he saw something that led him to the farm casino? It never would have happened if I'd held onto that damned Canon camera.* The sense of guilt was overwhelming and he wondered if somehow being clubbed in the head had made it worse.

He closed his eyes, trying to calm his mind. Reece knew there'd be more questioning the next day and he needed his sleep. He stared out past the dull white bars of his holding cell. A sixty-watt bulb hung from the ceiling behind its wire cage. He let his mind zone out back to better days. Reece remembered sitting in the dimly lit garage holding a flashlight and watching his father Al try to reassemble the carburetor for the GTO. They were done and it was time to put it back onto the dull gray manifold that sat on top of the engine. Al looked down at the metal can they'd been using to clean parts and saw four screws and a small coil spring. He'd put everything back together and still had parts remaining.

He looked up at his son dumbfounded and then watched as Reece tore down the carburetor and reassembled it adding the spring and the four Phillips head screws. They put it on the manifold and later Al let his seven-year-old son turn the key and start the car. At a young age he'd begun to tell his dad his ideas of how to put things back together, and for the most part Reece had always been correct. He remembered his father telling him, "You're going to be an engineer someday."

Reece stretched his arms above his head and groaned, looking toward the small rectangular window above the commode. It felt good to stretch. The space was small, but had all the necessary furnishings for an overnight stay.

He was still trying to piece together his fractured memory. The doctor had visited the night before, and suggested he was still suffering from a concussion, but he didn't require a return visit to the hospital. He'd informed Reece of an overnight stay for observation Tuesday night, and was told that he had no memory of the occasion. The doctor expressed concern and told Reece he needed cognitive rest.

"Wow, you're a carbon copy of your old man," Reece heard someone say on the other side of the bars. He sat upright, and saw a thick man who at first glance looked like Teddy

Roosevelt. Reece studied the man's tailored black suit, bushy gray hair parted to the left, and his shirt pulling at the center button behind the suit jacket, suggesting the need for exercise.

"You don't remember me, do you?" the man said, looking in at Reece like some primate in a zoo. "Mike Mobley. I worked with your dad when he was a detective."

Reece got to his feet and shoved a hand through the bars. "Good to meet you," Reece said, and then heard footsteps coming down the hallway.

"You can let Mr. Culver out of his cell. I'd like to have a chat with him in room six," Mobley said. He headed toward the room where Reece had talked to the public defender. The cell door opened with a "clank" and Reece stepped out. Officer Felps was standing in the aisle, smiling.

"Turn and face the bars," he said, taking Reece's hands behind his back and fastening on a pair of bright steel handcuffs. Felps led him down the hallway and into the room where he'd been questioned earlier. Mobley was inside sitting in a chair with his coat hanging on the back.

"Take the cuffs off and leave us," he said to officer Felps, waving his hand.

"Tell me what got you in here, Reece," Mobley said with a grin.

"I'm working on a missing person's case for a client of mine. She grew up at the home on Calvin Avenue here in St. Louis. I went there to look for clues about the disappearance of her mother Tracey Roberts."

"Okay, so you were in the house looking for clues," Mobley said. He was studying Reece's face like he was trying to find a resemblance between him and his father.

"The house was full of meth addicts, and one of them

managed to get my flashlight. I'd been attacked earlier and fired a single shot into the rafters to clear the place," Reece said.

"Okay, that explains the gunshot residue on your right hand. What happened next?"

"I waited for the place to clear. A little while later I bent down to grab my light, and that's when I got smacked in the head. That was it, lights out. The next thing I remember is those bozos of yours playing good cop, bad cop."

"Did you tell this to the detectives last night?"

"I never got a chance."

CHAPTER TWENTY-FOUR

MICHAEL ZIMERATTI WALKED down the overgrown dirt path from the main casino building to one of the galvanized steel sheds still left on the property from its days as a working farm. It was the kind of circular outbuilding that farmers use to store grain. He took a breath and blew out a stream of moist winter condensation, still wondering why Owen Roberts had decided to turn on them. Especially after all he'd been through. He knew Owen had a history with Shanks and Blackwell, but he thought it crazy for him to work against them with the FBI.

The steel clasp of the second padlock felt cold to his touch and he rattled the lock, trying to get it undone. Zimeratti heard Owen's chains scraping on the wood floor inside.

"You stupid son of a bitch. You still with us?" Zimeratti yelled as he pulled open the rusted door and stuck the barrel of the shotgun inside, tapping Owen's foot.

"Keeping me locked up like some goddamned animal, after all I done for you guys. Does that give you your jollies?" Owen snapped back.

"You're lucky Sam didn't let Blackwell have his way with you last night. Hell you might have ended up laying next to that dealer Rocco in his deathbed. Wherever that is."

"All you got a do is unlock these chains and we can get out of here. We can start over somewhere'" Owen said, pleading with Zimeratti.

"I brought you some food and a light bulb to give you a little warmth. I don't know what lies ahead for you, Owen, but no need for you to freeze to death," Zimeratti said as he set a cafeteria-style plastic tray down between Owen's outstretched legs and stood up to screw a hundred-watt light bulb into the overhead socket. "There's a switch for the light right here if you want it off."

Owen flinched at the sound of someone else banging on the side of the galvanized steel outbuilding, and he instantly rolled up onto his knees. Zimeratti pushed the rusted door open, bringing sunlight into the dim interior.

"Just me. Michael, you got a minute?" Shanks said. Zimeratti slammed the door shut and clinched both padlocks before joining in with Shanks' cadence, walking down a narrow path that led toward the woods. Tall clumps of grass scraped their boots as they walked and left streaks of moisture on their pant legs.

"I got to tell you, it didn't surprise me all that much to hear that Owen was working for the other side. Michael, we need to keep our eye on the ball. You and I both know Vinton is a troubled man. He always has been. I'm not saying Owen Roberts is the best of characters, but he would have done much better in life if he'd never crossed Blackwell's path," Shanks said. "We need Owen's help packing the business, so I want you to do your best to control Blackwell."

"That's like telling me to control a cobra," Zimeratti said.

"I've got a plan, Michael. In a few weeks we'll be past all of this and living the good life in a place where no one can get to us. Your old man, Anthony, was there for me more than a few times. I made him a promise and I'll stick to it."

"What sort of a plan are you talking about?"

"Not now, Michael, just keep your eye on the ball."

CHAPTER TWENTY-FIVE

REECE SAT IN Mike Mobley's office on the fifth floor of the downtown St. Louis police building, waiting for his return. He'd visited the same floor once before when Haisley had an office there and he'd tagged along with his dad. The walls were still a dull brown, and he doubted much else had been changed since his last visit.

He'd caught a lucky break when he recognized Officer Felps the night before and told him he was Al's son. It turned out that Felps had called Mike Mobley, the chief of detectives, and Reece was soon freed from jail.

He heard the heavy steps of someone coming, and Mike Mobley walked past and plopped down behind his prominent wooden desk. His cheeks were red and the tie he wore looked like it might be cutting off his breath. He smiled at Reece.

"I just talked to the DA. You're off the hook for now, but he still considers you a suspect," Mobley said.

"So what's that mean for me?" Reece said, having an idea.

"It means they may still have questions, but for now you're free to go."

Reece promptly stood up and headed for the door.

"Hey, if you have time, I'd like to buy you lunch," Mobley said, looking like the kind of guy who was especially fond of lunches.

"Sure, I got the time for a guy who sprung me out of jail."

The two men walked to the elevator, and they rode down a few floors in awkward silence. Just because they both knew Reece's father didn't mean they knew each other.

"I made a call and got your rental out of impound. It's parked right over there," he said pointing to the blue Mazda. "Let's take my truck, though."

They were listening to Garth Brooks and driving parallel to the Mississippi River when Mobley silenced the radio and turned toward Reece. "So, let me get this straight. A little over a year ago, you took a leave of absence from a high-paying job as an aerospace engineer to try your hand at investigative work."

"That's correct."

"And you've spent all that time trying to figure out who took your father's life while surviving on private investigation wages."

"Yup, that's about it," Reece said.

"Mind if I ask why you didn't keep your old job and hire a seasoned investigator?"

"Like you?"

"Well, like me except someone who investigates cold case murders for a living."

"You want the truth?" Reece asked.

"Give it to me."

"Because the St. Louis PD and the FBI both screwed up. I figured, what the hell, I'd give it a shot. I couldn't do any worse than they did," Reece said. "If I don't do it, no one else will."

"But you're in the prime of your life. You spent all those years going to school to get your education," Mobley said. "Not just any education, but an engineering degree."

"That's true, but once you have an education, it's for life.

Once I solve my father's case I can go back to what I did before."

"So that's your plan. You're going to solve Al's case and then go back to working for NASA?"

"Something like that"

Reece watched Mobley slow to peruse the parking lot and after realizing there weren't any places pull his truck up to the sidewalk a few hundred yards past the restaurant. Reece followed him toward the diner. Once inside, he looked up at the textured plaster ceiling and noticed a juke box in the corner playing Patsy Cline. It tugged at Reece's memory and took him back to a day he'd eaten lunch with his father in a similar place. He stared at the far wall in deep thought, picturing his father's face and his kind voice. He'd spent his whole life trying to earn his acceptance.

"I've been coming here for years. They got a great menu, and you can't beat the prices," Mobley said, sliding into an empty booth. "You okay, Culver?"

Reece heard his name and came back to the present time, crawling into the booth across from him. Mobley picked up a newspaper that had been left behind by the previous patron.

"This is what's wrong with our god damned country," he said. "If we could find some way to secure our borders and keep the drugs out, the crime rate in this country would no longer be a problem. It seems like every single case we get here in St. Louis has a connection to drugs."

"If I was in charge of this country, I'd make one change that would fix that," Reece said.

"Oh yeah, what would that be?"

"Have you ever heard of a MOA?"

"No, I can't say I have. What's that?" Mobley asked.

"It's a Military Operations Area. We have them all over the

country. It's where the military practices. There are lots of them out in the desert Southwest," Reece said.

"Okay, so what do MOA's have to do with the drug war?"

"We take twenty miles along each of our borders and make them Military Operations Areas. You post tanks, soldiers, and fighter jets in them 24/7. Anything that moves that's not supposed to be there gets blown to bits. Drug war over," Reece said watching Mobley shake his head.

"Good idea. You got any more Culverisms?"

A waitress came and dropped two red and white menus that looked like they were a relic of the 1960's in front of them.

"We already know what we want," Mobley said. "He'll have a number one special and I'll have a number six."

Reece looked at the menu and quickly figured that the cheeseburger and fries special Mobley had ordered for him would do the trick. "I'll have a Diet Coke too."

Once she had left, Mobley gave Reece a tight smile. "First off, I want to apologize for my over eager detectives. St. Louis is a much different place than the town you and your dad lived in. We have our hands full."

"They had me worried for a little while. I'm glad I recognized Officer Felps," Reece said, beginning to relax for the first time since driving into St. Louis three days before.

"Felps is a good guy. Your father and I used to go hunting with him along the river back in the day. Reece, speaking of your father, there's something I need to tell you," Mobley said.

"Yeah, what's that?" Reece said studying one of the waitresses as she served a group of college kids a couple of booths away.

"The night your dad went to that casino out in the country, he called me for backup. I've carried this burden with me for years, Reece."

"What are trying to say, Mike?"

"It was a Friday night. I remember it well because I had been chasing this gal Marci. Anyway, I finally convinced her to go out with me. It was my lucky night. We were back at my place and had polished off close to a fifth of bourbon," Mobley said, staring past him like he was reliving the memory.

"So, what's this got to do with my old man?"

"I remember Marci had taken my hand and was leading me down the hallway when the phone rang. I'd just made chief detective, so I had to answer it, but I wasn't in any condition to drive. I wouldn't have been any help to your dad that night."

"So what's that got to do with the night my dad got gunned down?" Reece asked.

"It was late—I'd say eleven or so—when I got the call from Al. He'd parked at a liquor store out in Malum. He'd been staked out all day at Anthony Zimeratti's house, trying to get pictures of Zimeratti with one of his mistresses," Mobley said. "Al was working for Mrs. Zimeratti's divorce lawyer."

"There's no way it was eleven at night when my father called you," Reece said. "I have the pictures from his camera and it was just before dark when he took them."

"Okay, maybe it wasn't that late. Like I said, I'd had a lot to drink." Mobley said, pursing his lips. "Did your dad ever tell you about the incident on the rooftop in East St. Louis when he and Haisley were partners?"

Reece wasn't sure why the conversation had turned in this direction. "Yeah, he told me all about it one day in the garage a year or two before he died," Reece said wondering where his story was going.

"When your dad was at Zimeratti's house, he spotted the guy that beat him to a pulp on that roof back in 05'. Your dad followed him that night, and the guy led him to the casino out in Malum. He'd turned into the liquor store parking lot across the street from the entrance to that place to call for some backup. I remember hearing him say he'd already tried Haisley but got no answer."

"So let me guess you blew him off that night for a piece of ass."

"I made the wrong choice, Reece. I was drunk and I—"

Reece stood up, slapped a twenty down on the table, and walked away, leaving Mobley and his BS behind. He smiled grimly at the cashier on his way out the door, trying to reel in the anger that threatened to explode.

He half expected Mike Mobley to chase after him, but then knew it would never happen. The fat bastard might miss scarfing down the rest of his French fries. That wouldn't happen. Not today anyway.

Reece thought about Crystal and his case. He needed a cab so he could get back to the Mazda rental car and head back to Tulsa. He thought about the streets they'd driven and remembered seeing a few cabs a couple of blocks over before they'd taken a left onto the street where the café was located.

He felt the rattle of his phone in his front pants pocket, reached in to pull it out, and noticed he had several missed calls. He answered.

"Yes."

"Reece, are you okay?"

"Yeah, why?" Reece said, startled. It was like his mother had ESP.

"Mike Mobley called me this past Thursday. The night you were supposed to take me to dinner," Helen Culver said.

"He did? What did he want?"

"He said I should hire you a good lawyer. I should get

Haisley involved if I needed to. He said you might have killed someone, Reece."

Her voice was edging toward hysteria, and he quickly corrected that notion. "He was wrong, Mom. It was all just a big misunderstanding."

"I don't believe you, Reece. Where are you now?"

"I'm on my way to get a taxi. I just had lunch with Mobley," Reece said.

"Reece, I hope you're not in danger. I can't afford to lose another member of our family. I don't know what you're involved in, but why don't you drop it? Let the police handle it."

"That's an idea," Reece said irritably.

"Are you coming back to Tulsa?"

"Yeah, I'll be there later today. Why?"

"Reece, honey. I don't think you're cut out for this investigation business you've gotten yourself into."

"Sometimes I wonder too," Reece said, wanting to end the call, but not wanting to hang up on his mother.

"Reece, if one of my boys was going to follow in his father's footsteps, I'd have thought it would have been your brother. He's the athletic one, the tough guy. Reece, you're an engineer. You went to school and did so well. How many investigators do you know who have a college degree?"

"Mom, most of them do."

"How about an expensive aerospace engineering degree?" Helen said. "Reece, you're not cut out to be a private investigator."

Reece held the phone out and stared at the end button. How dare she say that to him? "You know, Mom, I've sacrificed a lot for you, for this family. You'd think you'd be on my side for once. Maybe you could work at appreciating what I'm trying to do here."

He hung up after that, burning inside. First, Mobley confesses he was drunk the night of, and now his mother wanted to belittle him again. Why doesn't everyone just leave me alone? he thought bitterly. Then I'll solve the damn case.

CHAPTER TWENTY-SIX

VINTON BLACKWELL PUFFED on his cigar as he stood in the second-story window of the old barn. Below, Michael Zimeratti climbed into the passenger's seat of Sam Shanks' white Porsche and slammed the door. Vinton gnawed his lower lip, jealous of the increased amount of time he'd noticed Shanks spending with Zimeratti.

He walked down the creaking stairway, still mulling over what Zimeratti had told him about their needing Owen's help dismantling the casino over the next couple of days. He flipped his cigar forward into the air and watched the red cherry tip break off and slide into a pile of damp leaves. Vinton pulled his handgun from the breast pocket of his suit coat, pulled out the magazine, and ran his thumb across the copper-jacketed ammunition.

It was a short walk to the shed where they'd been keeping Owen, and on the way Vinton began to smile. He unlocked both locks and found his prey sitting down in a folding chair.

"You look like you could use some exercise. Let's take a walk. I need your help with something," Vinton said, unlocking the padlock that shackled Owens' leg to the steel U-bolt on the floor.

"What kind of help do you need?" Owen asked, acting like he was trying to stay on Vinton's good side.

"You'll see," he said as they walked abreast toward the casino. "You feel like driving? I got something I have to pick up. It's not far."

The two men climbed into the bench seat of a yellow cab over truck. Blackwell handed Owen the keys and pointed toward the dirt road that led out of the property. Owen started the truck and it zoomed loudly.

"You nervous or something?" Blackwell said, watching Owen's right knee shake as he took his foot off the accelerator pedal and shifted into drive. The truck crept forward, picking up speed.

"See them trees over there on the left side? That's where we're headed," Blackwell said. He leaned forward and slid a pair of stainless handcuffs from his back pocket. Owen stared out the windshield, focused on the uneven ground. Blackwell opened one end of the cuffs wide and came down on Owen's left wrist in a quick movement. The truck skidded to a stop.

"What the fuck are you doing?" Owen demanded.

Not replying, Blackwell picked up his foot and jammed it down on top of Owen's, mashing the gas pedal and sending the truck barreling into the tall vegetation toward a row of trees. After fifty yards the wheels of the truck started to spin in the rugged terrain.

"This is good. Shut if off," Vinton said, taking his foot off of Owen's. "Roll down your window and sit tight."

Owen stared over at Blackwell as he exited the truck.

"Do it," Blackwell said, pointing the gun at him.

CHAPTER TWENTY-SEVEN

REECE HELD UP a black plastic magnifier, eyeing one of the photos he'd been studying earlier. He was in a hotel room with two queen-sized beds. The book of matches in the cheap black plastic ashtray on the nightstand read "Executive Inn." In the photo, three men were standing on the porch of a large red-brick ranch in one of St. Louis's finer neighborhoods. The lawn was well kept with what looked like professional landscaping. Vintage muscle cars were parked single file in the long asphalt driveway. Large trees in front of the house were in full bloom, and he squinted trying to make out the faces of the men through the foreground of leaves.

One of the guys had long black hair pulled back over his forehead the way Pat Riley had when he coached the L.A. Lakers. He wore gold-rimmed glasses and had a diamond stud in his right ear lobe. Reece moved the magnifier to examine a squatty round-headed man with board shoulders who was pointing a finger at the first guy. He wondered if this fireplug showing attitude might be the boss.

The third man was tall and had thick blond hair with broad shoulders. In the next photo Reece saw the profile of the man's face with his Nordic features and light eyes. He held the magnifier up, but the foliage was blocking a head-on view of this guy's face. Reece wondered why his father had taken the photos. *What was he investigating?* Then he thought about what Mobley had told him back at the diner.

In the next photo the men were getting into cars. The third man was behind the steering wheel of a black Camaro, and the squatty guy was standing with the passenger's-side door open talking to someone outside the picture. The Pat Riley clone was in a blue Corvette. It looked mid sixties vintage. Reece pulled the magnifier back and spotted a woman in the passenger seat of the Corvette. This was the first time he'd noticed her. He lifted the magnifier focusing in to study the interior, but couldn't see much detail.

The next photo showed a large dirt parking lot filled with high-end cars in front of a black and white cobblestone barn. The building was long and at least two stories tall. It looked out of place somehow. He used the magnifier to look closer at the front door. It looked elaborate with two bright carriage lamps and a sign with fancy white letters that read "Malum Farms."

Reece stood from the bed and yawned, still mulling over his father's case. He thought of his mother, sunk in depression after her husband's beating on a East St. Louis roof top back in 2005. He couldn't stay mad at her. Not after what she'd endured the past several years. She was a proud woman, too proud to ask for help. She'd gotten past that and taken up a new career in real estate.

He had learned a few things about his father's cold case, and he couldn't help feeling angry about the way it had been handled. Someone at the St. Louis Police Department had called in the FBI after a few months of investigation. They wanted it off their plate. Six months after the FBI stepped in, the case was dropped and with it his mother's hope that her husband's killer would be caught. All along Special Agent

Stephen Cox, the guy heading up the FBI investigation, had his sights on something bigger, the crime boss who owned the casino.

Reece thought back to all the great times they'd had together, especially during his stint as a cop in the military. He'd finally found a way to connect with his stoic father. They'd spend hours on the phone talking about cases. He missed that. All the good times they'd had were too painful to remember. They had to stay pushed away out of his mind. It was still, even after a year and a half, too fresh to dwell on.

Not anymore, he reminded himself. After all this time he had returned to St. Louis. After he tracked down Crystal's mother, he was going to crack the case at last.

He glanced around the cheap motel room. He'd made great time driving back to Tulsa the night before and had chosen the same place he'd stayed at earlier. It felt good to rest after being locked up and harassed in St. Louis. After graduating with his degree in aerospace engineering from Parks College, Reece had packed his bags and headed west, never wishing to return to St. Louis. Now he'd come back. He was ready to even the score.

Reece's mentor, Haisley Averton, had taken a job as a senior detective in Tulsa three years earlier. Haisley had spent a lot of time with him, both while he was setting up his PI practice and afterward. It was like he was trying to make up for something he thought he owed Reece's father. Later on he figured out a second interest. They'd been out having a few beers one night when Haisley started talking about his wife. Reece thought it odd because he'd always been so private. He'd told Reece how tough it was when Mavis found out she couldn't have children. That was the night he realized he was probably the closest they'd ever get to having a son.

After a shower and shave Reece got dressed, put on his

Stetson, and bypassed the motel restaurant for something closer to edible. On his way to the downtown library he stopped off for some toast and a few cups of coffee. He sat on a stool at the counter, watching order tickets get clipped to a long wire that ran into the kitchen. Reece felt the rattle of his cell phone and pulled it from his brown corduroy jacket. Yet he recognized the number of his client Crystal and let the call go to voicemail. He didn't particularly want to tell her about his fiasco of the last few days. He heard his phone chirp, and he dialed voicemail.

"Hi, Reece, it's Crystal, I wanted to check in with you to see if you've turned up anything about my mother. I was wondering how you're doing on money. I know you told me $700 a day, and you've been on the case for seven days now."

He pulled the phone away from his ear before deleting her message. He needed every cent he could get, but didn't feel like talking to her until he had some solid information. Reece looked at the phone, and saw he had two more missed calls. Both were from Haisley. One was late Friday night, the night he'd called for help from the St. Louis jail, and the second from early Saturday.

Reece dialed Haisley's number just as the waitress dropped by and refilled his coffee cup. The aroma of the hot beverage pleased him.

"I guess you're okay, since you're calling me back on your cell phone," Haisley said, answering the call.

"Yeah, I'm okay now. I lucked out a little."

"What do you mean, you lucked out?" Haisley asked. "How did you end up in jail in the first place?"

"I was checking out the Roberts house where my client grew up. The place was trashed and filled with vagrants. I got jumped somehow, and woke up in an interview room in downtown St. Louis," Reece said.

"Are you okay?" Haisley said.

"Pretty good considering someone smacked me in the head with a pipe."

"Have you seen a doctor?"

"I had a concussion, but I'm good now," Reece said, not entirely convinced he was.

"How'd you get out?" Haisley asked.

"When they took me in to meet with the public defender, I recognized the name of an officer who used to work with my dad," he said as he started to think about Crystal's voicemail. "I guess Officer Felps talked to Mobley, or the DA, and they let me out."

"Where are you now?

"I'm back in Tulsa. I drove back last night,"

"If you're up for it, Mavis and I would like to have you over for dinner tonight," Haisley said.

"I've got some research to do, but dinner sounds good. I'll give you a call later."

Reece finished his breakfast, left a stack of money to cover the check and the tip, and headed out to the sidewalk. The air felt moist and humid outside, and he decided to leave the rental car in the spot out behind the restaurant and walk the four or five blocks to the library. He liked the safe feel that the city had, but started thinking about how Haisley had told him Tulsa had more murders annually than Denver. Reece wondered why, since Denver had a third again as many people. He figured it might have something to do with the mild climate of the city.

The downtown Tulsa Library had an industrial feel, and tables near the entrance were occupied by a cast of characters ranging from a bearded homeless man dressed in the remains of a three-piece suit to schoolchildren with their soccer moms in tow. Reece spent a few hours looking through old newspaper clippings for any articles about the disappearance of Tracey Roberts. He found a few and made copies of them. He was searching the name Roberts when he came across an article about the tragic death of Bobby Teeter, age seventeen, who accidentally fell to his death while hiking with his fourteen-year-old girlfriend in Tahlequah, Oklahoma, on August 5, 1997. Reece read the entire article, and found out that Bobby was the quarterback of the Edison high school football team.

A second article dated a few weeks later had more information on the accident, and some details about how the boy's girlfriend, Crystal Roberts, had been hospitalized after the accident for psychiatric evaluation. Reece copied both articles and searched for more, but only found earlier articles with the highlights from Bobby Teeter's football career.

He sat at the library table thinking about the accident and wondering if it was an accident, or if his client was a childhood psychopath. Reece's phone began to vibrate. He looked down at the display and saw that the incoming call was from none other than Crystal. *Spooky that she calls when I'm uncovering her past.*

"Hi," Reece said as he left the table and hurried outside to talk.

"Reece, did you get my earlier message?"

"Yeah, I got it."

"How is the investigation going? Have you found anything?" Crystal asked. Reece thought about the article he'd just read. "I visited the house where you grew up."

"Did you find my father Owen?"

"No, that turned out to be a dead end. Say, Crystal, I was

meaning to ask you. Have you seen your father since you were a kid?"

"No, and it's probably a good thing, because if I did see that bastard I don't know what I'd do to him," Crystal said ominously.

"When you called earlier, you mentioned my fees. This might take a few weeks to solve. There's not much to go on after twenty-two years."

"I understand, Reece. I can wire you more money when the bank is open on Monday. What hotel are you staying in?"

"I'm at the Executive Inn. It's off the highway on the north side of Tulsa. Room number 237," Reece said, wanting to tell her to add an extra $5,000 for pain and suffering.

CHAPTER TWENTY-EIGHT

THE WHEELS OF Sam Shanks' Lear 55 chirped as the main landing gear kissed the runway upon landing at Denver's Rocky Mountain Metropolitan Airport. The sun was long gone, having set over the mountains hours before, and the twin landing lights of the corporate jet parted the blackness as the plane made its way down the taxiways.

Shanks felt the forward motion cease and pulled at his lap belt, freeing himself from his plush brown leather recliner. Out the side window of the jet he spotted her still driving the same gray Maserati he'd helped her pick out at the dealership a few years before. The twin turbine engines of the jet spooled down to a welcome quiet.

After pressing the button to deploy the side air stairs, the co-pilot nodded at Shanks as if to say see you next time. Sam walked down the steps into the dry Colorado air. A gentle wind blew across the tarmac, and he reached down to fasten the bottom button on his signature blue blazer. He wore it everywhere like a uniform.

The sleek four-door coupe crept forward past the tail and stopped near the fuselage. The trunk popped open and the co-pilot hoisted three cardboard boxes from the rear of the jet and loaded them into the Maserati.

"Thanks, Jeff, I'll call you guys in a few days for the return trip," Shanks said.

"Very well, sir. Safe travels."

Shanks opened the passenger's side door and admired the tall brunette sitting with both hands braced on the steering wheel. Her eyes sparkled in the vehicle's interior lighting like diamonds under glass. He slid into the leather seat and sniffed the mixed scent of new leather and citrus perfume. It had been far too long since he'd last laid eyes on her.

"It's so good to see you, Sam," she said, leaning toward him. She slipped an arm around him as he wrapped both his arms around her. Their lips met and they held one another. Shanks felt the stresses of his world slipping away. It was good to have her in his arms once again. He had a plan for her, but he couldn't share it yet.

They both withdrew from the hug. She shifted the car into reverse and backed away from the jet. Her long brown hair flowed down over the shoulders of a yellow mid-thigh length Donna Karan dress. He let his eyes run down her body, admiring her tanned thighs.

"Are you hungry? Do you want to grab something before we drive up?"

"No, it's late. I'll eat when we get there," Shanks said as the acceleration of the Quattroporte pushed him back into his seat. Before long they were following 120th Avenue west toward the foothills paralleling the airport.

"How's business been?" Shanks asked as the woman slid her fingers under his left hand and squeezed. Her face was illuminated only by the glow of the car's instrument panel. She'd kept herself up well over the years despite the troubles she'd endured early in life.

"It's been busy at the Golden Spur since the holidays," she

announced in a businesslike tone. "That's all good, but things have changed since Evelyn made the announcement that she's going to retire after New Year's."

"Oh yeah, how so?" Shanks asked.

"She hired a general manager to run operations. I like having the help, but I've got to tell you, I hate this new guy, Derrick. He's a control freak and he seems like he's trying to make a name for himself."

"I'm sorry to hear that. It's never any fun when new people come to the party and think they're smarter than anyone else."

She down shifted and guided the Maserati from Highway 93 onto Highway 6. The tachometer showed the rpms building, matching the sound of the engine's acceleration as they sped off down the road.

"This is one sweet car, and from what I see, you're enjoying it," Shanks said.

"Very much. It's great for the curvy mountain roads."

About twenty minutes later she turned off the main highway and drove up a series of switchbacks through a forested area to a solitary log home at the top of a mountain. Incredible views stretched in all directions.

"I like what you've done with the place. You've got a yard now," Sam said.

"Yeah, I guess that's what you could call it. The deer up here love it."

"The house looks the same as it did when I brought you out here," Shanks said.

"Yeah, I've come a long way since those days," she said. "That reminds me. Does Vinton still work for you?"

"Yes, he has his talents." Shanks said as he followed her into the home and took a seat at the bar in front of the kitchen. The woman dropped her keys onto the black granite counter, pulled two long-stemmed wine glasses from a cabinet, and went to work pulling the cork from a bottle of expensive Cabernet.

"So tell me more about this Derrick person," Shanks said.

"Well, you remember we had the vault and the two safes. The safe in my accounting office on the third floor has always suited me for a place to keep the revenue from your ventures. It's separate from the main casino and has always been fine."

"Yeah," Shanks said, bringing his wine glass up to his lips and nearly draining it.

"Derrick had the bright idea at our last weekly meeting to change things around. He wants all the cash in the vault, and he wants to keep the large denomination poker chips in my safe."

"What does Evelyn think about that?"

"She's fine with whatever anyone wants to do. She left the planet, as far as I'm concerned. All she thinks about these days is yoga and buying a place in the Caribbean."

"It sounds like its time for you and I to come up with a plan for Derrick," Shanks said. "You've been laundering my money for over a decade. We can't let some new bozo come to town and ruin things for us."

"It gets worse. Last night I was out for a drink with him and Evelyn, and Derrick came up with the great idea to move all the money next week and then on the first of the month do a company-wide independent audit."

Shanks stiffened, and his reply came out as a growl. "Those are fighting words."

CHAPTER TWENTY-NINE

A LARGE DUAL-AXLE TRUCK with the name Maverick Gardening painted in green letters across both sides turned into the Southern Hills subdivision on the south side of Tulsa with a black Range Rover following close behind. The two trucks drove down a residential street lined with cars on each side, and slowed as the passageway between the cars became too narrow to proceed. The driver watched his rearview mirror, as if wondering what to do.

Melvin Phillips walked up to the driver's side window and rapped on it with his knuckles.

"Are you here for the golf tournament?" he shouted.

The driver cranked the window open. "No, Mister. We're here to do some gardening in the neighborhood."

"Gardening, huh? Whose house are you working on?"

The man in the truck hesitated and reached across the seat for his cellphone. Michael Zimeratti, dressed in a solid green gardener's outfit, emerged from the Range Rover and approached Melvin Phillips.

"What's the hold-up? We got work to do," Zimeratti grumbled.

"I was just trying to figure out what you're up to. This is a neighborhood watch area," Phillips said.

"We're here to work on the Austins' place. They're out of

the country, and their daughter Ann called saying that the place is overgrown with weeds," Zimeratti said, running his hand through his slicked-back hair.

"I know Chuck Austin. He's a good man. Wait a minute, I'll clear the way for you."

Phillips made his way down the street, stopping at each car to talk to its driver. A group of cars pulled to the side so that both trucks could pass. Soon the large one pulled past a long red brick driveway with a circular arch. Turning in reverse, he backed toward the garage of Melvin Phillips' seventy-two hundred square foot home.

Vinton Blackwell, who had been lying under a blanket in the backseat of the Range Rover, climbed out wearing dull green pants and a matching shirt with the name Maverick Gardening stenciled across one sleeve. He bent down and began working the multi-colored flowerbeds, appearing busy but studying the nearby houses for signs of life.

He worked his way down the right side of the garage, stopping every so often to pull a weed from the flowerbed. As he neared the side door of the three-car garage, he looked through the window. The side door was unlocked, he discovered, and once inside, he brushed the dirt off his gloves.

A sleek navy blue Aston Martin was parked on the far side of the garage, and Blackwell sniffed at what smelled like the inside of a basement. He pulled a small leather pouch from his rear pocket and went to work on the keyhole of the garage doorknob. With his cellphone held to his ear, he started talking.

"I've got the door unlocked. Read me the alarm code." The reply came instantaneously.

"Four-nine-six-two," he said out loud, reciting the code. Blackwell smiled, pushed open the garage door, and entered the home, setting off the beeping of the alarm. He flipped on a light switch and entered the code he had just been given. He watched the alarm status light change from red to green.

"Got it. I'm inside with the alarm off. Back into the driveway, and be ready for the left door to open," Blackwell said. He walked out to the door, and watched the large work truck pass by the house like he had planned and park a few houses down on the opposite side of the street. A white Ford van with the same Maverick Gardening logo painted across both sides backed into the driveway toward the garage door. When the van was almost all the way to the house Blackwell pressed the garage door opener, watching Zimeratti's progress as he waited for the door to fully raise and then backed the van in. Blackwell closed the garage door behind him.

Heading efficiently to the rear of the van, he opened both rear doors. He reached inside and unfastened a brown leather briefcase from the side. The interior of the van had been outfitted with a series of vertical compartments, each covered in fuzzy black material. Vinton had just pulled his briefcase out of the van when he felt a hand on his shoulder.

"What you got there?" Zimeratti said.

"Tools for the job. What's it look like? Stop standing around and let's get this done," Blackwell barked, not wanting to explain himself.

The two men entered the home with several others and fanned out. Zimeratti went to the foyer and scooped up a set of keys with a pink fob on them. Then he went to the basement, where Vinton Blackwell had gone with Melanie Phillips the night of the dinner party. Zimeratti pressed a four-digit code into a black keypad and swiped the set of keys past it. He heard a "beep," and the telltale sound of the lock on the stainless steel door of the Phillips' art vault "clicked" open. Zimeratti stepped inside and instructed the other men to grab each of the works of art, insert them into a felt bag, and carry them out to the van.

In the meantime, Vinton Blackwell searched the gigantic house for signs of a secret room. The night he'd met Melanie Phillips he'd found out that she and her husband had a private collection of paintings that would never appear on the auction block. Blackwell entered their master bedroom and ran his hand down a wall absent of decoration. He stopped, feeling what seemed like a joint in the wall. Blackwell set his briefcase on the Phillips' bed and pulled a small flashlight from his back pocket. He shined it onto the wall and worked his way along the seam, looking for a way in.

On the wall a few feet from the seam he found a small picture that looked like it had been hand-drawn in crayon by a youngster. Vinton pulled the framed portrait off the wall and uncovered a red button. He pressed it and the wall popped open. He replaced the picture and entered.

The room had two large wooden queen anne dressers, and on top of one sat a one-foot by one-foot painting on a miniature easel. He stared at the thick brush strokes and vivid colors of the Van Gogh. Paydirt. Vinton edged back out of the room and grabbed his briefcase. He reentered the small vault holding his flashlight in his teeth, opened the case, and pulled out a black felt bag. He shined the light on the small painting and admired the vase of yellow flowers the artist had painted more than a century earlier.

Blackwell joined the others in the garage and watched as they loaded the last of the black felt-covered paintings into the back of the white van.

"Where were you for so long?" Zimeratti asked.

"None of your goddamned business," Blackwell said. "Remember who got us this job, asshole."

Zimeratti turned toward Blackwell with his hand cocked to throw a punch. The painting in his other hand dropped and banged into the trailer hitch of the van. Both men froze at the sound of tearing canvas.

"Great move, idiot. I hope that piece of artwork wasn't priceless," Blackwell said.

The younger man looked up at him sheepishly and pulled the painting from the felt bag. It was a western that now had a perfect fist-sized hole in the center. Zimeratti shoved the torn painting back into the bag and walked toward a nearby tool bench.

"What are you doing?" Blackwell yelled.

"I'm leaving it. It's ruined."

"No, you're not. Bring it. We're running out of time. Let's finish this thing and get out of here."

Blackwell rounded up the other men and told them it was time to leave. Zimeratti climbed into the driver's seat of the van. Two other men climbed into the van through the sliding side door. Blackwell pushed the garage door opener and watched the van drive away.

He pressed the "9" button on the alarm panel and pulled the locked six-panel door closed listening to the alarm beep as it counted toward arming. With his briefcase in hand he walked out of the side garage door smiling. He'd just become a very rich man.

CHAPTER THIRTY

REECE DROVE SOUTH toward Haisley's neighborhood, listening to Waylon and Willie singing, "Mama, don't let your babies grow up to be cowboys" on the car's radio. He'd stopped at the candy store and picked up a big box of chocolates for Mavis. Hearing the ring of his cellphone from the center console of the rental car, Reece held the phone up and saw that the call was from his mother. He let it go to voicemail and stuffed the phone back into the console. The last thing he needed was to hear more of her garbage about how he wasn't cut out to be a PI.

Parking in front of their brick ranch, set among other well-kept homes along the street, he strolled up to the door and rang the bell.

Mavis Averton answered with a big smile. "Reece, you look great. Come in," she said, giving him a big hug. He smiled at her familiar face. Her dark skin was smooth except for a few crows' feet at the corners of her eyes. Her hair flowed down to her shoulders. Reece guessed that she and Haisley were in their mid fifties. She hadn't had an easy life being the wife of a black police detective in the Bible belt, but he had never heard a negative word from her. The two had met in college, when he was playing basketball and she was a cheerleader. They'd never had kids.

"Here, this is for you," he said, handing her the chocolates. "Thanks for remembering my birthday."

"Oh, Reece, you shouldn't have. We'll dig into these after dinner," Mavis said, running her hand down his forearm with a fondness reserved for longtime friends or family. "He's out back in his office."

"His office?"

"Yeah, after he got his dream car, he built a second garage out back. When he's not working, or watching basketball, he's out there doing god knows what," Mavis said with a laugh.

"It's pretty neat that you found a house close to where you guys first met. It looks great," Reece said as he headed for the back door. On the porch he saw a large wood building that matched the house in every detail. Haisley came around the corner on his right.

"Come on in, Culver. Check out my man cave."

Reece followed his friend inside and saw in the dim light of the garage a bright orange 1970 Camaro. The car Haisley had always wanted.

"Wow, buddy, this is something," he said, admiring the car.

Haisley motioned Reece past, and they walked through a door that separated the two halves of the building. The office was carpeted with finished walls, a ceiling fan, and a large-screen TV on one wall. The opposite side had a fax machine, copier, and several computers spread out across an L-shaped desk.

"I'm glad you're here, Reece," Haisley said, grinning at him.

"It's good to be here. I really like your digs."

"So how's your new case going? Did you find any new leads?"

"It's been slow, but I did think of something you could help with," Reece said as he watched Haisley pour two glasses of Scotch.

"What's that?"

"I was wondering if you could do some background on Owen Roberts."

A frown crossed Haisley's face. "Reece, there's something I've got to tell you."

"Oh yeah, what's that?" Reece asked, wondering if the name meant something to him.

"I've been helping with an investigation that involves Owen Roberts. It's part of a three-state task force," Haisley said, handing Reece a glass of Scotch.

"A task force, huh. I hope you're not working for the FBI. You know what happened the last time you got involved with them." Then he took a long pull of the Scotch, savoring the taste.

"Culver, you've got to learn how to trust people. Not everything is so black and white."

Reece didn't like what he'd heard, but he let it pass. "So what's this got to do with Owen Roberts?"

"I got a call from Special Agent Stephen Cox a few weeks after I retired."

"What'd he want?" Reece asked, knowing he wasn't going to like the answer.

"He needed some surveillance done. He knew south Tulsa was my home turf, and he offered to pay me for my time."

"What kind of surveillance?" Reece asked.

"Cox had spotted Owen Roberts and followed him to a farm south of town. Owen was living there and working on the place. Cox had been following a lead on Sam Shanks when he found the farm. It turns out Roberts is working for Shanks, and they've been operating an illegal gambling operation out of that property for years."

"Sounds like what they were doing up north," Reece said.

"That's why I got involved. That and the extra money don't hurt either. Do you know what healthcare insurance costs these days for a retired cop?" Haisley said.

"No, I can't say I do. Is it expensive?"

"Everything is expensive these days. I used to pay twenty bucks a week for the best plan they had, and it covered everything," Haisley said.

"You know what the problem is, don't you?" Reece said.

"I got my idea of what the problem is. Crooked politicians and lobbyists back in DC."

"Yeah, that's one part, but it's also how everything is set up," Reece said. "The entire healthcare industry should be non-profit. There are too many people getting rich off of sick people in this country."

"Hell, Culver, you got some good ideas. Maybe you should run for office."

"No, thanks. I don't have the stomach for politics," Reece said. "So, what we were talking about earlier, the task force. That sounds odd to me."

"It does why?" Haisley said.

"Why would the FBI farm out a surveillance job to a retired police detective? Don't they usually do their own work?"

"They usually do, Reece, but this task force is something they came up with after 9/11. It's a new concept for them."

"I guess that makes sense."

Haisley paused, and in his meaningful look Reece realized this was what he had been building up to the whole time. "Say, there's something I could use your help with tomorrow morning. It would mean getting up early, and it might be dangerous."

*

In the pre-dawn darkness Haisley shifted into low and eased his wife's green Ford coupe off the pavement onto a snow-covered single track. They had driven into the countryside south of Tulsa, a place where beef cattle were more numerous than people. They headed down a road cut through a forest of green plants, like something, Reece thought, you'd see in a jungle. The headlights painted a scene of old corn stalks from generations past that stretched ten feet tall in some spots intermixed with wide-leaved plants that threatened to overtake the road.

The air smelled fresh and sweet as Haisley continued toward what he believed to be one of Shank's hideouts. A large casino was hidden in back of this overgrown land. The road took a jaunt to the left, and Reece looked out the side mirror into the dark field behind them. He felt the car coming back right and up ahead saw a cluster of old structures with one long single-story brick building that looked like it had been constructed very recently.

They drove the last thousand yards with the headlights switched off and parked just short of a clearing. He followed Haisley to the trunk, and his friend unloaded matching black bulletproof vests and a pair of gun belts. The belts each had a holstered sidearm with a flashlight on one side, and several clips, and a leather compartment housing a set of handcuffs on the other. Reece took a vest from Haisley, put it on, and took one of the belts, wondering if he'd kept a few souvenirs from his days on the Tulsa PD. Reece felt a black 9mm semi-automatic pistol on his right side after clipping on the belt.

"You're familiar with a Glock, right?" Haisley asked.

"Yeah, I've shot these a few times at the range."

They walked single file through the tall grass. Halfway through, Haisley stopped and motioned to him. "Either this place is abandoned, or they're asleep. Let's be ready." Reece watched him pull his gun and continue onward. He looked for light, but the only thing he saw was the glow of a distant neighborhood to the east. The sky was devoid of stars and a gentle breeze rustled the foliage. The ground was rock hard. It was covered with a dusting of snow, but the traction was fine.

The two men suddenly heard a noise and froze. Haisley turned back toward Reece, pointing his gun to his left. They both stood listening. Reece heard what sounded like hooves, and guessed it was livestock. Haisley motioned for them to continue. They stepped out of the tall grass onto a dirt lot in front of the long brick building. To the left was a large barn, and to the right an assortment on galvanized circular steel outbuildings.

Reece followed Haisley and peered into a window of the brick building. He took a flashlight off his belt and shined it in.

"Looks abandoned to me. I was surveilling in that field just last week and there were over fifty cars parked in this lot," Haisley said. "It's starting to seem like this guy is always one step ahead."

"Have you told anyone else about the investigation?"

"No, you're the only other person who knows other than Special Agent Cox and the other people on the task force."

"Do you want to go in and have a look?" Reece asked, holding the Glock by its barrel and raising the handle toward the panes of glass on the exterior door.

"Can you break it quietly?" Haisley asked. Reece walked over to a large plant and tore off several of the thick green leaves. He held the leaves up to the glass and tapped the handle of his gun on them. It took two hits until he felt the glass give way and he reached through to unlock the door.

They entered shining their lights in a circular pattern around the interior. The center of the room had a couple of poker tables with stacks of chips, and a deck of cards in the middle of each.

"Looks like they left in a hurry," Haisley said.

"I wonder what spooked them."

Haisley was shaking his head. "I'll tell you, Culver, I'm starting to think this bastard has someone on the inside at the FBI."

Haisley and Reece did a quick search of the grounds and found several sets of deeply grooved tracks, the kind a moving truck would make on a wet dirt road.

"What now?" Haisley remained quiet and Reece followed him back toward the car. The sky was gaining a blue-orange tint, hinting at sunrise, and the trees to their west were filled with the chirping of birds starting their day.

"Well, this will change things with the task force. There goes my second income," Haisley said, kicking dirt next to his wife's car. The two men got in and Haisley drove back toward the main road. Reece had to admire Shanks' ingenuity. The landscape provided perfect cover for the work he and his men did at the farm, and unless someone flew over they'd never know it was an illegal casino. Yet the question was: why they'd moved out so fast?

"What's that?" Reece said, pointing toward a red flash of light. "Do you see it? Over in those plants, it looks like they left something behind."

Haisley drove off the road. The headlights illuminated the reflectors on the back of a small moving van that looked like it had been driven deep into the cover in an attempt to conceal it.

The front wheels of the car spun, losing traction in the deep foliage. Reece opened his door and got out. He walked toward the truck, curious about why it had been abandoned.

"Hold up a second," Haisley yelled from behind. Reece saw his friend digging through the trunk of his wife's car. He walked back and Haisley handed him a pair of latex gloves and blue cotton foot covers.

Reece pulled on the gloves, covered his shoes, and followed his friend toward the truck. The sun was up and he felt a cool breeze running through the field. They walked closer, climbing past tall plants, and he pulled his gun and held it outward. Every couple of steps he glanced downward, figuring they might find a booby-trap.

"Haisley, look for trip wires," Reece said.

"I was just thinking the same thing."

"Lets take this slow," Reece continued. The property had been abandoned, but Shanks had a history of leaving behind surprises.

"You smell something?" Haisley said, closing in on the truck a few yards ahead.

"Yeah, smells like death," Reece said, having smelled dead carcasses more times than he cared to remember.

"We got a body," Haisley said, looking into the side window of the General Motors truck. Reece came up behind and looked over his shoulder. The sweet smell of rotting flesh hit him. He instinctively brought his arm up to cover his nose and mouth with the fabric of his jacket, but the smell had already entered his lungs and he felt like retching. Inside the truck Reece saw an elderly man with short wisps of white hair parted to the side. The dead man's eyes bugged out, making his face look mask like. He still had his seatbelt on with his hands on the steering wheel, and Reece noticed the guy's right wrist was fastened to the steering wheel by a pair of stainless steel handcuffs. Three dark stains had long ago dried on the corpse's chest where multiple bullets had punctured.

"I've seen enough. Let's take a quick look in the back, and then I better call this in," Haisley said. "Looks like an assassination. Especially with those cuffs fastening his wrist to the steering wheel."

"Any guesses on who this is?" Reece asked, watching Haisley work on the truck's back door latch. After a few minutes they got it undone, but it took both of them to shove the heavy door open. Reece stood up on the back of the truck, holding the door up while Haisley went in with a flashlight.

"Just a bunch of old slot machines. I don't see anything that would help ID the body," Haisley said, backing out with a handkerchief held tight against his face.

"What's that?" Reece said, pointing at a large rectangular object covered in black felt. Haisley handed off the flashlight, and Reece crawled into the truck hunched over to avoid hitting his head on the ceiling. He took a breath and caught the smell of the decaying body up front. He dry heaved, and then took a second breath with his nose buried in the sleeve of his jacket.

Reece latched onto the felt-covered container. It felt wooden like a frame. He pulled it out of the truck, and welcomed the smell of fresh air as he stepped down onto the ground. Haisley peeled back the felt bag, holding the frame with his hands. It was a painting of several cowboys on horses near a stream. The detail was amazing, and if it weren't for the three-inch hole punched through the center it might have been worth something.

They closed up the truck, and walked back toward the car.

"Reece, I think you should probably take Mavis's car back to the house, and I'll call this in. If anyone asks I'll say I was dropped off to avoid detection, and on my way out found this."

CHAPTER THIRTY-ONE

REECE DROVE BACK to Haisley's house puzzling over who the dead guy was and who might have tipped off Shanks. It seemed like Shanks had always been one step ahead of law enforcement. He promised himself that once he solved Crystal's case, he'd spend some time working on putting Shanks and his men behind bars.

He parked the Ford in Haisley's driveway and climbed into his Mazda rental. The sight of the dead body had made him think of another dead body found out in the country, his father Al Culver.

Feeling unsettled, Reece took off down the street. He was hungry and the car's heater felt good on the drive toward the same diner he'd gone to every morning. Reece parked in the lot and stopped by the newspaper machine out front to see if any Sunday papers were left. He pulled the handle open and saw that the box had been stripped clean.

Reece took a seat at the counter and ordered coffee. The waitress smiled like he'd become a familiar face. A Sunday *Tulsa World* was lying on the seat next to him. It had been pulled apart, sticking out in all different directions. Drinking coffee, he paged through the sports section. The waitress returned to fill his cup and handed him another stack of newspapers. He glanced down at the local news section, and spotted an article about a recent burglary that had smashed the hopes and dreams of two Tulsa philanthropists.

Reece read the article and learned that Melvin and Melanie Phillips had planned to auction off their art collection to raise money for the construction of the new Melanie Phillips Cancer Center.

"Would you like something other than coffee?"

Reece looked up at the waitress. She stood holding an order book in one hand and a pen in the other. "Are you reading the article about Mr. and Mrs. Phillips?"

"Yeah," he answered.

"I hope they catch whoever did that. We really need that new cancer center. It's really amazing what the Phillipses have done for this town."

CHAPTER THIRTY-TWO

CRYSTAL DROVE WEST on Sixth Avenue, squinting into the rearview mirror. She saw her exit and veered right, cutting off another car just in time to make the turn, and heard the car's horn. The ramp circled around to the south, and after a few hundred feet she pulled into the Denver Federal Center. After driving a few blocks she turned in and parked in the lot where she and her boss George worked. As she stepped out, the howling wind lifted the edge of her dress. She reached down, stopping the dresses rise, and in doing so dropped her briefcase. All of her files slid out onto the ground beneath the car.

"Damn it." She picked up the leather case, straightened her papers, and buttoned the leather flap closed. On the way toward the building Crystal wondered why so many cars were parked in the lot this early on a Monday morning, then dismissed the thought, figuring there must have been a big meeting.

Fighting the wind once again, Crystal opened the first set of doors and barged into the building. She smiled at the same guard she saw most mornings and passed by security, holding up her badge. He nodded as she walked by and disappeared down the hallway into the right wing of the building. She past several doors for federal departments until she reached the seal on the door that read Colorado Federal Attorneys Office.

Crystal greeted the receptionist, walked past George Kendall's large office, and continued to her own just down the hall. She logged in to her computer and had started reading e-mail when she noticed the red light on her desk phone blinking.

"Hello."

"Ms. Thomas. Mr. Kendall is here and would like you to come to his office," the receptionist said.

"Tell him I'll be right down." Crystal said having anticipated this little chat. She grabbed her coffee cup and headed over.

"Crystal, come in and shut the door," George said.

"What's going on?"

"I'm going to take you off the task force," George said without looking up from his computer.

"Why are you doing that?" Crystal asked, sounding hurt.

"We have other priorities that need your attention."

"This is not fair, George. I've been on the task force with you since it started. Does this have something to do with the past week?" Crystal said, struggling to keep from slamming her fist on his desk.

"No, Crystal. First of all, what happened was a mistake and will never happen again. Second, you're the daughter of our informant, and that constitutes a conflict of interest for this office. We're lucky Special Agent Cox or one of the others hasn't made that connection. Third, Jim Burney is a junior attorney, and he needs your experience on his case."

"But George—"

"We are done here," George interrupted. "Go back to your office. I will be setting up a meeting this afternoon between the three of us, so you can transition smoothly onto Jim's case. Oh, and shut the door on your way out."

Crystal stared at the top of his downturned head and left his office. This wasn't over, not by a long shot. She went to her office to get her briefcase and headed to the ladies' room. She took the first stall, locking herself in. She sat down on the cold toilet seat and reached into her briefcase for her personal smart phone—but it wasn't there. How could that be? She pulled out the contents of the briefcase, hunting for it. It wasn't where she'd put it, and she felt a sense of dread.

Crystal tore into each of the three side pockets on the briefcase. She was desperate to find her phone, but only found an assortment of lipsticks, Kleenex, and an old boarding pass. She began to sweat. *Where could my phone be?* The video on it could easily ruin her career.

On the way back to her office, she retraced the events of her morning and decided she must have left it in the car. Crystal pulled open the office door and popped her head in.

"I have to run a quick errand. I'll be back shortly. Call me if anything urgent comes up."

"Sure thing, Ms. Thomas," the receptionist said.

Once outside, she felt the wind blowing even harder than before. The twin Colorado and American flags stuck straight out like postage stamps against the bright blue sky.

She pressed her key fob and watched the car's lights blink amber with a "chirp". She stopped at the door, and unbeknownst to her, the tip of her shoe nudged the smart phone she'd dropped earlier. Crystal slid into the car, started it, and rolled the side window down a few inches to get some air. After checking the glove box and coming up empty, she shifted into reverse, heading for home, and felt a slight resistance. She stepped harder on the accelerator and heard a crunch from somewhere under the car. She continued to back out but stopped when another car had backed out from the row behind, blocking her progress.

Crystal saw something smashed in the parking spot she'd just vacated. She slammed the transmission into park and jumped out with a sick feeling in her stomach. The horn of the SUV blared from behind, but she ignored it. Crystal walked toward the pile of smashed plastic—what remained of her shattered phone. One half looked fine except for the cracked screen, but the other side was cracked with chunks of plastic sticking upward.

The blue Ford Expedition was still waiting with the woman in the driver's seat. Crystal heard the horn blast again and felt like turning, and giving the driver the finger, or better yet approaching the SUV, and grabbing this asshole by the throat. She instead focused on the pile of plastic. With the cardboard backing of her notebook pressed against the pavement, she used her left hand to scoop up the pieces. She saw the cracked green circuit board with tiny white wires. With the end of a legal-sized envelope held open, she tilted the notebook downward coaxing the pieces inside, and prayed that the video would be okay.

*

Back at her apartment, Crystal grabbed the stack of her mail. She saw that one of the envelopes was different from the rest. With her thumb she flipped through the letters and stopped on a small taupe-colored envelope about the same size as a wedding invitation. She pulled the card out of the stack and brought it to her nose sniffing. The taupe envelope smelled like a mixture of paper and cardboard.

She shoved her thumbnail under the edge and slit it sideways, tearing open the thick paper. The inside was occupied by a single piece of stationary folded in thirds. Crystal unfolded it and began to read. It was like all the rest she'd received, except this time it mentioned going to dinner with a sophisticated gentleman. Crystal hurled the letter toward the center island. She didn't have time for it. Where was Tracey Roberts and why was she writing these stupid letters with no return address, especially after all of this time? Tears ran down Crystal's face.

In the kitchen, she set the remains of her phone on the center island before swinging open the refrigerator, where she found an ice-cold bottle of vodka. With the blue cork cap pulled, Crystal raised it to her lips. It smelled chemical and burned as she poured the liquid down her throat, waiting for it to calm her racing mind. With both hands she pushed the bottle away from her mouth, gulping to catch her breath. Her mind eased and her eyes felt funny. She returned it to her mouth and chugged some more.

After a long pull she set the Grey Goose on the counter. The alcohol was definitely entering her bloodstream. Wanting more, she reached for the bottle, but her unsteady hand back knocked the vodka over. She watched open mouthed as the frosted glass bottle rolled across the granite counter and stopped against the pile of mail. The small amount of vodka that remained was well below the neck and none spilled. She stepped back, wobbled, and gained her balance, reaching up to run both hands through her long hair.

From a kitchen drawer she pulled out an old copy of the yellow pages. She stared at the thick book, forgetting for a moment what she was searching for, then turned the pages until she found "Computers." She stopped on a listing for someone with an address on Broadway, picked up the phone, and staring past, watched the floor spin. *Why won't it stop?* She leaned over and felt like puking. Yet Crystal gained her composure and dialed.

"Lane's Phone Service," a man said.

"Doooo yoooo fiixxx smott phowns," Crystal slurred.

"All kinds. What kind of problem are you having, miss?"

"How late errr you opem?" Crystal asked.

"I'll be here all night"

CHAPTER THIRTY-THREE

THE BLACK RANGE Rover exited off Highway 24 just south of where I-70 runs through the city of Vail, Colorado. A thin veil of cloud cover approached from the west. The air was crisp and with the sun falling toward the horizon, the season's night chill had arrived.

"Hello, " Vinton Blackwell said, answering his cell phone. "Yeah, I'm just a few minutes away. I made good time," he said to the caller. He drove the truck fast, shooting gravel from his tires as he accelerated around a corner.

"If that's what you want, Sam, but I got to tell you, I don't care for Michael the same way I cared for his father, Anthony. He's careless. He punched one of the westerns through the trailer hitch of the van." Blackwell followed the road left at the Y and after a few turns entered a series of seven steep switchbacks that descended down the mountain.

"Okay then, I'll let it go," Blackwell said, ending the call. Annoyed as hell, he jammed his foot down on the brake, skidding across the crushed gravel road, and slammed his clenched fist on the dashboard. "Mother *Fucker,* after all these years of doing Shanks' business."

Something had changed about Shanks, and now Blackwell was the odd man out. That was fine, he thought. He'd always hated the prick for taking too large a share of the winnings.

What Shanks didn't know was that the Van Gogh would pay back for all those years of playing follow the leader.

Blackwell pulled left down a long paved driveway. A ten-foot wall rose out of the field on both sides of the pavement. The land was well manicured with tall pine trees and short mountain grass, devoid of the usual pine needle carpeting. The truck rolled up to a tall decorative gate fashioned into a scene of running horses cut into black steel plate. A short, stocky man in a blue blazer, looking like Shanks' twin, appeared from somewhere behind the wall and approached the Range Rover.

"You back here for good?" the guard asked.

"Yeah. Anything new going on around here since my last visit?"

"No, nothing but cold days and lots of snow," the guard grumbled, then went back into his shack. The decorative steel gate opened, cutting the frieze in half. Blackwell eased the truck down the driveway and parked in front of a large multi-roofed mansion sheathed with the same rock that made up the exterior wall.

He parked in a spot next to a second building, detached from the main house. Vinton opened the briefcase and eyed his prize. It was time to put it in a safe place that his boss would never find.

CHAPTER THIRTY-FOUR

HAISLEY AVERTON STOOD to the side as a group of men in white full-body clean suits loaded the corpse onto a gurney and zipped up the black body bag to the midpoint of the torso. Another man in a white suit was photographing the inside of the truck, and a woman with blond hair tucked under a cap was making a white mold of the truck tracks. Yellow crime-scene tape cordoned off the area, and several crime-scene vehicles were parked nearby.

The afternoon sun had climbed above the houses to the east and the air was still. A second photographer approached the gurney and took a series of photos. Haisley was trying to guess who the man in the body bag was. A fingerprint technician squatted near the open side door of the Penske truck, collecting evidence.

"Averton," a brown-haired man called. Haisley didn't need to see the detective's nametag. He recognized Dave Wheeler from his days in Homicide.

"So tell me again what you were doing here this morning?" Wheeler asked, pulling out a notebook.

"We've been working a case here," Haisley said, knowing it was all part of the drill, but wishing someone else had been sent to question him.

"We? I don't see anyone else here, Mr. Averton."

"I'm working for Special Agent Stephen Cox of the St. Louis Organized Crime Task Force," Haisley said, idly studying a patch of stubble Wheeler had missed when he'd shaved.

"So let me get this straight. You were here, all alone, working for the FBI?" Wheeler said mockingly.

"You got it. Cox has been working this case for years, and I was doing recon for a raid," Haisley said. "Listen, I haven't even had my breakfast yet. Can this wait? I'll drop by—"

"No, Averton. It can't," Wheeler interrupted. "This is a crime scene, and until I figure out what happened, you're not going anywhere," he added, pointing his finger toward Haisley's chest. Haisley stared at the detective and felt his temper flare. He wanted to punch him. He'd been one of the first black detectives to join the department, and while most of his colleagues had grown to accept him, Wheeler had always been a prick.

"Okay, get your pen ready. This is what happened. I was hired by the FBI to do surveillance on this property. I came here to fill in some blanks this morning. Here's Agent Cox's card. You can call him yourself. He'll vouch for me," Haisley said, slamming his palm against Wheeler's chest like he was killing a fly, and letting Cox's card tumble to the ground.

Wheeler braced himself, pulling his hand into a fist. Haisley held his ground a few feet away and stared at the balding man, hoping Wheeler would loose his cool and take the first punch.

"So tell me, Averton, where's your fucking car?" Wheeler asked, breaking eye contact and looking back toward the buildings.

"I had my wife Mavis drop me at the corner early this morning," Haisley said, not wanting to bring up Reece's name.

"Your wife? Is she working for the FBI too?"

CHAPTER THIRTY-FIVE

BACK AT HIS hotel, Reece smiled when he walked into the lobby and heard the clerk call his name. Crystal had wired the $7,000 she'd promised, and once again he was back on track financially.

"Do you know what time that bank across the street closes?"

"Five o'clock, Mr. Culver." Reece thanked the clerk and headed up the stairs to his room on the second floor. On the way up the breeze he was making reminded him just how bad he needed a shower. He was still sweating out the Scotch he'd had the night before with Haisley.

He felt the buzz of his cellphone and reached into his front pocket.

"Culver."

"Reece, I'm glad I caught you," his mother said.

"Yeah."

"Mike Mobley called and told me you're working with Haisley."

"Yeah, so what's he the *National Enquirer?*"

"No, Reece, he's keeping me in the loop. He's trying to keep you safe."

"Oh, is that what he's doing?" Reece said. "Well, Mom, I hope you're doing well, but I'm in the middle of something right now. I can't talk. You take care," Reece said, ending the call.

After pulling off his cowboy boots and stripping off his clothes, he jumped into the shower. The warm flow of water felt wonderful on his stiff back. He wondered if Haisley and the guys from his old precinct had found any ID on the dead guy.

At the bank a few minutes later, he walked up to the teller and managed to wire five grand to his bank account in Denver, keeping the rest in cash. On the walk back to the motel, he decided to give Haisley a call.

"Averton."

"Have you guys got a name for the corpse?" Reece asked.

"No luck on that. We'll have to wait on forensics."

"You still out there?" he asked, trying to see if they'd found anything else.

"No, I just got back to the house. We may be out of luck getting any more information, Reece. The guy they assigned, Detective Wheeler, hates my guts. He's a real peckerwood. If you know what I mean."

"I'm sorry to hear that," Reece said. "Hey, is there any chance you can get a list of the regulars who visited Shank's casino from your friend Cox on that task force?"

"That's doubtful. I just got off the phone with Special Agent Cox. He's disbanding the whole task force. They're convinced they've got a leak in the unit."

"How about the guys from Tulsa? Any chance the insider you told me about, what was his name? You know, the guy that plays poker. Would he know who the regulars were?"

"It's worth a try. I'll call you right back."

*

Haisley crossed the garage, past the Camaro, and entered his office, trying to remember where he put Agent Messerman's phone number. He shuffled through a stack of papers until he found a small scrap with the number on it.

"Hello, Agent Messerman."

"Jim, it's Haisley Averton. How are you doing?"

"Haisley, I just got off the phone with Cox. He's pissed that Shanks got tipped off, but thankful we didn't go in on the raid and get ambushed."

"Yeah, I guess that's one good thing, but it was a real shock this morning."

"I bet it was. It sounds like Cox is pulling the plug on the task force."

"Yeah, I just talked to him a little while ago. I can't blame him. It definitely seems like Shanks has compromised the TF," Haisley said.

"That's too bad. I really enjoyed working with you. So what are you going to do now? Go back to your retirement?"

"Yeah, for the most part. I've got a PI friend out of Denver who's working a case. Do you remember when we were briefed on Owen Roberts?" Haisley asked.

"Yeah, what about it?"

"The PI is trying to find out what happened to Tracey Roberts," Haisley said.

"That sounds difficult, especially after all these years."

"Yeah, it seems like a tough case."

"Well, it's been good working with you. Haisley. If you ever need anything, give me a call," Messerman said.

"Actually, Jim, there is one thing you could help me with."

"What's that?"

"Do you remember the names of the four guys you played poker with in those tournaments when you were on the inside?"

"Yeah, I've got them right here," Messerman said, reading off the names.

Now all Haisley had to do is find out if one of them was his dead man.

CHAPTER THIRTY-SIX

SAM SHANKS BRACED himself as the Lear 55 settled onto the runway at Guayaquil, Ecuador, with twin chirps as the landing gear kissed the asphalt. He peered out the small oval window of the corporate jet, looking for his contact. Pablo Escodar had worked the bar for Shanks in his St. Louis casino, and the two of them had developed a loyal relationship over the years.

The jet taxied to the ramp, and after the pilots shut down the engines the air stairs deployed. He heard someone walking up the steps and wonder if it might be Pablo, but became irritated when he saw the blue cap of a customs agent.

"Welcome to Guayaquil. May I see your passport, sir?" the agent said.

Shanks reached for his thick silver briefcase and produced the document.

"Very good, sir. May I ask how long you'll be in Ecuador and the nature of your visit?"

"I'm on a short vacation. Came to see your beautiful beaches," Shanks said, lying.

"And how long do you plan on staying?"

"Three days."

"Very good, Mr. Shanks. I just need to check the flight crew's documentation and we'll be done here.

Shanks left the airplane and walked to the hangar a few hundred feet away. He wondered where his friend Pablo was and why had hadn't arranged for Shanks to avoid customs. The hanger was lined wall to wall with an assortment of airplanes ranging in size from small single-engine Cessnas to a large Gulfstream corporate jet. He heard a noise and turned to see the face of his friend.

"Mr. Shanks, I'm sorry for my late arrival. I had some difficulties with airport security. I guess they've been having threats of some sort lately."

"It's good to see you, Pablo, my old friend. How have you been? What's it been, two years?" Shanks said, extending his hand and then falling in next to the man as they walked toward the rear door, where Pablo's Toyota Tundra was parked. The two men got in and the truck sped away.

"So you mentioned wanting to charter a large plane from Guayaquil up to the U.S. and back. What did you have in mind?" Pablo asked.

"I'll be needing something with a couple thousand nautical miles range capable of carrying large wooden crates. I was also thinking of using coffee beans stacked around the crates to make it less appetizing for customs to inspect the airplane."

"How about an Airbus A-320? I checked and the airline that flies out of Eagle-Vail flies them. How many passengers would you be bringing on the flight?"

"Ten to twelve people on the leg down to Guayaquil."

"And how about the second leg of your trip?" Pablo said.

"That's something we'll have to discuss further. I have a special request."

*

Several days later an orange and white cab drove out of the darkness into the well-lit area in front of the general aviation ramp at the international airport. Sam Shanks climbed out wearing khaki pants and a dark blue blazer with brass buttons. His bald head was moist with sweat, and he wanted nothing more than to find air conditioning. Shanks pulled a small flashlight out of his pocket and walked toward a man standing near a large twin-engine cargo plane parked just inside the hangar. The jet was solid white with no markings other than the tail number stenciled in black numbers on both sides of the vertical stabilizer.

"You must be the guy Pablo told me about," he said.

"Yes, how was your flight?" the man asked in a thick accent, offering his hand. "I've got the airplane all ready for you, Mr. Shanks."

"How long have you been flying A-320's?"

"I crewed for the airlines until the strike last year. Now I do specialty cargo," the man said. "Follow me. I'll show you the flight deck." He led Shanks up into the A-320 jet, then added:

"You guys got one of the nicest models that Airbus makes. It's got plenty of range for both legs of the flight, and the previous operator was hauling cargo, so the back is already set up the way you guys want it."

They walked through the elaborate flight deck into the rear cabin area. The first section had two forward lavatories, a full galley, and twenty rows of seating. He followed past the last row of seats, and watched as the man opened a solid door that led into the rear bulkhead. The floor beyond was flat with aluminum skids and a series of recessed aluminum rollers to bring pallets on board, and the walls held equally spaced D-rings for use in tying down cargo.

"This will work perfectly. What's the range of this aircraft?" Shanks asked.

"That depends on the load and winds aloft. The maximum

stated range at full load on the standard configuration is 3,200 nautical miles. It's 2,849 from Denver to Guayaquil, and another 2,700 miles down to Montevideo. This airplane has winglets, so it'll have better range. I'll get the specs on this model and e-mail them to you it that's okay."

"That would be good to know. You can send them to this e-mail address," Shanks said, handing a business card to the man. "I'm heading home tomorrow and I don't want to leave anything to chance."

CHAPTER THIRTY-SEVEN

THE NORMAN EXIT was easy to find and in no time the plethora of red OU flags confirmed that Reece was drawing near the home of the famous University of Oklahoma football team. He drove past the student union and watched a group of students all dressed in bright red uniforms march in four lines, each carrying a wooden rifle. He figured they were part of the drum corps, but they looked young to him.

Reece was hoping he'd be able to locate Kathryn Anders. The registrars would know where Ms. Anders kept her office, but that required locating a parking space, and Reece wasn't in the mood to overpay.

It was less than refreshing to find that only a decade later, parking was still one of the most precious commodities on a college campus other than beer. He remembered back to his college days in St. Louis, and knew that without a parking-permit you were virtually screwed. Reece was driving down a long line of cars parallel parked when he saw a small space between a jacked-up Ford dually truck with an empty gun rack and a new Lexus. It was tight, but he managed to get the Mazda sandwiched in.

He walked up the steps toward a tall red building, and the sweet chemical smell of new carpeting filled his nostrils as he went in. A long line of students was waiting at the counter for the Registrar. He entered the line and waited. Reece must have stuck out from the crowd because a nice woman waved him over and opened a new service window. He asked about Professor Anders' office number, and was told she was in the Arts building at the other end of the campus.

He set off at a fast clip, figuring if he hurried he could catch her before lunch. Maybe he could grab a bite with her while asking questions. People being questioned were always more free with their words when food was involved. Soon, Reece was walking up a flight of stairs in the Arts building, looking for office number 279. He rounded the corner and found it, but was disappointed to find that the door was locked. Professor Anders had a weekly schedule posted on her door. She was in class from 10:00 – noon, at lunch till 1:00 pm, and had office hours from 1:00 to 3:00.

He whiled away the time eating and surfing the internet until a glance at his watch told him that it was one-thirty. Reece felt lucky when he saw the professor's office door open and was about to walk in when he noticed she was talking to a student. Ms. Anders looked up, making eye contact as if to say, I'll be with you next and continued her conversation with the girl in her office. Reece turned away and noticed a group of Italian Renaissance reproductions running down the opposite wall. He studied each one, remembering a class he'd taken back in college. He'd always wanted to get over to Italy to see the paintings in person.

"Did you need something?" Reece turned, and for a moment didn't recognize the face. She didn't look like what he'd torn out of the newspaper article. She had long chestnut hair pulled back into barrettes, and he thought the look accentuated her high cheekbones, making her appear younger in person than in the picture. She was wearing a plaid dress with a green sweater draped over her shoulders. Anders looked like she was used to dressing conservative at school, but when she wore an outfit that was less baggy she'd have no problem hailing a cab.

"Yes, I was wondering if we could talk," Reece said.

"Are you a student?" she asked, studying his face.

"No, I'm an investigator," Reece said, handing her one of his business cards.

"Oh," she said. He followed the Professor into her office.

"Is this about a student?"

"No, it's about your aunt, Tracey Roberts."

A weird look came over her face. "What about my aunt?" she asked sounding annoyed.

"Crystal Thomas hired me to find her mother."

"Why would she do that after all of these years?" the professor asked.

"That's what I'm trying to piece together."

"And you think I'm the magic link that will help you solve your case?" she said, sounding sarcastic. The more he talked to her the more he realized he was in for a less than pleasant experience.

"I don't think anything, but if you've got a few minutes I have a couple of unanswered questions."

"What was your name?" Kathryn asked.

"Reece Culver," he said, extending his hand and adding a smile. Reece watched as the professor's attention shifted toward her office door. A tall red headed coed dressed in a grey OU sweatshirt and torn jeans was standing in the office doorway.

"Professor Anders, could I ask you some questions about

yesterday's quiz in AH302?" the girl asked, looking eager for them to finish.

"Yes Angela, we're done here. What can I help you with?" Kathryn said, ignoring Reece.

"Mr. Cooler, you'll have to come back another time. I have student matters to take care right now. That's what OU pays me for, not to answer questions from total strangers."

Reece wasn't putting up with this B.S. He walked to the office door and said, "Angela, the professor will be with you in a minute." He shut the office door and returning to the desk. "Now look, I didn't drive ninety miles to get a bunch of crap off of you. Answer my questions and we'll be done here. Got it?"

She reached for the gray desk phone. Reece put his hand on top of hers, keeping her from picking up the receiver.

"Stop or I'll call security," Kathryn Anders said loudly.

"Cut the crap, or I'll call the police and have you taken in for questioning. You did the appraisal of the artwork at the Phillips' home in Tulsa, and that artwork was stolen just the other day. Sounds like there could be a connection to you? Doesn't it? I'd bet the police would love to find out," Reece said.

Professor Anders removed her hand from the desk phone and crossed her arms, glaring at Reece.

"What year did my aunt go missing?" she asked.

"It was August of 1989. How old would you have been back then?" he asked, guessing she wasn't much older than himself.

"I would have been in the first or second grade. Crystal, my cousin, and I were born the same year."

"What relation were your parents to Tracey Roberts?" he asked, finding it interesting that she and Crystal were the same age.

"My father Charlie is Tracey's older brother. Tracey was the youngest of three children," Kathryn said as she reached up to flip her long bangs out of her eyes.

Reece studied her face. "Do you remember your father talking about Tracey back then?"

"A little," she said, then stood up, looking toward the closed office door. "I need to get to my students."

"In a minute," Reece said. "Does your father Charlie live in Oklahoma?"

"No, he lives on the outskirts of Denver. Are we done here?"

*

On the way to the rental car Reece dialed the number for a friend who worked for the Jeffco sheriff. Actually, Natalie was more then a friend. They'd dated for a few months a couple of years back.

"Jefferson County Sheriff's Office, how may I direct your call?" the receptionist asked.

"I'd like to speak to Deputy Natalie Gleason," he said. Walking down the steps in front of the art building, Reece looked at the students perched on each side reading books and talking in small groups.

"This is Natalie."

"Hey, Natalie, I'm sorry to bother you, but I was wondering if you could do me a favor."

"Depends what it is," she said, sounding stressed.

"It's not urgent, but when you get some time, can you do a multi-state search, and get everything you can on Crystal Ann Thomas? She was born Crystal Ann Roberts on August 26, 1982, in St. Louis, Missouri."

"What did this one do?" Natalie asked.

"She's a client who hired me to find her missing mother, but last week when I was at her childhood home I got jumped."

"Jumped? Are we talking punched out or shot at?"

"Neither. I was hit in the head with a blunt instrument."

"Did you see a doctor?" Natalie asked, concerned.

"Yeah, I did. Nothing can damage this thick skull of mine."

"Do you know what other states this Crystal person lived in?"

"Oklahoma, and Colorado, but there may be more. Also, I found a newspaper article about an accidental death near a place named Tahlequah, Oklahoma. See if there's anything more on that."

"I'll see what I can find," Natalie said.

"I should be back to Denver in a couple of days. Pick a place for dinner, and I'll take you out. It'll be my treat."

CHAPTER THIRTY-EIGHT

CRYSTAL WOKE FROM a nap on her red leather couch, realizing she was lying on something. She rolled halfway over and saw she'd been sleeping on the cordless phone. She looked over at the DVD player and saw that it was only three in the afternoon. Then she noticed the vodka bottle lying on the counter and pulled a hand to her head.

She stood up, stumbled, and almost fell, tangling her feet in the dress she'd stripped off earlier. Wobbling down the hall to the bathroom, she thought about George Kendall. The warm water felt good as she soaped up. She remembered the call she'd made earlier to the phone repair guy. It was time to pay him a visit.

In an old pair of jeans and a gray hooded sweatshirt she went to the kitchen and grabbed her keys from the counter. She also wanted to call her stepfather.

"Hello," a man answered in the rough voice of a longtime smoker.

"Hello, Vinton, is now a good time to talk?"

"Hey, Crystal, what's going on?"

"I've run into a little trouble at work," she said in a quiet voice as she tried to rub away the headache that was pounding in her forehead.

"A little trouble. What are you talking about?"

"I've been taken off of the task force because of my connection to Owen, but I have a plan to get back on."

"Whose idea was it to take you off?"

"My boss, George Kendall."

"Why do you think he did that?"

"I'm not sure, but I may have some leverage on him."

He didn't sound impressed. "It sounds like you figured out the solution to your troubles."

"One of them. The phone you gave me got banged up this morning at work," Crystal said, sounding apologetic.

"Crystal, I sure hope you were smart enough not to leave it sitting around the Federal Center. That place is crawling with FBI agents."

"Why do you say that?" Crystal asked.

"Because if the SD card or memory survived, it wouldn't take much for them to find your calls to me, and I don't want the feds snooping around up here."

Crystal was outraged that he would think she was that stupid. "I can't believe we're having this conversation. Sometimes you're such an asshole. I've got the phone right here in my loft. You need to learn to trust me," Crystal yelled, slamming down the cordless phone.

CHAPTER THIRTY-NINE

REECE SAT IN his rental car balancing his laptop on his knees and listening to Willie Nelson singing, "Blue eyes crying in the rain." He'd bluffed earlier with Kathryn Anders, figuring she had something to hide, and in a short time he'd pieced together the names of the individuals that were involved in the deal to appraise, and auction off, Melvin and Melanie Phillips' art collection. He'd found the hospital website and their public relations announcement about the upcoming art auction to be held in the hospital cafeteria on May 5th.

Purple and gold lightning flashed across the southern sky in the distance. He watched the approaching storm and looked down at the laptop wondering if the Phillipses were truly good people, trying to do nice things with their money, or if they had other intentions. Reece thought about the housing bubble that led the country into the current recession. So many people have been hurt as a result of the financial greed of so few.

He grabbed his notebook and thumbed through the sheets from the previous week. Reece came to the place where he'd written notes after visiting Ann Fletcher in her smoke-filled home. He'd taped in the concert ticket from the 1981 Rolling Stones concert in St. Louis, and below it the picture of Crystal and her relatives. Below the picture he'd written the names of her family members. Kathryn Anders was Crystal's cousin. *Interesting.*

Reece was scrolling through news articles on his laptop, looking for more information about Melvin and Melanie Phillips, when the phone rang. He checked the caller ID, not wanting to endure another call from his family.

"Hello," Reece said, recognizing the number.

"Hey buddy, have you got a pen?" Haisley said, sounding excited.

"Yeah, what have you got?"

"I talked to the FBI agent I worked with here in Tulsa. I got the names of the guys he played poker with at Sam Shanks illegal casino. Are you ready for them?"

"Yes."

"Dr. Hank Johnson, Tavo Sheave, Dan Kochi, and Melvin Phillips."

"Thanks, buddy," Reece said, writing them down. The name Melvin Phillips seemed to jump up off the page.

CHAPTER FORTY

THE EARLY MORNING sun streamed through the large A-frame window of the two-story log cabin high in the foothills above the town of Blackhawk. Still wearing only his towel, Sam Shanks wrapped his arms around the woman he'd flown in to visit. They exchanged a long and passionate kiss in her kitchen.

"Okay, here are the keys to my truck," she said, pulling away from the embrace. "Give me an hour or so to get settled in at work and then drop by. Do everything just like we discussed."

"Got it, and you said the clothes you bought are in the second drawer of the chest?"

"Yes, Sam. Come here, let me show you. I don't want to take any chances with Derrick. It all has to look like I told you. I don't trust that bastard. It's bad enough that Evelyn hired him."

"I got it. You'd better get to work or you'll be late."

"Okay, I'm going, but first," she said, motioning to him for another kiss. "Next time you need to get back here sooner. This three months not seeing you is getting old." Sam leaned into her and let his hands slide down the woman's firm back. They held one another close and kissed passionately. When the kiss was complete, he picked up his coffee mug and watched her exit through the side door. Before long she'd pulled the Maserati out of the garage and descended the steep asphalt driveway.

Sam tossed the towel onto the bed and pulled out the second drawer of the dresser. He got dressed into the outfit she'd purchased and slid on the same blue dress socks he'd worn with his dress clothes the night before. After wolfing down the rest of his bagel, he got into the woman's truck, wearing black jeans, a white t-shirt, a navy blue zip-up hoodie, and a pair of light brown Red Wing work boots.

Shanks eyed his image in the rearview mirror, getting into the character of a cabinet installation technician, and drove down the steep roads toward the Golden Spur Casino, where the woman took care of the books. He hated the idea of this new guy moving in on her territory. There were other ways of taking care of people like this, but attention was one thing they didn't need in this situation. Not when she had millions of dollars she'd laundered for him in her office safe.

He parked the Toyota Highlander in the side lot of the casino and strolled through the front doors, admiring the four neat rows of slot machines near the entrance. Making his way to the cashier's cage, he asked about the woman and was directed to a row of gaudy red chairs to wait.

"Bruce, did you have any trouble finding the place?" the woman said, after tapping Shanks on the shoulder. "Alan and Hank will help you bring the boxes up to my office on the third floor."

"You mentioned having common hand tools here at the casino," Shanks said.

"Yes, we've already moved the tool box up to the office. It has screwdrivers and such like you requested." she said, smiling at him.

"Good," Shanks said as he followed two men dressed in

black cotton dress pants, white shirts, and green vests with the gold embroidered logo of the Golden Spur across their chests. Out in the alley behind the casino Shanks found the crate that contained the three wooden cabinets she'd ordered from Staples. He and the other men tore off the plastic wrapping and carried the wooden boxes to the elevator and up to her office on the third floor.

"Okay, I want the tall bookshelf in the first room and these two cabinets in this room," the woman said to Sam as the workers brought the last of the boxes up to her office. "Thanks, guys."

Sam went to work, opening the first box and pulling out the pieces of wood for the bookcase. Behind him near the door to the inner office he'd stacked two of the remaining boxes in a manner that precluded anyone from entering.

Shanks worked fast and soon the five-shelf bookcase was assembled in the corner. The woman opened the safe and was in the process of loading the cardboard box with stacks of $50 and $100 bills when someone knocked loudly on the exterior door to her office.

"Just a minute!" she yelled after exchanging a look with Shanks, who had walked into the second room to assemble the cabinets.

"Hello, are you okay? Is the door blocked?" Derrick said.

"We're fine. What is it?"

"I don't like having the door blocked. It's a fire hazard."

"Derrick, the cabinet installer is here. What do you need?" she said.

"Nothing, I just thought I'd come see if you were okay."

"Why wouldn't I be okay?" she said curtly, rolling her eyes at Sam as she stuffed the last of twenty stacks of cash into the first box and interleaved the flaps to keep it from opening.

"The delivery is all set."

CHAPTER FORTY-ONE

VINTON BLACKWELL STARED out the second-story window of Sam Shanks' palatial home, watching the pink and orange glow of the eastern sky as the sun began to seep into the tree-covered mountaintops. He heard a steady moan followed by a screech of brakes and looked down just as one of the moving trucks was backing down the driveway. Blackwell bolted down the stairs and out the kitchen door. He rounded the corner of the garage and watched the long moving van back toward an open bay of the three-car garage.

The driver climbed down and walked toward the rear of the truck. Looking tired, the man unlocked a padlock before pulling a steel latch outward to unlock the right rear door. Pulling back on the handle, he opened the cavernous interior of the truck.

Blackwell approached the driver like a cat sneaking up on prey. He ignored Blackwell's approach and climbed into the back of the truck and started dismantling what looked like a false wall of cardboard boxes. The man tore a section down with his hands, throwing it back toward the open doors.

Michael Zimeratti climbed out of the passenger's side of the truck and waved at Blackwell without speaking. He then rushed through the garage door and into the house.

"How was the trip?" Blackwell said to the driver as he waved a lighter under the tip on an unfiltered cigarette.

"Good. We stopped in Amarillo and got one of them big steaks you told me about."

"Where'd you spend the night?"

"At the truck stop off the main highway." The driver walked back into the truck and untied a series of tie-down straps that held several large wooden crates labeled "Coffee Beans". With a cordless drill he took the wooden side off of both of the crates. Now they were set to load the first paintings into the house.

In the meantime, Michael Zimeratti went down to the basement of Shanks' large home. He passed a well-stocked workout facility, a large room with a fireplace and a bar, and walked toward a stainless steel door. The door had a black numbered keypad in the place of a doorknob. Zimeratti pulled his key ring from his pocket and swiped it past the keypad with a beep, then punched in his six-character password, and heard the door unlock.

Back upstairs, two men assigned to the back of the moving van waited as Blackwell and a shorter worker stood on the hydraulic lift holding a large felt-covered painting. As the lift was lowered toward the ground, both men braced themselves. The lift settled to a halt and the painting was handed off.

As Blackwell held the garage door open, two of the men carried the painting into the house and down to the temperature-controlled storage vault where Zimeratti was waiting.

Later, after the contents of the truck had been unloaded, Blackwell found Zimeratti standing outside the vault with an electronic tablet in his hands.

"You got everything inventoried?" Blackwell asked.

"Yeah, looks like some very high-value pieces. Sam will be very happy." Blackwell had to hide the smile that wanted to creep onto his face.

CHAPTER FORTY-TWO

CRYSTAL PARALLEL-PARKED HER Mercedes on Broadway and walked past an assortment of garish neon signs. Up ahead she saw the bar the guy on the phone had mentioned, and walked past, opening the door to a narrow red brick entrance sandwiched in between Roy's Saloon and a fortune teller.

She walked down a hallway lined with old-fashioned mailboxes on one side and a blizzard of concert flyers, ads, and posters on the other. The entryway smelled of mildew and stale beer. She pulled the paper from her jeans and checked the apartment number. The banister, in need of a new coat of varnish, sported an array of ancient knife scratches. Crystal walked up the narrow wooden staircase, reached out to balance herself, and then thought better of touching the sticky railing.

As she rounded the banister from the second to the third floor, she almost tripped over the boots of a man sitting on the stairs in the dim light. His face was covered with a gray beard stained with food scraps. He reached up toward her with glassy red eyes. She swatted toward him, just missing his face, and ran up the stairs.

"Aw, fuck you, whore," she heard him say.

At the end of the hallway on the third floor was #6. Crystal knocked on the door and then stood back with her right fist clenched just in case.

"It's open. Come in," she heard a man yell from within. She pushed open the door, and the smell of bacon hit her. It was the first pleasant smell she'd encountered since entering. She peered into the darkness. "Mr. Lane?" she yelled.

The lights were off, and the interior of the apartment was lit by a blue glow given off from two tables lined with computer monitors. A pile of electronics boxes was stacked in a U-shape near the computers.

"You the one with the smashed smart phone?" someone said as he came up behind her.

She turned, startled, and almost dropped her purse. "Yeah, I got it here. I hope you can get the video off."

"Bring it over here, and I'll take a look at it." Lane walked toward what looked like the kitchen. Crystal followed, wondering if the guy ever went outside. He was tall, pale, and so skinny she guessed she might outweigh him.

She was greeted by a stack of dirty dishes. A pan sat on the stove piled high with cooked bacon strips knuckle deep in congealed grease.

"Take a seat," Lane said, pointing at a wooden table that took up the majority of the room. She pulled the envelope that contained the remains of the smashed phone out of her purse and handed it to him.

The repair guy clipped a static strap running from a back mat on the table to what looked like a wristwatch band on his arm. He picked up a pair of tweezers and coaxed the pieces from the envelope on to the mat. She watched him methodically parse out the black plastic chunks, turning and inspecting each one.

"The phone is dust, but if we're lucky, I might be able

to grab the video," Lane said, looking up at Crystal. For the first time she noticed a split in his upper lip that looked like a poorly reconstructed cleft palate.

"How long do you think it will take? Could I get it tomorrow?" Crystal asked in an anxious tone.

"If you're not in a hurry, I can do it right now."

With a casual ease that spoke of experience, he pried open what was left of the mangled phone. He picked up the black anti-static mat and carried it out into the other room.

"Someone has been inside your phone," Lane called to her.

She walked in to make sure she'd heard right. "What do you mean?"

"You have some jumpers in here that aren't OEM."

"OEM, what's that?"

"Original equipment manufacture. It means the phone has been modified since it was built at the factory. I think someone's been tracing your calls, or maybe uploading them to another device." Crystal thought of Vinton, so eager to buy her a new phone. It made sense that he had done it to spy on her. She couldn't think of any other explanation.

"Can you get the video?" Crystal asked, not wanting to discuss who might have bugged her phone.

Lane didn't answer. Instead he turned on a soldering iron. He waited, eyeing her up and down in a manner that she didn't like, then spit on the metal tip of the Weller iron. She heard the spit sizzle and then smelled it. He wiped the tip of the iron on a wet sponge and touched it to a small green circuit board from her phone. Crystal watched wisps of smoke appear, and Lane blew toward them, coaxing the remnants away.

"Watch this screen here," Lane said, setting the soldering iron back into its green wire coil and flipping it off.

Crystal watched the video flicker and then come on. She

was kneeling in front of George Kendall's naked torso. He was on his back on the bed, his face a vision of ecstasy.

"Can you fast forward it?" she requested, uncomfortable with having a stranger witnessing her in action.

"This is good stuff," Lane said, leering at her. "I'm assuming you want a copy of it?"

"Yes, I'll be taking the only copy, and then I'm going to smash the phone so it doesn't end up on the Internet," Crystal said, watching his grin turn to a frown.

"It'll cost you $150, unless you want to let me have a copy for my personal use," he said, making an odd up and down gesture with his right hand. Crystal had a strong impulse to smash the pale bastard's face open and grab her phone. She felt her temper rising, but she needed the recording.

"I'll give you $200, and I get the only copy. If you try to keep a copy for yourself, you won't like the consequences," she said, glaring at him.

He reached under the desk and slid a DVD into the computer.

"Let me see the money," Lane said. Crystal reached into her purse and pulled out two crisp hundred-dollar bills. She plopped her hand down in front of the keyboard with both bills visible between her fingers, and reached for the DVD.

"I'll take that."

CHAPTER FORTY-THREE

REECE DROVE BACK toward Tulsa, fighting the strong sunshine that blazed through the right side of the windshield. He thought about what Kathryn Anders had told him. He knew that her father was Tracey Roberts' older brother. He knew that Crystal and Kathryn were the same age, yet apparently weren't close. Reece wondered if somehow Kathryn Anders might be tied to burglary at the Phillips home. If Melvin Phillips was a regular at the illegal casino, it was feasible that he was dirty. Maybe he wanted out of his marriage and had staged the burglary as a way of raising quick cash to end things.

Reece pulled out to pass a slow green 1970's vintage Volkswagen bus. He smiled after reading its bumper sticker, "Zero to Sixty in Fifteen Minutes." He thought of his friend Haisley back in Tulsa and pulled out his cellphone.

"Haisley, it's Reece, what's going on?"

"I just got off the phone with Mike Mobley," Haisley said.

"Did you ever get a name on that body we found?" Reece asked.

"Yeah, are you sitting down?"

"I'm sitting. Who is it?" Reece said.

"Owen Roberts."

"Holy crap ..."

"Culver, are you still there?" Haisley asked.

Reece could see his investigation going up in smoke. "I guess that confirms that there's a snitch on the task force."

"Yeah, that could explain his death. There's more, Reece."

"What do you mean, Haisley?"

"The weapon used to commit the crime was a .45 caliber."

"Sounds common," Reece said.

"The .45 caliber is common, but this one's different."

"How so?" Reece said.

"I talked to Mike Mobley up in St. Louis. I mentioned you and your case involving Tracey Roberts. We got to talking, and he faxed me the ballistics report from your father's case."

Shaken by this mention, Reece took his foot off the gas and let the car coast down a hill. The green Volkswagen bus came up fast in his rearview mirror and flew by him.

"Reece, the ballistics are a match."

"A match to what?" Reece asked.

"A match to the gun used on your father. Whoever killed Owen Roberts murdered your dad back in 2009."

CHAPTER FORTY-FOUR

SAM SHANKS RECLINED his plush leather seat in the Lear 55C/LR corporate jet as it crossed the Mexican border heading south. He was looking forward to catching up with the people at his new gallery in Montevideo and starting his latest endeavor as an art dealer. It seemed like an easy, painless way to spend his retirement.

Except for one lingering irritation. He picked up the satellite phone and punched in a number on the digital keypad.

"Zimeratti speaking."

"Michael, it's Shanks, how's your evening been?"

"Good, Sam, where are you?"

"On my way south. I have a few more tasks to take care of before I return." Shanks idly noticed the green flash of the navigation light at the end of the wing illuminating the thick clouds outside. "I have a little problem that I was thinking you might be able to help me with."

"Oh yeah, what sort of problem?"

"Vinton Blackwell," Shanks said.

"That guy. Whose problem isn't he?"

"I know what you mean, Mike, but he has had his uses over the past couple of decades. I'm just afraid his shelf life, for my purposes, is running out."

"So what are you trying to say, Sam?"

"I've got this idea I'm putting into place. The one I hinted at a while back when we were talking about your father. So anyway, when we finish our business in Minturn, you and I will be going one direction and the others will be going another. If you know what I mean?"

"I'm not totally following you, Mr. Shanks, but you've never led me astray. What does this have to do with Blackwell?"

"He's a slippery character, and I'd rather he not catch the plane out of Vail. I was thinking we might be able to use his stepdaughter Crystal against him. She'd be one of the people that I'd be interested in taking along," Shanks said.

Michael started to sound more interested, as Shanks knew he would. Michael always was watching her whenever she came around. "How were you thinking of using Crystal?"

"I was thinking if you were to befriend her. You know, good friends," Shanks said.

"Good friends. What makes you think she'd be interested in me?"

"She's on the run right now from the FBI. She doesn't know where to turn."

"Yeah, so?"

"Her world is not in order. Who better to help her than you?"

CHAPTER FORTY-FIVE

CRYSTAL PARKED HER Mercedes and walked lightly through the slick, ice-coated parking lot toward her office. A foot of snow covered the grass on the sides of the parking lot, and a clear blue sky peeked out from behind a heavy blanket of clouds moving rapidly east. She was glad she'd worn her winter fashion boots, and was impressed with their traction.

She returned the security guard's smile and walked past feeling new confidence before heading down the hall toward her office.

"Hello, Ms. Thomas. How was your drive in?" The receptionist asked.

"Good, I guess they sprayed the streets with magnesium chloride again. Oh, is George in yet?"

"He is, and if you're free he'd like to have a short meeting with you once you get settled."

"Tell him I'll be in his office at eight-thirty."

She walked to her office, logged into the computer, and began reading e-mail while sipping a cup of coffee. Her phone rang and she answered, "Hello, this is Crystal Thomas."

"Good morning, Ms. Thomas. We're in the Aspen conference room. Will you come join us?" George said.

Crystal grabbed her briefcase, feeling unsettled, and

walked down the hallway toward the conference room. Who was in this meeting? She had been planning to confront George with the evidence. She walked in and instantly recognized one of the three men with her boss George. It was FBI Special Agent Stephen Cox.

"Thanks for joining us, Ms. Thomas. We've been discussing the plans the task force had for the raid in Tulsa," George said, getting up to shut the conference room door. "The retired detective we had doing surveillance made a visit to the property to confirm the logistics we had planned—and found the place abandoned."

Crystal took the seat next to an unfamiliar man who had thick black sideburns, a pockmarked face, and a deep blue suit. George Kendall and Agent Cox sat across from her looking grim.

"Ms. Thomas, it's nice to see you again," Agent Cox said, extending his hand to greet her. Crystal smiled and shook his hand. The agent slid his fingers back toward a brown folder and stared at her meaningfully after placing his hand on top of it.

"I have something here that might tie into our problem," he said, pushing the folder across the table to Crystal.

Opening it, she recognized on the left side a photo of Owen Roberts taken ten years earlier with the date at the bottom. On the right was a photo of his gray face, eyes closed, lying dead on an autopsy table. Crystal fought back an unbidden wave of tears.

"We all know who this is, and your relationship to him. Gentlemen, if it's okay with you, I'd like a few minutes alone with Ms. Thomas," Cox said, waiting for her boss and the other man to leave. He got up and closed the door behind them.

"Ms. Thomas, I know this is no shock to you. I suspect

you're working for Sam Shanks, and you may have even been present when your father was murdered."

Crystal stood up from the table, feigning outrage. "You're full of shit, Agent Cox. I should call your office and report you. What, do you take some kind of pleasure in showing women autopsy photos?" Long streams of tears flowed from her eyes.

"I suggest you sit down, Ms. Thomas," he said quietly. "I could detain you for questioning right now."

Crystal sat down but continued to glare at him.

"There is a way you could save yourself a long prison sentence despite all you've done."

CHAPTER FORTY-SIX

AS REECE DROVE toward his Tulsa hotel, the sun was low in the sky and the temperature was dropping. Reece felt the rattle of his phone in his front pants pocket and peeled it out. He glanced down and saw he'd missed a call from his client, Crystal Thomas. Reece pressed the button for voicemail.

"Reece, are your there? If so, I hope you pick up. Oh well, I guess not. When you get this, give me a call. I need to talk to you."

Reece turned off the highway and headed toward the Executive Inn, his home base in Tulsa. His eyes felt funny and he considered pulling over. *Whoever killed my father just killed Owen Roberts. I was that close to the murdering bastard.* Suddenly the guilt he'd been carrying about the second camera and knowing he'd been the reason his father went back for more pictures seemed inconsequential. The killer was working for Shanks. It could be Shanks himself.

His cellphone started to dance around the plastic cup holder as it vibrated. Reece reached for it and answered.

"Culver, it's Averton. Where are you?"

"Just heading back to my hotel why?" Reece said.

"You okay? You sound funny."

"I'm fine. What's going on?"

"I got a call from Agent Cox. They're disbanding the task force," Haisley said.

"That's no surprise. It's obvious they've got someone working for Shanks," Reece said, turning into the parking lot of the Executive Inn. "It's starting to sound like Crystal is on the wrong side of all of this," he added. "I figure it was either Crystal or Owen that hit me in the head with the pipe, intending to frame me for murder."

"The thing that doesn't add up, though," Haisley pointed out, "is why she killed the homeless guy and framed you for it. She's the one that brought you into this in the first place."

"True, but what if someone else, someone trying to protect Sam Shanks, found out that Crystal hired a PI," Reece said, shutting off the Mazda.

"That makes sense. This someone is close to her, and they're using her to stay one step ahead. That would explain why Owen Roberts was murdered."

"There's one more piece to the puzzle," Reece said.

"What's that?"

"Kathryn Anders, the woman I interviewed over in Norman, was the art appraiser for Melvin and Melanie Phillips."

"What does Kathryn Anders have to do with all of this?"

"Melvin Phillips was a regular at Sam Shanks' poker tournaments. The past couple of months the newspapers have been full of publicity for the art auction the Phillipses had planned on holding to raise money for their new cancer center." Reece paused, giving Haisley time to process these connections. "A couple of days ago, the home of Melvin and Melanie Phillips was burglarized."

CHAPTER FORTY-SEVEN

SAM SHANKS WALKED down a tree-lined path admiring the progress the construction crew had made on his new home on the outskirts of Montevideo, Uruguay. He looked up at the banister that ran up the white marbled staircase. A cool breeze fluttered the beige shirt he wore and brought a chill. The sun was setting and he took a seat in his favorite chair on the expansive new patio that surrounded the infinity pool. He liked it here and he wondered if she might like it here too.

He yearned for the time when he'd be done. He was tired of running and worrying how long he'd stay one step ahead of the FBI. Shanks heard an airplane overhead and looked up, wondering if someone was watching him, waiting for the right time to pounce. He dismissed the thought as paranoid. Uruguay was friendly to foreigners with pockets full of American currency. No one knew about this place he'd built in the country. He was thousands of miles south of the places they'd look for him. If they came far enough, they would find the gallery, but it had no connection to him. He was safe here.

Shanks thought about his friend Michael Zimeratti and what he'd told him the day before. He reached into his pocket to retrieve his cellphone.

"Vinton, it's me. How are things up in Colorado?"

Blackwell sounded surprised to hear from him. "Good, we've got everything locked up in the vault downstairs, and I'm working on the plan, and details for our last job," Blackwell said.

"Did you have a chance to look over the inventory Michael put together?" Shanks asked.

"No, I leave that sort of stuff to Zimeratti. He's got to pay his way somehow."

Shanks looked down at the Tuesday edition of the *Tulsa World* newspaper, featuring an article describing the recent burglary at the home of Melvin and Melanie Phillips.

"There seems to be a discrepancy. I'm looking at a recent article from the Tulsa paper, and they mention a painting by Van Gogh. Vinton, you don't remember seeing a Van Gogh, do you?"

"No, that doesn't sound familiar. What was it of? Do they say in the paper?" Blackwell asked.

"It says here it was a one foot-by-one foot painting of a vase with poppy flowers."

"Poppy flowers? I didn't see anything like that."

Blackwell's voice was smooth as silk, without any catch of a lie in it. Yet Shanks knew better than anyone how little that meant.

"Tell me something, Sam," he went on, "if this Van Gogh was stolen, why would Melvin Phillips mention ever having possession of the piece?"

Shanks could think of a few reasons, but he merely said, "You make a good point, Vinton."

CHAPTER FORTY-EIGHT

GEORGE KENDALL SAT in a booth at his favorite lunch place a few blocks south of work. The management had affixed to the ceiling an assortment of junk to give the place some personality.

"Crystal, thanks for meeting me for lunch," he said.

"I wonder what they have on special today," she replied.

"Listen, Crystal, I'm sorry about what happened earlier."

"What are you talking about?" Crystal said, holding back the urge to laugh at him.

"I'm talking about the meeting in the conference room. The way we informed you of your father's death. It was Agent Cox's idea. He's convinced we have someone on the task force who's working for the other side."

Crystal was relieved when the waitress came to take their drink order. She wore a green vest covered in buttons that looked like they'd been collected back in the 1970s. Crystal took a deep breath. "Do they know who killed my father, Owen?"

"That's being investigated, but until they figure out who's spying, the task force is on hold. I'm sorry to do this to you, Crystal, but I'm going to have to lay you off. Without the task force, I don't have enough bandwidth to keep you on."

Crystal's face went slack. She felt a rushing of blood in her forehead and calmed herself only because she knew she held the cards to his future.

"Nice, you slimy son of a bitch," she said, shifting into a totally different mode. "Let me get this straight. Cox points the finger at you because of my dead father, and you lay me off so you can save your own skin."

Crystal reached into her purse. "You're really the pride of the department, aren't you, George Kendall?" She pulled out a small black portable DVD player and set it in the middle of the table. She opened it up so that the small screen pointed in his direction. She was close to breaking into a smile, but she held back. This was going to be fun.

"I wonder what would happen to you if this video somehow made its way onto the Internet? I wonder what your pal Special Agent Stephen Cox of the FBI would think?" she said as she pressed play, bringing the screen to life.

CHAPTER FORTY-NINE

REECE LAY FULLY clothed on top of his motel bed. He felt better being engrossed in his case and pushed the image of the Canon camera lying on the floorboard of his father's green GTO out of his head. He knew he was on the right track to solving his father's murder. Crystal's case had brought him to Tulsa, and Haisley had taken him to Sam Shanks' casino. Owen Roberts was dead and the murder weapon was the key to everything. *All of this is happening for a reason. Why am I still thinking about that goddamned camera? I'm going to solve all of this. I'm okay.*

Someone rolled what sounded like a cart down the sidewalk outside his hotel room. He heard a knock on the door.

"Housekeeping."

Reece got up and answered. "You can skip my room today. It's not dirty," he said to the Mexican maid before shutting the door. The older woman smiled and winked at Reece.

He fell back on the bed. His mind started roaming and pretty soon he was thinking about the ballistics report Haisley got from Mike Mobley up in St. Louis. The gun and bullets from Owen Roberts' murder and Al Culver's murder matched. Shanks or one of his men had to be the triggerman.

Reece's phone vibrated on the dresser adjacent to the bed.

"Hello," he answered, wondering if it was Crystal. "Oh, hi Mom, how are you?"

"Good, Reece. How's your missing person's investigation going? Have you found anything?"

Reece was surprised by her interest. He couldn't believe she was asking about something he was working on.

"Good. Actually very well, I found something that relates to Dad's cold case," Reece said.

"To Dad's case? What is it, Reece?"

He had to make a decision. As much as she deserved to know, he had another, vital consideration. "You've got to make me a promise, Mom."

"What's that?"

"You can't tell anything I tell you to the FBI."

"Why not? Reece. Won't it help them? I don't understand."

"It's complicated, Mom. They've got their own agenda."

As he knew very well, she had been suspicious of their investigation for a long time. So he believed her when she said, "I'm on your side, Reece."

"That's good, because I'm hoping this will crack the case wide open."

CHAPTER FIFTY

CRYSTAL SPENT THE afternoon at home waiting for a call from human resources to confirm her transfer to a new position with the Bureau of Land Management. She was still laughing inside about the look on Kendall's face when he saw the video. She'd spent the afternoon surfing the Internet while George made calls to all of his connections, then came into her office to tell her he'd found her a position at the BLM.

She was heading down the steps into her basement office when she heard the phone ring in the kitchen. She retraced her way back up the stairs and ran toward it.

"Hello," she said, out of breath.

"Ms. Thomas, this is Jocelyn Welders from Human Resources. I have your transfer paperwork here on my desk, and I was wondering if we could set up a time for you to come sign everything."

"Sure, Ms. Welders, what time were you thinking?"

"If you're free today how about three-thirty?"

"That works for me," Crystal said, sounding upbeat.

"Do you know where administrative building six is located?"

"Is that the tall red brick building with the fountain in front?"

"That's the one, Ms. Thomas. I'm on the third floor in Room 3989. I look forward to meeting you."

Later that day, Crystal got off the elevator on the third floor. She was wearing a conservative blue business suit and carrying a leather shoulder bag. She walked confidently toward Room 3989 at the end of the drab brown hallway. She stepped into a large waiting area with black bench seats and stacks of magazines.

"Good afternoon. I have a three-thirty with Ms. Welders," Crystal said to the receptionist.

"Have a seat Ms. Thomas, and I'll tell her you're here."

Crystal took an empty seat next to the magazines. She picked up woman's fitness and began to page through the articles, thinking of how much better her body looked than the woman standing in leotards doing yoga. She was fully engrossed in an article about pomegranates when she heard someone call her name.

"Crystal Thomas," the receptionist said. "Ms. Welders will see you now. She's down this hallway third door on your left," the woman said, holding the door to the hallway open.

Crystal walked down the hall and entered the third office on her left.

"Thanks for coming, Ms. Thomas. It's good to see you," Ms. Welders said, sounding a bit too cheery.

"It's good to be here," Crystal said.

"Okay then, if you'll sign these forms resigning from your old position, we'll get you set up for your new position with the Bureau of Land Management."

Crystal pulled her favorite silver pen from her purse and signed where indicated.

"Ms. Thomas, this packet has information about the BLM,

its policies, and charter. I think you'll find it a great place to work. What day would you like to start?"

It was time to turn on the waterworks. "Ms. Welders, I was planning to start Monday morning, but I've had a change in plans. I got a call last night, and my father is very sick. I would like to take some Family Medical Leave Act time if that could be arranged, so I could go take care of him."

The human resources woman seemed very receptive. "Oh yes, I can set that up for you. We encourage employees to take FMLA to take care of family members. How long would you like to take?"

"How about three months?"

CHAPTER FIFTY-ONE

SAM SHANKS SAT on the patio behind his newly built Montevideo home. It felt like it was the first time he'd had a chance to relax in over a month. Things were all going much too fast. Especially now that Blackwell had taken out Owen and he had one less man to get things done. He could hear the chirp of crickets in the distance but little else. The nearest road was over a mile away and all the land in between his home and the road was his. It would be paid off in full as soon as he transported his artwork to the gallery and sold it off at auction.

He had his work cut out and he knew it. With his cellphone in hand he scrolled through a list of contacts until he saw the name Escodar. Shanks highlighted the number and pressed send.

"Mr. Shanks, what brings me the pleasure of receiving a call from you this evening?"

"What are you, drunk or something, Pablo? Cut the crap. You got everything we talked about put in place?"

The sunny voice quickly reverted to its usual criminal hardness. "Yeah, I got it, but I'll need more money to put together the final parts of your plan."

"More money? I thought we agreed on a price."

"We did until you amended your plans."

"How much more?" Shanks asked, sighing.

"Ten thousand dollars ought to do it. Those dollars of yours still speak very loudly here in Ecuador," Pablo said. "I do have one question for you, though."

"What's that?" Shanks said, taking a sip of his Mojito.

"I wonder why you want to fly all those people down to Uruguay when you could set them up to take the fall for the crimes in Ecuador, and you could get away to Uruguay a free man."

Shanks was intrigued. He should have thought of this himself. "What did you have in mind?"

"When the A-320 arrives in Guayaquil, it will have to be fueled and serviced," Pablo said.

"Yeah, so what were you thinking?"

"It would be easy to require everyone to get off the aircraft for an hour or two while it's serviced. They'd be sitting ducks there in the jet center," Pablo said.

The proposed double-cross tickled him. "I like the way you think. The only problem is, the airplane will be full of my precious artwork."

CHAPTER FIFTY-TWO

THE LAST CAR pulled from the parking lot of the Murphy's restaurant adjacent to the Executive Inn. The bank sign across the street flashed Thursday and alternated between 2:38 am and 43 degrees in big bold yellow numbers. A door of a maroon Ford Explorer opened and someone dressed in a black sweat suit, ski mask, and dark running shoes stepped out. The driver closed the trunk with a click and walked into the shadows of the parking lot.

He carried a small cloth satchel bag folded under one arm and a five-gallon gas can in the opposite hand. Stopping in the dark, he looked up at the rooms along the second floor. He took slow steps up the covered stairway of the three-story structure. Halfway down the second floor hallway, the lone figure stopped at a door labeled Maintenance in cheap stick on metal foil letters and set down the red plastic gas can. He pulled a black vinyl case about the size of a cigarette pack out of the satchel and went to work picking the lock.

The door soon opened, and the arsonist stepped inside, pulling it closed behind. He pulled out a flashlight and turned it on. A wooden table was revealed in the center of the room, covered with tools. The arsonist pulled a long tube from the satchel and unrolled it, exposing a set of floor plans. Room 237 was just on the other side of the maintenance room.

He searched through the satchel bag and pulled out a stethoscope. With the head of the instrument held up to the wall, the arsonist listened to the sounds of a television set, along with the low roar of the in room heater fan. The arsonist put the stethoscope back into the satchel bag, rolled up the floor plans, and put them into the bag before taking it over to the door.

The room filled with the smell of gasoline as the arsonist poured the contests of the five-gallon gas can onto the wall and floor, taking great care not to get any on his shoes. With the gas can set next to the center of the wall the arsonist walked over to the satchel, took out a road flare, pulled off the end, and stuck the cap against the tip of the flare, lighting it. The arsonist held the thin red cylinder upward, admiring its bright red glow, and felt a rush of adrenaline. He picked up the satchel bag, opened the door, pitched the flare toward the gasoline-soaked wall on the opposite side of Reece Culver's hotel room, and left. That would take care of the annoying PI.

CHAPTER FIFTY-THREE

THE MORNING SUN streamed between the curtains hanging in the master bedroom of Crystal's Denver loft. She sat on the floor with a cardboard box between her legging-clad thighs and pulled strips of tape off a dispenser. The cordless phone beside her rang several times.

"Hello," she answered.

"Hey, Crystal. It's Michael Zimeratti. I wanted to call and see how things are for you these days."

She was glad to hear his voice. Whenever she came around, he always went out of his way to be nice to her. "Michael, it's good to hear from you. Things are good. How about with you?"

"Yeah, they're good here too. Hey, I was talking to Shanks and he mentioned you were having some difficulty with your boss. I was wondering if there's any thing I could do to help."

"Why would Shanks bring that up to you?" Crystal asked, not doing a very good job of covering up her annoyance. "What else did Shanks tell you, Michael?"

"Nothing really. Hey, I'm just down the street from you here in Denver. I was wondering if you'd like to join me for breakfast."

"Breakfast? Well, I'm kind of busy packing up my loft right now. How about you come by and we can make something here?" Crystal asked, liking the idea of having a strong man around to help her pack up the last of her things.

"I've got a better idea. I'd imagine the last thing you want while your moving out is dirty dishes. I'll get something to go and drop by your place. Are you in the mood for anything special?"

"How about you surprise me, Michael? I've heard you have great taste."

Crystal ended the call, wondering why Michael Zimeratti had decided to be so friendly. She'd seen him around when she was with her stepfather, but had never found him too interested in socializing. *Why would Sam Shanks tell Zimeratti about her job at the Federal Center?* She hated the thought of Shanks meddling in her business. Crystal knew from her stepfather that Shanks would control the whole world if he could figure out a way to pull it off, and she hated control freaks.

She set her phone down beside her thigh and went back to taping boxes. After a bit she started thinking about her loft and how much she'd miss it. Crystal remembered all the times she'd walked into the restaurants and bars of downtown Denver. The location had been great for her social life. It was her place. She'd bought it with her own money. It was a badge of her independence and now it would be gone. It was tough letting it go, but she knew something better was waiting for her out on the horizon.

Crystal opened the mailbox to the right of the main door of her loft and scooped out a pile of letters hopeful the post office had processed her move notice and would begin forwarding all of her mail to her new P.O. box at the Minturn, Colorado, post office. She flipped through the junk mail and came to her electric bill. She ripped it open and was looking at the amount she owed when she spotted another of the letters from her mother. This one had a heart hand-drawn on the back where the envelope had been sealed. She tore it open and read the hand written letter.

Dear Crystal,

I hope this letter finds you well. I'd really like to reconnect with you. I miss you dear and there is so much I'd like to share with you.
If I knew I could trust you not to tell Vinton my whereabouts I'd meet you tomorrow, but I have many reasons to fear this man. I know deep down you must fear him as well dear. He took many things from me including you and your brothers. I know you probably blamed Owen for my disappearing from the bus station all those years ago in Tulsa, but it was Vinton who played upon that day. Owen did make a deal to retire his debts, but it was Vinton Blackwell who followed me and tormented me.
I'm not too far from you now, but I have to be careful or else risk loosing everything including you. I do this because of what Vinton did to me back when he found out I'd given my love to someone else.
I have to wrap this up now, but I promise I'll write again.
I love you Crystal. Take care of yourself.
Love Mom

Long streams of tears flowed down Crystal's cheeks. She dropped the letter to the floor and slid the fingernail of her ring finger under the nail of her right thumb. The pain felt good. She felt anger towards her mother knowing that she was alive and had failed to contact her for all of these years while she blamed everything on Vinton Blackwell.

CHAPTER FIFTY-FOUR

HAISLEY AND HIS wife Mavis sat on their couch reading separate sections of the *Tulsa World* and drinking coffee. The television was on in the background, so Mavis almost missed the report about the fire.

"Hey, isn't that Reece's motel?" she said.

Haisley saw a recorded picture of three fire engines hosing down the Executive Inn earlier that morning. "Holy shit," he said, realizing rooms 237 and 238 had been gutted. "I think Reece told me he was in Room 237."

Haisley picked up the phone and dialed.

"Reece Culver Investigations. How may I direct your call?"

"Holy crap. It's good to hear your voice."

"What's going on? Is everything all right?" Reece said.

"It is now."

Reece was puzzled, not sure where this was going. "What's up, buddy?"

"Mavis and I were watching the tube and it looks like someone tried to take you out last night."

"Take me out? What are you talking about?" Reece said.

"There was a fire at the Executive Inn, and rooms 237 and 238 are fried to a crisp."

"Whoa, that's heavy news," Reece said. "I'm glad I decided to fly back to Denver yesterday."

"Do me a favor, Culver," Haisley said. "Watch yourself. Someone is gunning for you."

Reece hung up the phone, mystified by this turn of events. His trip to Tulsa had for the most part been a dead end, so how did he become a target? The arsonist was most likely the same person that used the .45 caliber semi-auto that killed both his father and Owen Roberts. That person was linked to Sam Shanks, or could be Shanks himself. He knew Crystal was tied to Shanks too, since she was the only person he could think of that would have told Shanks and his crew that Owen was working for the task force as an informant.

Reece pulled his cellphone out and dialed the number for the Jeffco sheriff.

"Jefferson County Sheriffs Office, how may I help you?" the receptionist asked.

"Yes, this is Reece Culver. Could you connect me with Natalie Gleason?"

"One minute, Mr. Culver."

As he waited, he kept retracing his steps in Tulsa, trying to decipher when he would have tripped a wire.

"Reece, how's the hunt for that missing person going?" Natalie asked. Reece could hear shuffling papers in the background. "When are you coming back to Denver?"

"I'm back."

"Good, did you find anything?"

"Well, I found some stuff, but not what I was looking for," Reece said. "Hey I was wondering if you got a chance to look into the favor I asked for."

"I did. You got any plans tonight?" Natalie said.

"No, I guess not. What'd you have in mind?"

"I was thinking we could do that dinner you promised, and I'd bring what I found on your girl Crystal."

Reece wanted to get one thing straight. "The dinner part sounds good, but Crystal's not my girl. I think she might be trying to kill me," he said, annoyed.

"You're right, doesn't sound like much of a girlfriend," she said breezily. "Tell you want. I'll make a reservation. How about you drop by my place at six?"

"See you then."

CHAPTER FIFTY-FIVE

TRACEY ROBERTS MADE excellent time in her Maserati, driving from the airport in Broomfield back to her log cabin above Blackhawk, Colorado. She was excited to show Sam what she'd come up with for transporting the laundered money they'd successfully smuggled out of her work safe. Shanks sat quietly next to her, having just arrived himself from South America.

"You'll be so pleased, Sam," she said as she led him down the stairs to the basement. She stopped on the bottom step and reached up, taking his head into her hands. He kissed her.

"Your eyes look bloodshot. Are you feeling all right?" Tracey asked.

"I guess I'm still a little jetlagged. I've been going nonstop trying to get everything in place." Seeing the concern on her face, he added in a brighter voice, "I can't wait to take you down to our new retirement home in Uruguay. You'll love it." He smiled as he recalled how much he'd enjoyed it. "Do you remember the time you showed me that kitchen you liked in a copy of *Architectural Digest*?"

It was her turn to be excited. "Don't tell me. You copied that kitchen in the new house."

"All of it," he said.

"You are something else. You really know how to spoil a

girl, don't you?" she said as she led him into what looked like a bedroom down in the basement.

"You didn't tell me you were a golfer," Shanks said, looking around.

"I'm not, but I think you're going to like what I've come up with," Tracey said, leading him over to a workbench. "Check this out."

"Looks like the back of a golf cart," Shanks said, pointing toward a molded plastic piece.

"It is. The guy I had make these customized cart-mounted golf bags gave me this to store them on during the winter months." Shanks eyed a black and green men's golf bag and a pink and white women's bag propped up against the wall.

"Can you do me a favor and bring the men's bag over here to the workbench? Just lie it down on its side," she said. "Okay, watch how this opens up. You're going to love this feature."

Tracey picked up a red cordless screwdriver and went to work on the golf bag, taking out four Phillips head screws. Two came out of the top plate that held the carry handle, and the other two came out from behind a zippered ball bag lower down.

"Okay, now grab a hold of the putter and pull it out like you're taking a golf club out of the bag."

Shanks followed her directions and was surprised when all of the clubs came out the top. All eleven clubs pulled out of the bag along with a circular black plastic section that held the false clubs in place. Each club had been cut off at varying lengths so that when the piece was secured into the top of the golf bag the clubs stuck out the top and looked normal.

"Okay, now reach down into the golf bag and pull on the black strap," Tracey said.

Shanks reached down inside the bag and pulled out the

nylon strap handle that was hooked onto an oval molded plastic case. He set it down on top of the bench beside the gutted golf bag.

"The combo is 7-9-23-12," she said.

Intrigued, Shanks dialed the numbers in and pressed the tab sideways. The case popped open and he stepped back.

"Cool."

"That's what I thought you'd say. It holds $1.4 million dollars.

Sam scooped up the stacks of hundred dollar bills held inside the case.

"There are twenty-four stacks," Tracey said.

Sam took her into his arms and they kissed passionately.

"You are one hell of a woman," Shanks said. "Thanks for coming up with this."

"Thanks, Sam. If you hadn't saved me from Vinton all those years ago, things would be different."

At the mention of Blackwell, Sam scowled. "You wait. You may have to save me from him before this is all over. If I don't kill him first. "

CHAPTER FIFTY-SIX

CRYSTAL BENT OVER a box and ran two strips of packing tape across the seam between the two flaps. Two movers were taking one of her leather couches out the front door of her loft, and several others were following with armloads of cardboard boxes. Michael Zimeratti stood leaning against the kitchen counter, reading through the documents Crystal's realtor had assembled for the sale of her property.

"That's the last one," Crystal said to the realtor as she walked over to join them in the kitchen.

"Okay then, the sign is up downstairs, and we've got you listed on the MSL. I'll call the stagers and have them position the furniture tomorrow. I wouldn't be surprised if we get an offer in the next week or so. I'll give you a call," the realtor said.

"Sounds great, Angela, I hope it sells quickly. Judging from what you said earlier, it sounds like these downtown lofts are a hot commodity." Crystal grabbed her purse and turned back toward Zimeratti, who was watching her with a big grin.

"You got any place to be today?" he said.

"No, what were you thinking?"

"We could spend the rest of the day together here in town before we head up to the mountains."

"How about you follow me in your car out to Golden and we'll see what trouble we can get into out there?" Crystal said, not wanting to take a chance on running into anyone from her old job in Denver.

A few minutes later, she was pulling out of the underground parking garage and following Zimeratti, who was driving his green Jaguar. They drove down Speer Boulevard until they got to 8th Avenue and then headed west toward the mountains. The sun was up above the foothills, and Crystal welcomed the warmth on her face as she followed Zimeratti.

She started thinking about Reece Culver and wondered if he'd returned from Tulsa. Crystal steered the Mercedes with her left knee and fished her cellphone out of her purse. She could see Zimeratti's car up ahead moving away with several cars filling in the gap between them. Crystal dialed Reece's number.

"Hello," he said.

"Where are you?" she asked

"In my office, why?"

"I thought you were going to call me when you got back to Denver."

He seemed distracted. "Was I?"

"I need to see you, Reece. I have some new information about my mother's case."

"What sort of information?"

"I've received several letters from her."

"You have? That's interesting," Reece said, sounding a lot more interested. "Handwritten or typed?"

"Some typed and some handwritten, but I know they're from her."

"Do they have a return address?"

"No."

"Then how do you know they're from your mother?"

"I just know. What are you doing right now? Can I come see you?"

"I'm busy working on another case."

That wasn't the answer she wanted to hear at all. Not when she was so close to finding her mother. "I have to go out of town for the afternoon. But try to get unbusy, because I want to talk to you."

CHAPTER FIFTY-SEVEN

SAM SHANKS SAT in the study of his Minturn, Colorado, home sorting through the last of his business papers. He'd set up a trust in Michael Zimeratti's name to transfer the ownership of his Minturn property. He was now officially renting the property from the trust. With the document in place he was making good on a promise he'd made to Zimeratti's father Anthony years past to look out for his son.

His thoughts turned to Tracey Roberts and what had happened all those years ago when Vinton Blackwell found them together at Tracey's condo in Santa Barbara. Blackwell went into a fit of rage and proceeded to trash the place until Shanks finally got him under control. Everything seemed fine and Sam left thinking he'd placated Vinton. Sam rubbed his hand over his head, thinking about what he'd put Tracey through. Not until she called him from the hospital several months later did he realize how demented Blackwell was. He'd beaten her and held her captive in his van in the desert. Tracey snuck away one night naked and half out of her mind and made it to a fire station. She'd been hospitalized and treated for anxiety and hysteria.

Sam pulled away from the memory. It was painful recalling what Tracey had endured. He thought of Crystal and Owen and the family life Tracey once had back in St. Louis. She was in a better place now. Shanks had succeeded in giving her a new life. Owen, even though he tried, wasn't worthy of her.

Shanks knew Tracey liked the life they'd built together since he'd smuggled her away to Blackhawk. She'd become educated and successful in a place far away from Blackwell's threats. Sam had managed to see her from time to time, and over the decade and a half since California they'd built a lasting relationship. He yearned for the time when he would take her away to Uruguay. Shanks thought of Blackwell—he had to be killed. He was the only thing standing between Sam and Tracey and their happiness.

Shanks felt the vibrating ring of his cellphone and answered. "Hello."

"I've got a big problem down here."

"What kind of problem Escodar?"

"It's with Customs. The agent I paid off was fired today. They're cracking down on security. I don't know if I can solve this problem in one week," Pablo said, sounding frantic.

Shanks was used to unexpected problems, and he quickly grasped a possible solution. "What if we didn't need Customs? I've been thinking about the plan you had earlier. What if I was on a separate flight on the Lear with just a few pieces? The most precious pieces."

"What do you have in mind, Mr. Shanks?"

"What if we had everyone get off the Airbus in Guayaquil while they service the plane? The pilots will escort them to the lounge on the second floor of the jet center. There will be a celebration with champagne. That should buy some time."

"Okay, I could put that in place easily. What else did you have in mind?"

"The mechanics will find a problem with one of the engines while the plane is being serviced. They will open the doors to the cargo area to gain access to a control box or something like that. The mechanic will make a call to the local authorities and inform them that they are working on a suspicious aircraft," Shanks said.

"That all sounds feasible. I like the part about your people celebrating. They won't know what hit them when they're arrested."

"I'm hoping that's the case … but there's one problem I have with it now that I think about it. Do you remember Michael Zimeratti from our days up in St. Louis?"

"Yeah, Anthony's son. What about him?"

"I don't want him going down with the others. He needs to be spared."

CHAPTER FIFTY-EIGHT

REECE STOOD AT the corner window of his office late in the day on Friday, staring west toward the mountains. The usual cast of characters was walking up and down Colfax pedaling drugs, sex, or both. The ballistics report Mike Mobley had faxed to Haisley had changed things. Now he had confirmation that his father's case, Crystal Thomas's missing mother Tracey, and Owen Thomas's death were all connected. He was curious to see what Natalie had found. He needed some clue to follow forward. Reece thought about Crystal and the letters she mentioned. *Were they from her mother, or were they a trick from the trigger man?*

It didn't take long for him to find the address and telephone number for Charles Anders on his laptop. He dialed the number, but the call went to voicemail. Reece hung up figuring he'd rather see Anders in person.

Reece thought about his mother and her earlier interest in his case. Maybe he'd managed to make her realize he was serious about catching the people that murdered her husband. He decided to give her a call.

"Hey, Mom, am I catching you at a good time?"

"Yes dear, I'm just watching TV. Is everything okay?"

"Yeah, things are fine," Reece said.

"Have you found any more clues in your case?"

"A few."

"Reece, I want to apologize to you. I'm sorry I didn't take you seriously earlier. I'm proud of what you're doing, and I appreciate you putting your career on hold to solve Dad's case."

Reece couldn't believe his ears. He wondered for a moment if she was using some kind of ploy to get information for Agent Cox. He held the phone away and laughed to himself. He was being paranoid. If he couldn't trust his own mother, whom could he trust?

"Reece, you were going to tell me something you found. You can tell me. I did some soul searching and you're right. That FBI agent screwed up. Just like you said he did. I was so messed up back then. For a while I didn't remember how the police handled Al's case. They botched it."

"I'm sorry about that, Mom. I'm sorry they dropped the case, but I'm going to fix things," Reece said.

"I hope you can, son, but I don't want you taking chances. I want you safe. If you need to call Haisley—he can help."

"Yeah," Reece said.

"Will you do me a favor? If you need help, will you call him?"

"Sure," Reece said.

"Oh, I wanted to thank you for letting me use your rental car. I talked to the nice man at the Toyota dealer. They need to keep my Camry for a week. It is the transmission, after all. They have to replace it, but it's still under warranty."

"Mom, you can keep the rental for as long as you want. It's paid for. Just let me know when you turn it back in."

"You're such a good son, Reece. I love you," Helen said. "Tell me, what did you find on your case."

"When I was in Tulsa, I helped Haisley with some

surveillance for a case he's been working. We found a body," Reece said.

"A body. Oh, my goodness. Like a dead body?" she said, raising her voice in shock.

"Yes, a dead body. But that's not the big deal. The important part of the news is the ballistics report."

"Yeah, so what does that mean?"

"Whoever shot this dead guy we found used the same gun to kill Dad."

"Oh no!" Helen Culver said. "Reece, be careful. Promise me you'll be careful, son."

*

After feeding his dog Manchego, he took him for a quick walk, still thinking about the case. When he returned to the apartment he filled the dog's water bowl before locking up his apartment and walking down the stairs to the GTO. Reece scanned the surrounding buildings, just in case anyone had followed him from Tulsa. He knew someone wanted him dead, but he still wasn't sure who it was. His instincts were pointing to Crystal, or someone working for Sam Shanks. Yet he'd made a handful of enemies solving cases over the past couple of years, and knew it could be totally unrelated.

Reece had stuck the key in the ignition when the thought of what happened to his hotel room in Tulsa came to him. He climbed out, got on his hands and knees, and looked underneath the car. He traced the exhaust pipes from the headers coming off both sides of the engine to the twin mufflers, and back. He spied several old wires running down the left fender well that were taped together with black electrical tape. Reece searched the bottom of the car. Everything looked as it should, and he reminded himself to take it to the car wash. Nothing was out of the ordinary. Next he popped the hood, and looked around, wishing he'd brought a flashlight, but decided he was being paranoid. He got back in, turned the key, and listened. The starter barely turned the engine over, then it started with a roar, and he eased his foot off the accelerator.

The oil temp gauge sat on zero and then jumped up as the engine warmed. The temperature was coming up, and he thought of his expired tags. Reece got out, walked around to the license plate, and saw that the month sticker was an eleven, and the year a ten. He was four months over due on his registration. He made a quick decision to try to cover up the stickers and get new tags the next day.

Reece, leaving the car running to charge up the battery, walked over to the grass plot next to the street. He dug his hand into the dirt beside a tree. With a palm-sized glob of mud he returned to the car and smeared the brown muck across the plate, covering up the stickers. It was a quick fix, but he thought it just might work for the night. Reece stood up from his squat, just in time to hear the engine sputter and die. He jumped in and hit the key. The starter made a clicking noise and he knew the battery was toast.

After walking out to the curb in front of Chui's Chinese he looked for a cab. Two woman dressed in short blue jean skirts with a collage of poorly done tattoos were leaning against a street sign on the opposite side of the street. One of them grabbed the frayed edge of her skirt and flipped it up, motioning for him to come join them. The last thing he needed tonight was a hooker.

Reece spotted a cab going the opposite way as it passed the two women, and he waved hoping the cab would spot him. The cabbie continued down Colfax for another block and then pulled a U-turn. That was more like it, he thought. He jumped in the backseat and they headed west down Colfax toward downtown Denver.

*

On the way to the restaurant, Natalie told him about a recent case she'd worked involving a motorcycle gang from Los Angeles that had relocated to Denver and taken over a large chunk of the cocaine trade from a rival gang. Nineteen months after placing an undercover officer in the gang, they did a city-wide sweep, arresting most of the bad guys.

"Reece, you seem kind of down tonight. How did your trip to Tulsa go? Are you any closer to finding your missing person? What was her name? Tracey?" Natalie said. Reece looked over at her face, tinted in the red glow of a traffic light. "Not by much. The whole thing was a waste of time. All I did was blow through lots of money and tons of time. I'm starting to hate this damned case."

Natalie pulled her Toyota FJ Cruiser into the restaurant parking lot and hunted for a spot. It took two revolutions around the building to find one. Once inside, the hostess took them to the table. Reece watched Natalie slide into the booth and took the seat across from her. The waitress came and Natalie suggested red wine.

"So tell me what you got on Crystal. I can't take the suspense," he said, smiling at her after the waitress left with their order.

"Yeah, I guess that was why we came here in the first place," Natalie said. "You always get what you want. Don't you?" She flipped up the flap on her large purse, pulled out a brown folder, and slid it across the table.

"You know most of the events of her childhood, so I won't bore you with any of that, but I think you might find it interesting that her stepfather has no history of employment in this country."

"What do you mean, no employment?"

"I went one step further than what you asked, and took a look at the Social Security records for her birth parents and stepparents. Her stepmother, Diane Blackwell, worked at a bank for twenty years, and has spent the last ten years working at a horse riding facility. The stepfather, Vinton Blackwell, got a social security card when he was twelve, and spent two years working as a paperboy. After that there is no history of employment."

"None at all? That's interesting," he said, sensing that something was up with Natalie, but he couldn't put his finger on it. Reece was about to speak when he heard her cellphone ring.

"I've got to get this. I'll be right back," she said, holding the phone to her ear. He figured it was work- or boyfriend-related and she didn't want him listening.

Reece started reading Crystal's file. The first section was a detailed account of her life from the time her mother Tracey went missing, to the six months she'd spent in the orphanage, and finally to her adoption by the Blackwell family. Vinton Blackwell had volunteered at the orphanage. The next section detailed the accidental death of her high school boyfriend while on a camping trip in Tahlequah, Oklahoma. He skimmed over that section since he'd found most of the information at the Tulsa library.

Reece looked up—and almost bit his tongue. Crystal Thomas rounded the corner, walking into the aisle at the far end of the room. He slammed the file shut and shoved it under his left thigh. She smiled, noticing him, and walked up to the table.

"Reece, what a surprise," she said sliding into the booth across from him.

Reece smiled back, extremely conscious of the file lying awkwardly underneath his leg.

"You don't mind if I join you for a few minutes, do you?"

"It doesn't look like I have a choice," he said, then broke into a smile to temper how his words came out.

"Are you here with a date?" she asked, looking around.

"I'm here with a friend, but she left to take an urgent call," he said, not really wanting to explain. Natalie walked by the table heading away from them. Reece noticed her making an OK sign with her index finger and thumb.

"So, what's new on the case? Have you gotten any closer to finding my mother?"

He stared at her, silent, wanting to ask if she'd hit anyone in the head lately, or if she was surprised to see him alive after setting fire to his motel room. He wasn't entirely sure the culprit was Crystal, but Reece figured she was in deep enough with Sam Shanks to know about what happened to him in St. Louis.

"I've gotten a few good breaks, and I'm closing in," Reece said, lying to her.

Crystal was immediately delighted. "Is she in Denver?"

"No, not Denver, but I'm getting close," he said, not wanting to tell Crystal that he was at a dead end.

"How do you know that, Reece?" she asked, leaning forward.

"So tell me about those letters you mentioned. Do you really think they're from your mother?" Reece said, ignoring her.

"I do. I could show them to you if you have time."

Reece suddenly realized that Crystal's offer could be the key to solving everything.

He stood from the table, thinking about the folder he was exposing by doing so. Yet he had to force the issue. He waited, feeling trapped between the leather booth and the table. She at last stood up as well.

"Come on, let's go," she said.

Reece followed, leaving the folder behind. He knew Natalie would see it when she returned. They walked through the parking lot to a bright red Mercedes coupe, and Reece slid into the passenger's seat. The interior had the same citrus scent she'd worn the day she came to his office. He glanced sideways and caught a glimpse of her exposed thigh, then looked up. She smiled at him seductively.

"It's so good to see you, Reece," Crystal said as she started to back the car out of the parking space.

"No, let's stay put. Do you have the letters?" Reece said.

She shifted the car into park and pulled up the emergency brake. Forcing the slit on the side of her leg to rise almost to her waist, she turned toward the back and pulled a brown leather bag from the cramped backseat. Reece couldn't help looking down at her firm thigh. She was in some kind of shape.

"Here," she said, handing him a three-inch thick stack of taupe envelopes held together with a wide rubber band.

"So she's been writing you for a while," he said.

"Yes."

"Can you tell me the gist of what she's been writing?"

"The first letters told about her struggle of staying one step ahead of a man who I assume was my father Owen. Then her tone changed and she seemed happier. She talked about a sophisticated man—"

"Did this man have a name?" Reece asked, interrupting.

"No, no name, but she said he liked art and was classy compared to Owen."

"How often have you gotten the letters?" Reece asked.

"Sometimes once a week, then once a month, and sometimes they come in batches."

Reece pulled a penlight out of his pocket and shined it down onto one of the letters.

"Reece, it's dark here in the car. Why don't we go back to your apartment and we can read them together where there's more light?"

Reece was mighty tempted. She hadn't done much to push down her skirt, and the invitation was waiting right there. Yet he knew he had to reconvene with Natalie. With these letters, her information might provide a whole new set of leads.

Swallowing a lump down his throat, he opened the door, turned back toward Crystal, and said, "I'm sorry, it'll have to be another time. This could be the break we need."

CHAPTER FIFTY-NINE

VINTON BLACKWELL DROVE his black Range Rover down the Sands Springs Expressway heading back toward Tulsa. The high beams of a semi truck on the opposite side of the road blazed into his eyes, and he pulled down the visor trying to block it out, but at the same time keep his eye on the blue Mazda 6 in front of him.

The arson at the hotel room had been the perfect solution, except Reece Culver wasn't there that night. Vinton clenched his fist, glad that it would be so easy to ram the car and push it off the upcoming bridge. Traffic was light, and in the darkness Culver's blue Mazda would be over the side of the bridge before he knew what hit him. The deep waters of Keystone Lake would be cold this time of year, and if the crash didn't kill him the cold would.

Blackwell knew the perfect spot. During the first third of the bridge the drop was a straight shot into the deep waters. He watched the red taillights of the car ahead and mashed his foot down on the accelerator of the Rover. The speedometer was climbing past eighty as he closed in on the back of the Mazda. Vinton let his truck drift to the left over the passing line and aimed the right side of his front bumper at the left rear panel of the car. He was closing fast and going at least thirty miles an hour faster than the Mazda.

Blackwell smiled, still pressing the gas pedal to the floor. He flinched as the front bumper of his truck collided with the Mazda, launching it at an odd angle up and over the guardrail. Sparks shot off the front of the Range Rover as it slammed sideways into the railing just past the spot where the Mazda went over. Vinton jammed on his brakes and swerved back left, gaining control of the truck. He eyed the rearview mirror but couldn't see the Mazda. He counted himself lucky when he saw the highway all the way behind was free of traffic. Blackwell wanted to stop and watch the Mazda sink into the cold waters of the lake, but he couldn't draw attention to himself.

He figured he'd read about the crash on the Internet after returning to Colorado. He chuckled as he imagined Culver fighting for his life as the car sank into the murky water of the lake. Blackwell pulled up a nice visual of Culver's teeth chattering and blood gushing out of a head wound as it mixed with the water.

*

Helen Culver ripped at her seatbelt, frantically trying to get out of the sinking Mazda. The car was upside down and the cold water had drenched the blue dress she'd worn to her friend's house to pick up the containers of canned fruit. They'd been canning fruit together every year since she'd moved to Tulsa, and Sheila Hampstead was a joy to be around. Her friend had wanted her to stay over and watch a movie because it had gotten dark, but Helen had insisted on returning home to check on her cat.

She screamed, hoping frantically that someone might hear. Maybe a trucker saw that crazy black truck that smashed into her from behind. She remembered perfectly the image of the man with his thick white hair. She'd looked in the rearview mirror just as they collided. He was smiling. His face was lit up somehow. Who would smile when they were crashing their car into someone else? She thought of her Bible beside her bed. *Oh God, help me.*

She gulped at the last of the air above her head. It was pitch black inside the sinking car. The water was so cold and her head hurt where it hit the steering wheel upon impact with the water. She pushed the fabric of the deployed airbag away from her face. At last Helen found the seat belt release down on her right side. She squeezed it and felt the weight of her body settle downward against the ceiling of the rental car. The windows felt cold on her fingertips, and she could see nothing but darkness past the glass. She madly scratched the door and window, trying in vain to get it open. Her ears popped and she took a breath, but the air was gone. Coughing and choking, she thought of her dead husband Al.

At least this way, she wouldn't miss him anymore.

CHAPTER SIXTY

THE NEXT DAY, out behind his apartment Reece tightened down the bolts on the red and black heavy-gauge cables running to the new battery, then slid the red rubber cover over the positive battery terminal of the GTO. He opened the driver's-side door and waited for his dog Manchego to jump into the backseat.

Reece thought about the file on Crystal that Natalie had given him the night before. Nothing in it contained more than circumstantial evidence, but it appeared that she was responsible for the death of her boyfriend fifteen years earlier in Talequah Oklahoma.

She'd moved on from that relationship and had eventually married someone by the name of Paul while attending the University of Oklahoma. She'd graduated with her pre-law degree in 2003—a few years after her first husband died in a freak waterskiing accident on Lake Tenkiller. The only witness was Crystal who, it was speculated, was driving the boat when her husband, who was practicing for a waterski jumping competition misjudged a ramp and drowned. It took divers more than a week to find the body, and Crystal had to be hospitalized for two days with severe hysteria.

A year later, in 2004, she met her next victim while attending law school in Denver. Reece thought back to the newspaper article he'd found the day Crystal came to visit him at his office. He recalled it announcing the death of her husband Nathan in a skiing accident at Vail the previous winter. Wow, all three men she became involved with died. Not a good track record.

He'd looked through the letters Crystal had given him the night before at the restaurant with Natalie, but hadn't found anything that led him to believe they were from Tracey Roberts except that the last few had been written in women's handwriting. They certainly gave no clue as to her whereabouts.

He headed toward Sixth Avenue, heading for the on ramp to I-25 south. He pulled one of his disks from its case and pushed it into CD player. It was Willie Nelson singing Kris Kristofferson's "Help Me Make It Through the Night." Reece hummed along with the tune, trying to match the twang of Willie's voice. The expressway was crowded and it took a while to get down to C-470 and the ramp to the city of Littleton. He was meaning to pay a visit to Charlie Anders.

Reece checked the address on the piece of notebook paper he'd used as he pulled into the empty driveway of the large brick ranch-style home. It looked like it had been built in the mid 1970's and showed a lot of pride in ownership with its well-manicured lawn. The front door was freshly stained, looking newer than the rest of the home. Reece exited the GTO, hoping his dog Manchego would be okay alone in the car.

The doorbell was the kind that rang with multiple notes and began chiming as soon as he pushed it. No one answered, so he pushed it a second time. A bright yellow Ford T-bird was parked in the driveway, so Anders should be home.

Reece went around the side of the two-car garage and heard the squeal of a table saw ripping wood. When the grating sound stopped, he gave the door a rap with his knuckles. In a few seconds the entrance pushed out toward him, and an elderly man with thinning white hair emerged. He wore a dull green hat with the logo for the 82nd Airborne sewn into the front in yellow thread.

"Yeah?" the old man said.

"Mr. Anders, I'm a friend of your daughter Kathryn's," Reece said, stretching the truth as he held his investigator's license up. "If it's not too much trouble, I need a few minutes of your time."

"Investigator huh," Anders said.

"Your daughter might be in trouble, Mr. Anders. It won't take long. I just have a few questions," Reece said.

Charlie Anders stared at him, unconsciously taking a few steps backward into the garage.

"You see, there was a burglary in Tulsa, Oklahoma. The thieves took a lot of valuable art. Your daughter Kathryn was involved with the family that was burglarized," Reece said.

"Kathryn, involved in a burglary. How so?"

"She wasn't involved in the burglary. She did the appraisal on the art that was stolen. The family intended to donate it for the construction—" Reece said before Charlie Anders cut him off.

"Yeah, yeah, I know all about Melvin and Melanie Phillips. Rich people," Anders said. Finishing Reece's sentence seemed to make up his mind about whether Reece was legit or not. "Yeah, I guess I got time for some questions. Come on in."

He turned and made tracks through the sawdust-covered garage. Reece took a whiff and welcomed the smell of fresh sawn lumber. Anders led him into the kitchen of his home and walked over to the refrigerator.

"Are you thirsty?" he said, reaching up to remove his hat and then placing it on top of the fridge. A shower of sawdust rained down on the floor.

"What did you say this was about? Is my daughter in some kind of trouble?" Mr. Anders said, seeming like he'd forgotten what Reece had just told him.

Reece smiled at the old man, unsure if the visit was going to be a complete waste of time. "Your daughter's not in any kind of trouble."

The old man opened a cupboard and pulled out two short crystal glasses. "Scotch or bourbon?" he asked.

"I'll have whatever you're going to have," Reece said, looking at his watch. "There was a burglary in Tulsa about a week ago. Your daughter did some work for the family that was burglarized," Reece said. "I just need to tie up some loose ends, Mr. Anders."

"Yeah, okay. That sounds good to me," the man said as he reached into the cupboard and pulled out a bottle of single-malt Scotch.

Reece could only hope that Kathryn Anders hadn't called her father and warned him that an investigator might be coming to ask questions.

"Don't mind the mess. I'm still getting used to being a bachelor," the old man said. He pulled a yellowed layer of newspaper pages off the couch and motioned for Reece to sit. Anders began to talk, and Reece soon learned that he'd served in the 82nd airborne as a career military officer retiring at the rank of lieutenant colonel back in 1979 after his last deployment to Honduras, which was part of the military operation named Golden Pheasant.

They shared a tray of cheese, crackers, and hard salami while sipping their single malt. Reece was content to let him talk, wanting him to warm up for the questioning to follow.

Charlie Anders told him how he and his wife had raised several pairs of chocolate Labrador retrievers over the years after Reece had commented on a picture in the kitchen. Reece told him about his dog Manchego and could tell the old man was warming up to the idea of being interviewed.

"Do you have the dog with you today?" Anders asked.

"Yeah, I do. Manchego's out in the car."

"It's probably hot out there. Why don't you bring him in? I'm sure I've got some treats he'd like. Hell, it's not like I'm going eat the damn things myself," Anders said with a chuckle.

"You sure you want him in here?"

"Yeah, let your dog stretch his legs. I got a nice big backyard."

Reece went to the car and brought his dog Manchego back to the house on the leash. Anders rubbed the dog's ears and pointed to the ground. Manchego instinctively dropped into a sit and then sank all the way to the ground. Anders reached into the end table next to his recliner and pulled out a box of dog treats. Manchego rose into a sit, eyeing the man intently, and was rewarded.

"So, what did you want to know about my older sister Tracey?" Charlie asked, setting down his glass of scotch.

Reece didn't remember asking anything about Tracey, and the man's question confirmed he'd spoken to his daughter Kathryn.

"I do have a few questions, as a matter of fact. First off, what did you think happened to your sister back when the police reported her missing?" Reece asked, pulling his notebook out of the side pocket of his down jacket.

"Well, I guess at first I thought it was some kind of mistake, but when I went down to the station, and they told me she'd left the kids alone overnight at the bus station. I immediately suspected foul play."

CHAPTER SIXTY-ONE

EARLY SATURDAY MORNING a strong wind buffeted Crystal Thomas's red Mercedes on the drive toward Vail. She thought about Reece Culver, curious about what he was doing with the constant supply of money she'd been sending him. She thought about the scene in the car the night before and knew she had stirred him, despite his hasty escape. Reece Culver was right where she wanted him. Close to her, but not close to the things she wanted to keep hidden.

The phone ringing in her purse pulled her out of the daydream.

"Hello, this is Crystal," she said, not recognizing the number.

"Crystal, it's Michael Zimeratti. What's going on?"

"Oh hi, Michael."

"Are you still up for some skiing?"

"Very much so, I'm just about there."

"Good, I've got our lift tickets, so just park in the lot I told you about and I'll meet you by the lift."

Crystal hung up her phone and exited the highway for the Vail ski area. She found the lot Michael had mentioned, and after parking she gathered up her ski gear and took the bus to the base of the lift where they'd arranged to meet.

She had arrived first and stood staring at the mountain,

imagining what it would be like to ski down it. Someone touched her left shoulder from behind. Crystal ignored it, deep in her own thoughts. She knew Michael was behind her, but she didn't want to seem too eager, whatever game he was playing. He patted her left shoulder again and she turned to see him standing on his skis, grinning at her.

"Hi," he said.

"Good morning."

"Did you spend the night up here or drive up this morning?" Michael asked.

"I came up this morning. I had the road to myself and it was good to clear my head." Crystal banged the tip of her ski pole onto her boot ,knocking off a big chunk of snow, and stepped into the binding of her left ski, clicking the boot into place. She followed the same routine with her right and jammed both poles into the snow to push off into a glide on her skis.

*

Michael Zimeratti followed Crystal into the lift line, admiring how trim she looked in her form-fitting black ski pants. He was rapidly warming to Shanks' idea of starting something up with this beautiful creature. She was spunky and unpredictable, and Michael liked the idea of banging Vinton Blackwell's stepdaughter.

The sun peeked out from the thick white clouds, warming his face where the ski helmet and goggles didn't cover. He poled his way up next to her.

"What a great day to ski. I'm glad I called yesterday. This is a great idea," Michael said, grinning at her while devising a plan to wine and dine her later that day. He'd done it so many times before with his Italian machismo. He had the money, charm, and wit to get almost anything he wanted. He could already picture Crystal standing next to him in his warm steam shower.

"Let's take this one up and then head to the back bowls. I can't wait to ski some black diamonds," Crystal said with a hint of competition. The couple in front of them skied toward the quad lift and waited their turn to hop on. Michael waited, letting another couple go, and then followed Crystal and skied into position ahead of the approaching lift. The chair kissed the back of his thighs and lifted him into the air. He scooted backward against the rear pad, getting settled, and slid his ski poles underneath his thigh for safe storage and free use of his hands.

A man and a woman shared the lift with them, and all four rode up the steep slope. The trees were covered with a fresh dusting of snow and the air felt crisp to Michael. At the top they skied off side by side and took the first black diamond run to their right.

Zimeratti let Crystal lead, admiring her form as she sped off down the steep run, carving turns back and forth. He loved skiing and had raced on the high school ski team back in Chicago, before his father's decision to move the family to St. Louis. He looked ahead and saw Crystal a hundred yards in front, skiing back and forth following the steep fall line down the mountain. The wind blew through his hair on the sides of his helmet and felt good. He needed to get out and do this more often. Skiing helped him reconnect with his youth.

Up ahead, she slid sideways, stopping at the top of one of the stair steps on the ski run. He himself did a hockey stop, shooting snow sideways at her, and came to a halt only a few feet above.

"Nice, she said, grinning at him despite all the snow sprayed on her. "God, I love it up here. I never want to set foot in Denver again."

"You shouldn't have to. You've paid your dues long enough."

Her mouth twisted into a frown. "Paid my dues? What do you mean, Michael?"

"I mean, you've been daddy's girl long enough. It's time you do something for yourself."

Crystal looked away from him into the tall pine trees to one side.

"I'm not sure I'll ever be done helping Vinton. He's done so much for me in my life. He saved me from that orphanage. He adopted me and put me through law school. I owe him my life," Crystal said.

Michael pulled his helmet off and pointed his skis downhill, gliding forward until his left ski slid in between hers. He was close to her and wanted to grab her, but waited.

She stiffened, almost as if bracing, as he tried to take her into his arms. She turned her head sideways, looking down the slope. "We should keep going. We came here to ski."

"No, not yet," Michael said, planting his lips on her cheek. Crystal turned toward him with a funny look. He was trying to read her. He wanted to figure her out. He decided to take a chance and pressed his lips against hers. She kissed him back, halfway at first, and then gave in. They both dropped their poles, and she wrapped her arms round him, kissing him like she meant it.

"It's okay, Crystal. I've got the means to help you now. You can free yourself from him. I see it in your eyes. You love him, but he scares the hell out of you too. You—"

"No," Crystal screamed, pushing away from him. "You don't know what you're talking about."

"It's okay. You can tell me. I'm here for you. You can tell me all about it," Michael said, moving closer to her again.

"I do love Vinton, or at least I've tried to. It's not been easy," Crystal said with tears streaming down her red face in the bright sunshine.

"It's okay, baby. I'm here for you," Zimeratti said. He watched her come toward him with her lips parted. They kissed and ran their hands over one another for a satisfying long while. Despite the cold, he was getting plenty heated.

Finally, he suggested they finish the ski run. He followed her once again, thinking about her relationship with Vinton Blackwell as they skied. Zimeratti had always wondered if she'd been sexually abused. A guy like Blackwell didn't care about anything but what he wanted.

After a few more runs they got in the line for the three-person chair lift that ran to the back bowls of Vail. The strong sunshine felt good beaming down onto his face. He noticed the stern look on her face and wondered what she was thinking about.

"Michael, I was wondering if you know what Shanks is planning to do next. He must know Agent Cox is still looking for him. Especially since you guys bugged out of the casino back in Tulsa just before his planned raid."

"That's probably true. Shanks has been out of the country for the past few days, coming up with a plan, but there are a few problems."

"Problems? What do you mean?" Crystal said, skiing into the lane in front of the coming chairlift. Michael followed and they settled onto the green padded seat as it came and took them up the slope.

"We have more personnel problems," Michael said, unbuttoning his helmet and clipping the strap to his jacket.

"Personnel problems. What do you mean? Is there someone

else in Shanks' organization working for the feds?" Crystal asked.

"No. Someone has stolen a major piece of artwork."

"Who?" she asked, pressing against his shoulder.

"It's just a suspicion right now, so I really shouldn't be talking about it."

"That's not fair. You've brought me this far. Who does Shanks suspect is stealing from him?"

"It was the job we did in Tulsa. An article afterward in the paper listed the works of art we got," Michael said. "There was a small Van Gogh painting of yellow poppy flowers. It's valued at something like $55 million."

"Yeah, I've heard of that painting. It's one of Van Gogh's small works. What did the article say about it?"

"It was listed as stolen during the job, but when we inventoried the paintings, it wasn't one of the works in the vault," Michael said.

He imagined that she had a good idea who could have stolen it. "Maybe it was never taken. I'm sure that sort of thing happens all the time."

"It wasn't a case of insurance fraud, Crystal. It's your stepfather, Vinton Blackwell. He wants out."

"You're mistaken, Michael," she said too quickly. "Vinton would never steal from Sam. They're like father and son."

The chairlift reached the top of the mountain, and Michael pushed up on the steel bar they'd been resting their skis upon. He watched her ski off the chair, wishing he'd never brought up his suspicions about her stepfather. He knew he'd hit a nerve. He wanted to help her, pry her free of her controlling stepfather. Zimeratti knew Blackwell wouldn't be joining them in Uruguay. Shanks had been losing interest in Vinton ever since he'd killed the blackjack dealer in Tulsa. Shanks wanted rid of his nemesis, and setting him up to take the fall in Ecuador was the perfect plan.

Zimeratti watched the top of Crystal's pink helmet disappear down the ski terrain. Straightening his skis, Michael shot down the steep hill after her. He was gaining speed when he caught an edge on a sheer piece of ice. Crouching downward, he began sliding out of control and braced, ready to fall. He managed to turn and slide, then pulled upward, and was back in control. Michael slid to a stop, glad he hadn't crashed. Pivoting, he looked back and saw a bunch of skiers coming.

Michael pointed his skis downward and picked up speed racing down the mountain. As he turned back and forth, carving turns, Crystal had stopped up ahead on the edge of a stair-step section. He skied toward her. She turned back, making eye contact with him, and then pushed off, zooming downhill. Michael felt his tired thighs burning. He needed to stop and rest. He wasn't as young and tireless as he had been in past years. Crystal was going straight down the hill, not turning to control her speed. Zimeratti worried about her. If she fell, she'd break a leg. She was so sensitive, yet so in command when she wanted to be.

He came down the hill and saw that she'd stopped a few hundred yards before the roped-off area that led to the lift. She was waiting for him. He came up alongside her and stopped. Michael smiled but stayed silent, waiting for her to make the first move. She motioned toward the three-person ski lift that serviced the steeper terrain and stepped left, skiing toward it. He followed and skied into the lift line behind her. They were all by themselves and got right to the lift. She scooted onto the chairlift bench and he followed, taking a seat beside her with his thigh pressed up against hers.

Crystal took off her helmet and goggles, and clipped them

onto the side of her coat. Zimeratti followed suit and pulled his sunglasses from his pocket. He looked over at her, expecting to hear angry words, but she was smiling.

"The bright sun feels good," Crystal said. She turned back, looking down the hill toward the empty chairs behind them. "We've got the whole lift to ourselves."

"It's probably the terrain. No one has the guts to ski this stuff," he said with satisfaction. Down below them, the steep slope was narrow, mottled with large sections of snow-covered rocks. The wind had picked up and the chair bobbed. He grabbed the pole beside himself to hang on. The chair was rising above the slope, until they were at a high point a couple of hundred feet above the rocky slope. The wind tore at them and he sank down into the collar of his coat, blocking his face from the biting cold. Down below, he noticed, more skiers were finally getting on.

"Ahh!" Crystal yelled.

"What's wrong?"

She sounded like she was in awful pain. "I've got a cramp in my left calf. Oh, it hurts so bad, Ahh."

"What can I do? Can I help you?" Michael said, rubbing the top of her thigh with his gloved hand.

"Can you reach my boot? Get the top buckle undone. That would help. Oh, ouch, it hurts. It's like a knife. Can you reach it for me?"

He leaned toward her and shoved his ski poles under his right thigh to free his hands. Michael let go of the bar on his right, and with his left hand pressing down on the seat of the chairlift leaned out over her legs. He was reaching for her boot, trying to grab the buckle.

"Ahh, it's so bad," Crystal said in an agonized voice.

Michael touched the buckle of her hot pink ski boot with

the tip of his index finger, but it wouldn't unlatch. He felt her hand on his shoulder and was thankful she was keeping him in his seat. He looked down at the jagged snow-covered rocks a couple of hundred feet below. The wind was blowing hard, and the chair lift was swinging side to side in a steady rhythm.

"Can you get it? I've got your shoulder," Crystal said in a weak, pain-ridden voice.

Michael leaned out farther toward her boot. Finally he had the buckle. It flipped open.

Without warning, her hand on his back gave a hard shove. He slipped forward, off balance, and reached desperately for the bar on the side of the chair lift, but missed it. He felt himself falling. The rocks far below came up at him much too fast to survive.

CHAPTER SIXTY-TWO

CRYSTAL WATCHED MICHAEL Zimeratti's body plummet toward the rock-covered slope below. Michael let out a faint scream just before he hit the ground with a splash of snow. She smiled, then turned back and yelled.

Crystal saw the top of the mountain coming. She started smiling broadly, thinking about how easy it was to fool Zimeratti. Now he wouldn't be able to carry out whatever foul mission Sam Shanks had planned for her stepfather.

Crystal saw the ski patrol sign next to the lift and knew she needed tears to be convincing. She took herself back to the day the police found her and her two brothers alone in the bus station. A feeling of true sadness and dread came to her. Crystal bit down on her lip, feeling the pain and fear of her childhood. She thought about the last time she saw her brothers. She felt the flush rise up within her, and was back at the day she rode to the orphanage with a female social worker in Tulsa. Tears bubbled up in the corners of her eyes. Crystal was afraid and all alone. Soon she was crying and moaning, rocking back and forth on the chair lift.

The look on the face of the young ski lift operator in the lift booth confirmed she was in the right state of mind. Crystal skied off the lift but almost immediately kicked off her skis and hobbled in her bulky ski boots toward the lift operator's hut. The man jumped out of his seat and opened the door.

"Oh God, I need your help. My friend. He fell, oh God, oh God, I hope he's..." Crystal screamed through her tears.

"Your friend fell off the lift?" the lift operator yelled, hitting the bulbous red button on his operator's console. The ski lift wheel above their heads groaned as it slowed and came to a halt. The lift operator ran out his hut and looked down the long line of the lift carriages, dumbfounded.

Crystal saw the faces of two skiers that had been following her up the slope about ten chairs back. The horror they showed confirmed that Michael didn't make it. She fought off the urge to smile.

"Come this way," someone said from behind. A handsome ski patroller in a red ski suit had appeared. "It's okay we'll take you down to him," the man said, taking her arm. The ski lift started back up, and then she followed the man in his red ski patrol outfit with a large white cross on his back. He was talking on a radio and pulling her with him. The handsome man stopped and motioned for Crystal to get her skis on.

Together they headed down the slope, him towing an orange plastic sled, the kind they use to take injured skiers off the mountain. Two other ski patrollers joined them. She kept concentrating on the orphanage. The tears came easy. She was sniffing and snorting and crying as she followed the others down the steep slope toward Michael Zimeratti's broken body. Crystal had seen him fall head first off the chair and slam into the jagged rocks. She knew he couldn't survive a fall like that. He had to be dead.

That was good. She wouldn't want him to be able to tell anyone what happened.

CHAPTER SIXTY-THREE

REECE TOOK A long swig of his scotch and savored the relaxation he felt coming. Charlie Anders was on his feet coming toward Reece with the bottle. Reece held up his hand, signaling he didn't want more, but the old man ignored him and poured the liquid into his highball glass until it was half full. Reece watched him retreat to his recliner. His dog Manchego was now permanently parked at his side, and every once in a while the old man would reach into his box of treats and reward the dog.

"So, what were we talking about?" Anders said. "I mean, I know what we were talking about, but what was your questions?"

"When the police reported your sister missing. Did you suspect her husband, Owen Roberts?"

"Well, Reece, I guess I did at first. I guess I thought she and Owen might have gotten into a fight and something happened, but the few times I met Owen, he didn't seem like that kind of a guy."

"What kind of a man did he seem like?" Reece asked, not knowing anything other than what he'd heard from his client.

"He seemed like a caring man, vulnerable somehow."

That was completely at odds with the portrait he'd gained

so far. "Mr. Anders, do you know why Owen didn't take custody of the children?"

"Call me Charlie," he said. "Well, I guess I'd say he didn't have the money to take care of three children on his own. A few weeks before Tracey disappeared, she came over to the house. We were living up in Claremore, Oklahoma, back then. I remember how upset she was when she'd found out he was gambling away their savings."

"Did you or your wife ever hear from Tracey again after 1989?"

"No, not a word, which if she was still alive seems very odd to me. Tracey and I were pretty close growing up, and during the few months she lived in Tulsa with the kids, we saw her at least once a week if not more."

Reece pulled out the concert ticket he'd borrowed from Ann Fletcher's house and handed it across the couch to the old man. "Does this mean anything to you?"

Anders took the ticket from his hand and read the date off the top of the Rolling Stones Concert ticket. "Where'd you get that?"

"I visited Crystal's Aunt Fletcher a week ago. I saw this on the bulletin board in the room Crystal used to stay in when visiting. I did some quick math and came to the conclusion that this had to be something from her mother Tracey," Reece said, hoping he wouldn't be irritated by the small theft.

"How is Ann Fletcher?"

"She seemed reasonably well for an old woman on oxygen with a tobacco habit," Reece answered in full honesty.

"Still smoking those damn cancer spikes," Charlie said. "Reece, this concert ticket has a lot of history to it. My sister was very unhappy back then. That was when she first discovered the true character of the man she'd married." Charlie raised his glass and drained the yellow liquid down into the ice. "That was the summer after she started nursing school. Sometime during the previous winter she'd discovered Owen had a compulsive gambling problem, and had squandered their entire bank account, and the boy's college fund to support his habit," Charlie said, looking sad for the first time. "I remember asking her about her concert after she came back.

Reece had been idly studying the walls of the den as he listened, and he noticed that almost every picture contained the old man and his wife.

"It took a long time for her to tell me the whole story. She went to the concert that November of 1981 with a pack of girls from school. They met some guys and she liked one of them more than the rest. His name was Vinton. He was tall with piercing green eyes and long blond hair. I think she used the term dreamy."

Reece came sharply to attention with the mention of the name. Vinton was an unusual name, and in this context there couldn't be more than one of them.

"Tracey left the concert with this guy, and they spent the next three months touring the west in his Volkswagen bus. I remember Owen calling in a panic the day after the concert. He was going to call the police and file a missing person's report, but then he told me about a fight they'd had, and he decided to wait a few days. I got a postcard in the mail from Tracey telling me she was okay. She just needed a little break from Owen."

Reece was paying close attention. That ticket stub had turned out to be gold.

"Three months into her trip with this guy Vinton, she found out she was pregnant with his child. They had a big fight, and he left her at the Berkley bus station with fifty bucks," Charlie said with a frown.

"Do you remember this Vinton guy's last name?" Reece asked.

"Yeah, Vinton Blackwell."

"What happened next?" Reece asked, wanting to hear the end of his story.

"Tracey called Owen, and he told her to come back home. She had the baby the next August, and they named their new baby girl Crystal, after Owen's mother."

CHAPTER SIXTY-FOUR

CRYSTAL TOOK THE exit off I-70 for Minturn. The traffic had been light, and she gunned the Mercedes, enjoying the slingshot effect as she cruised around the circular exit ramp. She watched the speedometer climb past seventy on Highway 24, then slammed on the brakes as she neared the exit for Line Shack Road. The car slowed instantly, handling like it was on rails. She jerked right onto a gravel road, slowing as she tapped the brake pedal. She smiled breathing in the fresh scent of the pine trees.

"Papa, I'm on your road. Can you get the gate for me?" she announced into her cell phone.

"You made good time. I'll meet you out in the drive," he said in his usual rough voice. The road straightened and she passed the point where Meadow Mountain road broke off, running south. She continued onward downshifting the transmission and curved around the switchbacks descending toward her stepfather's home.

A large black decorative entry gate rose in front of a river rock two-story villa, set in the valley below snow-covered peaks. She felt warm and calm. She approached the property and saw Vinton dressed in brown corduroy pants and a blue down jacket, sitting on his black Polaris ATV beside the gate. She stopped just inside the property and left the engine running while she got out and ran up to him. He scooped her up into his strong arms and hugged her.

"Oh, Papa, it's so good to see you."

"You too, Crystal. I've missed you," the man said.

As always, her gaze focused on the clouded green cataract in his left eye. She could smell his aftershave, and she admired his strong chin and longish white hair. They held one another in a prolonged hug. She thought back to the day she had met him at the orphanage and first admired his green eyes, wondering if he was a sorcerer. Since she'd grown up, her estimation had sunk quite a bit. He wasn't perfect, but he was all he she had. He was the only man who'd ever taken care of her.

"Let me get the gate and I'll ride up to the house with you," he said, pulling away from her.

Crystal watched him walk back toward the gatehouse. He was fit for a man in his early sixties. She'd always been attracted to him in a way that felt different than a father. She'd told herself the attraction was okay since they weren't related. She knew he felt the same way somewhere deep down in his heart.

Crystal followed Vinton into the house and deposited her bags on the bed in the upstairs guest bedroom. She joined him in the kitchen, and the smell of his famous ham, egg, and cheddar sandwiches pleased her.

"Are you hungry?" he asked, turning toward her with a plate full of steaming food.

"I'm always hungry for your sandwiches, Papa," Crystal said, feeling herself relax for the first time since the plane ride to St. Louis.

"Here, take a plate, and come this way. I want to show you something," he said, walking toward a door on the other side of the kitchen. Crystal followed, and they descended the stairway into the basement. The room was finished in rich oak paneling with a large pool table in the center, and an assortment of black and white photos hung eye level on three of the exterior walls. On the east wall there was a mahogany desk and matching chair.

"I couldn't tell you about this until now, Crystal. This is what we've all been working for the past year." He pointed at a large easel near the knee-high windows on the west wall. It was covered with a large map of North and South America. Crystal walked up to it and ran her finger down a blue magic marker line that stretched from Vail, Colorado, to Guayaquil, Ecuador, and then downward to a circle in Uruguay, South America.

"What's this, Papa?" she asked, pointing at the circle.

*

Later that day Crystal scooped up a box of forwarded mail at the Minturn post office and retreated to her red Mercedes. The thick veil of clouds that had brought snow the night before had lifted, and bright sunshine was streaming down on her car. She set the box on the passenger seat and scanned through the letters in the pile until she spotted what looked like another letter from her mother. She slid her thumbnail under the envelope flap and tore it open. Pulling out a single piece of stationery, she read the letter.

Dear Crystal,

I hope the time is near for you and I to reunite. I still fear Vinton, and hope I can trust you. I know you guys are close, but there are things you still don't know. I don't want to

be the one to break these things to you, dear, especially not in a letter.
I know he has most likely done things to you, dear. Especially when you were young. He is a bad man and you are good. Don't ever let him convince you otherwise.
I'm hoping we can meet one day soon.
Love, Mom

The mention of "bad things" set in motion a train of thoughts. As they whirled about in her mind, she let the letter drop into her lap and drifted into a distant memory. She saw Vinton Blackwell and his wife Diane. They were all eating breakfast together back in Oklahoma. She remembered having her long hair twisted into braids like her favorite character on television. She was excited to be going camping with her stepfather. Diane had loaded up one of her horse trailers and was going to compete in a horse show.

They'd set up the tent and gone for a hike together in the wooded slopes of northeastern Oklahoma ,near Tahlequah. She remembered how special she felt having Vinton all to herself. Later that night, after roasting hotdogs and marshmallows over a campfire, she'd watched him change as he emptied what was left of a bottle of booze. Vinton became quiet and sullen. They went to bed in their tiny tent and she remembered being scared of the noises she heard outside the tent.

She remembered how good it felt when he wrapped his arms around her from behind and held her close. She wasn't scared anymore and didn't care what kind of animals were out past the thin fabric walls of their Sears tent. All was good.

Then Vinton Blackwell did something no parent does.

Crystal was jerked sharply into the present. She found

herself staring at the floor of the Mercedes and shouted, "No!" That cruel memory hadn't visited her in so long. As she sat there, numbed by the realization, she paid no attention to the tears streaming from her eyes.

CHAPTER SIXTY-FIVE

REECE LAY IN bed with the ceiling heater vent blowing warmed air toward his face. His thoughts turned to Vinton Blackwell and the facts he'd learned while talking to Charlie Anders. Reece was certain Vinton Blackwell was the man he was after. He was the one who'd killed his father in 2009, and it made sense that Blackwell would take Owen Roberts' life.

Reece had started a pot of coffee when the phone rang.

"Hello."

"Culver, I got Mobley here with me at the hotel. We'll be over to your place in thirty minutes. If you got a girl loving you up, turn her loose. We've got work to do," Haisley said.

"You're in Denver?"

"Yeah, we flew in this morning. This whole damn thing is heating up, Culver. Cox is going one hundred miles an hour, and if we don't get in the game, he's going to screw this thing up again and we may never get Sam Shanks."

"Who put you in charge?" Reece asked, not liking to take orders.

"Cox and his crew are in Colorado Springs chasing leads. Mobley talked to him this morning."

"I hope that fat bastard kept his mouth shut," Reece said, referring to Mobley.

"I'm buying breakfast," Haisley said cheerfully, and Reece realized Mobley was listening to that end of the conversation. "We'll go to that place you took me to, Pete's on Colfax. We'll be over to your apartment in a few minutes."

Reece ran a comb through his hair and brushed his teeth. He started thinking about his mother and the last time they'd spoke. He needed to give her a call and see how she was doing. He had washed up and just pulled on his second Tony Lama boot when he heard what sounded like an army of feet tromping up the steel stairs out back of the apartment.

The pounding reminded him of Mobley, and how much he still didn't trust the fat cop. Maybe he had some connections they could use.

Reece opened the door and saw a fat, red-faced man wearing a cowboy shirt and jeans panting as he fought to breathe in the mile-high atmosphere.

"You guys want to come in for a bit and rest?" Reece asked, watching the corners of Haisley's mouth pull up into a smile.

"No, we're good. You got any notes you want to bring to breakfast?"

Reece grabbed his notebook and locked the door to his apartment before following the two men down the stairs to a black Chevrolet Tahoe parked beside his GTO. He climbed in the backseat and the stale air inside the truck hit him. It made him feel like he'd entered a gymnasium. Haisley took the driver's seat and was in gear before Mobley had gotten his door shut and his seatbelt fastened. Reece caught the tension between the two of them as Mobley gave him a hard look in the rearview mirror.

"So, Reece, where are you in the case? Have you uncovered anything new since we last spoke?" Haisley said, heading toward Pete's.

"No big leads, just some more background," he answered, lying through his teeth. He figured Mobley had teamed up with Haisley as a way to feed information back to Agent Cox and his team.

After breakfast, Reece put his suitcase into the back of the Tahoe and went back upstairs to lock up. Manchego sniffed at him and barked as if to say, what about me? Earlier he'd made a call to his landlord and arranged for Noi to take care of the dog. Reece had a flash of Charlie Anders' dog and wondered if he should have left Manchego with him.

He climbed into the truck, and Haisley asked him, "What's the best way to go?"

"If you stay on Colfax, you'll see the exit for I-25 up ahead. We'll take that north, then catch I-70 west."

Haisley peeled out into traffic, and Reece smiled. The old man hadn't lost his old policeman's ways about commandeering the road.

"Mike, what's the latest with the Task Force?" Reece asked, leaning forward over the bench seat until he caught the stench of Mobley's smoke-laden breath.

"It's been disbanded. The last I heard, Cox had a lead in Colorado Springs and was pursuing that."

Reece caught Haisley eyeing him in the rearview mirror, and he nodded in return. He wasn't trusting Mobley with a thing.

"So, how's the case in St. Louis going? Did you guys ever figure out who shot the homeless guy at the Roberts house?" Reece asked, changing the subject.

"We've got some leads but no arrest yet," Mobley answered, sounding annoyed that he'd brought it up.

Reece heard a ringtone and watched Haisley dig his cell phone out of his coat pocket.

"Hello?" he said, sounding like he didn't recognize the incoming call.

"I'm in Tulsa, where are you?" Haisley said, sounding irritated and obviously lying.

"I'm working on something else right now. What kind of help do you need, Agent Cox?" Reece cringed at the name.

"What part of Colorado?" Haisley said, taking the exit off I-25 onto I-70 at the mousetrap section of the highway. Reece leaned toward the side of the truck as they took the curve going a little too fast.

"What makes you think they're in mountains?" Haisley asked.

"Oh, I see. Well, I guess I could book a flight. Where are you guys staying?" Haisley said, merging onto I-70 heading west.

"Okay, the Hampton Inn. Sounds good. I'll give you a call when I get to Denver."

CHAPTER SIXTY-SIX

SAM SHANKS ROLLED out of bed and looked out across the valley of his Minturn home, thinking about his soon to be new home in Uruguay. He had a thought of Michael Zimeratti and wondered if he and Crystal had hit it off. Distracting her could only make their lives easier.

He was still not sure exactly how he would handle Vinton Blackwell, but very much liked the idea his friend Pablo had recommended when he was making arrangements in Ecuador. The hard part would be getting Blackwell to stay in Guayaquil while the broken A-320 was being repaired. He knew Vinton wasn't good at sticking to the plan. He always wanted to do things his own way. Shanks needed to be in the rented Learjet halfway to his new home in Uruguay when the police arrived at the jet and took Blackwell into custody with an airplane full of what was left of the stolen art. Crystal and Michael Zimeratti would be with him in the corporate jet. The only thing he wondered was if the FBI would be satisfied with taking Blackwell into custody instead of himself. Maybe he'd stash a couple of kilos of heroin in the baggage compartment to make the capture a little sweeter.

Once Shanks was dressed, he walked into the kitchen and smiled at the smell of fresh toast and coffee.

"Hello, Mr. Shanks I was hungry, so I took the liberty of making something to eat," Crystal said, smiling at him.

Vinton Blackwell looked up from the sports section of the *Denver Post* just long enough to frown. Shanks couldn't get rid of him any sooner. He casually took a seat at the table across from the two of them.

"We've got that one last job you guys have been planning, and then we'll box everything up and head down to South America like I told you," Shanks announced. "Have you had a chance to fill Crystal in with the details of our trip, Vinton?"

"Yes, she knows all about it," Blackwell said, not looking up.

"Is there anything good in the paper?" Shanks said turning over the front page to see the headline.

"Son of Chicago businessman dies in accidental fall from Vail chair lift."

Alarmed, he saw the picture of Crystal Thomas kneeling in the snow next to the ski patrol sled with Zimeratti's lifeless body wrapped inside. Her lipstick was smeared and long streams of mascara-colored tears had stained her red cheeks. Sam was ready to explode as he looked up from the article.

"What did you do to him?" he yelled, rising from the table with the newspaper in his hand like he was about to hit her with it.

Blackwell jumped up from his side of the table. "What are you talking about, Shanks?"

"This!" he said, plopping the paper down in front of Blackwell and storming from the kitchen.

"What happened, Crystal?" Vinton asked, quickly grasping the gist of the article. "We needed him for our last job. What's wrong with you?"

"You should talk," she said crossly. "He told me what you

did to Owen. If anyone is a murderer in this kitchen, it's you, Papa," Crystal said, standing up from the table herself.

"The timing, Crystal. Why did you have to do this now?"

"He was plotting against you with Shanks, Papa. I did it for you."

"What do you mean, plotting?"

She checked the doorway Shanks had exited through, then lowered her voice. "They know about the painting you stole from the Philips house. The one with the yellow poppy flowers in the vase. Shanks knows you took it. He thinks you're up to something, Papa."

"He does, does he?" Vinton said, waving his arms angrily and sending his coffee cup flying to the floor with a crash.

Sam Shanks came back through the door. "What's wrong with you people? Are you both fucking mad?" He pointed his finger toward Crystal. "Michael Zimeratti was like a son to me. We grew up together back in Chicago."

"Don't you talk to my daughter that way," Blackwell yelled.

Shanks charged at him, grabbing his arms and reaching for the pistol he'd stuffed in his pocket.

Blackwell seized the weapon and tossed it to the side. Enraged, Shanks grabbed Blackwell's wrist and pulled him to the ground. Crystal ran to get the gun. The two men grunted, struggling as they wrestled on the floor. Shanks got Blackwell by the throat and the larger man began to choke and cough.

"Stop it. You're going to kill him," Crystal screamed, firing the gun into the wall.

Shanks looked over at her but held his grip on Blackwell's throat. Crystal, realizing she couldn't shoot him, instead dropped the gun on the table and jumped onto Shanks' back, wrapping her arms around his shoulders. Sam Shanks was smaller than Blackwell but well muscled for his size, and was no stranger to a wrestling mat. He tossed Crystal aside like a horse shaking off a fly. Blackwell started making choking noises and fought for air.

Satisfied he had made his point, Shanks let go of his throat and stood up.

"Enough of this. You will behave now, or…"

"Or what?" Blackwell said sarcastically, rubbing his throat. "Or you'll kill me?"

CHAPTER SIXTY-SEVEN

REECE HAD TAKEN the wheel, driving the Tahoe toward the Vail/ Eagle County Airport. Mobley sat in the backseat, smoking a cigarette with the cold mountain air pulling at the ash. Haisley was in front, poking the buttons of a hand-held GPS receiver.

"I think I'm going to take a rain check on this flight if you guys don't mind. I hate small planes," Mobley said, flipping his cigarette out the window.

"That's fine, Mike. Reece and I got it covered," Haisley said distractedly.

"Weren't you going to check in with that detective you know on the Vail PD?" Reece asked, figuring Mobley had to be good for something other than smoking, eating, and smelling up the truck.

"I'll take the truck and go pay him a visit while you guys take your joy ride," Mobley said.

Whatever, Reece wanted to say, as long as you're not with us. He pulled up at the fixed based operators hangar on the south side of the airport, and he and Haisley jumped out. Mobley waved and drove away.

"You want to fill me in on what Cox was telling you a while back when he called?" Reece said.

"They're at the Federal Center in Golden. He's been

working with another federal agency, and they think Shanks is somewhere in the mountains west of Denver. He told me to fly into Denver to help out."

"So, it sounds like we're a few steps ahead of Cox for now."

"It seems that way. I didn't want to say anything in front of Mobley, but it sounds like Cox is hell bent on catching up with Vinton Blackwell. He wants to offer him immunity in exchange for his testimony against Sam Shanks," Haisley said, walking across the blacktop toward a high-winged Cessna airplane.

"Cox wants to give that psychopathic murderer immunity? You just got to love the way the FBI does business," Reece said.

"I hear you, Culver. If we get to him first, maybe that won't happen."

"There's no maybe about it," Reece said, opening the right-side door of the Cessna 172. "Have a seat and I'll get the pre-flight done."

"Is there anything I can do to help?"

"No, it will go faster if I just do it alone." Reece walked around to the left wing of the airplane and started his inspection. On his way around the plane he noted a spot on the end of the elevator where someone had used a generous helping of silver duct tape to keep the plastic end cap on. He wasn't worried since the fiberglass was merely decoration, and if it did decide to come off in flight, it would depart in the slipstream of the airplane and not harm anything.

Reece climbed into the airplane and, after fastening his seatbelt and ensuring Haisley had done the same, he pulled the red mixture knob all the way out and then screwed it in three turns. He pulled the black throttle knob out, then using the first digit of his index finger as a gauge, pushed the knob back in about a quarter of an inch. Reece flipped a switch and heard the whine of the fuel pump and studied the fuel pressure gauge priming the fuel injected Lycoming engine. With the switch flipped off the whine ceased. Reece turned the ignition key with his left hand while pushing in the throttle with his right. The engine caught and chugged a few times before roaring to life with a pleasing spurt. Reece let the engine warm and eyed the oil temperature guage as the small white needle climbed into the green.

He reached up to the stack and tuned the communications radio to frequency 135.575 for the Automated Terminal Information Service. A recorded voice read off the weather conditions, winds, and other information and at the end of the recording announced, "You have information Romeo." Reece turned the radio frequency to 121.8, pressed down on a small black button on the front of the control yoke and started speaking: "Eagle ground, this is Cessna 5484 Kilo with information Romeo. We're at Bronson FBO and would like to taxi to the active for takeoff ."

"Cessna 5484 Kilo taxi to runway 27 and hold short. Contact Eagle tower at 119.8, good day."

They taxied toward the west, and he listened to the radio chatter on his green David Clark headphones.

"You ready to go flying?" Reece asked as he pressed down on one of the rudder pedals and swung the tail end of the Cessna around so they were facing into the wind. Reece ran through his preflight checklist and gave Haisley a thumbs up, "Eagle tower, this Cessna 5484 Kilo ready at 27 with Romeo for takeoff."

"Cessna 5484 Kilo, you are cleared for takeoff on runway 27. Winds 220 at 13," the eagle airport air traffic controller said. Reece looked over at Haisley with a smile, taxied onto the runway, and pressed the black throttle knob all the way into the dashboard. The one hundred and sixty horse powered engine spooled up, and the Cessna roared down the nine thousand-foot runway.

Once airborne, Reece headed east toward the town of Vail. As the mountains passed below, he scanned the ground for the type of house he figured Shanks might inhabit. He turned to look at Haisley, and saw his bald black head moistening with beads of sweat.

"Is there any way to get some ventilation in here?" Haisley asked. Reece reached over and turned the vent near the top of the door on the right side of the airplane and felt a blast of crisp cold air.

"The best time to fly is early in the morning or late at night. I'm afraid it will be bumpy like this for most of our flight," Reece said, rolling the plane right into a bank and looking down at the tree-covered terrain below them. He glanced back toward the folded map on his thigh.

"That looks like Line Shack Road there. You see that big house with a rock wall around it at the end of that road there on the left? Looks like the sort of place Shanks might use to hide out."

Down on the ground several men were standing next to a black SUV that was parked next to two semi tractor-trailers, and other men were unloading one of the large trucks. The plane rocked sideways, hitting some bumps, and Reece pulled the throttle out, lessening the engine's RPM and causing the airplane to begin a descent.

"Feels like we're dropping," Haisley said, looking over worriedly at Reece.

"We're not dropping. We're descending so we can get a better look."

"Is that safe?" Haisley said. "I mean, is it okay if we go this low while we're over the mountains?"

"I can handle it. Just sit back and enjoy the ride, Averton," Reece said. "Looks like they're either moving in or out."

"My guess is they're moving out if those guys are who we're looking for."

Reece rolled the plane right again and added power, taking them north away from the large estate.

"That's the Vail ski area down there," Reece said as they overflew snow-covered trails carved into a forest-covered mountain. "There's another big property over this way," Reece noted, flying toward a large white-fenced property with a main log cabin and several smaller buildings. "I'm thinking we should head back over that first house with the moving trucks."

They flew close to the first place they'd spotted, and he saw a group of men near the front of a black Range Rover. "Haisley, can you get our current position on your handheld GPS?"

"Already got it, Culver."

Their mission accomplished, Reece called the tower on the radio and got clearance to land. Three miles off the end of the runway and a couple of thousand feet above pattern altitude, Reece dropped the left wing and pushed down on the opposite rudder, putting the Cessna into a forward slip and losing altitude at an alarming rate. A hundred feet above the approaching runway, he eased up and squeaked the wheels onto the runway in a smooth landing.

"Now I see why your nephew calls you the flying cowboy. That was one cool landing, Culver."

"I'm glad you liked it."

After taxing back to the parking spot in front of the FBO, Reece started to tie down the airplane.

"Hey, take a look at this," Haisley said, pointing at a hole punched through the left wing of the airplane about a foot from the tip. Reece bent down and looked up through the hole. There was blue sky on the other side.

"Looks like a bullet hole."

"I'd say we found the hideout."

CHAPTER SIXTY-EIGHT

SAM SHANKS AND Vinton Blackwell stood in the front yard.

"Who the hell do you suppose that was up in that airplane?" Shanks yelled, pointing his finger toward the taller man's chest.

"I imagine it was just some flight students out doing maneuvers," Vinton said calmly.

Shanks reached into his pants pocket for his ringing cell phone. He walked away from Blackwell as he answered his call.

In short order he returned. "Okay then, thanks for the call. I'll make it up to you later," Shanks said, ending the call.

"Who was that?" Blackwell asked.

"None of your goddamned business," Shanks growled.

The two men stared at one another like dogs ready to fight. Shanks' lower lip was twitching and Vinton pulled his hands into fists. Shanks finally turned his back on Blackwell, walking back toward the house. His phone rang again.

"Yeah, what is it?"

"You saw them too. What did you make of it?" Shanks said.

"Two men. Did you get a look at them?"

"Yeah, I see, so what'd you do a stupid thing like that for?" Shanks asked. "Remember our plan. We don't want any attention. The last thing we want is someone reporting gunshots."

"Who was that?" Blackwell asked, coming up behind.

"The gate guard. He took a few shots at the plane the second time it came over," Shanks said, exasperated. "We've got to get all of this shit under control or we're going to lose what we've all worked so hard for." Shanks turned his fury on Blackwell. "Do me a favor. Get that daughter of yours back in line and don't let her pull any more stupid tricks."

"You be careful what you say about Crystal," Blackwell yelled right back. "If it wasn't for her, your buddy Owen would have led us straight to prison. She's sacrificed a lot for you, old man."

"Who are you calling old? I've had enough of this. If you're going to continue to work for me, you'll get yourself together," Shanks said. "When we get to South America, you and your daughter can do what you want, but between now and then you both still work for me."

*

Later that day, Shanks stood in his upstairs bedroom, brooding about Blackwell and all he'd done to ruin Tracey Roberts' life. He'd been thinking about her each night when he'd drift off to sleep and found the thoughts of a woman he once loved comforting. That's not to mention what Blackwell had done to Owen Roberts. Owen had been a snitch but deserved better than to have been handcuffed to the steering wheel of a truck and gunned down in cold blood. Vinton Blackwell was a problem and needed to be taken care of.

He stared at his image in the dresser mirror in his bedroom. Blackwell had to be taken care of but how? Shanks liked the idea of Ecuador, but he wanted a sure thing. He considered the plan for the upcoming burglary. He thought about tipping off the police so that Blackwell would be caught inside the home red-handed.

"No good," Shanks said out loud. *That would only bring the police back here.*

"Vinton Blackwell is a dead man," Shanks said out loud, grinning at himself in the mirror.

He heard a creak outside his bedroom door and turned to see who was there. The door to the laundry room squeaked just down the hall. Shanks walked to his bedroom door and looked down toward the adjacent door. He caught the scent of cigarette smoke and went down the hall to see who had the nerve to smoke in the upstairs of his home. Before he'd taken his second step, he knew who'd be there. Shanks thought of his earlier comment spoken out loud. He cringed, not wanting a confrontation.

Blackwell emerged from the laundry room with a lit cigarette hanging out of his mouth.

"I heard you to talking to yourself in there. You crazy bastard, are you losing it or what?" Blackwell said with a knowing smile.

CHAPTER SIXTY-NINE

REECE THOUGHT ABOUT the phone call he'd just received from Haisley's wife, Mavis Averton. The Toyota dealer in Tulsa had contacted her the day before. They'd been trying to reach his mother Helen to let her know the Camry was ready to be picked up. Mavis didn't seem too worried about Helen and mentioned maybe she'd gone out of town for a few days with one of her lady friends. She'd gone on to tell him that Helen and her friends were selling canned fruits at local swap meets to make extra money. Reece had asked why the dealer called Mavis. How the dealer had gotten her number? She'd told him they found a small phone book in the center console with her number in it.

It seemed weird to him that his mother didn't answer her cell phone. Reece picked up his phone and dialed his mother's number once again. It went right to voicemail like the phone was turned off.

"Mom, it's Reece. When you get this, give me a call. I hope you're doing okay. I love you."

Reece propped himself up with two pillows at the head of his motel bed and paged through his notes on his laptop. He still wasn't clear about whether Tracey Roberts was alive and if so, where she was hidden. At least they'd gained some clarity. It made sense that Blackwell and Shanks were working together at the enclave in the mountains, and the bullet hole in the wingtip of the rented Cessna confirmed that he'd been flying over the right place.

Reece felt the vibration of his phone in his pocket and pulled it out to answer.

"Hello."

"Reece, it's Natalie. How are things going up in the mountains?"

"Good. I think I've figured out where Sam Shanks and Vinton Blackwell are holed up."

"Do you want me to set something up with the local sheriffs office so you guys can go in?"

"No, let's hold off on that until I verify we've got the right place," Reece said. "So, what's going on down in Denver?"

"I did a little more digging and found an arrest of Vinton Blackwell in Santa Barbara County, California, back in 1997," Natalie said.

Reece sat up abruptly. "That's great. How much time did he serve?"

"One week in the county jail and then he was released on a technicality," Natalie said.

"A technicality?"

"They forgot to Mirandize him," Natalie said. "They had to release him, and by the time they got to a point where they could charge him with another crime, he'd vanished."

"Interesting. Does the case file tell who he assaulted?"

"Tracey Roberts," Natalie said. "Isn't that the name of your missing person?"

Reece ended the call and sat staring at his phone. *So Tracey Roberts is alive, or was back in 1997. I wonder where she is now.*

CHAPTER SEVENTY

VINTON BLACKWELL STOOD at the kitchen counter of his Minturn villa, contemplating a hunch he'd had for the last week or so. The house was quiet. He headed up to the second floor, on his way to Crystal's bedroom. The scent of her perfume pleased him. He thought of how nice it was having her living with him. It was good to have a woman around.

On the table beside her bed he spotted a thriller novel. Blackwell picked the book up and paged through it, not sure what he was looking for. He considered looking under her mattress and then dismissed the thought. *No one puts anything under the bed anymore.*

He noticed a jewelry box on the dresser. The box was finished in dark mahogany, a little bigger than a cigar box but with twice the depth. Vinton opened it and found a wad of folded papers. He went through them. They were the papers Crystal signed the day she transferred jobs at the Federal Center. He folded them back up and placed the sheets of paper back into the box. Pressing the lid down, he noticed it wouldn't close all the way. The last thing he wanted was for Crystal to discover he'd been snooping through her things. He needed her for one last burglary. Especially now that Michael Zimeratti was no longer around. Crystal would be a perfect replacement.

Vinton pulled the papers and a tray of rings out of the box and set them to the side. He pulled out a second green felt tray that held an assortment of gold and silver necklaces. Who had bought all of this jewelry for her? Underneath, he found three taupe envelopes. He picked up the first one, examined the postage mark and noted that there was no return address.

Blackwell read the letter. Who ever wrote it was telling Crystal that she'd met a sophisticated man who was charming and was going to take her away. At the bottom of the letter he saw the name Tracey.

"That fucking bitch! I should have cut her throat when I had the chance!" Blackwell shouted. He thought of the last time he'd seen her. He'd done savage things to her, things that would drive a person crazy. The vein in his right temple was throbbing. He wanted to kill someone. *Crystal. I'll slit her throat. No, not Crystal. What's wrong with me? I need her.*

He stormed out of the bedroom and ran down the stairs to the kitchen. He was headed for the knives in the butcher's block. He pulled out the meat cleaver and slammed it down against the marble counter leaving a white mark where the sharp edge hit the polished rock.

Maddened by his thoughts, Vinton picked the knife up and pressed his thumb against the blade, drawing blood. *I should have ended that bitch when I had a chance. Another man. That's what she did last time back in Santa Barbara. I thought I taught her a lesson. I put her in a god damned mental institution. Wasn't that enough?*

CHAPTER SEVENTY-ONE

AFTER EATING LUNCH, Reece climbed into the Tahoe wearing jeans, hiking boots, and a ski jacket. He and Haisley had filled Mobley in on what they'd seen from the air and their plan to go see what they could turn up on foot. Reece drove the truck west on I-70, following Haisley's directions as they navigated to the waypoint he'd saved on his handheld GPS receiver.

He hoped they'd get a chance to verify that Blackwell and Shanks were at the compound they'd seen from the air. He'd decided not to mention the bullet hole in the wing to Mobley, but because of it he'd brought along his gun, and a box of bullets.

"Take the Highway 24 exit to Minturn. It's just ahead," Haisley said, sounding like he was excited. Mobley had his window down, smoking and coughing in between puffs. It reminded Reece of Crystal's Aunt Fletcher and her oxygen, and he thanked himself for never picking up the habit.

"You're going to take a left onto Line Shack Road up here," Haisley said. Reece followed his directions and took them onto the forest-lined road. The gravel ricocheted into the fenders of the truck, and he noticed the air coming out of the vents had cooled considerably since they'd left the hotel.

Reece guessed it was about ninety minutes or so before

sunset, and was hopeful they'd have enough time to see something. He could feel his adrenaline building and was excited to be getting close to the man who'd murdered his father one and a half years earlier. The road turned to rough gravel, and after a mile or so they took a left at a place where it split off in two directions forming a Y. He heard Mobley rummaging through his backpack and wondered what he was doing. Reece eyed him in the rearview mirror, then glanced back ahead. The road was dropping downhill and traversed a series of sharp switchbacks.

"There's a good spot up there on the left. It looks like an old logging road. Pull off there," Haisley said. Reece put the truck into four-wheel drive and eased down the trail until they came to a spot where several trees had fallen, blocking further progress. As they got out of the truck, Reece noticed once again that Mobley had put on a bulletproof vest and a sidearm in a holster. Reece had to question if Mobley knew more than he'd let on.

They used the GPS to move up a hill on their right. Mobley lagged behind the whole way, wheezing and coughing, and Reece figured it wouldn't be long before he turned back. He topped the hill with Haisley just behind—and saw a large stone house to the west. It was about a half mile away in a straight line, but probably a couple of miles by road. Reece took the lens cap off the camera and cranked the zoom, pointing toward the house.

He thought of his father and the photographs he'd taken at the Malum Farms casino on the last day of his life. He wanted revenge, and he needed to get Vinton Blackwell not only to settle the score, but also to redeem himself.

Reece spied the same trucks he'd seen from the air, but the black Range Rover was gone. He heard crunching and looked over to see Mobley making his way out of the forest to their right.

"Do you think you could pick a steeper hill to climb?" Mobley blurted out, still wheezing. His face was bright red and his hair was wet with sweat.

"You better sit down, Mike," Haisley said, pointing at a large rock. Reece stared at the house through the lens and saw movement near the front door. He started snapping off pictures, hoping to get something he could analyze later.

"That looks like Shanks," Haisley said. Reece looked to his left and saw him squinting through a pair of large green military-issue binoculars.

"Let me see," Mobley said, jumping up from the rock. Mobley took the binoculars from Haisley and stood watching the house.

"We got those bastards," Mobley said, making his first complete sentence since scaling the hill.

Reece followed the others down the hill toward the Tahoe in the dim light. The sun was dropping fast, and the last bits of light were yielding to darkness. Haisley was just ahead and Mobley was leading the way, cracking twigs underfoot and griping every step of the way. Reece smelled smoke and wondered if there was ever a time he didn't require a cigarette. As Reece slid downward at a weird angle in the loose footing, he grabbed the rough bark of a pine tree, trying to slow his descent

They got to the truck, and Reece backed the Tahoe out of the woods and onto the gravel road. It was almost dark and he drove slowly with his high beams on, remembering the switchbacks they'd descended earlier.

"When we get back to the hotel, we need to come up with a

plan. I don't want to wait on this. I don't want Cox stepping in and blowing this thing." Reece said.

"We're with you on this, Reece. We'll figure something out, and put these bastards behind bars for good," Haisley said.

As Reece drove around one of the switchbacks, he saw a flash of light through the trees. He turned left, driving up the steep road, and curved back to his right. Coming around the corner, he saw a large moving van pointing straight at them with its high beams on. It was coming fast and he was blinded. Reece hit the brakes and the Tahoe started to skid in the gravel toward the left shoulder. The truck stopped just short of a steep cliff, but the headlights were shooting off the steep drop into blackness.

"Back up, back up!" Mobley yelled.

Reece slammed the transmission into reverse, stomped on the gas pedal, and took them backward away from the cliff. All the while the moving truck was just sitting there in the middle of the road. Reece slowed their retreat as he neared the curve and wondered if he might be able to pull a U-turn.

"We've got company coming up behind us fast," Mobley yelled.

"Guns," Haisley said, then bumped Reece's arm with his palm outward as if to say give me yours, but Reece kept both hands on the steering wheel and yanked left, shooting the tail end of the truck to the right for a U-turn. He hit the gas, pulling them forward in the opposite direction. They shot down the hill toward the other moving van. He saw a chance to slip past the truck on the right side, but couldn't be sure if there was enough room. It was now or nothing.

"Hold on, I'm going for it !" he yelled. As they got close to the truck, it looked like he was going to make it. They were just about past when Reece heard the truck's engine rev and felt their rear bumper smash into the side of the Tahoe. He floored the gas pedal, hoping to shoot by.

The bumper of the moving truck was grinding into the side of the Tahoe, and Reece could hear the metal crushing. They were sliding sideways. The Tahoe was starting to tip, and the right front tire was off the side of the cliff. Reece bit his lip and cringed.

"Holy shit!" Haisley yelled.

Reece pulled his foot off the accelerator and thought about trying to reverse, but it was too late. He jammed on the brake pedal and felt the nose of the Tahoe going over the side. In the rearview mirror the face of the truck driver was giving him a shit-eating grin. Reece squeezed the steering wheel in anger and held on.

The Tahoe capsized and started rolling sideways down the steep embankment. In the rapid revolutions Reece lost all sense of which way was up. He heard the engine of the Tahoe rev and Mobley talking loudly, but not making sense. Pushing his feet past the brake pedal into the floorboard, Reece tried to brace himself for some kind of stability. The noise was horrendous with snapping trees and scraping metal.

He heard the other two groaning. Reece closed his eyes and hung onto the steering wheel. His ears filled with the sound of breaking glass. At any second he expected the Tahoe to explode into a fireball, killing them all.

When the noise stopped, Reece lay in a daze. His head was throbbing the same way it had the day he'd been in that St. Louis interrogation room. He smelled gas and fought to open his eyes. He could feel gravity pushing his head into the ceiling. The Tahoe was upside down, and he was still strapped into the truck by the seatbelt across his lap and shoulder.

Reece opened both eyes and looked out the shattered

windshield. A large tree limb had punctured it a few inches to the right of his head and scraped the side of his face. He struggled with the seatbelt and unlatched it, falling down into a crumpled mess on the headliner. Reece tried the door, but it was jammed shut. He heard a groan from somewhere behind and looked into the rearview mirror to see what it was. The mirror was gone. Reece heard voices in the distance yelling. They were coming closer. He pulled desperately on the door handle, rocking back and forth trying to get out. He could still smell that gas and was beginning to panic.

Something touched his left shoulder and Reece looked over. Haisley was poking him with a tree branch. He was outside the truck, kneeling on the ground. His forehead was stained with blood and his eyes were bloodshot.

"You got to get out of there, Culver. Can't you smell the gas?"

Reece tried the door again and Haisley ran around the front of the truck to help. The two men tried, but they couldn't get it to budge.

The smell of gasoline was intensifying and the voices up above were getting closer. Reece could make out their words. Shanks's men were coming for them. He had to get out. He thought about kicking out what was left of the front windshield, but he was in an awkward position and couldn't get his legs up to kick out the glass.

"Use my side, Reece. You got to get out before this thing blows."

Crawling across the ceiling, Reece got to Haisley's door. He spied a small gap where Haisley had kicked it open to get out earlier.

He squeezed through and felt the steel door frame scrape hard across his back. Reece tried to stand up, but he was dizzy, and he dropped instantly to his butt. He was trying to stay conscious. His head was spinning and he felt his left eye twitching. To calm himself, Reece took deep breaths. He smelled the gas and tried once again to stand. He was on his feet, but he felt wobbly. The voices up above him, Shanks men, were getting closer.

"Where's Mobley?" Reece said under his breath.

"He's right here, but he doesn't look good," Haisley said.

Reece felt the twinge of a smile and felt like asking if Mobley ever looked good. Using the truck for support, he made his way around the back of the Tahoe and saw Mobley's backpack. He reached inside for it, watching a trickle of fluid run down the slope toward his boot. He sniffed the air and realized it was gasoline.

Reece stumbled around the truck toward Haisley, with the backpack hoisted over his right shoulder. It was heavy and he wondered what Mobley had brought along. Haisley had the heavy man propped up against a tree and was wiping blood out of his eyes with the back of his shirtsleeve. Mobley wasn't moving.

The voices from above were getting louder. Reece heard a gunshot and felt Haisley's hand on his bicep, urging him down the hill. No words were spoken, but Reece knew what Haisley wanted. Together, they picked Mobley up, and with him leaning down with an arm around each of their necks started skidding down the steep slope. Mobley grimaced fiercely in pain and Reece was glad he was still alive.

They hobbled their way down the loose-scree slope, gaining distance from the truck. Reece could distinguish the voices and figured there were two or three men hot on their trail. He reached into his coat and felt his gun in the right pocket and a smashed box of ammo in his left. He kept skidding down the mountain, trying to keep from dumping Mobley. They started going out of control, and Reece grabbed a tree to slow his descent. The rough pine bark scraped his hand, drawing blood. He felt the pain and took a deep breath. He almost went down sliding across a patch of ice and then stepped in between two branches, stopping when his foot sank into the deep snow.

Up above, he could hear tree limbs breaking near where the truck had come to a stop. Reece pushed Haisley's shoulder and held his finger to his mouth.

The two men stood silent, listening, and could make out three voices.

"Do you see tracks? Which way did they go?"

They pressed on, edging down and to their right, away from the truck and the men who were hunting them. The forest was pitch black now and Reece started to feel lightheaded again, squinting to see.

He lost his footing on some loose shale and stumbled. Haisley made an "oomph" sound, and all three of them went down, sliding toward who knows what in the darkness. Reece's foot caught a tree and he spun sideways, coming to a stop. He caught someone's arm and stopped him too. Reece lay there, stunned, catching his breath. For the first time he had a chance to notice the beauty of the starlit blackness above.

CHAPTER SEVENTY-TWO

THE STEEP TERRAIN was covered in loose pine needles, rocks, and downed trees. The forest was more sparse here than in other areas below the road and made it easy for the Chevy Tahoe to skid down the slope. The air was already chilly and Shanks could feel the temperature dropping as night set in.

"Hold your fire," Shanks yelled from the steep slope above them.

"They'll get away," the second man protested.

"If you hit the gas tank, we'll have a hell of a mess and the police will come. You'll ruin everything," the first man yelled, losing his footing and going down with a thump.

"We've got to track them. We can't just let them go," Shanks said.

"I think they're over this way," the first man said, shining the beam of his flashlight down past the Tahoe.

"Okay, you two take the right side and I'll go this way to the left. If you find them sleeping later on, use your knives and slit their throats. We can't afford to let these intruders go. They came snooping and now they have to pay the price," Shanks said.

The men split off as Shanks instructed and worked their way down the mountain. The two on the right stopped every couple of feet to shine the light from side to side, determined to catch the three who had escaped.

Shanks pulled out his cellphone and dialed his house.

"Hello," one of his men answered.

"It's me. Get one of the others to help you and come fetch the moving trucks. Leave a car on the road with the keys under the mat, so I have a way back to the house."

"Do you want me to get Blackwell or one of the others to come help you?" the gate guard asked.

"No, I've got it under control," Shanks said. He shoved his phone into his pocket and continued down the mountain in the darkness. To the right he spotted the flashlight beam from one of his men sweeping back and forth. After going a good ways, Shanks stopped his descent and stood leaning against a large pine tree. The rough bark of the ponderosa felt good on his back.

What wasn't so good were the bastards in that Tahoe. Where the hell did they come from? He couldn't help but suspect that they were the same people who had buzzed the property in the plane. If so, that meant they were organized. Although he didn't think they were cops.

Having such loose ends at a time like this made him very angry. When he found those bastards, they were going to pay for their meddling. He'd make sure to set coyotes on them and rip them to pieces.

CHAPTER SEVENTY-THREE

"YOU OKAY?" HAISLEY asked.

"Yeah, I guess so," Reece said, pushing up into a sitting position. He pressed his left hand down into the snow-covered rocks, and a wrenching pain coursed through his left shoulder. Reaching across his chest, he searched his shirt for blood. It felt dry. Blood wasn't a good thing to be leaving behind in this kind of country. It would bring predators at night and make tracking them easier once daylight hit. Reece figured he could dispatch any animal that came calling with his .357 Magnum, but knew the sound of gunshots would draw Shanks' men to their position.

"How about Mobley?" Reece asked, listening to the silence of the night. He jerked at the sound of voices over to their left.

Haisley whispered, "We need to get some distance between us and them. If we can get enough far enough away, we can make a small fire. That's the only way we're going to be able to survive the night."

"Sounds like a plan," Reece said.

"Mobley seems to be compliant with coming along, so we've got that on our side," Haisley said, sounding like he was back on the force.

"I think that's north," Reece said, pointing and then realizing that Haisley couldn't see him in the darkness. "If we walk far enough, we'll get to I-70. It's north of here and there should be cell towers along it."

They stood up, and Reece went first, with Mobley behind and Haisley following. Moving tree to tree, the men felt their way across the mountain. The chill of the night was setting in with the sun's heat long past. Reece was glad they'd worn hiking boots and ski jackets, but each time he grabbed onto a tree he felt a spike of pain shoot through his shoulder. He knew it was injured, but there was no time to stop, especially with Shanks's men tracking them.

Going blind was going to take forever. Reece passed Mobley off to Haisley and moved ahead at a faster pace. He heard something below them and stopped to listen. It was the rushing water of a stream or river. That filled him with hope, because wherever that water was going would lead to civilization.

Reece could hear Mobley groaning as Haisley brought him down the hill. If there was a mountain stream below, they would probably find a flat spot where they could camp for the night and, if need be, clean up the large man's wounds.

"You hear that?" Reece whispered.

A heavy hand landed on his back. "What is it?" Mobley grunted, slurring his words.

"Sounds like a stream. We have to go another five hundred feet or so, and we can take a break,"

Reece cast an eye back up the slope they'd just traversed. It was pitch black now, and all evidence of daylight had been erased from the mountaintops.

Reece pressed on, taking small steps. The trees were spaced farther apart in this stretch, and he felt dirt skittering under his feet. He took a deep breath, smelling the fresh earth, and felt his shoulder throb. *A hit of Charlie Anders single malt scotch would taste pretty sweet right about now.*

"Haisley, this seems like a good place to stop and make a fire," Reece announced at last.

"Look up above," Haisley said.

Reece turned toward him and saw the lights of both trucks driving along the switchbacks.

"Maybe they've given up."

"I think we should keep going a while longer. We're too easy of a target for them here. The Tahoe is straight above us," Haisley said.

"Yeah, you're probably right. It's Mobley I'm worried about."

"He's come this far. He can go a little farther."

Reece wrapped his arm around Mobley's round back and coaxed him forward. The ground was smoother down here, with only an occasional rock. The water to the left trickled, making its way south along its rocky course. Reece stuffed his hand into the front pocket of his jeans and held it there. That position seemed to provide some relief from the throbbing pain. Mobley was covered in sweat and wheezing hard. Reece willed him along, pulling forward.

"You up there?" he said when he lost track of Haisley.

"Yeah," Haisley said a long way off.

Reece pulled Mobley toward the distant spot. He could just make out the shape of large, jagged rocks ahead of them. They seemed darker than the darkness he was squinting to see through.

Reece felt a hand grab his left forearm, and he groaned in pain. "Let go," he managed to say.

"You hurt too?" Haisley said, releasing his grip.

"Yeah, I tore up the shoulder on that fall."

"Check this out, I found a good place to build a fire, and I found this in Mobley's pack," Haisley said, waving the beam of a small flashlight at Reece's feet.

"Careful with that. As dark as it is, that light can be seen for a long way. They might still be out there tracking us."

Reece dropped to his behind and lay back, gazing up at an array of stars. The sky was clear black and the heavens above looked brighter than he'd ever seen. The cold ground felt good under his back and Mobley had gone quiet. Reece was hoping he'd finally passed out. The night was dead silent. Haisley volunteered to scout for firewood, since he had full use of both of his hands.

Reece caught himself drifting toward sleep. He knew he needed to stay alert, but the thought of sleep was too sweet to ignore. He was beat. A twig snapped somewhere out in the woods. Still dozing, he ignored it, savoring the promise of rest. Another branch snapped and he sat up sharply, listening and straining to see out past the rocks. He thought of his gun and reached inside his coat, finding it in the inside pocket. Listening hard, Reece heard another limb snap, closer this time. He shifted over to the U-shaped rocks they'd taken shelter in and peered around the corner.

Mobley groaned, and Reece reached back, putting a hand over his mouth to quiet him. Mobley reached out with both hands and tried to pry Reece's hand from his mouth. He was twisting his head side to side.

"Did you hear that?" Reece heard someone say a few yards past the big rocks. Mobley struggled with Reece trying to get free from his hand. He bent down next to Mobley's head: "Shut up or we're dead."

He held his gun out, ready to fire if Shank's men discovered them. Reece heard a voice again—only this time it was farther away. He dropped the gun to his side and eased his grip, hoping they'd decided to go the other way. He knelt up and then got to his feet. Looking around one of the rocks, he spotted a light dancing as one of the men walked downhill away from him. He just hoped Haisley hadn't gone looking for firewood in that direction.

CHAPTER SEVENTY-FOUR

VINTON LOWERED THE bundle of tie wraps and the pliers to answer his vibrating cell phone.

"Blackwell. Yeah, did you find the bodies?" Vinton said, cradling his phone between his chin and shoulder. He picked up the white oval inspection panel from the red cloth underneath the wing of the Lear 55 corporate jet.

"Those two are some of my best men. If they're still alive, they'll track them down and take care of the problem." Blackwell picked up a pile of Phillips-head screws and inserted the tip of the screwdriver into one. He poked it through the hole in the inspection panel and turned the screwdriver clockwise, tightening the screw into the nut plate inside the wing. Then repeated the process with all six screws.

"Shanks went too? Was he alone? Good. Okay then, call me if they need help. I like nothing better than hunting in the dark."

Blackwell fished out the bottle of white gloss nail polish he'd brought along and touched up the screw heads that held the inspection panel in place. He fetched the red cloth from the floor of the hangar and reached into the landing gear well, rubbing it on a glob of black grease. Then brought the cloth out and smeared dabs of grease onto the sides of the oval inspection panel underneath the wing.

He knew the pilots would do a walk-around inspection before boarding the plane, and he didn't want to give them any reason to suspect work had been done. They'd figure things out eventually, but at that point it would be too late.

CHAPTER SEVENTY-FIVE

REECE HEARD A noise behind them. He slipped back from the side of the rocks and listened. "Hold it right there," someone yelled in the distance.

Reece instantly thought of his friend Haisley. He'd been gone too long.

"Take it easy with that gun," Haisley yelled.

"Oh hell," Reece muttered under his breath. Getting to his feet, he set off walking as quietly as he could up the hill toward the sounds.

"Where are the others?" someone said.

Reece stopped in his tracks about twenty yards above them. The wind was still and he could hear their voices plainly. He could see one of the men shining a flashlight into Haisley's face. Reece had to help Haisley before it was too late.

"There down by the river. We found a downed tree for shelter," Haisley said, lying.

Reece inched closer, shuffling his feet forward, trying his best to keep quiet like a savage sneaking up on prey. He wished he'd brought a knife like the big Buck knife his father used to carry when they went pheasant hunting along the Missouri River.

The man with the light followed Haisley toward the running water down slope of them. Reece picked up his speed, closing the gap between himself and Haisley's captors. Along the way he considered his options. He decided the best move was to knock the light loose. Reece knew his eyes had adjusted to the darkness, but the men with the flashlight would be at a disadvantage without their light.

Palming a rock in his hand, he threw it out past the men. The rustle got the desired reaction. They stopped and pointed the light in that direction. Reece could see the man pointing out toward the forest on Haisley's right side. He knew his friend was left-handed and if given the chance would seize the gun. Reece took aim and fired a single shot. Gold flame leaped from the barrel of his gun, and Reece watched the man go down.

Haisley started struggling with the second man and a shot rang out, ricocheting off a distant rock. Reece held back, wanting to help his friend but not wanting to get shot. He saw the man on the ground writhing. The flashlight was shining back at him and the guy was shuffling in an awkward rhythm toward the gun. He knew if he didn't stop him Haisley would be dead.

Reece sprinted toward the downed man and stepped on his hand just as he reached for the revolver. Haisley and the second man were wrestling viciously on the ground nearby. He picked up the gun, stuffing it in a pocket. It was pitch black except for the light from the flashlight.

A second shot fired and Reece heard an "umph." The bullet had found a target and he hoped it wasn't his friend.

Reece struck the wounded man in the forehead with his revolver, knocking him out. He shined the light toward the two struggling men and saw Haisley pinned on the ground by the guy he was fighting. He saw the gun on the ground near Haisley's right arm. The man on top of him was bleeding from the left shoulder, but had a knife pointed down toward Haisley's neck. They were deadlocked. Haisley was holding him off, but the knife was just a few inches from his throat. Reece aimed and fired.

The man with the knife collapsed on top of Haisley. Reece sprinted toward his friend and watched Haisley roll away as the guy collapsed into the dirt.

"You okay?" Reece asked.

"Thanks, Culver. I owe you one."

"You owe me two, actually."

They took the guns, ammo, and flashlight from Shanks' foot soldiers and headed back to collect Mobley. Reece was tired and ready to make a fire, but he knew the gunshots would bring on reinforcements.

Haisley pulled Mobley to his feet, and they headed along the river. They had gone a long way when, out of nowhere, the cellphone Reece had taken off the guy he'd knocked out started to ring from within his coat pocket. He pulled the phone out, flipped it open, and checked the lit caller ID window.

"Does it have a name?" Haisley asked.

"Blackwell."

Reece and Haisley set Mobley down against a big tree.

"This looks like a good place to spend the night. You think we should risk a fire?" Reece said.

"I doubt they could find us now, as far as we've come. Besides, the hunt will be on tomorrow at daybreak. Our tracks will be easy to spot."

"Yeah, I'm with you. Probably a good idea to warm up and get some sleep so we can cover lots of ground tomorrow," Reece said.

When Haisley said he was ready, Reece opened the cylinder on his revolver and pulled out a .357 Magnum round. With his Leatherman in hand he pried the copper bullet from the casing. Haisley shined the flashlight down onto a wad of dead grass that was surrounded by a teepee of small sticks he constructed. Reece dumped the black powder from the bullet casing onto the grass.

"We need something to ignite this with. You got any ideas?"

Haisley made a face and unzipped Mike Mobley's backpack, rifling through the contents. That reminded Reece of Mobley and his cigarettes. He started to search the big man's pockets.

"What are you doing?" Haisley asked.

"Looking for his lighter." He knew Mobley had to have a lighter, but he went pocket by pocket and came up empty. Reece did find a cellphone in Mobley's coat pocket and opened it. He looked up at Haisley, who was giving him a funny look as if to say what are you doing, but instead of explaining he began scrolling through the list of calls. Reece counted nine calls to the same number over the course of the previous week. He studied the area code and knew it was Colorado, but to whom? Reece highlighted the number and pressed send. The caller ID on the phone showed the name Stephen Cox. Reece couldn't believe his eyes. He slammed the flip phone shut before the number began to dial.

"Motherfucker," Reece growled, still looking at the phone.

"What?" Haisley asked.

"You're never going to believe it," Reece said, setting Mobley's phone down on a flat rock beside his knee.

"Believe what?" Haisley asked.

"He's got nine calls to Stephen Cox over the past three days."

"Let me see," Haisley said. Reece handed him the phone and watched his friend review the calls himself. "I was wondering how Cox figured out Shanks was in the mountains of Colorado."

"I'll bet when he was lagging behind in the trees he was calling Cox, giving him our whereabouts," Reece said.

"We ought to make tracks and leave this scumbag behind to fend for himself."

"No, that's not necessary," Reece said, reaching over to take Mobley's cellphone. He set the phone down on the flat rock and smashed it with a baseball-sized rock. "That should take care of it."

CHAPTER SEVENTY-SIX

HAISLEY AND REECE took turns keeping watch in the miserable cold. When the sun came up the next morning, the air felt harsher than it had in the dark. They wrapped Mobley's leg in a makeshift splint, and Haisley made a sling for Reece's left arm out of bath towel he'd found in Mobley's pack.

They set out just before sun-up, knowing Blackwell and his men wouldn't be far behind. They still didn't know what to do with Mike Mobley, but had searched every inch of his backpack and pockets in an effort to avoid any more surprises. Reece took the now empty water bottles from Mobley's pack and held them one at a time to let the rapidly moving stream fill them. He leaned out, reaching as far as he could with his good hand, trying to catch the fastest water. Reece figured it might save them from ingesting giardia parasites or swallowing some other form of bacteria that they weren't equipped to handle. With the water bottles full they headed north, hoping to find the highway. Mobley seemed a little better after a night of rest next to the fire, but the pain in Reece's shoulder had grown worse and he knew he needed medical attention.

They hiked all day, following the flattest ground they could find with no sighting of anyone or anything. It was rugged country, and as he walked Reece's thoughts ran all over the place, ranging from what it must have been like as a frontiersman, to Vinton Blackwell, and finally to Crystal Thomas and her missing mother. He'd all but forgotten the case and was concentrating now on catching Vinton Blackwell. The man he was now sure murdered his father.

Up ahead, Haisley was gathering rocks at a spot where two large trees had fallen, forming a giant T. Some big boulders on the western side formed a windbreak, and it looked like a good spot to stop for the night. As Reece latched onto a big branch of dead pine with his good arm and dragged it back, he started to think about food. He formed a picture of a big juicy steak in his mind, and that would have to do.

Suddenly, Haisley came running over toward Reece. "Did you hear that?"

"Hear what?"

The two men stood motionless, listening to the forest. The wind was rustling the branches of a stand of trees beside them. Then Reece heard the rumble of an engine far off in the distance, back toward where they'd left the Tahoe.

"They're on motorcycles."

"In this terrain?" Haisley said, looking at the mile-wide scree field they'd just traversed.

"How many miles do you think we've covered since we left the truck?" Reece asked.

"I don't know, why?"

"It might not be Blackwell. This is a national forest. Maybe they're spring hunters? Let's find some food and kill it while we have a chance," Reece said.

Haisley started prying the brass out of a .357 Magnum round, and Reece figured they had a half hour of sunlight left before it dropped below the horizon. They got a fire going and started discussing ideas for finding food. The stream was farther away now, down in a canyon to the west, but if they could find something to make a fishing hook and something resembling line, they might have a chance of catching a rainbow or brown trout.

"What's that noise up in that tree?" Mobley said, coming to life.

"It's a squirrel, why?" Reece said. He smelled the distinctive smell of cigarette smoke and glanced over toward the heavy man. "Don't you think this might be a good time to give those up?"

"It helps me when I have an empty stomach."

"Shush, give me your gun, Reece," Haisley said, sounding parental.

Reece handed him the gun, and his friend aimed up into the tree. Then Reece too saw a fat squirrel standing out toward the end of a branch, twitching its tail.

Haisley fired two quick rounds, and the squirrel dropped, hitting the ground a few feet away. Reece pulled out his Leatherman and started stripping what little meat there was from the bundle of fur. Haisley grabbed the flashlight and headed out toward a copse of pine trees.

With a three-foot limb from an aspen tree Reece sharpened both ends and placed two large rocks on each side of the fire pit, He pushed the aspen limb through several chunks of squirrel meat and laid the branch across the fire. Before long Reece smelled the scent of meat cooking, and felt like everything would be okay.

He heard a couple of more shots ring out in the distance, and Haisley arrived a few minutes later with two more dead squirrels for their dinner. Reece bit into the first chunk of cooked squirrel meat and smiled. It was a little tough, but he wasn't complaining. Now all he needed was to get back to civilization, before Shanks and Blackwell disappeared. Worse, before the FBI offered Blackwell immunity.

CHAPTER SEVENTY-SEVEN

SAM SHANKS PRIED open the window to the laundry room in Vinton Blackwell's Minturn villa. He knew Crystal and her stepfather were away and he had the house to himself, but that didn't help him. Shanks was nervous and out of his element. He was the planner and manipulator, the brains behind the operation. He hadn't been on the action side of his crimes in decades.

Shanks started casing the house, searching for anything that could hide a small painting. He started on the second floor, not wanting to be caught up there if Blackwell came earlier than he guessed. One room had a row of bookshelves, and he looked behind the books for the small Van Gogh, but found nothing except dust balls. Through the dormer window to one side he saw the first glimpses of daylight. He had to hurry or he'd be caught.

The bald man left the room and hurried toward the next, picking up the scent of Crystals perfume as he entered her bedroom. He saw a rolltop desk and searched it, knowing the small painting could be hidden anywhere. A sudden squeak erupted out of nowhere, and he froze in his tracks, listening. It must just have been the settling of the house, he decided after long seconds. A bead of sweat rolled off his forehead and splattered on the leather insert of the desk. Shanks pulled out his shirttail and blotted up the perspiration, not wanting to leave any trace of his unannounced visit.

He sprinted down the stairs and went room by room, searching for any sign of the painting or the black felt bag it might have been stored in. He spotted a page from the architectural plans on the kitchen counter and searched the cupboards. Streaks of light shone through the windows, looking like someone with a flashlight was outside.

Shanks ran for the basement door and found it locked. He knew he'd found the right place, but he wasn't sure how to unlock the door with the tools he'd used to enter the laundry room. *Where would they keep the keys?* Casting about the kitchen, he saw a brass key rail in the shape of stallion hanging above the microwave oven.

Going to it, he examined the key rings, searching for the one that would most likely open the door. He saw a single brass key and snatched it from the hook. It turned out to be the right guess. With the door opened, he replaced the key before slipping down the stairs. He wanted the Van Gogh more than anything, for the incredible price it would bring. Besides, he'd be able to stick it to Blackwell one last time.

Shanks rummaged inside a cabinet at the base of the stairs. He went through the built-ins on the adjacent wall but came up empty handed. The house creaked above him, and Shanks froze. Madly he tried to think of a possible excuse for breaking into Blackwell's villa. He was a sitting duck down here in the basement.

He wondered if Blackwell would be bold enough to take him on after all of these years. The fight they'd had in the kitchen of his home after he'd found the newspaper article about Michael's death surprised him. It had been too easy to subdue his hired gun.

The furnace kicked on behind a door under the staircase, and Shanks startled with surprise. He considered that room and dismissed the thought quickly, knowing no one would store a priceless painting next to a furnace. Turning around in a wide arc, Shanks spotted a small wooden desk on the opposite wall. It was covered in envelopes and papers, looking like it hadn't been touched in years. He peered down behind the desk, thinking it might be the perfect hiding place for a small painting. No such luck.

He spotted a briefcase leaning against the side of the desk and pulled it out, noticing how light it felt. Shanks sat in the desk chair and set the briefcase on his knees. He tried to open it by pressing the two tabs sideways, but it was locked. *What series of numbers holds the clue to opening this case?*

The answer came to him. He entered them and pressed the brass tabs sideways. The top of the leather case popped open. He nearly lost his breath when he saw the painting inside. The priceless Van Gogh with its vivid yellow and red poppy flowers was staring up at him. The wooden frame was old and distressed, but the picture looked like a museum piece. He pulled the felt bag from his back pocket and slid the priceless artwork inside, taking care not to damage it with the now continuous beads of sweat dropping off his forehead. Shanks picked up a pile of the envelopes off the top of the desk, shoved them into the briefcase, shut the lid, and stuffed it back alongside the desk where he'd found it.

CHAPTER SEVENTY-EIGHT

REECE FOLLOWED HAISLEY and Mobley up toward the top of a forested hill and knew they'd made it when he heard Haisley yell, "Woo Hoo! Look at that, boys."

They looked across a small valley toward a string of tractor-trailer trucks driving east on I-70. Heartened by this discovery, they walked another few hours before the feel of firm hot pavement met the soles of their boots. Reece pulled out his cellphone and for the first time had coverage. He thought about whom to call and handed the phone to Mobley. He watched him closely as he dialed the number for the Vail detective he'd met a few days before. Mobley got through and told Detective Hughes about their predicament, and current location at the guardrail of the entrance ramp onto I-70 east at the Edwards exit. Reece watched Mobley hang up and grabbed his phone back.

"What's wrong with you, Culver?" Mobley asked.

"Plenty. Look, when this friend of yours comes to pick us up, I don't want you running your mouth. I want Vinton Blackwell, and I don't want the Vail PD or anyone else getting in my way. You understand?" Reece said, staring down at Mobley.

"Reece, I think you'll like Detective Hughes. He's a real

good guy. One of us," Mobley said, sounding much more alert than he'd been earlier.

Reece walked a ways down the guardrail and heard someone following. He turned to find Haisley staring down at his own cell phone, then making a funny look.

"What's going on, Haisley?" Reece asked.

Haisley grabbed Reece's good arm and tugged him a few paces farther away from Mobley, then leaned close. "I've got a bunch of missed calls from Agent Cox."

"You going to call him and check in?" Reece said, alarmed.

"No, read this last text message," Haisley said, passing his phone.

Reece read the screen of Haisley's phone: "Suspect Sam Shanks is in Vail Colorado. Closing in on his location. Call when you get this."

Reece handed the phone back to Haisley, and they exchanged a meaningful look. Haisley pointed as a gray Crown Victoria pulled up beside the guardrail a few yards behind them. A tall silver-haired man in business attire got out, carrying a trio of bottled water containers.

"You guys look like hell," Detective Hughes said, handing out the water.

"We feel like hell," Reece said, glad to be back to civilization.

"What the hell happened?"

Mobley supplied the lie: "We blew a tire on our Tahoe and went over the side of a cliff."

Reece watched Hughes, knowing he probably wasn't buying Mobley's explanation, but he didn't feel like he needed to do any explaining.

"Let's get you guys stitched up."

After driving into town, Hughes dropped them off at the Vail Valley Medical Center. Reece got a couple of X-rays and it was determined that he had a tear in his rotator cuff, and would need to be scheduled for surgery the following week. Haisley got a few stiches for a head wound. Mobley remained at the hospital for observation with a banged-up knee, three broken ribs, and possible internal injuries.

Hungry as hell, they found the same restaurant they'd eaten burgers at several days earlier and discussed their options.

"I think we should go have a chat with Mobley and make sure he doesn't give us up," Reece said, starting to feel the effects of the pain meds the doc had prescribed.

"I've already taken care of Mobley. Detective Hughes knows the story about Cox too, and as far as I can tell, he's not cooperating with the FBI."

"That's good to know. Thanks for taking care of our liability."

Reece felt his phone rattle in the front pants pocket of his jeans.

"Hello?"

"Reece, it's your brother Raymond. Have you heard from Mom?"

"No, I haven't," Reece said, surprised by the call. When did his brother ever call him?

"She's missing, Reece."

"Missing? What are you talking about?"

"Well, it all started out when the Toyota dealer called Mavis Averton looking for Mom," Raymond said.

"Yeah, Mavis called me, but she thought Mom might have gone out of town with some of her friends. Are you saying that wasn't the case?"

"Reece, that was over a week ago. No one has heard a thing from her."

"Have you called the Tulsa police?"

"Yeah, we did three days ago and no one's seen a thing."

"So you filled a missing person's report?" Reece said.

"Yeah."

"How about my rental car?" Reece said. "The blue Mazda 6. I lent it to Mom just before I came back to Denver so she'd have something to drive while her car was in the shop."

His brother sounded eager about this possible lead. "I don't know about that. Maybe you should call the rental car place and report it missing too."

"Sounds like a plan, Raymond. Hey, call me if she turns up. I'm hoping she just went out of town or something, but this doesn't seem like her. I hope she's okay."

Reece ended the call, feeling prickles of dread dancing down his spine.

"What's going on, Culver?" Haisley said.

"It's Mom, she seems to be missing."

Haisley was immediately alarmed. "That can't be good. Are you going to go back to Tulsa to look for her?"

"That's what I should do, but we're too close to catching these guys."

Reece stared down at the table, thinking about the last time he'd spoken to his mother. Then he thought about the rental car and reminded himself to call the rental place in Tulsa.

"What's your plan for catching Blackwell and Shanks?" Haisley said.

"The last time I talked to Crystal, she invited me up to Vail to go skiing. I'm thinking I should call her and take her up on the invitation," Reece said, knowing she was the best chance he had at getting close to Blackwell.

Haisley was not too receptive to this idea. "I don't know, Reece. You're pretty beat up. You're in no condition to ski, and that crazy bitch will do anything to protect her stepfather."

"I know, but we can't just wait around until Cox shows up and offers Blackwell immunity so he can put Shanks behind bars. We're talking about the guy who killed my father."

CHAPTER SEVENTY-NINE

SAM SHANKS CRANED his neck sideways, surveying the green roof of Vinton Blackwell's villa as the Lear 55 turned in a steep bank, pointing one of its wings toward the ground. He spotted Blackwell's Black Range Rover parked behind his daughter Crystal's red Mercedes and began laughing to himself. The plane bumped violently and his smile vanished. Shanks gripped the armrests of the plush leather recliner, wondering if something was wrong. The jet rolled back to wings level and he could feel the sensation of being sucked downward in his seat. He stared at the house, wondering if Blackwell had managed to get off one last shot.

"Sir, it might be a good idea to fasten your seatbelt if you haven't already," one of the pilots announced over the intercom. "We've met a few patches of turbulence this morning. Once we get up to cruising altitude, it should be smooth sailing."

Shanks cinched his lap belt tighter and leaned back, but felt the plane roll right into another turn. He clenched his teeth and gripped both armrests. The plane rolled back level and he could feel the acceleration of the twin turbofans pulling them upward toward thinner air. He thought of his new home situated in the center of the two thousand acres on the outskirts of

Montevideo and the priceless paintings stowed in the rear baggage compartment.

Before long he'd be free from his life of crime in the U.S. Selling the paintings in South America would bring its challenges, but Shanks had connections to more than a few people in that part of the world. He knew that wealth went hand in hand with ego, and people with ego were always interested in collecting things of value.

Shanks imagined the surprise on Vinton Blackwell's face when he discovered the missing Van Gogh. He wished he'd been able to video the event, but just knowing he'd beaten Blackwell was good enough. He bit his lip at the thought of double crossing the psychopathic killer. It worried him. Blackwell would have been better off dead. He thought about Michael Zimeratti meeting his death while skiing with Blackwell's daughter. He'd underestimated Crystal, as he was sure many men before him had. She was dangerous and better off left behind.

The co-pilot undid his seat belt and climbed out of the Lear jet's cramped cockpit, heading toward the bathroom. He pushed open the cockpit door and glanced over at their sole passenger Sam Shanks.

"We're past 35,000 feet. It should be smooth the rest of the flight until we stop for fuel, Mr. Shanks."

"Good, I don't like bumps," Shanks said.

Suddenly both men heard a loud "pop" outside the airplane.

"What was that?" Shanks said, seeing the baffled look on the co-pilot's face.

"Not sure."

The airplane rolled violently to the right, going inverted, and Shanks watched the pilot slam face first into the wooden credenza between two seats in the row ahead of him. Blood streamed from his nose, and he lay motionless, then pushed himself up, and crawled back toward the cockpit.

Deep inside the left wing of the Lear 55, a small explosive device triggered by a barometrically activated fuse had exploded. This sheared off the attachment hinges of the left aileron. As an airplane climbs upward, the barometric pressure drops. Because of this fact a bomb's fuse maker can dial in the precise altitude that the device will explode. In this case that altitude was 36,400 feet above ground level.

Panicking, Shanks looked out the window of the inverted airplane and felt the downward rush of G's, as if something was pulling down on him. Up ahead the pilots shouted loudly in the cockpit. The airplane rolled back level, and he looked out the side window toward the wing. Something was wrong with the aileron. It was flapping violently in the wind. He watched as a big piece of torn white metal separated from the wing. He gripped the armrests of the plush leather recliner. The nose of the airplane pitched downward, and Shanks banged his head into the seatback in front of him. His guts tightened and he felt like puking as the airplane spun violently.

Shanks thought of the Van Gogh parked safely in its wooden crate in the rear of the plane, then Vinton Blackwell, and then he wondered whether he'd survive. Somewhere up in front of him one of the pilots was screaming, "Mayday, Mayday! Denver Center, this is Lear 557 Sierra, Sierra. We are declaring an emergency 120 miles south of Eagle Vail. I repeat, we are going down."

CHAPTER EIGHTY

THE WARM WATER felt good on Reece's aching shoulder as he stood in the shower. He'd been filthy the whole time in the hospital. Reece reached up with his good arm and rubbed the spot on his head where he'd been struck in St. Louis. The wound had healed, but it still hurt when he pressed on it. That reminded him of Crystal and he decided to call her after he got dressed. He needed her to get to her father, Vinton Blackwell, but he had added motive now.

Reece had called the rental car place in Tulsa and reported the car stolen. He wasn't sure it was, but he figured it would intensify the hunt for his missing mother. The call he'd received earlier from his brother Raymond was gnawing at him. The police had questioned a trucker that thought he saw a collision on a bridge over Lake Keystone west of Tulsa. It was nighttime and he'd been driving past in the westbound lanes when he saw a black truck rear-end a blue car on the opposite side of the highway. Raymond told him they were going to investigate the trucker's statements and planned on searching the lake for the car.

Reece toweled off and did his best to get dressed without using his left hand. It was tough doing the things he was used to now that he was a one-armed man, but at the same time made it even more important to follow through with catching the bastard that took his father's life, and might have killed his mother. Reece thought about his mother driving the Mazda rental car and felt a tremendous pang of guilt. *I hope she's okay.*

Reece stood at the window of the hotel room with his cell phone in his hand. *I should call Raymond and tell them. No, that won't do any good. If it was Mom in the Mazda on the bridge, the damage is already done.* Reece struggled with himself, knowing what he should do, but wanting to catch Vinton Blackwell now, worse than anything. He rubbed his eyes, feeling exhausted. If only he had some time to get away from all of this and think things out. But he had run out of time. For all he knew, Special Agent Cox and the FBI were hot on Sam Shanks' trail and they might catch him and Blackwell first.

He picked up his phone, ready to call Crystal, his ticket to catching Blackwell. He focused his mind and thought through what he'd say when she answered.

"Hi, Reece, how's the investigation going?" Crystal said.

"It's going well, Crystal. Hey, I just got up to the mountains for a meeting and I wondered if you wanted to get together for a drink, or something tomorrow?"

"Tomorrow, yeah, I guess we could meet," she said with a hint of reservation in her voice. "I heard the snow is still good. Do you want to make it a day of skiing and then have dinner up at my villa?"

"The dinner part sounds good, but I'm not sure I'm up to skiing right now."

"I have extra skis and boots if that's what's in the way of your hitting the slopes with me," Crystal said.

"How about you pick me up at seven and we'll take it from there," he said.

"What hotel are you in?"

"I'm in the Marriott in Vail. You know the place right?"

"Ok, how about I meet you in the lobby?"

"That works great." He finished the call, wondering if his call had just precipitated a hotel fire at the Marriott later that night. He and Haisley in fact were staying at the Sheraton in Avon.

Reece heard the door open and Haisley came in with a broad smile on his face. The bandage on his forehead had a small red bloodstain in the middle, but other than that he looked like his old self.

"You know any place to get a squirrel steak in this fancy ass ski town?" Haisley said.

He walked past Reece and threw his torn ski jacket on one of the queen beds.

"Not in this town, but I know a good place up in the hills," Reece said with a chuckle. "What did the rental car people say when you told them about the Tahoe?"

"I decided to hold off on that. Buy us a little time, so we can solve this thing before we get the police poking around out by Shanks' place. I went with Hertz this time."

"What do you say, we go pay Mobley a visit?"

*

Reece followed Haisley down the hospital hallway toward Mobley's room. He spotted the nurse who'd taken care of him and gave her a big smile. *Oprah* was turned up loud on the television set hanging down from the ceiling in Mobley's semi private room, and he failed to notice their arrival.

"Since when do you watch Oprah?" Haisley blurted out.

Mobley scrambled for the remote, hidden in the covers of his hospital bed. The television went black and he looked up, smiling guiltily.

"What's the prognosis? Are you going to live?" Reece asked.

"I got surgery coming tomorrow on the knee, but the ribs are healing up well." Mobley looked heavily sedated and he talked with slurred speech.

"Sounds like they got you pumped up on some good meds," Haisley said.

"You had any visitors other than us?" Reece asked.

"Just Hughes. He came by earlier. He's a really nice guy. Said when I get healed up, he'd take me fishing on his boat."

"I hope you're keeping your mouth shut about our little camping excursion," Reece said sternly.

The nurse came in and told them:

"You need to run along now. It's time for his bath."

They left the room and had gone halfway down the hallway when Haisley grabbed Reece's bad arm and yanked him into an empty patient room.

"What the hell are you doing? That's my bad arm," he cried.

Haisley looked over at him from his position at the door. He had it cracked and was peeking out. He turned back with his index finger to his lips.

"It's Cox. He just got off the elevator, heading this way," Haisley said darkly. "He just went into Mobley's room. Let's get out of here."

CHAPTER EIGHTY-ONE

CRYSTAL SAT IN the kitchen of the villa, suspicious of the call by Reece. "Hey, little girl," Vinton said, coming around the corner. "You ready to take a trip with me?"

"Sure. Papa, when are we heading down to South America?"

"We aren't."

"What do you mean? I thought that's what you and Shanks had planned. You've been spending all your time getting that plane ready to haul the paintings out of the country."

"I've changed my mind. I don't trust Shanks anymore. I've made other plans for us."

"What other plans?" Crystal asked.

"We're almost done here. We've got a flight to freedom on Friday afternoon," Vinton said, taking her into his arms. She hugged him back at first and then grew uncomfortable as he tightened his grip the way you would with a lover. She wanted to tell him to stop, but thought better of it. On one level she'd spent much of her life trying to gain his love and acceptance, but on another he scared the living hell out of her.

She broke loose from his grip, but he held onto her at arm's length. He was acting weirder than his usual unpredictable self. She needed him to get away and she figured at some point she'd strike out on her own, but now wasn't the time. Crystal had to play along.

"I've got a favor to ask."

"What's that? she said in a meek voice.

"I need you to take care of Reece Culver. He's been snooping around Sam's place, and we don't need any loose ends biting us."

"It's interesting you bring Reece up, Papa. I have a ski date with him tomorrow morning, and then I thought I'd bring him back here for the night. I can take care of the loose end then," Crystal said with a devious smile.

"You sound like you have a thing for that guy," Vinton said, distrusting his daughter. "Do what you will with him, but I want him dead. At this point Reece Culver is the only thing standing between us and our freedom."

*

Later that afternoon Crystal walked into the True Value hardware store in the city of Edwards. She was wearing tight blue jeans and knee-high brown leather boots. She caught the clerk eyeing her physique and nodded sexily at him. With a shopping basket in hand she headed down the nearest aisle. After picking out several items, she approached the counter in front.

"Did you find everything you were looking for?" the clerk asked.

She emptied the basket and set down a roll of duct tape, a hundred-foot length of cotton rope, and a selection of clamps and other hardware.

"Are you doing some work on your cabin or something?"

"Just getting some supplies I know I'll need next summer," Crystal said. "Oh, I forgot one thing. I'll be right back," she said as she ran to grab a box cutter.

After paying, she loaded the bag into the trunk of her car

and drove to the veterinary hospital where one of her ski buddies worked.

"Hello, I'm here to pick up a package of supplies from Pete," she told the receptionist.

"Let me see here," the older woman said, searching under the counter. "What kind of supplies?"

"It should be a cardboard box with the name Crystal Thomas. It's for my dog."

"Oh, I see it. Here you go," the woman said. "It looks like you prepaid over the phone. You're all set. I hope your dog feels better."

"I hope so too," Crystal said, although she knew one dog that wasn't going to feel better tomorrow.

CHAPTER EIGHTY-TWO

THE INTERIOR OF Rebecca's Roost looked more like a museum showing the past hundred or so years of Colorado history in a large collection of black and white photographs than a drinking establishment. Haisley and Reece took a seat on a pair of dark stools near the center of the long wooden bar. A youngish barkeep with long red hair had her back to them cleaning glasses in a series of three stainless steel tanks. The first was filled with what Reece suspected was soap, the second a rinse, and the third some kind of bacterial agent. It was the last sink that made him question whether or not he felt thirsty.

Haisley pulled the laptop computer out of its carrying case and began thumbing his way through the property records of Eagle county hunting for the names Shanks and Blackwell.

"Are you okay?" He asked.

"What do you mean, am I okay?" Reece said, lost in thought.

"You just seem out of it today."

"I guess I just have a lot on my mind," Reece said, fighting to make the words he was thinking flow from his lips. His shoulder had gone numb from the meds and he was pain free, but his mind was getting cloudier minute by minute.

"I'd imagine you do have a lot on your mind, considering

you have a date with that black widow who hired you. How many times has she tried to kill you now? Was it two or three?"

The bartender turned around with a funny look on her face and after a few seconds smiled. "What can I get you two to drink?"

"What beers do you have on draft?" Haisley said still nose down on the computer.

"We have Budweiser, Coors, Amstel, Ranger India Pale Ale…"

"That forth one. The Pale Ale. I'll have a glass of that," Haisley said cutting her off.

"Would you like a pint or half pint?"

"Oh, after what I've been through lately lets make it a full pint," Haisley said looking up from the laptop for the first time and smiling at her.

"How about you? What can I get for ya?"

Reece stopped looking at the television set on the right side of the bar and made eye contact with her. He'd been chewing on the thought of paying Crystal a visit at her villa that night, but he knew he'd be better off sticking to his plan. Especially with Vinton Blackwell roaming the neighborhood. "I'll take something strong. Is there such a thing as vengeance?"

"You mean a drink named vengeance?" She asked striking a pose with her hand on her hip.

"Yeah a drink. That's what I meant," Reece said not sounding too convincing.

"I've heard of something called sweet vengeance," she said leaning over the bar toward Reece. "If you'd like one those I'll need to look it up."

"You've got me interested. What are the ingredients to sweet vengeance?" He said watching as she walked over to the cash register and start poking at the screen with her index finger.

"Here it is. It's actually a shot. Not a cocktail. It contains 1 ounce of Southern Comfort Fiery Pepper, and a quarter ounce each of orange and cranberry juice. Is that something that sounds good to you?" she said returning to the bar rail in front of Reece and locking eyes with him.

"The concept sounds good, but I'll pass on that drink. How about a couple of fingers of single malt scotch?" Reece said.

"I've got a bottle of Glenlivet 18. Sound good?"

"It does," Reece said watching her walk down the rail to his left and disappear through a set of double doors he figured led to the kitchen.

"You got any hits in that property book?" Reece said looking over at Haisley.

"The only thing I see that looks close is a house under the name Trenton. That house is on the same road where we saw Shanks' place." Haisley said oblivious to the interaction between Reece and the barkeep.

"Maybe he's renting," Reece said.

"Oh, wait a minute, I got a 2,700 square foot two-story here that's south of that first location, owned by Crystal Thomas. I'm guessing that's the villa you'll be visiting tomorrow," Haisley said.

"Good, so you'll know where to come pick us up when I get her confession."

"Speaking of confessions, I was thinking we should go pay Detective Hughes a visit and see if he's on board," Haisley said.

"Yeah, that's probably a good idea. It might be good to get Hughes dialed in to Shanks and Blackwell in case I get delayed."

Reece looked up as the doors swung open and the bartender returned with a fresh bottle of Glenlivet. He watched her twist off the blue top, pull a fresh glass of the shelf, and pour a generous helping of the single malt. The bartender smiled at him and disappeared back through the double doors. Reece took a sip savoring the taste and started thinking about what was ahead of him the next day. He knew what he was planning to do was very risky. Going to Crystal's lair was a fifty-fifty shot. If things turned out well, he'd catch the man who killed his dad. If things turned out bad, he'd be joining his father six feet under.

CHAPTER EIGHTY-THREE

VINTON BLACKWELL SAT in his truck watching the line crew service the Airbus A-320. He pulled his cell phone from his coat pocket and dialed.

"Aspen Jet Center, how may I help?" a young woman answered.

"This is Mr. Blackwell. Are we all set for my Friday flight?"

"Yes, Mr. Blackwell. Everything is ready. Just use the key-card I mailed you and enter the hangar via the side entrance. The pilots have been briefed about your dietary wishes and your destination."

"Good," Blackwell said, ending the call.

He arrived back at the villa just as Crystal was unloading her trunk.

"Do a little shopping?" he yelled from his window, then got out and walked up to her.

"Yeah, you never know what you'll need when you're having a dead man over for dinner," Crystal said.

She followed him into the kitchen with the box under her arm, along with the bag of hardware she'd bought. Crystal turned the key in the basement door and followed her stepfather down.

"Have you got your bags packed?" he asked.

"All packed. When do we leave?"

"I'll swing by Friday around nine am, and pick you up," Vinton said. "If you have any trouble at all with that clown, send me a text and I'll come put him out of his misery."

"What are you thinking, you're going to finish the job the third time around?" Crystal said sarcastically. "First you knocked him senseless in St. Louis, and then you torched his hotel. What did you have in mind this time?"

Vinton's face turned red with fury. He walked over and grabbed her roughly by the throat. She coughed, pawing at him desperately, and started to choke. His grip tightened, and for a moment she thought she was going to die.

Then he let go. "Don't forget who's running the show, little girl. None of the other men in your life have done a damn thing for you."

Crystal coughed, trying to regain her composure. "I know that. I," she said coughing loudly. "I was only joking."

CHAPTER EIGHTY-FOUR

REECE SAT IN the lobby of the Vail Marriott, watching the hands of a big circular wall clock tick toward seven o'clock. His shoulder ache was coming back and he searched his jeans for the bottle of Vicodin, telling himself he could handle Crystal better if he put a dent in the pain.

Needing to do something, he jumped up, grabbed another cup of coffee from the breakfast bar, and retreated to the men's room with the intent of sawing one of the big white pills in half. Both stalls were full, and the room smelled. He glanced down at his watch: 6:50.

A stall door flew open and an elderly man walked out in a bright yellow Descent ski outfit, looking like he was ready for the Olympics. Reece took the stall, and felt the warm seat through his jeans, guessing the old guy had spent the better part of an hour in there reading the crumpled-up *Denver Post* cast aside on the floor. He took out his Leatherman, and noticed that the blades still carried the stain of squirrel's blood from their dinner a few nights earlier in the wilderness. He didn't have time to clean the thing, so he gripped one of the white pills in the jaws of the pliers and squeezed, breaking it into small chunks. He stuffed what he thought was half the pill into his mouth and chased it with hot coffee. It was a foul tasting concoction but he managed to choke it down.

Reece capped the pill bottle and left the stall. The same old man was toweling off. He reached toward his lips with a funny look and brushed at something. Reece didn't have the faintest clue what the guy wanted. Not something to do with the Olympics, he guessed.

A few minutes later, the front door of the hotel slid open and Crystal appeared, dressed in a bright pink ski parka with white fur circling her collar along with skin-tight black stretch ski pants. She had a funny look on her face as she approached him.

"Hi, Reece, I like your cowboy look," Crystal said. "What happened to your arm?"

"Oh, nothing much. Just a little tumble."

"So, I see why you were not up to skiing today. I wonder if that will interfere with any other activities," she said, sounding playful.

They walked out to her hot car, and after driving around the valley to show him the sights they stopped off for coffee. From there they went to the factory shops in Dillon and ate lunch. They spent the afternoon bumming around and then headed back up to Vail. He was enjoying himself, but was keeping his guard up for a chance to catch her on something. Soon they were roaring up a mountainside toward the villa that Reece knew her father owned. The place had a huge deck off to one side, and that's where Crystal led him once she parked the car.

Two steaks on a plate were waiting for them, and Crystal stabbed hunks of meat with a large stainless steel fork plopping them down on the gas grill. The heat radiating out felt good on his torso. Reece battled the urge to close his eyes. He was physically relaxed, but knew danger was near.

"How do you like your meat?" Crystal asked.

"Cooked," he answered.

"Does that mean medium or burnt like an old shoe."

"Medium will do," he said.

"Do you like drama or comedy?" Crystal asked, pulling her steak off the main part of the grill and turning up the flame under his tenderloin.

"Are we talking real life or movies?"

"I was talking movies, but I guess it concerns real life as well," she said, giving him a sassy look.

"I'd say drama is best for both, unless I'm in the mood for something funny," he answered, watching her walk into the kitchen with a slow back and forth.

After dinner, they settled in on one of the plush leather couches in the den, bringing in the bottle of cabernet they'd shared at dinner. They started watching the movie *Unstoppable*. She reached for her wine glass, and as she brought it to her lips he watched the red nectar disappear like blood drawn into a vampire.

"That's the last of it," she said. "Would you like me to open another bottle?"

"Sure, if you'll join me."

Playing voyeur once again, he watched her glide across the floor in her stocking feet. Reece grabbed the empty wine bottle and walked toward the kitchen himself, feeling a much greater level of intoxication than he'd normally felt after a couple glasses of wine. He saw an open basement door just beyond the refrigerator. He deposited the empty wine bottle into the trash, and was contemplating a descent down the basement stairs after her when Crystal came running up with a bottle of red in each hand. She slid to a hault and planted a kiss on his cheek.

Taking the corkscrew lying on the kitchen counter, she reached for two long-stemmed glasses and coaxed him to follow her toward the stairs. He knew exactly what she had in mind.

CHAPTER EIGHTY-FIVE

HAISLEY SAT ON the bed in the hotel room, flipping through the television channels. He couldn't find one that suited his interest, but that wasn't what was bothering him. The worry that filled his thoughts was of Reece Culver sacrificing himself to catch a killer. Haisley knew Reece was desperate to catch Blackwell, but he wished he'd persuaded his dead partner's son to do it another way. He knew Reece had something to prove not only to himself but to his mother. Haisley picked up the phone and dialed Detective Hughes.

"Hughes, it's Haisley Averton. I thought I'd check in with you."

"Haisley, how are you guys healing up?"

"Oh, I guess as good as can be expected for a bunch of old-timers. Hey, I was wondering if you'd heard from that FBI agent we told you about."

"Yeah, I just got off the phone with Agent Cox. He's not too happy with you."

"Oh yeah, what's his problem?" Haisley asked, knowing the answer before it came.

"He said you're working for that PI of yours, Culver, when you should be helping him."

"He didn't happen to mention his plan to offer that career

criminal Vinton Blackwell immunity in exchange for testimony against Sam Shanks."

"No, he didn't mention anything like that. What's your interest in Blackwell?" Detective Hughes asked.

"Vinton Blackwell gunned down my old partner from the St. Louis detectives squad back in 2009."

"Okay, that explains your interest, but why does this PI have such a hard-on for Blackwell?

"My partner, Al Culver, was Reece Culver's father," Haisley answered.

"Okay, I got it. So, do you guys have a plan to catch these guys?"

"We're working on that right now. Is there a good time I can drop by and have a chat with you?"

"Now's as good a time as any. You know where we're located?" Hughes asked.

"Yeah, I got the address right here," Haisley said ending the call.

Haisley left the hotel and made the short drive over. The interior of the Vail Police Department was nicer than Haisley had ever remembered a police headquarters being. He checked in with the receptionist and waited for Hughes to come out to the waiting area. Haisley wondered what type of cases a detective in a ritzy ski town might see in the course of his career.

"You look better than the last time I saw you, Averton," Hughes said, walking up behind Haisley's chair.

"Yeah, I feel a lot better too. It's amazing what a good night of sleep, a hot shower, and some food will do," Haisley said as the two men walked past the reception area toward the detective's office.

"You want to fill me in on your plan, or should I just wait and clean up the bodies after you guys play hero?"

"I'm counting on your help catching these guys, Hughes."

"Call me Mark."

"Okay, Mark. Like I said, I'm counting on your help, but catching Blackwell isn't going to be easy. Agent Cox and the FBI have been tracking Shanks and his people for close to a decade. I worked with him on the task force he had going. I know all the background on the case. I also know they want Shanks. He's the big fish, but Vinton Blackwell is worth taking down too. He's got blood on his hands from at least two murders."

"Murders? Who were his victims?" Hughes asked.

"I told you about my partner, and he most likely murdered an Owen Roberts a few weeks ago," Haisley said.

"He sounds like a muy busy hombre. So, what's your plan, Averton?"

CHAPTER EIGHTY-SIX

REECE FELT THE fullness of his bladder but resisted waking as long as he could. He held his eyes closed, slowly coming to. Crystal was on his right side with her warm leg over his thigh. He had no memory of getting from the couch to her bedroom and was worried about it. He was thankful to see he was still wearing his boxers.

He reached for the side of the bed to free himself from her leg, and felt a lightning bolt of pain shoot down his wounded left arm. He cautiously slid out from under her. She cooed as she turned over onto her side, took a deep breath, and then let it out like steam from a kettle.

He stood next to the bed, making sure she was still asleep. Reece donned his shirt but left his Tony Lama cowboy boots on the floor. Taking short steps, he made his way out of the door, down the hallway, and to the top of the stairs in the blackness of the early morning. Making sure to remain silent, he went down the steps. He was still feeling the effects of the Vicodin- and wine-laced euphoria. The bathroom at the bottom of the stairs was a welcome relief. Reece peered out of the bath toward the dark kitchen while toweling off his hands and saw the dim green light of the microwave oven display.

Something metallic caught his eye near the knob of the basement door. He felt the pull of intrigue and slid in his sock covered feet across the smooth hardwood floor. She'd left the key in the knob. Reece pulled gently on the door. It opened, and he went down the stairway, pulling the door shut behind. He hoped Crystal would stay asleep long enough for him to find out why she'd kept the room under lock and key.

Reece stepped off the bottom step into a large carpeted room. He flipped on the light switch, illuminating a finished basement. A large antique pool table occupied the center, and the exterior walls were covered in an assortment of both black and white and colored photographs. He started near the stairs and stopped at each photo, observing Crystal's family history.

It was chilly down there, and he slid his hand into the pocket of his blue jeans. He was pleased to find that he'd brought his cell phone. Reece gazed at a picture showing a face that very much resembled the description of the man who'd beaten his father on the rooftop of the apartment building several years before his death. The man was standing with his arm around a girl who had long red hair. It was Vinton Blackwell and his stepdaughter Crystal. He went to the next picture and recognized the same man a few years older standing next to Owen Roberts and the same girl.

Reece pulled out his cell phone and typed a text to Haisley.

"I'm in the basement. She's still in bed. There's a photo history of Shanks and Blackwell down here. Be ready to move. I'm going to break the news to her." He pressed send and saw only two bars of reception on the phone. He could only hope the text message reached Haisley.

He advanced to a desk in the corner with several envelopes pilled on top of one another. The top envelope contained a bunch of old receipts and bills. Reece scanned through the scraps of paper and other items on the desk. He found a crisp white envelope unlike any of the others. He peeled open the gold clasp and reached inside. He pulled out a stack of passports from two different countries in South America and three others in Europe. Each had the name Vinton James Blackwell. Reece rifled through the drawers of the desk and found a folded-up map of North and South America with a line running from Vail to Uruguay. Reece paged through the passports and noted that the two for South America were new.

He pulled his cell phone out and sent Haisley another text. "Found maps and passports in Blackwell's name for both Ecuador and Uruguay. Check Eagle Vail airport. Is this what Shanks is up to?"

*

Up in her bedroom, Crystal slid her hand across the cold cotton mattress in search of Reece's warm body. He was gone. Startled, she opened her eyes and sat up, blinking as she adjusted to the dark. Stumbling through the night, she made her way into the bathroom, feeling the effects of the night's wine. She ran both hands through her hair and smiled at the pleasant memory. If her PI had proved to be a bust otherwise, at least he could deliver in bed.

Through the small bathroom window she saw light outside. Crystal rose from the toilet, reached to flush, and then decided against it. *What's he up to*? She pulled back the bathroom window curtain and looked out toward the forest. The ground below was dark except for a sharp wedge of light shining outward from the basement.

Back in the bedroom, Crystal glanced down at the red iridescent 5:07 on the clock-radio beside her bed. From her closet she pulled out a fresh pair of jeans, a shirt, and her favorite barn coat. As she dressed, she mulled over what she was going to do about Reece. They'd had so much fun the night before, but now it was time for a different kind of fun.

*

Down in the basement, the thought of Vinton Blackwell and Sam Shanks getting away with their stolen cache of art masterpieces made Reece's stomach turn. He had to finish up down here. His luck with Crystal could change at any minute. She was volatile, just like her stepfather.

He flipped open the phone and typed out another message.

"Haisley – you've got to get to the airport and stop Shanks and Blackwell. They're headed to South America."

Reece sent the text and put the cell phone on silent mode. He couldn't risk the noise it would make if Haisley decided to call him back. His shoulder throbbed and he thought about his pills, but knew he needed to stay sharp. He moved along the wall, eyeing the last few photos taken at what looked much like the casino farm he'd visited with Haisley in Tulsa. All of this would be good evidence later on—if there was a later.

Reece heard a noise from overhead and raced to flip off the light switch. He stood motionless in the dark basement, thinking about escape, but he couldn't go yet. He needed a confession. It was vital for Crystal to realize how Blackwell had been playing her and come willingly.

Reece had mounted the first few steps on his way back up the basement stairs when the basement light came on, and the door above flew open. Crystal raced down the stairway toward him with a revolver pointed at his chest.

"You bastard. Why did you have to ruin it? What are you doing down here?" Crystal screamed as she pulled back on the hammer, cocking it. Reece held out his hand to say stop. She was barreling down the stairs toward him. He retreated backward into the basement and almost tripped off the last step.

"We were having so much fun, and now you had to come

here snooping, and break my trust. You're just like all the others," she shouted.

Crystal kept backing him up, pointing the gun with a mixture of anger and fear in her eyes. She looked disappointed, but at the same time had the set face of a killer. It was a face he'd seen before.

"Get up onto the pool table. Lie down, legs out," Crystal demanded.

Reece was watching her closely, and calculated if he should try a grab for the gun.

"Do it or I'll shoot you right now, you bastard."

He hopped up onto the pool table, and as he lay back, he felt the cold slate press against his flesh. He watched her open a cupboard on the far wall and take out a plastic bag. She fetched several lengths of rope, each with a loop on one end. It was obvious that she had premeditated her plan before having him over, and it sent chills down his spine. She really was the black widow she appeared to be. Haisley was right.

He'd miscalculated. She was deadlier than he'd imagined. She spun around with the gun and jabbed it toward him, as if to say, lie back down. With the rope in one hand she roughly looped it around his right hand and cinched it tight. He struggled to pull back against the rope as she ducked underneath the pool table, tying down the other end. The thought of driving his fist into her head when she came up occurred to him, but he didn't have enough slack. Reece focused, fighting the pain in his shoulder. He needed his wits.

Crystal worked her way around his body, poking the gun toward him each time he sat up from his prone position. She looked evil, like a changed woman. He remembered about the newspaper clippings he'd found in the library. His thoughts turned to the file his friend Natalie from the Jeffco Sheriffs had given him, and all the other men Crystal had killed. She tied his feet in a fashion similar to his arms, running the ropes to the legs of the pool table.

He yanked against his right wrist, trying to buy some slack. As Crystal held the gun in her left hand, she reached down to slip the loop over his left wrist. She shoved the gun into her waistband. He could feel his torn rotator cuff stretching as she pulled it outward and wrapped the other end around one of the metal support poles that rose from the basement floor to the wooden joist that spanned the ceiling.

She savagely pulled his wounded left arm, straightening it out.

"Aaaaahhh!" he screamed.

"Feels good, doesn't it?" Crystal said coldly.

Reece chastised himself for not calling for help. He'd sent three messages to Haisley about his findings and going to stop Shanks, but he'd screwed up not calling in the calvary.

"Why are you doing this, Crystal? Didn't you enjoy yourself last night? I thought we had something. A connection," he said, trying to reason with her.

"You're in the way, Reece. You don't fit our plans."

Crystal walked back to the cupboard where she'd found the ropes. He watched her retrieve a cardboard box with the words "Veterinary Supplies" stenciled across it in large black letters. He wondered what the box contained and knew it wouldn't be good. Reece once again pulled against the rope, but all he ended up doing is burning the skin on his right wrist.

Crystal set the box next to his left foot and pulled out a large glass syringe. Reece heard the ring of a phone in the upstairs kitchen, praying she'd run to answer it. Crystal heard it too and set a clear plastic box down onto the green felt.

"Don't move," she ordered, then ran up the stairs. She

began talking on the phone and Reece could hear her muffled voice. While she was gone, he seized the chance to struggle vigorously against the ropes. He managed to pull some free slack with his right arm. He strained hard against the rope and jabbed his fingers into his pocket. He could feel his cell phone buried against his thigh. Reece pulled and twisted his body, trying to gain more slack in the rope. His right wrist ached from the rope abrading it. Reaching farther, he finally touched the phone with his middle finger and concentrated on easing it back until it dropped out of his pocket and onto the pool table. He rapidly hit the keys, writing a text, and hit send.

Reece heard footsteps thudding across the ceiling. Crystal was coming toward the basement door. He shoved the phone under his right buttock and lay back, staring at the ceiling.

At the top of the stairs he heard Crystal say:

"Sounds good, Papa."

Reece rolled toward the staircase and in doing so felt a shot of pain course through his left shoulder. He could see her coming down the stairs, still talking on the cordless phone.

"Was that Vinton Blackwell on the phone?" Reece asked.

"No, it was your father calling to ask if you're still as stupid as you were when he was alive," Crystal said nastily.

She was angry now, and Reece wondered what Vinton had said to her. She climbed up onto the pool table. He thought about fighting back, but the slack he'd created in the rope wasn't enough to allow him to grab her throat. Crystal straddled him, sitting on his pelvis. The sexual connotations of the position reminded him bizarrely of the night before, but she looked nothing like the person he'd sexed. Her face was screwed up and her eyes were sharp and focused like a predator's.

She reached back toward his left shin and opened the clear

plastic case. Crystal took out a vial of fluid and a syringe, then pulled on a pair of yellow latex gloves. Reece wondered if the bottle contained cyanide. He knew it was lethal enough to penetrate the skin and kill a person. That explained the gloves. If it was, she'd done her homework.

She poked the needle through the rubber opening on the clear glass bottle and pulled back on the plunger, drawing the liquid into the syringe.

"Did Vinton tell you he murdered your father Owen in cold blood," Reece asked, playing for time.

Crystal glared at him and continued preparing the syringe.

"You know what happened when your mother disappeared, don't you? Owen made a deal with the devil to get rid of his life-long gambling debts to Shanks," Reece added, hoping to shake her.

"Shut up. I tried to love you just like all the others, but you betrayed me. The only man who's ever loved me is Papa. My father Owen abused me. He abused my mother. He deserved to die," Crystal muttered.

She held the syringe in her hand and pointed it down toward his chest. Reece pulled against his feet, trying to gain some leverage so he could flip her off. He wasn't going to meet his end like this.

"It's no use trying to struggle, Reece. This will all be over for you very soon," Crystal said in a deep, evil voice.

"It was a trade, Crystal. Vinton doesn't love you at all. I'm sure he abused you too. He's been using you all these years to stay one step ahead of the FBI."

That time he hit the mark. Crystal snorted, looking hurt. She set the bottle down by his foot, frowned at Reece, and held the needle straight up into the air.

"Crystal, your mother ran off with Vinton Blackwell in

1981. She met him at a Rolling Stones concert," Reece said in a soft voice.

"No, that's not true, my mother would never do anything like that. She was a good woman," Crystal said, on the verge of tears.

"Vinton got your mother pregnant and left her on the street in California. It was Owen who took her back. It was Owen who raised you as his own daughter until your mother disappeared."

Crystal's look changed and she seemed to be considering this scenario. He hoped she'd believe him and cut him loose. She set the syringe down on the pool table near the side rail, put both hands down on his waist and leaned forward, staring into his eyes. She slid her hands down onto the pool table with her wrists against his hips. Her hands were getting too close to the phone, and he tried to shift his hips to block them.

Crystal's lips quivered and Reece wasn't sure what she was thinking, but he knew he was getting to her. Then her hand hit exactly what he didn't want her to find.

"What's this?" she said, holding his phone up and poking at the buttons. "You fucker, you've been sending text messages."

She cocked her arm and hurled the phone across the room. It hit the wall and he could hear it shatter.

"Crystal," a voice yelled down the stairs from the kitchen above.

CHAPTER EIGHTY-SEVEN

HAISLEY HELD HIS phone to his ear and ran out the front entrance of his hotel.

"I hope you guys block off the airport before they get away."

"Even if the plane gets airborne, they'll be able to stop it. Ever since nine eleven the air force has made a habit of scrambling F-16's to escort planes down," Detective Hughes said. "I just hope your boy Culver is okay. Whose idea was it to send him to that villa alone?"

"It was his damn fool idea. I tried to stop him, but he insisted," Haisley said. "Once he gets an idea in his thick head, there's no stopping him."

"Okay, Averton, we've got eyes on the plane out here at the airport. One of my guys is on the far end of the ramp with binoculars on that Airbus at the east end of the airport. It's got to be the one we're after. There are no markings on it other than the tail number. We've got a call into the FAA to see who it's registered to, but we're also playing this close to our chest so we don't tip off the FBI."

"Don't let that happen. Stop that plane. Hey, I just got a text from Reece. They're headed to South America."

"Will do," Hughes said, ending the call.

Haisley pulled his handheld VHF radio out of his

police-issue backpack and listened to the frequency for Eagle Vail airport ground control. A male voice on the radio announced:

"Eagle Vail ground, this is November 768 bravo. We'd like to taxi from hangar six to the ramp."

"768 bravo, taxi to the west end of the ramp and hold."

"Eagle Vail ground, 768 bravo taxi to the west end and hold," the pilot said, reading back the clearance.

"It sounds like Shanks is on the move. I hope Hughes makes it there in time to catch them," Haisley murmured out loud.

He barreled down Highway 24 and cut sharply onto the gravel road that led to Vinton Blackwell's villa. After a few hundred yards he slowed his rental car and pulled off to the side. Haisley thought about what to do next and checked his phone for cell reception. Fine specks of snow dotted the windshield of the car and he hoped the plane might have to return to the ramp to de ice, but then thought about who was flying it and doubted that would be the case.

Haisley pulled out his GPS and figured he was still a couple of miles shy of the villa. He continued down the gravel road, hoping that Reece was still in one piece. Driving slowly around a curve, he spotted, a half-mile away, a black Range Rover parked in the driveway behind a bright red Mercedes.

"I guess it's time to go on in."

CHAPTER EIGHTY-EIGHT

"PAPA, DOWN HERE," Crystal yelled.

She rolled off of the table and hopped down to the floor. At the same time Vinton Blackwell came down the basement stairs. His face matched those in the photos Reece had seen earlier, with the same green eyes that Crystal had. This was the man who was responsible for his father's beating and murder. Rage welled up inside him, a hatred more overwhelming than anything he'd ever felt. He wanted to fling himself off the table and strangle Blackwell with his bare hands.

Instead Reece once again stretched his right arm out toward the edge of the pool table. Hearing a new sound, he worked his wrist back and forth, scraping the rope against the underside. He hoped the rough edge of the table would cut through.

Crystal ran to her stepfather with her arms out and hugged him with the same intensity she'd used to hug Reece the night before. It was all too weird. It seemed demented to Reece, and he hoped for his sake he'd gotten through to her.

"We'll have time for hugs later, Crystal. Let's put an end to this scum bag, so we can get to the airport," Blackwell said.

"Don't you want to tell her what you did with her mother?" Reece blurted out, still hoping to hit home with Crystal.

"She's going to see her mother later this week, Culver,"

Blackwell said, picking up the gun from the pool table. He flipped open the cylinder and studied the number of bullets, then snapped the cylinder closed and pointed the gun at Reece.

"She knows you're her real father. She knows you killed Owen Roberts to cover your tracks," Reece said, knowing he might be speaking his last words.

Blackwell held the gun out at him. For no good reason Reece noticed the glossed over film on Blackwell's left eye. He remembered his father Al describing it to him when he'd visited the hospital after the beating. That clouded green eye looking down at him on the rooftop in East St. Louis just before he'd lost consciousness. Vinton pulled the hammer of the revolver back and squeezed the trigger.

*

At the last second Crystal lunged toward Blackwell, knocking his arm sideways. The hammer of the .38 fell and sent the bullet meant for Reece's head into the wall. His ears rung from the loud blast, and he watched Crystal struggle with her stepfather, trying to wrest the gun away. Reece moved his arm back and forth, trying to get free.

"What are you doing, woman?" Vinton said in a mean voice.

"Tell me about how you met my mother Tracey at the Rolling Stones concert and you guys ran away," Crystal said, backing away at last.

Blackwell lowered the gun until it was pointing toward her. While the two were focused on each other, Reece pulled at the loop on his right arm and felt the rope snap under the table.

"Is it true that you got my mom pregnant and then left her on the street?" Crystal screamed. She was hysterical.

"What did he tell you, Crystal? You can't trust him. He's

one of them," Vinton yelled, turning back toward Reece with the gun.

"Is it true that I'm your daughter, Papa? You played me. You are just like all the rest."

Enraged, Blackwell turned back toward his daughter and fired. She grabbed at her stomach and slumped to the floor. Seizing the opportunity, Reece lunged toward the syringe and snatched it in his hand. The pain in his shoulder screamed as he pulled against the ropes. Vinton stared down at his wounded daughter, writhing in pain on the basement floor. Blood oozed into her blouse and stained through the barn coat she wore.

Reece stretched against the ropes with the syringe in his fist and stabbed downward into Blackwell's neck. The syringe shattered, slicing the web of skin between Reece's index and middle fingers. Jerking violently, Blackwell wobbled on his feet and turned back toward Reece, pulling the trigger. Reece flinched, but the bullet penetrated the basement wall, missing his head by mere inches.

Stricken by some lethal poison, Blackwell dropped to his knees beside the pool table. Reece rolled back, lying flat, and stared over the side at Blackwell. He was trying to stay low in case another bullet was fired. Blackwell took a final croaking breath and hit the floor face first with a thud.

Reece felt a burning sensation in his index finger. He held his hand up and saw that some of the fluid from the syringe had run down his finger. More drops were dribbling down from the tip of the needle onto his hand. He dropped the syringe instantly and rubbed his hand against the green felt top of the pool table, trying to get the poison off his skin.

Reece felt a wave of nausea and he became lightheaded and flushed. He stared at the ceiling in a daze. He could hear Crystal moaning on the floor. He thought about Blackwell.

He'd finally avenged his father's death, and most likely his mother's. *I guess it's all right to die now.*

Reece's vision narrowed and the paint above him looked like it was bubbling—just before the room went dark.

CHAPTER EIGHTY-NINE

HAISLEY TOOK OFF at a sprint, ignoring the pain of his stiff left knee. He had to get to Reece before it was too late. He had his gun out as he ran. He'd heard a gunshot a few seconds earlier on his way to the villa. Adrenaline surged through his tired body and he urged himself to run faster. He heard the roar of an approaching car and turned back to see a Vail police cruiser skidding to a stop behind the black Range Rover. Haisley flashed them his old badge.

At a full run he raised his right leg and smashed it into the front door of the villa. The door swung open, and Haisley crashed into the wall on the opposite side. The cops ran past him.

As he got up off the floor he saw an ambulance coming down the gravel road. He fought to catch his breath, feeling the altitude.

The house was quiet, and he could feel his heart pounding in his chest. Haisley ran up the stairs and went room-to-room. He caught up with one of the policeman, who wheeled around with his gun drawn, and then smiled lowering the weapon when he realized who it was.

"Clear," the other officer yelled from the room on the opposite side of the stairs.

"This floor is empty," the officer beside him yelled.

"The basement," Haisley said, running down the stairs with the second officer following. They found the basement door in the kitchen and started down the stairs. The familiar smell of gunpowder filled Haisley's nostrils, and he allowed the first officer past with his gun out, hoping to find Reece Culver alive and well.

"Call a second ambulance. It looks like we've got three wounded," the officer yelled, entering the basement.

Haisley found Reece lying on top of the pool table. His eyes were closed and Haisley wondered if they were too late.

The officer behind him squatted down next to Crystal and felt for a pulse.

"This one's still breathing."

CHAPTER NINETY

THE WALLS OF the Vail Valley Criminal Center were molded of steel gray stone, and the room had the fresh smell of new construction. Haisley didn't like that he'd been excluded from the debrief between Detective Hughes and Special Agent Stephen Cox, but he figured Hughes would fill him in on the details.

His thoughts turned to how bad Reece had looked the night before when he'd gone to visit him in the intensive care unit. The doctors were keeping quiet and that bothered him. Haisley felt his phone rattle in the breast pocket of his sports coat. He reached in.

"Averton." He paused, then said, "Oh, thanks for getting back to me." He listened to the report and said flatly, "So she's pulling through. That's good. When do you expect she'll be released from the hospital?"

The door to the conference room opened, and Special Agents Cox and Messerman stepped out. Cox gave Haisley a nasty look, but Haisley ignored it as he stood up and walked in past them. The room was filled with a long tan table with sixteen chairs around its perimeter. Detective Hughes and the two policeman Haisley had stormed the villa with seven days earlier sat on one side, and a young woman with a yellow legal pad sat alone on the opposite side.

"Thanks for inviting me," Haisley said, taking a seat next to the lone woman.

"What's the latest on Reece Culver?" Detective Hughes asked.

"He was still in a coma last night. I figured I'd swing by and check on him after we're done here," Haisley said, sounding morose.

"This is Jennifer Warren, the assistant DA here in Eagle County," Hughes said. Haisley turned and reached out to shake hands.

"I think we're okay, Mr. Averton, but we really wish you'd have let the police enter the villa first," Ms. Warren said.

Haisley listened with a stony face. There was no way he would have waited to find out what happened to the son of his old partner.

"We really need to get Mr. Culver's statement about what happened. The initial investigation seems to show that Ms. Thomas came to the aid of Mr. Culver and had an altercation with her stepfather, Vinton Blackwell, but without talking to Mr. Culver this is all just speculation."

"How about Crystal Thomas? How bad are her injuries?" Haisley asked.

"The bullet from Vinton Blackwell's gun missed all her vital organs. She's a lucky girl. She's due to be released from the hospital today, but we're going to keep an eye on her until we get a statement from Reece Culver. We may be charging her."

*

The next day Haisley and his wife walked down the hallway of the Vail Valley Medical Center. Haisley had called Mavis after riding with Reece in the ambulance. He'd told her how Reece had almost lost his life stopping the man who had murdered his partner. Mavis had filled him in on the search for Reece's mother, Helen, and the missing rental car.

Another witness had come forward saying they saw a woman who resembled Helen Culver filling a blue Mazda 6 with gas near Padre Island, Texas. Haisley had made some calls to friends at his old precinct in Tulsa and found out that they were now eighty percent certain that Helen Culver had been rear-ended by a black Range Rover and she had died when the car sank to the bottom of Keystone Lake. The search for her body had been complicated because of heavy spring rains in Tulsa and the fact that the Arkansas River runs through the center of the lake.

Mavis had wanted to know every detail about how Reece had been poisoned with the sodium cyanide from the syringe he'd stabbed into Vinton Blackwell. Haisley had told her that Reece had apparently cut his finger while trying to get loose from the ropes on the pool table, and the chemical had entered his bloodstream through the fresh wound.

"I'm glad you helped Reece figure out where these people were," Mavis said.

"It wasn't me that figured anything out. It was all Reece on this one."

"I wish we had better news for him about his mother," she said.

"I'm thinking we should hold off on telling him anything about his mom until he's out of the woods medically."

"Yeah, you're probably right. Poor guy."

"Mr. Averton?" Haisley heard someone say from behind. A tall brown-haired woman in a long white lab coat and green scrub pants was approaching him. "I'm glad you filled us in on the situation with Mr. Culver's mother. He didn't have anyone listed on the next of kin form other than his mother."

Haisley wondered what she meant by that. "Next of kin?" he said. "Reece was pulling out of it last night."

"Let me take you into the room. It's down the hall this way," the nurse said. Haisley and Mavis followed her to an area that was different from the one Haisley had visited the night before. The hallway was painted a light bird's egg blue and he thought it looked more like a maternity ward than intensive care. They passed several doors and near the end of the hallway the nurse led them into a well-lit room.

Haisley and his wife followed, eager to see Reece. An older man with a bald head was lying partially reclined in a hospital bed with his right arm in a sling and bandages covering much of his face. The television set was on, and the man in bed was concentrating on *Oprah*. Haisley looked at him and wondered where Reece was.

"Mr. Drumwell, how are you feeling?" the nurse asked, walking over to the side of the man's bed as the channel on the TV flipped to ESPN.

Haisley looked past him at a second bed with a curtain pulled around it. He saw two sets of legs below the curtain. It looked like a doctor and the nurse were attending to a patient. He wanted to barge in, but thought better of it. Mavis stepped up next to him and patted his arm.

Haisley watched the curtain slide back and could see a patient in the bed, but he couldn't see the face. An oxygen mask covered the person's nose. An IV bag hung beside the bed and clear plastic tubes ran toward the patient's exposed arm. *It looked like a man, but was it Reece?* The skin on his arm was cherry red.

"That should bring him out of it if we're lucky," the doctor said, leading the nurse out from behind the curtain. "Keep an eye on his vitals." The doctor made eye contact with Haisley and seemed shocked to see people in the room. His demeanor changed and he began to smile.

"Is that Reece Culver?" Mavis said.

"Yes, it is. Are you family?" the doctor asked.

"No, but we're the closest thing he has to family right now," Haisley said.

Mavis reached into her coat, pulled out a Kleenex, and rubbed her eyes. "Can we see him?"

"Yeah, that should be alright," the doctor said as the nurse walked to her side. Mavis and Haisley followed her up to Reece's bed. Haisley looked down at him wondering why his face was bright red with a hint of greenish yellow. His eyes were flickering and he wondered if he was dreaming or suffering. Mavis sobbed and Haisley wondered if it had been a good idea bringing his wife along.

"Let's take this off," the nurse said, lifting the oxygen mask from Reece's face.

"Is it okay if I touch him?" Mavis asked looking sideways at her.

"That's fine. I'll leave you alone," the nurse said as she walked past the curtain and pulled it shut.

Reece's eyes were still closed, but Haisley thought he saw his lips move. He bent down close to his ear and felt his wife's hand on his back.

"Culver, are you okay?"

Reece's eyes opened and he turned his head toward Haisley. "I guess so. I'm not dead yet."

EPILOGUE

THE ROCKY MOUNTAINS were gleaming white with a covering of fresh snow. Haisley and Reece sat at a table outside the Jefferson County Courthouse. The building was known in some circles as the nipple of justice because of its protruding periphery atop a circular base.

"Hey man, I'm sorry about your mother," Haisley said.

"Yeah, it sucks, but I'm glad they found her body. I hope it was quick and painless," Reece said sadly.

"Well, it should feel good that you got the guy that was responsible for her death," Haisley said.

"Yeah, I just wish I hadn't loaned her my rental car."

"You got to let that go, Reece. The past is the past," Haisley said.

Reece stood up as a white van with the logo for the Jefferson County Sherriff's Office pulled into parking place a few yards away.

"Hey guys, what's going on?" Natalie said, walking toward them.

"Good to see you," Reece replied.

Natalie came to a halt facing them and said, "Reece, I'm very sorry for your loss. Hey, if you need anything, anything at all, I'm just a phone call away."

"Thanks."

"Did you get everything set up?" Natalie said.

"Got it," Reece said as Natalie took a seat on the opposite side of the table. They waited in silence for a while and Reece checked his watch.

"Looks like she's here," Natalie said as the three of them watched a silver Maserati Quattroporte zoom into the parking lot.

"We'll meet you guys inside," Reece said. He and Haisley walked into the courthouse and made their way down to one of the interview rooms that were normally used for meetings between jail inmates and their attorneys.

Soon after, Natalie escorted Tracey Roberts into the room. The walls grimly reminded him of the room back in the St. Louis jail.

Reece and Haisley sat on a bench along one of the walls and watched as Natalie and Tracey Roberts took seats on the opposite side of a table. Reece heard a loud noise and turned to see Crystal Thomas being led into the room wearing orange Jeffco Jail attire. Mother and daughter started talking, and before long they were both in tears. At one point Natalie allowed them to exchange a hug. The guard returned to the room and took a tearful Crystal back out to the jail facility.

Reece and Haisley followed Natalie and Tracey Roberts out into the hallway.

"Mrs. Roberts, this is Reece Culver and Haisley Averton. They're the men I told you about," Natalie said.

"Oh, Mr. Culver, thank you so much for bringing Crystal and me together. This means so much to see my daughter again after all of these years," Tracey said.

"You're welcome, Mrs. Roberts."

"Well, I guess I'll be on my way. Thanks again," Tracey said as the four of them reached the top of the stairs and filed into the main atrium.

"Mrs. Roberts, there's one more thing," Reece said, motioning toward a hallway that led off to the left. Natalie led the way and Tracey followed with Reece and Haisley a few steps behind. Tracey had a lightness in her gait that hadn't been there when he'd seen her earlier. Reece hurried ahead and opened the door to a conference room, motioning for Tracey to go ahead. She entered first. A man dressed in a blue suit was standing just inside the door.

Tracey turned back toward Reece with a funny look on her face as if to say, "What are we doing here?"

Reece shut the door and moved out of the way.

"Mrs. Roberts, my name is Special Agent Stephen Cox with the Federal Bureau of Investigation," Cox said, holding out his identification. "If you'll please have a seat, I have a few questions."

Tracey looked over at Reece and dropped into one of the chairs on the opposite side of the table from Agent Cox.

The door to the conference room opened, and a man wearing a beige sports coat, brown pants, and a green tie entered.

"What are you doing here? What's this about?" Tracey said, standing from her seat.

The man in the sports coat pulled out a black wallet. "Mrs. Roberts, I'm Agent Derrick Johnston with the Internal Revenue Service, Criminal Investigation Division."

Agent Cox walked over to the door, opened it, and motioned for Reece to leave.

"Ms. Roberts, I believe you too have met previously at the Golden Spur Casino in Blackhawk, Colorado," Cox said as he closed the door behind Reece.

Reece found Haisley sitting on a wooden bench on the opposite side of the hallway.

"Good job, Culver. So, what's next for you?"

"I've got a job interview down at Caulder Space Systems next Monday. Between now and then I'm going to get some rest." He clapped the older man on the shoulder. "You know, maybe I'll catch a flight down to Cabo San Lucas. You wana join me?"

www.ingramcontent.com/pod-product-compliance
Lightning Source LLC
Chambersburg PA
CBHW020515260626
47156CB00006B/2011

* 9 7 8 0 9 9 1 5 8 2 4 1 9 *